What people are saying about …

The Project Restoration Series

"*The Renewal* is a sweet, gentle, authentic story that sneaks up on you and grabs hold of your heart. It's an unanticipated gift, a tender unfolding, a tale of two people who carry heavy emotional burdens and their struggle to finally shed those burdens and find new life. This is a very special story written by a very special author—a book of quiet peace, intense realism, and poignant, God-inspired truth. I'll remember this book for a long time to come."

Kathleen Morgan, author of *As High as the Heavens* and *One Perfect Gift*

"*The Renovation* is a beautifully crafted story about the broken relationship between a man and his son, and the joyful restoration of a mended heart and an old mansion. Engaging characters move the story along at a wonderful pace."

Lori Copeland, author of *Simple Gifts* and *Monday Morning Faith*

"In a captivating and evocative story, Terri Kraus skillfully weaves distance, longing, forgiveness, and redemption into a cast of unforgettable characters. This is a book to savor and ponder."

Nancy Ortberg, former teaching pastor at Willow Creek Community Church and author of *LookingforGod*

"Renovate your reading schedule to include this great new title by Terri Kraus! In *The Renovation*, Kraus crafts a tale that both tugs at the heart and tickles the funny bone."

Cyndy Salzmann, author of the highly acclaimed Friday Afternoon Club Mystery series

"Terri Kraus has woven an absorbing and deeply felt story of forgiveness that touches both the magnificence of heaven and the tenderly drawn detail of human relationship. Subtly and with compassion she explores the struggle of ordinary people finding their way through the complex emotional legacies of past pain, to the simplicity and peace of experiencing God's forgiveness and love. This is a compelling, memorable, honest story, offering hope and deepening faith."

Penelope Wilcock, author of *The Clear Light of Day*

THE RENEWAL

A PROJECT RESTORATION NOVEL

THE RENEWAL

by

TERRI KRAUS

David C Cook

transforming lives together

THE RENEWAL
Published by David C. Cook
4050 Lee Vance View
Colorado Springs, CO 80918 U.S.A.

David C. Cook Distribution Canada
55 Woodslee Avenue, Paris, Ontario, Canada N3L 3E5

David C. Cook U.K., Kingsway Communications
Eastbourne, East Sussex BN23 6NT, England

David C. Cook and the graphic circle C logo
are registered trademarks of Cook Communications Ministries.

This story is a work of fiction. All characters and events are the product of the author's
imagination. Any resemblance to any person, living or dead, is coincidental.

All Scripture quotations are taken from the King James Version of the Bible. (Public
Domain.) *A Paraphrase of the Lord's Prayer* by H. Hastings Weld is taken from *Godey's
Lady's Book,* vol. 41 (Philadelphia: L. A. Godey, 1850), unnumbered front matter.
"If I Should Fall Behind" from *Lucky Town* © 1992 Bruce Springsteen.

LCCN 2008940795
ISBN 978-0-7814-4890-1

© 2009 Terri Kraus
Published in association with the literary agency of Alive Communications, Inc.,
7680 Goddard St., Suite 200, Colorado Springs, CO 80920

The Team: Andrea Christian, Ramona Tucker, Amy Kiechlin, and Jack Campbell
Cover Design: Brand Navigation, Bill Chiaravalle
Cover Photos: Getty Images, PhotoAlto Agency;
Getty Images, UpperCut Images; iStockphoto

Printed in the United States of America
First Edition 2009

1 2 3 4 5 6 7 8 9 10

111908

To Jim—
kindest husband, finest father,
brilliant writing partner, patient travel companion,
best friend

*To preserve and renew
is almost as noble as to create.*
—Voltaire

"If I Should Fall Behind"

We said we'd walk together baby come what may
That come the twilight should we lose our way
If as we're walkin' a hand should slip free
I'll wait for you
And should I fall behind
Wait for me

We swore we'd travel darlin' side by side
We'd help each other stay in stride
But each lover's steps fall so differently
But I'll wait for you
And if I should fall behind
Wait for me

Now everyone dreams of a love lasting and true
But you and I know what this world can do
So let's make our steps clear that the other may see
And I'll wait for you
If I should fall behind
Wait for me

Now there's a beautiful river in the valley ahead
There 'neath the oak's bough soon we will be wed
Should we lose each other in the shadow of the evening trees
I'll wait for you
And should I fall behind
Wait for me
Darlin' I'll wait for you
Should I fall behind
Wait for me

—BRUCE SPRINGSTEEN

PROLOGUE

SHE REACHED UP TO PULL down the rear door of the minivan. It slammed shut with a determined, decisive thud. The back of the vehicle was stacked high with moving boxes, but not so high as to obscure her vision for the drive south that would take her and her daughter to a new life, a new beginning.

She carefully placed one last box—the one full of things she most treasured, each carefully wrapped—inside on the front passenger seat. It had to be kept close, safe, and within reach, not in the back with everything else.

She ran her hand over the lid. This one last box held a baby book, yearbooks, family photos—and an old moss green velvet-covered book that was her great-great-great-grandmother's diary.

Amelia Westland, age thirteen years
Glade Mills
Butler County, Pennsylvania
July 5, 1875

Oh, such a glorious day. On this, my thirteenth birthday, Mother and Father presented me with this perfect blank diary with the most lovely green velvet cover, acknowledging how much writing and observing means to me. I have pledged to them to keep record of my life, so upon reflection many years hence, I shall see the hidden hand of God, His works visible and evident in my days and weeks and years. I shall copy Scriptures that I am hiding in my heart, that I might not sin against our Lord. I now commence doing so.

Father has voiced that this harvest will be the best ever. Corn, wheat, sorghum are all poised to bring abundant yields. Even our vegetable garden behind the house is overflowing. Mother and I will have much to do this fall, putting up for the winter. She has purchased four additional cartons of a new type of Mason jar.

I will trust God and live my life as Reverend Wilcox urges, as a servant, humble, waiting on His command. Father claims that, if I continue to devote myself to learning, and if God wills, my future has no limits—like the sunset over our farm here in Glade Mills, wide and forever. I dream of becoming a schoolteacher. Dare I indulge such a hope?

For I know the thoughts that I think toward you, saith the LORD,
thoughts of peace, and not of evil, to give you an expected end.
—JEREMIAH 29:11

CHAPTER ONE

Present Day
Butler, Pennsylvania

HIS HANDS SHOOK A LITTLE—not just from nervousness, but from every-thing else … things he'd gone through, most likely. At least that's what he told himself. He took a deep breath, then another, before pulling at the door han-dle and exiting the truck. He reached back into the cab, over to the passenger side, and removed a thick stack of paper flyers from the box with an Insty-Print logo on the side. He straightened them into a neat bundle, adjusted his baseball hat over his short blond hair, and stepped to the sidewalk.

At thirty-three, Jack Kenyon was starting over, though he didn't call it that and wouldn't call it that—at least not yet.

I can do this. I can do this.

A friend back in Franklin had helped him with the design of the flyer. Each sheet of paper was an advertisement for Kenyon Construction, a firm whose total physical assets fit into the locked compartments of a silver pickup truck parked on a quiet residential street just north of downtown Butler, the county seat of Butler County in southwest Pennsylvania.

Jack Kenyon *was* Kenyon Construction.

Quality Construction. Expert Carpentry. Free Estimates.

Jack carefully rolled up the paper and placed it between the door-knob and the doorframe of the first house. He walked slowly, rolling the next sheet as he walked, and slipped that into the doorjamb of the second house he passed. The flyers cost him seventy-five dollars to have printed; the design was free. The flyer featured three pictures of the Carter Mansion—his last place of employment—in Franklin, Pennsylvania, a few hours north of Butler. Ethan Willis, his boss on that job, had said he could use the photos.

Distributing handbills had been Ethan's suggestion. "That's how I started. It's cheap and direct."

So that's what Jack was doing: rolling flyers, slipping them under doorknobs and between doorjambs, hoping one of the thousand pieces of paper would lead to work … and soon. He didn't have much of a financial cushion left. A few weeks. Maybe a month—two at the most. At the end of sixty days, if he didn't have a job lined up, he'd have to reconsider his options.

But he didn't want to reconsider his options. He was pretty sure he was nearly out of options.

Hurrying, he turned the corner at Cedar Street and stopped short, almost stumbling, almost dropping his bundle of flyers. An attractive woman with dark brown hair held back with a thin gold band stood in the middle of the sidewalk. She was holding the hand of a small girl, and both of them were staring up at the building in front of them. Carved into a stone lintel above the brick building's main doors were the words MIDLANDS BUILDING, and it was for sale.

The two didn't appear to notice him.

"Sorry," Jack said as he gathered the flyers close, trying not to let them spill.

The woman's face was as hopeful a face as Jack had ever seen. The young girl—her daughter, no doubt—was four years old, maybe five. She stood placidly. She didn't urge, didn't demand motion. She simply stared, taking it all in, as only a child could do.

Jack instantly attempted to create a story in which all the elements fit together. He was good at that sort of puzzle solving.

"Are you going to buy it?" he said as he removed a flyer for Kenyon Construction from his stack and cautiously offered the flyer to her.

Without looking directly at him, she said, "Actually, I just bought it."

She extended her hand and took his flyer without even looking at what the paper said.

———⊶∘⊷———

Holding her daughter's hand, Leslie Ruskin stared up at the old landmark building, squinting ever so slightly in the Sunday-morning brightness. The arched second-story windows stared back at her, like big eyes with heavy brows—a little dirty but solid with dignity, exuding tradition and timelessness. Something about the place had been irresistible to her. After looking at a half dozen others, in a town with many historic structures, she'd somehow been drawn back to this building, to this corner, in this town. Her attraction made no sense to her, but she heard something—a whisper, a murmur, from the stone and brick and mortar. And she knew she had to own this one specific spot of Butler geography.

Her daughter, Ava, scrunched her small shoulders together and scratched her nose with her left hand.

A car slowly rolled past along the side street, but other than that noise, the neighborhood was quiet. A dog barked, perhaps a block away. It was not an angry bark. It was a "Hello" bark.

"Are we going in?" Ava asked, turning her entire body to face her mother.

Leslie didn't look down, not just yet, and shook her head. "Not right now, sweetie. Mommy just signed the papers that say she is going to buy the building. We haven't paid for it yet. It takes awhile."

"When you buy it, then do we go in?"

Leslie squeezed her daughter's hand. "Yep. That's when we go in."

"Why is it called Midlands Building?" Ava asked.

She was too young to read, but Leslie had told her what the words over the main entrance said.

"I'm not sure, honey. I'll ask the man at the bank. Maybe he'll know."

"And I get my own bedroom?"

"You do."

"The one with the balcony?"

Leslie bent down, almost kneeling, next to her sweet Ava. Dark, wispy hair framed her daughter's innocent face; wide eyes were deep brown, just like her own. She wore a curious expression, as if she knew more than she let on. As if this was the lost place of her dreams … the dream home she'd talked about for weeks.

"No, honey. The balcony is off the living room. Your bedroom will be in the back. You'll be able to see the big tree right outside. Remember?"

Ava stared up again, taking in the small balcony, framed with wood painted dark green and enclosed with screen. She nodded. She didn't smile, but she didn't frown, either.

Leslie couldn't tell if her only child was happy or sad. They had left Greensburg, the only home Ava had ever known, less than a month before this moment. And for that last month, they had been living in an extended-stay hotel on the north side of Butler, living in two rooms, with a refrigerator not much larger than one in a child's play kitchen.

"How many days until we can go in?"

Leslie thought for a minute, trying to remember the hundreds of details surrounding her offer to buy this building: the seller's agreement, the need for an inspection, allocating tax funds into escrow, setting a closing date, putting her earnest money into another escrow account, conducting a radon test and a title search, and insisting on a seller's disclosure form.

"Maybe two weeks, sweetie. No more than that." Leslie was confident her right decision would be rewarded—soon they would have a real home again.

But two weeks was almost a lifetime to Ava. Even a single week was a long, long time to her. As a result, Leslie knew her daughter would probably ask the same question every morning. Ava could worry—a trait most likely inherited, or acquired, from her mother—and setting a moving date far enough away might free her from worry.

"Okay."

Leslie stood and looked up again, staring at the oddly screened balconies. Only one apartment unit, she knew, was occupied. Leslie could pick from the other two. She stepped back to decide which of the two empty units looked best from the outside and almost bumped into a young man hurrying around the corner.

The tanned, chiseled face, the short sandy blond hair, the medium athletic build barely registered in her mind. There was only the brief flicker that he was handsome, with that dangerous, tempting look—the same look that had proved Leslie's undoing before. He handed her a sheet of paper and asked if she was buying the building. Leslie replied that she just had.

It was only later, many hours later over breakfast at Emil's Restaurant, as Ava nibbled on her chocolate-chip pancakes, that Leslie looked at that sheet of paper. She needed a contractor, and Kenyon Construction sounded honest.

Trustworthy. Dependable. On Time, the flyer stated.

Maybe it was a sign.

Leslie hoped it was a sign—a good sign after so many months without a sign. Everything in their lives had gone gray and grayer. They were both ready to see sunshine again.

Leslie told herself over and over that this old landmark would be their new beginning—some sort of magical, wonderful new beginning they both so desperately needed.

Amelia Westland, age thirteen years, one month

Glade Mills

Butler County, Pennsylvania

August 21, 1875

Mother and I put up twenty-six quarts of tomatoes, sixteen quarts of cherries, two varieties of pickles and relishes. Yet to be done are beets, pole beans, peas, and corn. Today I helped Aunt Willa make blackberry preserves. Aunt Willa visits from Butler. She is exceedingly amusing and is oft happy, not downhearted, even though Uncle Jacob was killed in the War, so soon after they were wed, after a courtship of long standing. Mother is pleased that Aunt Willa has a penchant for schooling me in the ways of a lady. She has the voice of an angel, and she plays the piano. Sometimes she teaches me silly songs and we laugh and laugh. I take the greatest imaginable pleasure in her company. Today she taught me this poem, instructing me to recite it with my head held high, shoulders back, hands clasped at my waist, in a clear voice:

The Daisy
With little white leaves in the grasses,
Spread wide for the smile of the sun,
It waits till the daylight passes
And closes them one by one.
I have asked why it closed at even,
And I know what it wished to say:
There are stars all night in the heaven,
And I am the star of the day.

Yea, the LORD shall give that which is good;
and our land shall yield her increase.
—PSALM 85:12

CHAPTER TWO

JACK KENYON SPENT ALL OF Sunday and most of Monday distributing his flyers—almost all of them, saving fifty or so, just in case. He focused on the northeast side of Butler, north of Jefferson, east of Main. That's where the good houses were built—older, larger, most of them well maintained and preserved with care, some not so well preserved. The early moneyed settlers and Butler entrepreneurs built north of the railroad tracks, cutting into the steep ridge that protected the downtown, building ornate and highly wrought homes with layers of ornamentation. Jack viewed this as fertile geography.

Monday afternoon he visited several lumberyards and building-material suppliers in the Butler area—Dambach Lumber, Cook Brothers Brick, and Butler Millwork—checking out their stock, setting up accounts if possible, asking about contractors' discounts and delivery options, and introducing himself to whatever manager happened to be on duty.

Small contractors, especially small contractors who have just started in the construction business, were often considered horrible credit risks. They operated on a shoestring, and a bad decision or two often doomed many to crash and burn. Jack knew that most every lumberyard had a fluttering of returned checks pinned to an office bulletin board, all angrily stamped *Non-Sufficient Funds*—all written by people exactly like himself. He thought the personal introductions, without asking for credit at the outset, might set him apart from his less creditworthy competitors. This was another tip he'd learned from Ethan Willis, his former employer in Franklin.

Jack extended his hand to a rather large man, all chest and arms and neck, standing in the doorway of the office at Cook Brothers Brick.

"I'm Jack Kenyon," Jack said, as confidently as he could. "I'm just starting out. Wanted to introduce myself. Let you know that I want to be a good customer."

"Burt Cook," the man responded. "I sort of own the place."

Jack looked over his shoulder. "It says 'Brothers.'"

Burt unfolded his arms and still managed to appear massive. "Yeah, I know. But it's just me. I always wanted a brother growing up. My parents said that one of me was enough. But Cook Brothers Brick sounds better than Cook Brick. Cook Brick is plumb hard to get out of your mouth."

Obviously Burt had not yet grown tired of repeating the story.

"You new to the Butler area?" Burt asked.

"I grew up in Pittsburgh—south of Pittsburgh, actually. I'm new around here, I guess. Started handing out flyers a few days ago. Have to start somewhere."

Burt nodded as if he understood. "You got an extra flyer? You can put it up on the board over there. Sometimes we get amateurs in here trying to do things themselves and they look for a little help. And sometimes the big crews need an extra hand. You never know."

"Thanks. I'll put one up. I have a few in my truck."

Jack loped out to his truck and in a minute was posting the flyer in the middle of the board.

Burt leaned against the counter and folded his arms back over his chest. His arms barely made it across. "Why Butler? Why here? Must be better places to pick than Butler. Not that I'm nosey or anything. Just interested."

Jack wasn't bothered by the question. In truth, it was a question he'd already posed to himself dozens of times. He thought he'd come up with a succinct, clear answer and decided to try it in an out-loud way.

"Butler's a nice town. Not too big. Not too small. It doesn't seem like a fancy place. It feels honest. Lots of old buildings. Seems like a good place to start a renovation business. Close enough to Pittsburgh, if you need a big city. Far enough away to not be bothered."

Burt nodded, as if satisfied, then added after a bit, "Well, it's nice to meet you. Hope to see you back here, Mr. Kenyon."

Jack offered a half wave in reply and walked back to his truck, confident that he'd made a good impression.

That went well. Nice to know I still have it.

"Leslie Ruskin. I called yesterday about enrolling my daughter in kindergarten. Ava Ruskin."

The woman behind the battered desk craned her wrinkled neck forward, as if making sure that Ava was indeed a child.

A brass nameplate holder sat on the woman's desk, but the holder was empty, as if waiting for the school district's central office supply to provide an updated name. The unnamed woman's eyes narrowed in a permanent, angry squint, the kind only a civil servant with a lifetime position can have.

"Ruskin?"

"Yes, Leslie Ruskin. And Ava. She's five, and I want to enroll her in kindergarten. We've just moved to the area."

"You're late. Students registered for school last spring. School starts next week."

Leslie fought hard to keep control of her voice. She was not angry, she seldom got angry, but panic began to form inside. She knew this was simply a misunderstanding and not worthy of panic. Yet there it was. She had never moved anywhere, all on her own, at any time in her life, and she now realized that moving was much more complicated than she'd imagined.

Grandma Amelia experienced a lot of upheaval in her life. She overcame some big obstacles. I can handle this. I can.

Leslie took a deep breath before responding. To handle things in an appropriate manner, to relax in order to banish stress was a necessity—that was something she'd read in a *Reader's Digest* article while standing in a long checkout line in the grocery store.

"I explained this yesterday when I called. We just moved into town. We didn't know we were going to be here until a few weeks ago. On a permanent basis, I mean … in this school district."

The woman behind the desk pursed her lips. "Registration is over. Has been for months. I don't know if we can do anything about this."

Leslie looked back over her shoulder to make sure that this building was indeed a school and that she had not entered a business. She could see the lettering on the banner that hung over the office windows facing the dark, unlit hall. Even though the letters were backward, she could easily read the hand-painted words: WELCOME STUDENTS TO THE EMILY BRITTIAN ELEMENTARY SCHOOL.

Leslie looked down at her daughter. Ava seldom seemed perturbed by anything. She might worry, but she didn't grow anxious. Or perhaps, more truthfully, she simply did not *show* her anxieties like her mother. She smiled back up at her mother, then rubbed her nose with her hand.

"I called yesterday. The woman I spoke to said all we would have to do is come in to the office with Ava's birth certificate, her state health form, and proof of residency. I have all of those. And the custody papers. She said I needed those as well. The woman said if I had all that, my daughter could be registered. I have all of that with me. Just as requested."

"What woman?" the nameless woman asked, a little harsher than Leslie thought appropriate.

"I can't remember. I'm not sure I asked."

The nameless woman all but threw her hands in the air in response. "Well, no one told me anything about this."

Leslie drew in a deep, calming breath to fight her rising anxiety.

"The lady's name was Wilson," Ava said firmly, unexpectedly. "You said 'Mrs. Wilson' on the phone, Mommy."

Leslie was often amazed by what her daughter chose to remember, or could remember. She was like a sponge.

"That's right. It was a Mrs. Wilson," she said with triumph.

The woman behind the desk scowled. "Dr. Wilson? Figures. New principals—they think they know everything." And under her breath, just loud enough for everyone in the room to hear, she added, "As if she knows how any of this is supposed to work."

Leslie stood, awaiting instructions, and gave her daughter's hand a gentle congratulatory squeeze. The day grew brighter during that squeeze, and the tight band of tension forming around Leslie's heart suddenly loosened.

"Here—fill this out. This one too. And I need to make copies of everything you have."

Ava sat, her legs swinging in midair on the hard plastic chairs by the door. Leslie carefully filled out the six pages of forms, stopping for a short, painful moment every time she wrote Ava's father's address as different from their own.

"Kenyon Construction."

Jack waited for someone to say hello.

"Hello?" he finally said into the phone.

After what felt like a long silence, Jack heard the snuffling of an old woman's voice. "I have this paper. It says free estimates. Is that true?"

"Yes, it is," Jack answered brightly.

"Then you come and tell me how much it will cost to fix this, okay?"

Jack tried to get a description of what it might be that was broken, but the voice kept repeating, "Free estimate, right?"

Instead of trying to decipher the problem over the phone, Jack asked for the address. He hurried to his truck, making sure he had his clipboard, tape measure, and digital camera. He checked and made sure he had a supply of business cards as well, snugged in a package with a rubber band.

I can do this.

The address was an older home, gently sagging from age, and had been one of the first homes to receive one of his flyers. He tapped on the door. He heard shuffling, and the thin curtain on the inside of the door was pushed aside. Jack could see the top of a head, then an eyeball behind thick glasses.

"What do ya want?"

"I'm Jack Kenyon."

"Who?"

"Jack Kenyon. We just talked on the phone."

"What?"

Jack had no idea of what words might work. Then he smiled to himself. "Free estimate."

A tumbler was turned, and a chain was removed from the hasp.

"Free estimate, right?" the old woman nearly shouted as Jack handed her one of his business cards.

Jack yelled back, "Yes. Free."

He stepped inside. The living room nearly overflowed with a dusty mix of dark furniture, lamps, bags, newspapers, and magazines, plus three televisions on a standard church-issue folding table, and four calendars—two from the previous year—tacked on the closet wall. The room, done in ocher paint, smelled of Vicks, cats, and wet newsprint.

The best way to make the old house better would be to tear it down, Jack couldn't help but think.

"The back door sticks. How much will it cost to fix it?"

Jack might have told her, had the woman been able to hear, or had she appeared to have some resources, or appeared to be … more normal, that he was not a handyman but a carpenter who specialized in renovation, not repairs.

She shuffled off down the hallway, her blue faded housedress fluttering around her thin calves like leaves rustling in a quiet fall breeze. She walked with her hand out, her fingers tapping against the wall for balance.

"I would have called one of the kids … but they got their own problems. Not that they would care if I did call them. They figure, 'Why spend the money on the old lady?' when it just means they'll get less when she dies. Now what kind of attitude is that? I tell you—kids these days."

She stopped and turned to face Jack. The kitchen was nearly as cluttered as the living room. The smell of cats was stronger. Cans of food were stacked on the counter, unopened, in shaky pyramids. The old woman stood no more than five feet tall, so the upper cabinets were out of reach. The countertops were not.

On second thought, maybe she was shorter than five feet.

"I can't open the back door anymore. Is it busted? How much to fix it?"

Jack pushed against it, turning the knob. It gave just a bit. He pushed harder, with his shoulder this time, and the door popped open. A gust of warm air either entered or left—Jack wasn't sure which.

He looked down. The weather strip on the threshold had popped loose and was bent over, acting as a wedge.

He held up his hand. "I'll be back in a second."

Using a pry bar from his truck, he bent the strip back into place and hammered in five small roofing nails. They weren't exactly right for the job, but the proper nails would not hold as well, and he didn't have any wood screws in his toolbox. He opened and closed the door several times. Nothing was binding. He was dead certain his repair would outlast the rest of the house.

"There you go. Good as new."

The old woman—gray, bent, wrinkled, nearsighted—stared hard at him, her hand braced against the wall. "How much?"

Jack waved his hand. "This one is free. No charge. Only took a minute."

She shuffled closer than Jack would have preferred. "Free? Really?"

"Yep. No charge."

She put her hand on his arm, her fingers cold despite the room's warmth. She looked harder at his face through her thick glasses. Her fingers trembled. She drew even a step closer. "I … I could make you lunch."

Amelia Westland, age thirteen years, two months
Glade Mills
Butler County, Pennsylvania
September 5, 1875

I am now two months older than when I began this diary, and I am afraid, very afraid, despite my prayers, despite the reverend's assurances. There is a scourge of pox sweeping the county, and many people have died or are suffering—high fevers, terrible pain, horrible sores. The church will no longer hold a wake for people who have passed from this disease, for there are too many and some believe the illness will jump from the dead to the living.

Father and Mother try their best, but I know that the specter of death worries them. I hear them whisper in the dark after they believe I am asleep. Mother has the most doleful countenance at times.

I struggle to pray. I struggle to believe. I know that God is good, that He is love, for that is what the Holy Scriptures reveal, but I have seen small neighbor babies, covered with scabs, howling out in pain. How do I have faith? How do I remain unafraid?

My limitless future, as Father had described, has diminished to a faint glimmer, until the passage of this plague.

> *Yea, though I walk through the valley of the shadow of death,*
> *I will fear no evil: for thou art with me;*
> *thy rod and thy staff they comfort me.*
> —PSALM 23:4

CHAPTER THREE

"Do we take the furniture with us, Mommy?" Ava asked as she carefully packed her three dolls in a pink child-sized suitcase, placing each one just so, aligned at right angles, with little doll clothing neatly placed between them as padding.

Leslie looked at her daughter. "You mean the furniture in this room? No, this belongs to the hotel. Our new home has some furniture in it already. And we'll go on a shopping excursion to get what we don't have. Doesn't that sound like fun?"

Ava zipped her doll suitcase. "No. But I'll go with you."

Leslie gave her daughter a hug.

Maybe she'll grow to like shopping. But maybe it's a good thing she doesn't enjoy shopping ... for now.

They sat on one of the beds, side by side, in the bedroom of the two-room suite. This would be their last night in the hotel. They didn't have much to pack, but Leslie wanted to be out early in the morning. The Midlands Building would be hers, officially, at eight o'clock the following morning. The current owner, the First Bank of Butler, or at least the director of commercial real estate, said she could have gone in the previous night. But she remembered what her husband, her *former* husband, had said before they had bought their first home, back when things were normal and good. "Never go into a house before the papers are signed. If something gets busted, or was busted before you got there, they'll try to pin it on you. Nope. Wait till the ink dries. That's what you do so you don't get ripped off," he'd said.

Leslie didn't think anything would happen but was unwilling to take any chances. Not now, after risking so much … and signing so much of her future away.

"Tomorrow morning we'll get our breakfast here, since it comes with the room, then we'll go to the bank to get the keys," she told Ava. "Then we can start moving in. We'll do a little cleaning, and we'll set up the kitchen. It'll be so much fun."

Ava kicked her feet as they hung over the side of the bed. "Does the television there get *Dora the Explorer?*"

Leslie promised herself that she'd no longer lie to her daughter—about anything. "No. I don't think so. That show is on cable, and we don't have cable at our new house."

Ava's mouth turned down. She looked at her feet, now still. She folded her hands in her lap. "Oh."

She didn't cry, as Leslie thought she might. Ava had fallen in love with *Dora the Explorer* during their stay in the hotel. She did not plead or ask "Why not?" or demand that Leslie try to get cable television, even though they couldn't yet afford it. She simply stared ahead and kept whatever thoughts she had inside, in a place Leslie knew was out of reach.

The new owner of the Midlands Building came to a decision: She picked the middle apartment for their residence. The apartment on the east side had remained rented, with long-term tenants—the Stickles, a pleasant older couple. Leslie knew the apartment on the west side of the building was a bit nicer, a little larger with more windows and more closet space, but it would also be easier to rent. The monthly income it generated would help them remain solvent. For Leslie, it was an easy choice.

At the top of a wide stairway was a landing. Behind the apartment door, a cozy entryway opened into a spacious living room that had an original fireplace with a marble mantle and cast-iron surround, and enough room for a small dining table that Leslie would need to purchase. French doors opened from the living room onto the screened balcony at the front. Off the living room was the kitchen, and behind it, a surprisingly wide hallway led to two cozy bedrooms, with a bath in between at the end of the hall. The apartment had high ceilings and very tall arched windows, hardwood floors, and thick, dark-stained wood moldings. Leslie was relieved all the walls had been painted a fairly standard off-white, which wasn't exactly stylish, but at least wasn't ugly and wouldn't clash with anything. There were also several pieces of decent-enough furniture to help fill up the space until she could upgrade to her own.

After bringing in their luggage, a few boxes of kitchen supplies and linens, and her box of things most treasured from the front seat of the minivan, Leslie attempted to connect their small television. The building had been built well before everyone "had" to have a cable connection but had an antenna on the roof, and the wire ran to all three apartments. Feeling electronically inept, she stared at the end of the wire, then at her television set. She could see no match in connection styles. She looked over and saw Ava sitting quietly on the sofa, holding two of her dolls in her lap. Leslie stared back at the television again. Until she could get help hooking it up, without some sort of antenna there would be no reception at all.

Leslie wanted to weep in that moment, feeling as if she'd failed her daughter again. She bit at her bottom lip. The wire from the roof culminated in two silver horseshoe-shaped connectors, but every connector on the back of the television was round and shiny.

"Will our television work here, Mommy?"

Leslie peered out from behind the set. "It will, sweetie. But I think I need to buy a special plug."

Ava nodded, as if she understood. "At the Radio Shack place?"

"There's a Radio Shack in town?"

Ava pointed north. "It's by that store where you bought us popcorn."

"Really?"

That was five minutes away, by the hotel they had just left. While Ava did not read, not really, she did recognize logos and brand names with ease. McDonald's she'd known from age two.

"Well, honey, after I bring the last of the boxes up from the minivan, we'll go there and see if Mommy can find the plug that makes it work. Maybe tonight. Or tomorrow, for sure."

Ava offered a satisfied smile. "Okay."

<hr>

After fixing the old woman's back door, Jack received two other calls for estimates. That made three calls from his door-to-door advertising. One caller wanted a new roof. Even though he was hungry for work, Jack had made a promise to himself before he started that he would not do roofing. That was hard, dangerous work, and a single contractor had no business even attempting to roof a house; even flat roofs could be dangerous. He explained this to the caller, stating that he'd be better off with a company specializing in roofing.

The second call offered more promise. A young couple, the Pettigrews, recently married and in their first home, wanted to redo their kitchen and bath. It was a job Jack could easily handle alone, but he also knew young couples often lived on a pretty thin budget. He promised them he'd come by to give them an estimate the following day.

As dusk settled over the town, the streetlights clicked on all at once, as if some master switch had been flipped. Jack sat in his one chair and looked out his one window in his *very* small efficiency/studio apartment on Jefferson Street. He had propped the window open with a paint stirrer, so the noise of the traffic was diffused. Every red-light cycle, a buzzer would sound at the intersection of Main Street and Jefferson, a half block away, for at least fifteen seconds. He had asked his landlord, who lived in the apartment on the first floor, about it.

"For the blind people. When it buzzes, they know it's safe to cross," he'd explained.

Jack had stared out the window for several nights and had yet to see a blind pedestrian.

But I guess there must be visually impaired people in Butler. Why else would they install a buzzer?

Gratefully, the buzzer ceased buzzing at 10:00 p.m.

I guess blind people go to bed early.

This evening, he was not tired. He had not done physical work all day.

He had passed out more flyers—black-and-white copies he'd made at a fast-print store. He'd stopped at a few more construction suppliers and had talked to some contractors he'd met. He'd asked about work or jobs they had been offered that were too small for their crews. Everyone had been polite and helpful, offering advice on what areas would be a good source of jobs, and where not to go.

He had known starting a business would not be easy. He had no illusions about what might be in store. Ethan Willis had done it—started small and built himself up gradually. Now, with all the notoriety that came with the Carter Mansion renovation in Franklin, Willis Construction had become a very successful restoration business.

If Ethan could do it, so can I, Jack told himself. *I can do this. I know I can.*

If all else failed, Jack knew he could get a sales job in one of the several warehouse-type do-it-yourself home improvement centers around town. He did not want to, but he would go that route if forced. Jack knew that he was a natural-born salesman. He knew, without being smug, that he had a way with people—that they quickly trusted him, that they would buy things from him and believe him.

But I don't want to wear an orange apron.

He stood up.

I don't look good in orange ... but then, who does?

He ran his hand through his hair.

I am good at one key part of that sort of job: making people like me and trust me.

He stared at his face in the small mirror over the sink.

But ... isn't that one of the reasons I got into the trouble I did?

The buzzer sounded again. Jack decided that staring out the window at the street below felt a tad bit desperate. He was not desperate yet. He slipped on his sneakers and padded down the dimly lit steps of his new home.

This is just until I get on my feet. Then I'll buy a small old house that needs renovation, work on it in the evenings, sell it, buy another, and start over. I can do that.

He walked down Butler's main thoroughfare, named, appropriately, Main Street, North and South, with Jefferson Street the dividing line.

Main Street was actually Route 8—the William Flynn Highway—but that would not suit a downtown street sign.

I wonder who William Flynn was?

Butler had once been a very prosperous town, the site of steel plants and glassworks, home to thousands of immigrant workers. A few steel firms still remained, but the labor force needed to run them had shrunk. Over the years, malls and shopping centers and megaplexes had emptied downtown Butler of much of its retail viability, but there were many signs of a rebirth.

Historic buildings were being renovated. Landmarks were being restored rather than demolished. Large planters with seasonal flower arrangements lined the sidewalks, and banners on the vintage-style light posts highlighted performances at the historic Little Theater and exhibitions at the town's museums. Jack passed several new restaurants and specialty stores and a few empty storefronts with WATCH THIS SPACE signs posted in them.

He stopped at the window of The Iron Works, a motorcycle service, repair, and customizing shop that had taken over the entire street level of an old department store. He could see the holes in the stone surface of the second-story facade where the old establishment's name had once been but could not decipher the letters or the name from those sparse clues. He stared inside the darkened shop. In the window stood, or leaned, an elegant old motorcycle, from the halcyon days of American motoring, a restored and refurbished Indian Motorcycle, with its shift lever on the tank. They called it a suicide shift because, to shift gears, a rider had to let go of one side of the handlebars. No doubt it had caused any number of accidents with new riders.

He looked at the Indian for a long time, wishing he hadn't been forced to sell his own motorcycle to fund his fledgling business. But certain sacrifices were necessary. He tried not to dwell on that fact.

He walked west a few blocks. He caught the thick, greasy, and wonderful scent of hamburgers frying on a grill. He hadn't had dinner. Sometimes he skipped the meal. His appetite was not what it once was.

Across the street was a storefront tavern, with a palm tree painted on the side of the old brick wall. The leaves had been outlined in green neon, with THE PALM written in neon script. Even from where he stood, he could hear the faint humming drone of the lit neon gas, like a large bee in a harness.

I could eat something.

A second neon sign hung in the window: BEST BAR FOOD IN TOWN.

I'll just get a burger. That's all. I do have to eat.

He halted on the second of the three steps up to the front door of the bar. It was just a momentary hesitation, as if his feet were in debate with his brain. His feet won, and he opened the heavy door and entered, blinking his eyes in the murkiness of the darkly paneled room. It was early; the place was nowhere near full. A few older men sat at the bar. One or two of them turned as he came in, looked, then turned back to the television mounted on the wall. ESPN was on: A trio of old athletes behind a desk jabbered loudly at each other.

Jack took a seat at the long wooden bar with its deep, rounded bull-nose edge and leaned his elbows on the thick surface. Behind it he could see a dim image of himself reflected in the long smoky mirror behind the bar. It all felt so comfortable, so familiar, so inviting.

The bartender walked up slowly, as if not wanting to spook him, and asked, "What will you have?"

Jack inhaled deliberately and waited to answer. "A burger. No, a cheeseburger. You have fries?"

"We do. Evenings only, though."

"Then fries with that."

The bartender, an older man with glasses that slipped too far down on his nose—glasses with yellowed, oversized plastic frames that were only in style in bars like this—nodded. "What to drink?"

Jack looked over at the shiny brass pulls on the bar. He knew which beer each would dispense, dark to light, with their thick heads of foam nestling at the top of the frosted glass. He might have licked his lips, just a little, as if tasting a memory. He looked over to the rack of bottles behind the bar, amber and gold and clear, knowing the hard, tight taste of each. He looked down at his hands and counted. He put his palms flat on the bar and waited. He didn't want to look up and didn't trust himself to speak.

The bartender must have seen this small, secret dance before—a dozen times, a hundred times—from men just like Jack.

"How about a Coke? A big glass of Coke with ice?" the old man said softly, with a hint of understanding.

Jack looked up and saw the bartender's eyes, knowing, sympathetic. He nodded, thankful, unhappy, unsatisfied, relieved. "Yeah. Sure. That would be great. A Coke."

The bartender walked away, toward the back, and called out through an open service window, "Cheeseburger with."

A moment later he came back with a big glass of Coke and carefully set it in front of Jack. "It'll be okay. It really will. You keep at it, okay? Your burger will be up in a minute."

And Jack took a long sip of the drink, wishing that it were true, not believing that it was.

I can do this….

As Jack walked back to his apartment later that evening, he thought of calling Ethan Willis, his former boss. He'd learned so much from Ethan—about historic restoration, about life. Jack considered Ethan to be the closest thing to a wise man that he knew. He knew Ethan's cell number and that Ethan would be glad to take his call. But even as Jack picked up his cell phone, he began to doubt.

What am I going to tell him? That I passed a test? Maybe he's busy.

He plugged the phone back into the charger on the kitchen table.

Maybe tomorrow. Maybe during the day. That's when I'll call.

He lay down on his single bed.

And it wasn't that much of a test.

Amelia Westland, age thirteen years, three months
Glade Mills
Butler County, Pennsylvania
October 19, 1875

Great sadness has come to our family. I have lost my beloved Aunt Willa to the pox.

I know not what else to commit to paper. Are any words sufficient to hold my grief?

'Tis a parting to which there will be no reunion on this earth, but only someday, in heaven.

They that sow in tears
shall reap in joy.
—PSALM 126:5

CHAPTER FOUR

IT WAS EARLY THE NEXT morning when Leslie and Ava finished unpacking. Leslie carefully disassembled the stack of cardboard boxes that carried their kitchen supplies and linens and slid them between the refrigerator and the wall. *We might need these later,* she thought.

One last box remained packed and unopened. That special box would be unpacked last, when she could find a safe place in the apartment for the contents. Nestled among the thickness of white tissue paper, along with Ava's baby book, family photos, her school yearbooks, was the diary of her great-great-great-grandmother, whom both Leslie and Ava called Gramma Mellie, more properly Amelia Grace Westland.

The diary would go on her nightstand.

Leslie had read the diary from the late 1800s a hundred times, perhaps more, and still read and reread from the fragile pages often, trying to understand the struggles, grasp the courage, and draw strength from the words and faith of her ancestor.

Most of their other possessions had found a place in their new home. They had a sturdy white kitchen table, four matching wood chairs, a comfortable sofa in soft green, a pair of not-so-unattractive side tables, two beds with almost-new mattresses and box springs, five lamps, and two dressers. Leslie also had some colorful posters of her favorite art exhibitions from the Carnegie Museum of Art in Pittsburgh, still safely rolled up in a long cardboard tube and in need of frames.

It was enough for now. Before they'd left their hotel room, Leslie had carefully copied the names, phone numbers, and addresses of every secondhand furniture and resale shop in the Butler area from the fat Yellow Pages in the nightstand drawer. There were a lot of them, and Leslie hoped she would be able to fill in their furnishing gaps over the next few weekends. In the past, Leslie had scoured resale shops and garage sales looking for hidden treasures for her home. Now it was not so much treasure that she was searching for as bargains—to save the limited money she had.

She hoped to find some good school outfits for Ava as well as home furnishings. At Ava's age, Leslie remembered being very, very particular about what she wore and quite specific about what she refused to wear—the style, the color, the type of buttons, the accessories. Ava seemed not to care at all. Clothing to Ava was not what it once was to her mother. Colors, fashion, and design seemed beyond her. As long as it didn't pinch anywhere or wasn't tight, Ava was happy.

On the kitchen table was the flyer she had received from that man just after making her offer on the building. She knew no one else working in construction in the Butler area to call. She picked up her cell phone and dialed the number.

It rang only twice.

"Kenyon Construction."

Now I remember something else about our first meeting. His voice—unusual, rather deep, thick, and somewhat throaty. He sounds like that actor who voices all the movie trailers. But Mr. Kenyon's voice is less breathless, and somehow ... he sounds more trustworthy.

Leslie introduced herself and asked if he might be available sometime in the near future to give her an estimate on a series of projects.

"I know the building is old," she explained, "but it's solid—that's what the building inspector said—and I want to do some updating on the interior of the empty apartment before I list it for rent. Do you do that sort of work, Mr. Kenyon?"

"I do. Working with older houses is what I do best. How about tomorrow morning?"

"That would be great, but after nine o'clock, if you could. I have a family matter to attend to early in the morning. And it isn't really a house.

It's more like a three-flat building, with a big empty retail space on the first floor."

"That's okay. I'm sure I could handle any changes you might want to make. I'll see you tomorrow at nine o'clock, then."

"That's fine. I'll be done with the family matter by then, for sure."

She looked over to her daughter and offered her biggest, brightest, most comforting smile possible.

Ava didn't smile back. Clearly she knew what her mother meant by "family matter," and she wasn't falling for it.

Jack rose much earlier than nine. No building project waited for him—not yet. He had no business to attend to. He thought of visiting a few more stores that catered to the construction trade, getting there early, but did not.

There's something about this morning. His thoughts, jittery and dislo-cated, circled back to the evening before at The Palm.

Maybe I tempted myself too much. Maybe that's why I'm on edge now.

He sat at the table with a pencil, a solar-powered calculator, a recent contractor's guide to prices, and a half cup of instant coffee. He was almost finished with the estimate for the Pettigrews—the young couple with the outdated kitchen and bath.

He sketched a rough drawing of his proposed kitchen layout, the lines precise and angular, almost as if it had been done by a professional drafts-man. Jack took pride in being able to draw 3-D renderings of kitchens and bookcases and all manner of architectural and structural details. He drew out a rudimentary trim profile, made a list of the lumber needed, multi-plied the board feet times the prices, listed the cabinets required, added an estimate of the cost of various flooring options—hardwood, tile, and vinyl. He consulted his guidebook. He added midrange prices for kitchen appliances and a new set of bath fixtures—tub, sink, and toilet. He tapped at the calculator.

He could quote $15,000 for the job—$15,000 and change, if he used stock cabinets, the least expensive fixtures, laminate on the counters, and vinyl on the floor. From that number, he began to add extras: granite countertops, custom cabinets, built-in stainless steel refrigerator and commercial stove, hardwood floors. In just a few strokes, that initial figure ballooned easily to $40,000.

Jack brushed off the eraser residue from the estimate.

If they wanted him to do the work and picked the low price, he would be busy for a month and make a profit of at least $3,500. If they opted for the higher prices, he'd make more. People often stretched themselves financially. At any rate, Jack's payoff would not be a fortune. In fact, it wasn't much at all. But it would be a start. And, hopefully, he would build from there.

I know I can do this.

"Why, don't you look pretty?" Leslie said as she took a few steps back from her daughter.

Leslie had picked out a feminine, but not frilly, outfit: a bright yellow jumper with a patterned blouse and tights. This was her one school outfit that was purchased at full retail price. Leslie had already stockpiled a wardrobe of garage sale and thrift store finds—all in perfect shape and quite stylish, for pennies on the dollar.

It is what we do now, Leslie told herself. *There is no shame in saving money.*

Leslie held out her hand and Ava dutifully took it. They walked down the steps of the Midlands Building, onto North Street, over three blocks to Washington, then up one more block to Emily Brittian Elementary School, passing houses in which other children were being readied for school.

Ava was about to enter kindergarten.

Leslie chattered along as they walked, asking if Ava was excited ("A little"), scared ("No"), and if she was going to miss her mother ("Of course, but just a little"). Ava had been to school before, a preschool at the Congregational Church in Greensburg, but that was only three days a week and only in the mornings. Kindergarten in Butler meant that Ava would be in school all day long—from 8:00 until 2:30.

Leslie did not like the long hours but knew she would have to find a job—not immediately, but soon. If she had to work a full eight hours … well, she would figure those details out when she had to.

"You remember you're going to be there almost all day, right? Through lunch."

"I remember."

"And that Mommy packed you a lunch."

"Peanut butter and jelly, and Goldfish."

"And your name is on your lunch bag."

"A-V-A. That's easy to spell."

"And that your teacher is Mrs. DiGiulio and that she seems to be very nice."

"Mrs. Di … DiGiulio. That's a hard name."

Leslie stopped at Main Street. The crossing guard, an older man, maybe just retired, waved them across, his stop sign high in the air. Leslie was still worried. Traffic moved too quickly through the school zone, she thought, and this crossing lay at the bottom of a big hill.

What if a runaway cement truck lost its brakes?

"And you get milk at lunch. And I think they have a nap time, too."

Ava looked up and shook her head. "It's quiet time. We don't have to sleep. I bet too many kids went to the bathroom while they were sleeping."

"Ava!" Leslie said, not really upset. "Who told you that?"

Ava shrugged. "I dunno. Maybe I thought it myself."

Now the two of them, mother and daughter, stood in front of the Emily Brittian Elementary School, three blocks off Main, in a quiet, modest neighborhood. Leslie had not let go of her daughter's hand the entire walk.

"That's your door to your class, Ava: 2A. You have your own special door. Everyone else goes in through those big doors in the middle of the building."

Ava nodded. "You showed me that when we visited."

"I just want to make sure you know where to go. I don't want you getting lost or trampled by the bigger kids."

A score of mothers and a few fathers, and their daughters and sons, were milling about, waiting for the kindergarten door to open. A tension, or apprehension, flittered about the sidewalks. Even if the children wanted to, none of them were playing on the swings or the slide or the other playground equipment. It was the first day, after all, and no parent wanted a child to start school with dirty knees or elbows. Leslie noticed that some parents appeared to be relieved. Others looked blasé, most likely going through the experience for a third or fourth time. Only one or two showed any tender emotions.

For Leslie, this was a first and a last experience, all rolled into one. With Ava as her only child, Leslie would only get one chance at this, so each experience with Ava was both joyful and bittersweet. The doctors all agreed: Ava was the first and the last.

There were no older children on the school grounds this day. Kindergarten started a day before the rest of the grades. "We don't want to overwhelm our newest students," Leslie had been told. "In the past, with all the commotion going on, some of our more sensitive kindergarteners just had too much to handle."

A bell sounded from inside the building, echoing in the empty halls. The door opened, and Ava waited until her mother started for the door. The little girl did not hesitate but walked, with purposeful steps, into her classroom.

"And who are you?" Mrs. DiGiulio asked as she bent down to the child's level, her voice bright and happy. Her graying hair and soft wrinkles revealed a mature teacher, to be sure.

Ava stuck out her hand. "Ava Ruskin. I'm in this class. This is my mom. We just moved to Butler."

"You did? Where did you come from?"

"Greensburg. We lived in a big house there until my daddy got a divorce."

If Mrs. DiGiulio was surprised, she did not show a single ounce of it. She kept smiling and took a large laminated nametag, fastened to a length of yellow yarn, and placed it around Ava's neck.

"This matches your dress, Ava. See? This has your name on it."

"A-V-A. It's easy to spell."

"And it will help all the other students know your name too."

Mrs. DiGiulio stood. "It was nice to meet you, Mrs. Ruskin. We will see you back here at 1:00—right? Early dismissal today. They'll all be tired by then."

Leslie waited outside the door, watching as Ava found the desk with her name on it and sat down. She turned only once to face the door, and when she saw her mother still standing there, gave just the slightest nod, acknowledging her presence, then turned back to face the front and the smiling Mrs. DiGiulio.

Leslie waved. Maybe Ava saw her. Maybe she didn't. Leslie forced herself to turn and walk away. Other parents were talking—old friends, perhaps. Leslie wanted to meet them, but not today, not now.

She just couldn't.

She hurried down the sidewalk, turned the corner, and hurried to the end of the block. There she was alone. No one could see her break into sobs … sobs that racked at her heart. The tears would not stop.

Her heart was breaking, as she knew it would—not only for herself, but for her daughter, who would never experience her father seeing her in her little yellow jumper on her first day of kindergarten, and for a little girl who would never again have a big house to live in.

Leslie cried for a while, maybe four or five minutes, until she could compose herself … at least enough to keep walking.

She had an appointment to keep.

I've got to pull myself together. I can do this.

———————

Jack Kenyon stood in front of the Midlands Building and looked up at the peculiar screened porches built around the small balcony of each of the three second-floor apartment units. Even from the street, he could see that they had been done by an amateur: two-by-fours all around, hardly substantial, with two-by-twos dividing the larger spans. The entire structure may have been screwed into the original metal balconies, and even though Jack was not familiar with the building codes in Butler, he was pretty sure that none of it was up to code. Whoever was hired to do the construction work might have to bring the building back to code. He made a mental note to tell the owner when she showed up.

The majority of Butler's historic downtown buildings seemed to be constructed around the same time—1870s to 1890s, Jack was almost sure, and the Midlands Building was no exception. On its cornerstone was carved *Erected 1897*. It had become a landmark, with its classic flat Italianate roofline with a deep cornice that had ornamental brackets, and a secondary cornice separating the two floors. It occupied the corner of North and Cedar streets and boasted of a recessed diagonal main entrance with an etched glass transom. Large display windows flanked the main double doors on both sides, with high kickplates below the glass area, that were about three feet off the sidewalk, and etched transoms of their own. As he peeked around the building, Jack could see that there were secondary entrances on the building's sides, leading to the upper story. He could also see that, except for the peculiar screened balconies that had been added perhaps fifty years ago, the exterior, at least, had worn the years well—nearly all original and in good shape.

What's inside might be a different story.

"Hi! You're here early. I'm Leslie Ruskin."

Leslie extended her hand to Jack.

He remembered her from his first day at passing out flyers. She may have been close to Jack's age, maybe a few years younger. He was never good at estimating ages. She had full lips, medium brown eyes, maybe a shade darker, and a heart-shaped face. Her short-to-medium-length brown hair was cut in an almost angular bob and had highlighted streaks in it. Jack never understood the hows and whys of the hair highlighting process, but on her, it looked good, almost natural. She was very pretty, he thought, in a young mom sort of way.

No. That's not it, not nearly. She's much more than your standard soccer mom. I wonder what she's doing buying a building like this? Seems like a big step for a woman. For such a pretty woman.

She was wearing a close-fitting white T-shirt, nothing fancy, tucked into her jeans, with a black belt and flat shoes. It looked, to Jack, like a no-nonsense choice of attire. Without analyzing it, he hoped he would get this job—regardless of the scale of the project.

More than pretty, really. Much more.

"So you bought the place," he both asked and stated at the same time. "When I saw you the other day, I was kind of joking. I mean, I saw the For

Sale sign and saw how intently you were staring at the place, so I made the offhand comment."

"You know, I wondered why you asked that. I thought you might have known somebody at the bank," Leslie answered.

"Nope. Just a guess." He smiled.

Leslie bobbed her head, as if wondering what to do next.

"Why don't you show me around?' Jack asked. "You said there was an empty apartment. You want to start there?"

She took a key ring out of her pocket, a simple silver hoop with a few keys—not like most women, Jack noted, who possessed a hundred keys attached to some horribly oversized key charm. Her style was much simpler. He wished his wife had been that way.

"There are two apartments that share this street-level entrance and a stairway," Leslie was saying. "The unit on that side," she said as she pointed down the street, "has a separate entrance—but it's rented now, so ... I don't think I plan on doing anything to that one. At least for now."

She turned the key and pushed the door with her hip. Jack couldn't help but notice how she moved and how well her jeans fit. The door squealed a bit and popped open.

"Hinges need oil," she explained. "But I can't find where I packed that little can of 3-IN-ONE oil."

Jack brushed the comment aside. "I have some in my truck. I'll do it before I leave. Complimentary. Like peanuts on an airplane."

"Really? Thanks a lot."

"No problem." Jack gave her another broad, easy smile.

The stairway to the second floor was wide, with a high ceiling and dark wood wainscoting. "It all needs to be painted, but I think I'm going to try to do some of that myself. I painted some rooms of our old house," Leslie said as they made their way up the stairs.

"Where did you live before?" Jack asked, then quickly added, "Just curious. I'm not prying." He didn't want to be one of those contractors who became too friendly too quickly with their clients.

"Oh no, that's okay. We lived in Greensburg. South of here."

"Oh, sure. I've been through Greensburg. Seemed like a nice place to live."

They reached the second-floor landing, shared by both apartments.

Leslie appeared to be deciding something. Then she spoke. "My daughter and I moved here a short while ago. Her father and I divorced. I wanted a new start, and we chose Butler. My great-great-great-grandparents lived here once upon a time. I don't know much about them, but the town's in our family history, so I thought this would be a good place. What goes around, comes around."

Jack didn't respond. He didn't really know how to respond. But he was glad she'd told him. Saved him the problem of trying to decipher the puzzle a single mom and child presented.

"So I bought this place, with the intention of renting out the other two units—or the other empty unit, and eventually the lower floor, hopefully."

She unlocked one of the doors and they entered the empty apartment. Similar to her own apartment, it opened into a small entry, and they went through it to the light and spacious living room, with its fireplace and five large arched windows, all original from the 1890s, Jack guessed, and walnut trim—or trim stained to look like walnut—throughout. It was too dark for his tastes, but it looked to be in good shape. The windows may have been replaced once, but they were still old.

"Wow, what a great space. And a fireplace," Jack said.

"All three units have one." Leslie answered.

She led him into the kitchen—battered, nicked, out-of-date, worn hard, badly in need of renewal.

Jack whistled.

"I know," Leslie said. "It needs everything. For sure, we need new countertops. I guess you should price out laminate. I would love to use granite or something like that, but I don't have that sort of budget."

Jack took measurements and jotted down notes. He tried to focus on the notes on his clipboard, and not on Leslie. "New appliances? Cabinets?"

Leslie appeared to take another look at everything, then nodded, almost reluctantly. "I don't want to spend more money than I need to bring this place back, but these all have to go. I think the refrigerator is from the 1970s. The appliances in our apartment only look to be several years old, but these relics have seen their days."

"Will you buy the new appliances? Or is that something you want me to include?"

"Can you? I mean … do you do things like that?"

Jack put his clipboard on the counter. "I can. Might be less expensive if you let the store deliver them all together for a flat fee. I'll give you a separate price on that. And I'll quote new stock cabinets, as well as quoting the cost of just refacing the cabinets. The bases look solid enough."

The living room needed new drywall on one side; the entire west wall was cracked and peeling.

"The man from the bank said the roof was bad in that area and it had leaked," Leslie explained. "The previous owner put on new tar and gravel last year. Said the leak stopped, but this wall has to be repaired."

The bathroom's shell was serviceable; the original tile was so old that it was back in style, but in surprisingly good condition. But a new tub, toilet, and sink would be needed.

"I can put the new fixtures in and leave the vintage tile alone," Jack suggested. "Cheaper—and I think it will look nice. New lighting will help a lot. And a thorough cleaning."

The two bedrooms were plain and simple. Leslie wanted new wire shelves and poles installed in the closets, which were fairly large—unusual for this era of building.

Jack finished his notes. "What about your place?"

"We're not doing anything to our unit. Not yet. Maybe later," Leslie quickly replied.

"And the downstairs space?"

Jack looked at his potential customer, trying to read her expression, hoping that he wasn't being obvious about it. It was evident she hadn't fully considered that part of the building.

"Well, we should look at it. I guess. You know, I'm not sure what to do about it. Maybe you can give me an idea."

Back down on the sidewalk, Leslie tried one key, then another. Finally, with the third, the lock opened and she swung in one of the heavy wooden double doors.

"When I bought this place, I figured the two rents, and my job—when

I get one—will pay the bills. I guess I should start trying to rent this bottom floor soon as well. But I'm not sure what to do with it."

"What was this before?" Jack asked. "Did the people at the bank tell you?"

Leslie walked to the center of the room. It was a large space. Very large. Jack estimated at least four thousand square feet. Arched display windows ran around the two sides of the building, separated by brickwork, each arch capped by a granite keystone. Pillars stood, like mute guards in an empty hall, their round shafts painted, now peeling. They were topped with simple Greek capitals. There was a large fireplace in marble and cast iron centered on the side wall.

"The people at the bank said something about a locksmith shop, but there's too much space here for a locksmith, isn't there? And it's all too grand."

"Unless he was a really successful locksmith," Jack answered. "Or maybe he only used a portion of the space. Left the rest empty. Or rented it out to another business."

There was a space at the rear, with three doors. Jack walked back and saw that there were two very dated restrooms. He turned the fancy doorknob of a third closed wooden door, which was large and heavily carved, and found that it was locked. Probably storage space, he guessed.

"Wow—this is a really old door. Interesting carvings. Do you have a key for it?" he asked.

"No," Leslie answered. "The man from the bank said that the lock on that one door was jammed. Maybe it's because he couldn't find the keys."

Jack jiggled the doorknob one more time to see if that might spring the door open. It did not.

"You'll need to get a locksmith in for this," he suggested. "That space will be important to prospective tenants."

Leslie nodded. "Sure, I can do that."

They turned back to the front space. Leslie gingerly shoved an old, empty cardboard box with her foot.

Jack looked up at the ceiling. Tin squares all around, painted white, a few bent, some peeling. Dropped lighting fixtures dotted the space—from their look, last upgraded in the 1950s. The floor was all hardwood, in thinner strips than currently used. He pegged the floor installation to be original to the building.

"This is a really nice space. Wonderful architectural details. Needs cleaning more than anything. A few repairs. Floor needs sanding and refinishing. Maybe a few patches. New restroom fixtures, for sure. A few repairs on the ceiling. New lighting. Painting."

Leslie nodded along with his assessment but stopped. "But if I found a tenant, wouldn't they do all that work?"

Jack took out a penknife, knelt down, and scratched at the bottom of one of the pillars. "These are concrete. That's good. Plaster might hide problems."

He stood and slipped the knife into his pocket. "New tenants? Yes, probably they would do their own build-out—fix it the way they want, I mean. But this place is kind of a mess. Hard to see past that. You know: A clean house sells quicker than a messy house. The few repairs, like the bathrooms, will have to be done. And they won't be that expensive."

Jack walked to a front window. "Tell you what: I'll work up a quote for the job upstairs. If you like it, and hire me, I'll do the cleanup down here, and I'll only charge you the reduced rate that builders charge for cleanup. I can do the cleaning on the weekends myself. Should only take a few weekends to get everything done. Since I'm starting out too, every little bit helps. If you want the restrooms redone, or any other of the repairs, those I'll charge at my regular rates."

Leslie appeared relieved. "Good. I'll keep that in mind when I review your quote."

"I'll have it for you tomorrow."

Leslie appeared surprised.

"You said you're starting over," Jack answered. "Nobody wants to wait when they're starting over."

All that morning, Leslie's thoughts kept going to Jack. She knew he was the type of man who possessed an effortless charm—the sort of affability women found irresistible, the ability to be everyone's friend.

I wonder if he's unattached. He's so good-looking … highly unlikely.

Ava unwrapped her peanut-butter-and-jelly sandwich. She spread out her Goldfish, which had been tucked into a Ziploc bag, in straight lines on her desk. In the store, she had seen and had wanted the individual bags of Goldfish, but her mother had insisted that the bigger bag was exactly the same Goldfish and so much less expensive. One of things today that made up for not having Goldfish in its own bag was that she got milk in a little carton, all her own. Mrs. DiGiulio walked down each aisle, making sure that everyone's milk was opened.

The teacher clapped her hands properly—not mean, but like when you're chasing a cat out nicely—and all her young students looked up. A few were already chewing, but Ava had waited for someone to say it was time to eat.

"Children, it's almost lunchtime," she said, pointing at the clock. "When the little hand and the big hand meet at the top, then we eat."

Ava squinted. The hands were just *this close* to each other.

"And when the clock's hands are together, we should do what the clock does—join our hands together and pray before we eat."

Mrs. DiGiulio looked so happy, Ava thought, happier than any adult she had known, except for one lady on television, and that didn't count because her mom said those people were just actors and it was all make-believe. Mrs. DiGiulio didn't seem to be pretending at all.

"Okay, hands together," Mrs. DiGiulio said, then added, "you can all repeat after me: 'God is great. God is good. Let us thank Him for our food. Amen.'"

Ava looked up.

Her teacher was beaming. "Now let's all enjoy our lunch."

Ava chewed quietly, with her mouth closed, as her mother had always insisted. The boy in front of her was sort of bouncy. He had two chocolate cupcakes with a squiggle of white frosting on each top, wrapped in a cellophane wrapper. He turned in his desk and looked at the soldierly straight line of Goldfish that Ava was deliberately, systematically eating one by one. His name was Trevor. Ava didn't like the name Trevor, but this Trevor seemed nice.

"You want a cupcake? I only eat one. That's all my dad says I'm allowed to have at one time, even if I'm still hungry or starving. He says I have to bring one of them home, for later."

Ava considered the offer. She really wanted the chocolate cupcake, because her mom never bought them, but she wasn't sure if this was the polite thing to do—or even if it was allowed.

She raised her hand.

It took Mrs. DiGiulio a moment to notice, and she hurried to Ava's desk.

"Trevor wants me to have his second cupcake and not bring it home like his dad said. Can he do that?"

Mrs. DiGiulio bent down and gave the little girl a little hug. "Of course he can, Ava. Trevor, that's such a nice thing for you to do. You tell your daddy that Mrs. DiGiulio said it was okay to share."

Ava reached over and as she took the cupcake, she said firmly, "Thanks, Trevor."

"My dad won't mind. He can go to the store and buy one for himself."

As Ava ate the moist, delicious, sweet, sweet cupcake, she stared at the back of Trevor's head, as if memorizing the way his red hair fell just so over the collar of his slightly wrinkled blue shirt.

Jack left the Midlands Building just before noon. Feeling good about his prospects, he decided to treat himself to lunch—at a real restaurant. His usual midday meal consisted of something ordered at a speaker from the cab of his truck, or a quick ham-and-cheese sandwich he made himself at his apartment.

He thought that he and Mrs. Ruskin—or Ms. Ruskin, or was it Miss Ruskin?—had hit it off nicely. He just didn't know what to call her. Using her first name, Leslie, might be too presumptuous—and again, he told himself he didn't intend to be one of those contractors who confused a business relationship with a personal one. He wanted to keep business *business*, if at all possible.

He picked a counter stool at Emil's, a restaurant on Main Street that appeared to have been in business for decades, judging by its facade. The restaurant always seemed crowded, Jack had observed.

How else do you know if a place has good food or not?

Emil's had large, sparkling clean windows and warm lights, and it seemed like a friendly sort of place—not fancy, but nice, in a "comfort food" kind of way. He would have gone back to The Palm tavern, but he knew it would be too easy, too tempting, to transform this lunch into a small liquid celebration. No matter how little the celebration was, it would prove too much for Jack to deal with. Emil's was more of a family place and safer by far.

"Menu?"

A young waitress—cute and blonde—held out a folded menu, in plastic with leather reinforcements as a frame. Jack categorized restaurants by their menu: an illuminated menu board on the back wall was cheapest, a slab of laminated plastic with color photos of all the food was next, a folded menu with some plastic and some leather was next on the expensive ladder, and finally, a menu tucked into a thick, padded booklike folder with a gold elastic string holding it in place was the most expensive of them all.

He immediately glanced at the prices, recognizing that he hadn't yet found any paying jobs. The prices weren't bad. He could afford a BLT and fries and coffee and tip and still have change from a ten-dollar bill.

The waitress stood in front of him with a pad in one hand and a pen in the other. Not smiling, but not frowning either, she waited as if she had all the time in the world to wait for his order alone.

He immediately would have ordered the BLT, but the meat loaf special caught his eye as well. *Mashed potatoes. I haven't had mashed potatoes in months.* "How's the meat loaf?"

The waitress, wearing a nametag that had *Judy* written out in raised black letters, leaned closer to him—almost too close. But Jack liked that. She was very cute. He had been alone for a long time, and this sort of unexpected intimacy made him take notice.

"What's your second choice?" she said softly, almost whispered, as she leaned in even closer to him, closer than a waitress normally got to her customer. She was almost touching his right ear as she spoke.

"A BLT?"

"A wonderful choice. I recommend it, but on Italian bread. With lots of mayo. We're using fresh tomatoes from the owner's garden. You won't be sorry. A better pick, really."

"Okay. But can I get mashed potatoes instead of the fries?"

She reached down and touched his arm. "For you, of course."

She wrote down his order. "What did you say your name was?"

"I didn't, but my name is Jack. Jack Kenyon."

She gave him her best smile … or so Jack thought. When she put out her hand for him to shake, he was sure that it was her best smile.

"It is so nice to meet you, Jack Kenyon. I hope you become one of my regulars."

She held his hand longer than needed, then walked away with a swaying purpose in her steps, ripped his ticket from her pad, and headed for the kitchen.

Jack watched her every step.

Is she this friendly with everyone?

There was an inverted coffee cup at every placemat. He turned his over and looked down the counter. Judy was at the small kitchen window, laughing with the cook. She slipped his ticket into the round rotating holder.

I wonder how old she is?

"Trevor gave you a cupcake?"

Ava nodded.

"Why?"

They had stopped at the corner of Main and North, waiting for the buzzing light to change.

"He saw me eating Goldfish."

Leslie waited. There had to be more to the story than that. But she had just read in a parents' magazine at her old doctor's office that you shouldn't push a child to tell you more than they were ready to tell. Yet she was so anxious to hear how her daughter's first day of school went.

"Did you like Mrs. DiGiulio?"

"She's real nice. And funny. She read a story about a chipmunk and made her voice go all squeaky. Everybody laughed."

Leslie held tightly to her daughter's hand as they hurried across the street. She looked up the hill, toward Locust Street, worried afresh about runaway cement trucks.

"Did you like all the kids in your class?"

Ava shrugged. "I didn't meet them all. But they seem nice. I like Trevor. He's funny. He has red hair. And he wiggles a lot."

Leslie was sure she was missing something, but Ava was talking and that was a good thing.

"What else did you do?"

Ava sighed theatrically. "We did colors. We had story time. We learned where our cubbies are. Our paint shirts go in them. She talked a lot about the rules. I don't remember all of them."

"Rules?"

"Like no talking. You have to raise your hand if you need to go to the bathroom. Like that."

They were at their corner. Leslie reached into her pocket for her keys. She had purchased several decorated white cupcakes earlier in the day at Friedman's Market, a few blocks from their new home. She hoped that the earlier cupcake from Trevor wouldn't dim the surprise.

"Cupcakes!" Ava shouted when she entered the kitchen. "With smiley faces! Can I have two of them?"

"One for now," Leslie said as they both sat at the table, on two of the four chairs they owned, and carefully peeled off the paper wrappers. "Do you want milk?"

Ava nodded. "We get milk at school in little cartons. I like that."

They ate in silence. The cupcakes were very tasty. Leslie was certain they had been baked fresh in the bakery right in the store. Ava carefully folded the crinkled paper wrapper and put it on her plate, then drank the rest of her milk.

"If someone doesn't say they have something, does that really mean they don't have that?" Ava asked as she put her empty glass on the table.

"Like what? Who doesn't have what?"

Ava's mouth looked compressed into a sour pucker, as it always did when she was concentrating on something.

"Trevor never said he had a mommy. He just talked about his daddy. Does that mean he doesn't have a mommy?"

Leslie waited to answer. After all, Ava did not often mention her father, but it didn't mean that she did not have a father.

"Maybe, sweetie. Maybe Trevor's mommy is away."

"My daddy's away."

"He is, but you still have a daddy."

Ava looked at the clock on the wall. "Mrs. DiGiulio is going to teach us to tell time. What time is it now?"

"Two o'clock. Almost—a few minutes till two."

Ava slipped off the chair. "Can I watch television? Maybe *Dora the Explorer* is on."

Leslie had indeed found an adaptor plug that matched the wire from the roof and plugged nicely into their television set. Times had changed since Leslie was a little girl. Despite not having cable, they still received ten different channels. In a moment, Leslie heard the familiar theme song.

"Mommy! *Dora the Explorer*! Our television has *Dora the Explorer*!"

Leslie hurried out to join her daughter on the green sofa. She was certain the episode was a repeat, or even years old, yet as she slid her arm around her daughter, she noticed her wide, happy smile.

Thank you for small favors, Leslie said to herself, aiming the thought at no one in particular.

"Oh, and Mrs. DiGiulio taught us how to pray today. I liked it. It was a rhyme."

Leslie, surprised, would have asked Ava more. But the animated program had started, and the child leaned forward, unwilling to miss a single moment of her favorite show. So Leslie kept silent, regardless of the theology involved.

───◦◦◦───

"Kenyon Construction."

"Hello, Mr. Kenyon. This is Leslie Ruskin. I'm sorry I wasn't at home when you stopped by. I must have been at the grocery store."

"No problem at all. I hope you got my estimate."

"I did."

She had gotten it, looked at the bottom number—the total estimate of costs—and realized that she could just afford to have it all done and still leave a small cushion in the bank. She looked at each individual number, not truly knowing if the amounts were high or low, but they seemed reasonable. Of course, Leslie had seen all the remodeling shows on television and read scores of articles on picking contractors—how to avoid being taken, how to ensure work done to code—but in the end, it all came down to trust. And, somehow, she trusted Jack Kenyon. She trusted him because he had not insisted on doing more work than she wanted. He had offered to work on the first floor cleanup at a reduced rate, and, well, he had an honest face and an honest approach.

That was enough for her. But she did hear echoes of her ex-husband. *Always knock 20 percent off an estimate. See what they do then. Maybe they come back with a 10 percent reduction. That's how you beat them at their own game.*

"The final number, Mr. Kenyon—can we do any better than that?"

No doubt Jack was prepared for this. "I really estimated down to the bone—"

She waited, thinking he was going to keep talking.

"—but what I can do is split any contractor discount I get on items I purchase for you. The cabinets for example—I put in $4,000 for them. If I get a better discount—let's say an extra 10 percent, I'll split that with you. So on the cabinets, you could knock off $200 or so. How's that sound?"

Leslie grinned to herself. It wasn't what her ex-husband would have called substantial, but it was something.

"When can you start, Mr. Kenyon?" Leslie asked, her voice eager.

"Would tomorrow be too early? I'll need to take final measurements for the cabinets," Jack answered, his voice sounding equally eager. "What time tomorrow?"

There was a hesitation. Then, "Would 7:30 be too early?"

Amelia Westland, age thirteen years, four months
Glade Mills
Butler County, Pennsylvania
November 12, 1875

It is the worst of all worlds. In less than three weeks' time, since I last recorded my thoughts, I have lost my saintly mother, and finally, two days prior to this day, my dear father succumbed to this horrible illness and passed.

My tears are without end. I can find only small comfort in the fact that they have all traveled on to God's greatest reward—a life in heaven without pain nor sorrow nor sickness.

Yet, I am left here alone. The crops have been left to rot in the fields, for it was harvest time when Father was stricken. The furrows of soil, once so promising with their rich, yeasty smell, now lie frozen, bleak and hopeless. There is no one to hire to work the land. Most able-bodied young men have left to avoid this scourge.

I call out to God: What shall I do? What shall become of me?

Reverend Wilcox performed both funerals. He knows I am now alone. My father had nothing of real value to leave to me. The farm was not paid for. Only the spare furnishings were ours and the few items of clothing each of us possess. Surely the bank will recall the acreage and claim the house and affects be held in payment for accounts now far in arrears. I assume that my few books will be regarded as effects and taken as well, and it frets me greatly, since they are most precious to me.

In my sadness I sometimes pray for death to come and free me as well. Then I would be with Mother and Father again. I miss them so. Why, God, have I been spared?

> *Blessed are they that mourn: for they shall be comforted.*
> —MATTHEW 5:4

CHAPTER FIVE

JACK PARKED HIS TRUCK AROUND the corner from the Midlands Building. It was only 7:00, and he did say he would be there at 7:30. He wanted to be the sort of contractor who was true to his word, and while thirty minutes was a minor point, it was still a point. Early might not be welcome.

He rustled through the bag from McDonald's. He had eaten the hash browns on the ride to the Midlands Building and now started in on the breakfast sandwich. The coffee was nestled into the cup holder on the dashboard. The radio scratched out traffic reports for Pittsburgh, which he did not need. Jack had not yet decided which radio station he would listen to. While living in Franklin, the choice had been easy. There was only one station that played decent music coupled with clear reception. In Butler, he faced all sorts of choices—the Pittsburgh stations were all close enough to find good reception on a basic truck radio, and even the local station offered a fairly current playlist of his kind of music.

He folded the visor down to block the early sun. Held tight with two thick rubber bands was a creased picture of a small girl—blonde, prettier than the prettiest flower, sitting on a gleaming motorcycle, eating a strawberry ice-cream cone. It was his favorite picture, a picture he could not look at without aching, without remembering, without tasting the sharpness of pain and regret.

He flipped the visor back up and squinted.

He listened and ate, and consulted his watch every five minutes. At

7:25, he allowed himself to leave his truck and walk slowly to the front door. He was carrying his clipboard and wearing his tool belt, with hammer, twenty-five-foot measuring tape, two carpenter's pencils, and one new black felt-tip pen, all snugged into their proper spots.

He brushed back his hair with his hand and pressed at the bell. Above the bell was a slip of paper, taped next to the buzzer: *L. Ruskin.*

From upstairs, a faint buzz echoed. Jack waited. He knew how frantic mornings with a young child could become. Less than a minute passed and Jack saw a glint of the door opening on the landing above. He saw four feet coming down the steps.

"Good morning, Mr. Kenyon. Here's the key to the vacant apartment. And this one opens the front door of the building."

Leslie handed both keys to Jack. They were tied together with a twist-tie from a bread package. He noticed Leslie's daughter staring up at him. He saw the young girl tug at her mother's hand. She bent down and her child whispered in her ear.

"This is Ava," Leslie said when she stood back up.

The child waved at him, still silent.

"She knows not to talk to strangers. Ava, this is Mr. Kenyon. He will be working on the apartment next to ours. He's no longer a stranger, okay?"

Jack extended his hand to the child and held her hand as delicately as he could. "Nice to meet you, Ava. Are you going to school now?"

Ava nodded vigorously.

"Do you like school?"

She nodded again, even more vigorously.

"Are you going to say hello?" her mother asked.

Ava shook her head, indicating no but smiling, as if holding back a conspiratorial giggle.

Leslie shrugged, took her daughter's hand, and slipped past Jack in the small vestibule of the Midlands Building.

"We're walking to school this morning, Mr. Kenyon. And then I have a few errands to run. I should be back by eleven o'clock."

She is a very, very pretty woman, Jack thought to himself as he watched them walk out of the building and down the sidewalk. At the corner, Ava turned back and waved to Jack like a sailor heading out to sea, waving with her whole arm, shoulder, and most of her body, her grin visible at the half-block distance.

I wonder … she's divorced … but is she unattached? That beautiful and unattached? I could ask … or should I keep this first job purely business?

Jack walked up the stairs, slowly, wondering about Leslie, and then, in a rush, feeling the guilt and the pain, feelings he knew were always there, lurking at the edges all along. He tried to force it away by remembering Leslie's encompassing smile and Ava's wave, but it was of no use today.

Not even his own legendary charm could keep his morning from turning gray and cold.

———⊰◦⊱———

To fight this, I need to stay busy … very busy.

By 9:30, Jack had created a list of what materials he would need to start the project. He had only asked Leslie Ruskin for a payment of 10 percent of his estimated costs up front. Many contractors insisted on a full one-third, but he thought, at this point, that amount might cause concern from any wary customers. So instead of a larger initial sum, Jack had asked her for smaller payments to be made every week—like a paycheck. "If you get worried at any point along the job, you tell me. We'll work it out," he'd insisted.

Two-by-fours; plasterboard; wallboard screws; three kinds of nails: rough construction, finish, and trim; several sheets of interior plywood; paper runners for the floor; a bucket of finishing plaster; wallboard tape; wallboard compound; electrical supplies: tape, wire nuts, new outlet covers; and tubes of white caulk and adhesive—it would fill up the back of his pickup. It would take him all morning to purchase everything, then haul it all upstairs. The rest would come later.

There would be no assistants on this job to do the grunt work. Jack would be the grunt, the rough carpenter, the wallboarder, the taper, the finish carpenter, the gopher, the cleanup crew. No carpenter liked doing all of that, but every small contracting firm was made up of guys who had to know how to do it all. Besides roofing, the only other aspect of construction that he'd hire out would be plumbing. He could install a disposal unit, he could swap out old faucets for new, he could install a dishwasher—but anything more than that, he would call for help from a subcontractor.

And electrical. He had caused enough sparks in his day. He would call an electrician to do any real electrical work. He could rewire an outlet, and install a light fixture. But adding a *new* outlet—knowing which wire to pull from where—was beyond him. He didn't anticipate needing advanced plumbing or electrical on this job and had already resigned himself to a lonely few weeks.

By noon, he was back at the Midlands Building and began the process of hauling all the materials upstairs. He immediately began to envy the big contractors, who would have their supply yards deliver trucks filled with materials to be offloaded with cranes and lifts. No, today he muscled up six sheets of four-by-eight drywall. The single sheets, not all that heavy, were awkward and unwieldy, and required careful handling, and a special drywall sheet carrying tool, to manage them up the stairs. And Jack was not about to get off to a bad start on this job by racking dents and dings in the existing stairway and halls. By one o'clock, everything was upstairs and Jack was sweating through his shirt.

He was hungry and recalled the days working for Ethan Willis on the Carter Mansion in Franklin. At noon, precisely on the hour, all work would stop and the crew would gather somewhere in the building, or on the wraparound front porch, or on the lawn, for lunch. Sometimes, someone would volunteer to make a fast-food run. And sometimes, someone's wife or girlfriend would make cookies. Lunchtime would be laced with talk and laughter.

Today, by himself, Jack unwrapped a single sandwich—prepackaged ham, yellow American cheese, unwrapped from a plastic sleeve, two packets of mayonnaise taken from a Subway store last week, and half a bag of potato chips, which he did not like, and which had been stored above his refrigerator for the last two weeks.

At lunch, they won't be all that bad. I guess I'll just need to be hungry, he'd thought when he'd packed them.

Even though he was hungry, the chips did not taste any better. The salt left him thirsty, and he wished he'd driven over to The Palm for a cheeseburger. But he was thirsty … really thirsty, so maybe it wasn't such a good idea. He finished the bottle of water he'd bought at the drugstore, went to the sink, let the cold water run for a while, then filled it up again.

He walked to the double french doors that led to the balcony. He undid the latch and opened them, letting the fresh autumn air inside. He looked at his watch. It had taken ten minutes to eat his lunch and drink his water. Instead of immediately going back to work, he took his refilled water bottle out onto the balcony overlooking the street, all screened in, and sat in the abandoned lawn chair that had been left by the previous tenant.

It was warm for the time of year. He sat and watched the cars roll by on Cedar Street, a block off Main. There was not a lot of traffic on the side street, but enough. He wondered if he should buy a radio at the discount center north of town. He liked music while he worked. Since he would be working alone, he thought it all the more important.

But I'm not spending more than fifty dollars on it. And I don't need a CD player or anything fancy. Maybe even less than fifty dollars ...

———◦◦◦◦———

Leslie opened the *Butler Eagle* newspaper to the classified section and spread it out on the kitchen table. The afternoon sun was streaming in through the tall expanses of windows, and, even with them open, it was getting warm in the apartment. There were shutters, old and hanging crookedly, on the bottom halves only.

I'll need to get some wood blinds for those soon, she thought as she flipped on the wall switch for the ceiling fan over the table.

She filled a glass with ice and grabbed a Diet Coke from the refrigerator, then poured the soda. The air started moving and she felt a bit cooler. The apartment had three window air conditioners—one in each bedroom and a larger one in the living room—but they were noisy and expensive to run, Leslie knew. The ceiling fan would have to do.

She leaned against the counter and took a sip of soda, then looked around her for a long moment. In the harsh afternoon sun, everything appeared washed out and without color. She had to fight back images of the house they'd lived in before, when her family was complete, before her husband's cycles of mania and depression. It had a gourmet kitchen and central air-conditioning. Crisp white trim that set off the buttery-colored walls. Beautiful thick white plantation shutters and custom-made tailored valances on the windows. A big, sunny backyard, where she'd designed and planted an English-style garden around the flagstone patio. Outdoor furniture with an umbrella table. She had loved that house, felt at home in her neighborhood, had put so much of herself in the decorating and the gardening, and the day she had to leave it was one of the darkest in her life.

She knew it was useless to look back, that it was just "stuff." Most of the time she tried to focus on the positive—what she still had—not what was gone. Most of the time she was able to resist the urge to wallow in self-pity over what had happened in her marriage, her world … at least most of the time. But there were some days when fighting that urge was harder than others, when the sinewy threads of hurt and anger and failure and loss tried to wrap themselves around her heart once more. And today, as she stood all alone in the half-empty apartment—*her* apartment that didn't feel like hers, didn't feel at all like home—was one such day.

I'm living someone else's life …

She took in a deep breath through her nose, then exhaled through her mouth slowly, a relaxation technique she'd learned at a yoga class at the health club in Greensburg. She did this until she had calmed herself a bit and her tightening stomach muscles relaxed. Then she sat down in front of the newspaper.

… but I can try and make this mine. If Gramma Mellie could do it, so can I.

Flipping to the beginning of the employment listings, she tried to focus.

She scanned the list of ads, her eyes following the path of her finger as it moved down the page.

Asphalt Worker. Assembly. Drivers. Food Service. Machinist. Nail Tech. Welder.

Wrong category, she thought as she found the Sales and Marketing area.

But unless she was interested in working in "the exciting field of Identity Theft Protection" or wanted to sell "Quality Stone Veneer," nothing caught her eye. Under Situations Wanted, among the ads for Childcare and Live-in Home Companions, a twenty-seven-year-old country western singer was in need of a guitar player, and Lingerie Parties Ltd. was looking to expand. A smile crossed her lips, as she tried to envision what that would look like, but she didn't see anything promising.

She closed the newspaper, and was ready to toss it in the recycling bin, then had another thought and opened it again. She found the Real Estate section and went to the Rentals area. Under the Store/Office/Garage heading were several office spaces for rent, and a few storefronts available in the downtown area, but nothing over 1,000 square feet.

Good! No competition …

She imagined someone at the *Butler Eagle* office would help her with the wording of a rental ad for the first-floor space, but she had no idea how much she could ask per month, and there were no prices included in the rental classifieds. She thought about calling the real-estate agent who had listed the Midlands Building, then glanced at her watch: *2:15.* Time to get Ava at school.

—————

Frank Adams glanced at his Rolex watch—the stainless steel and gold model with an additional small dial for a different time zone.

Two fifteen in the afternoon eastern time. That's if I set this right. And that makes it 9:15 p.m. here? Is Paris on Europe Standard Time? Does Europe have a standard time? And did we change our clocks when we left Butler? I should ask Alice. I think she's wearing two watches today.…

He pressed one button on his chunky watch, which he thought started a stopwatch, but the button didn't do anything.

Maybe the button is for the time change. I wonder where I put the manual for this thing?

Frank sat outside a café, on the Left Bank, in Paris, along the Quai Voltaire, across the Seine River from the Tuilleries Gardens, sipping café au lait with his wife, Alice, his long legs splayed out in front of him.

I would ask her what the button is for, but I don't think I'll get the answer I expect. And what is a Quai, anyhow?

"If this is the City of Lights, why can't I read my newspaper?" Alice asked.

The restaurant was hemmed in by a long row of antique shops and vintage fabric boutiques—all of which were open late for a special city-wide design exhibition, but the nearest streetlamp was a quarter of a block distant.

Having shopped most of the afternoon and evening, weaving their way in and out of dozens of "funky" (Alice's word) French boutiques and show-rooms, the couple welcomed the chance to sit down and enjoy a relaxing meal of steak frite—a large, thin slice of beef, marinated and grilled, served with a mound of crisply fried, skinny-cut potatoes, and a salad.

"Meat and potatoes," Frank declared, "but done in the French man-ner. French-esque, as it were."

Alice pretended to scowl at him when he reduced things to simple equations. She said it made him sound provincial. She leaned back in the rattan chair and shook out her long, thick auburn hair, then snapped open a compact mirror and reapplied her lipstick.

"I absolutely *adore* the idea of another Alice and Frank's … Frank," she said, smacking her lips together to smooth the color. She snapped the compact closed. A cool breeze came up off the river, and she pulled her pale pink cashmere pashmina shawl closer around her shoulders. "Butler is simply *dying* for it. I can tell. Maybe they don't know it yet, but they *need* us, Frank. They do. The poor citizens have been bereft of style for years and years. Think about it … the closest place to buy a book—a good book—is out at that *horrid* mall, and heaven knows one can't find a decent croissant for miles and miles. And there's no good coffee, either. That swarthy fellow with the ice-cream/coffee shop on Main Street—he's like a bad version of an aging Backstreet Boy. How could *anyone* go in there more than once, other than to gather new material?"

Frank nodded, then looked out on the glistening water, the golden light of the lampposts flittering off the ripples. A sightseeing boat filled with passengers floated past slowly, its bright lights sweeping the facades of the old buildings along the river, briefly interrupting the soft glow.

"Oh, yes—Cunningham's. He is awfully amusing, though. And they do have good ice cream."

Alice did her best to appear perturbed by her husband's defense of the man. "I also saw a gift shop going into the empty space on Main and Vogel before we left, but it looked *so* … unchic," she said. "Is *unchic* a word? Or would it be *chic-less?*"

Alice continued the thought, smiling hard, in an American way—brittle, if you asked a proper Frenchman.

"I would say it would be 'in the manner of non-chic,'" Frank answered. "Or, wait! *Sans chic.* That's it. They're both French words, aren't they? *Sans* and *chic.* That's what they should call the place."

Alice sipped at her café au lait, making a rather loud, un-French-like, un-chic-like, slurping noise. Even the waiter looked up from whatever it was that was keeping him so totally bored with everything.

Alice ignored him, and her husband. "With the wonderful, wonderful things I'm finding here to sell, we'll have the natives of Butler simply dancing in the street—they'll be so astounded."

Alice leaned forward and put her hand on one of Frank's.

"I really, *really* liked the look of that empty building on North and Cedar—you know, the one with the arched windows and the fireplace and the quirky green screened porches on the balconies. It's a *landmark*, Frank. It had a For Sale sign on it. We should have asked about it before we left home. Perfect size. Great location. I can't get it out of my mind. You can see it too, can't you, Frank?—a retro-metro feel—ohhh … I like that: *retro-metro.* Dark woods, walls in dark*ish*, but not *overly* dark colors, deep colors, or, rather, colors with *depth*. Some outlandish artwork—big art!—vintage posters, maybe. Large ones. Lots of glass shelves with cool halogen track lighting for sparkle. Some recessed cans for drama. Simple, understated, casual, yet elegant. A European café/bistro, right in the heart of middle America."

Frank pressed another button on his watch, and the hour hand seemed to jump forward an hour for no good reason.

"Okay," Frank answered, obviously not paying any attention. "We'll have to get right on it."

"Oh, don't talk to me about going home, Frank," Alice said with a bit of a whine, despite the fact that Frank hadn't mentioned a word about going home. "I can hardly *bear* the thought of leaving Paris. You know how depressed I get at the end of a holiday." She sighed deeply. "I'm homesick for Europe already, and we've only been here a few months. Can one be homesick for a place where no one understands a single word one says?"

Frank had his watch up to his right eye, watching the hand slowly sweep. "I don't know, babe."

"Give me that watch, Frank. If you can't pay attention to me when I'm whining, I want that watch."

It was a familiar game to both of them. Frank turned away and stuck his watched arm under his other and clamped up tight.

Alice sat and glared, smiling as she did. "And in addition, we will just simply *have* to find a baker that can do authentic French baked goods for Alice and Frank's, Frank. That's all there is to it."

She huffed once.

"Are scones French?" she asked.

Frank turned back to her and they both began to laugh, a big, bold, rolling American laugh, until the waiter came over and interrupted their good time and chattered away at them in a language neither of them understood.

"Hi, I'm Trevor's father. Mike Reidmiller. Trevor has told me all about your daughter."

Leslie's hand felt small inside his large, almost massive hand. Yet for a man, his handshake was surprisingly gentle. If teddy bears came in human form, Mike Reidmiller would be one of that species—sort of round, but in a pleasant way, with a neatly trimmed dark beard, thick dark hair, and a wide, eager smile.

"Well, I want to thank you for the cupcakes. Ava says Trevor insists on sharing. I hope that it's not a problem," Leslie replied.

Mike Reidmiller had sought out Leslie while they waited for the bell to sound, announcing the end of kindergarten at the Emily Brittian Elementary School. Both were standing in the dappled shadows of the large oak tree on the corner of the school ground.

"Trevor pointed Ava out to me yesterday, and I saw you then, but by the time Trev got his backpack together, you were gone."

Leslie waited, unsure if that required an apology or some manner of explanation. She decided that it did not.

"Anyhow," Mr. Reidmiller continued, "Trev goes on and on about

Ava, and I thought I should say hello. He says that Ava and you just moved to Butler."

"We did, a little over a month ago. We really like it."

Mr. Reidmiller looked over to the playground, as did Leslie, both checking on their children. "Is Ava your only child? Trevor said she was, but sometimes I have difficulty making sure everything he says is really real, and not just something he wants to believe."

"She is an only child, Mr. Reidmiller. And I have the same problem with Ava. I guess it goes with the age," Leslie replied with a smile.

"I know this is probably way too forward, because I've been so out of practice. Trevor said that Ava said that you're divorced. I know it's none of my business, but you know how kids talk and tell all sorts of details that perhaps parents don't want to be made public." Mr. Reidmiller waited for a moment, with what Leslie interpreted as his best nonthreatening look, then continued. "I'm sure Ava has heard all sorts of stories from Trevor as well."

"She didn't tell me all that much, really. She likes him, but Trevor must be some sort of cipher to Ava. She did say that he didn't talk much about his mother, though," Leslie said, as kindly as she could.

"Yeah, that's Trevor," Mr. Reidmiller said, as if admitting to some secret.

The happy screams from the playground seemed to diminish slightly, as parents arrived and students began heading home.

"So I guess I need to tell you that I'm a single parent as well."

Leslie waited again. She seemed to wait a lot lately, not knowing how people expected her to respond and trying her very best not to try and meet someone's else's expectation of just what she should be and just how she should act.

"So … I don't know anything else about you, Mrs. Ruskin, but since we're both single parents … well, I thought maybe we could get coffee sometime. Maybe at Cunningham's—the new ice cream and coffee shop on Main Street? My cousin owns it and he could use the business."

He waited, and Leslie was certain he was hoping for an affirmative reply. The date of Leslie's official divorce decree was less than one year old, though her emotional divorce had occurred much earlier. She knew that, at some moment in time, in the future, some man, somewhere, might just ask her out. Part of her wanted that to happen, and there were moments she wanted it to happen soon, when she wanted to be with a man very badly.

I'm young. I guess I'm sort of attractive. I still want to be with a … in a relationship with a … dating a …

She'd always known dating would be in her future, yet she had no idea what to say now and how to decide.

Does my new life start from here?

Leslie had made one very disastrous choice, based on looks and lust, and she had no additional training in how to avoid making another one choice as inopportune as the first.

Ava picked this instant to charge at her mother full speed, hair flowing behind her pretty young face as if caught in the wind. Her lips opened with a gigantic grin and she called out, "Mommy!" as she opened her arms wide. Leslie bent to receive her daughter and scooped her up, holding her close. She turned back to the invitation at hand.

"Mr. Reidmiller …"

"Mike. Mr. Reidmiller is my father," he said with a grin.

"Mike, thank you for the invitation. I would—"

Just then, Trevor came screaming toward them, his Thomas the Tank Engine backpack windmilling as he ran, straps flapping, his scream not of fear or terror, but of sheer joy of being five and out of school on a warm, pleasant fall afternoon.

"Mike, thanks for the invitation. I would like that, but maybe in a couple of weeks. A rain check, okay? We're still getting settled in, and I've got a contractor that started the work on my place this morning and … well, a lot on my plate."

She knew for certain that having to face a man, a cup of coffee, and possibly uncomfortable silence, was more than enough to cause beads of sweat to form on her forehead and her stomach to ache ever so slightly.

Mr. Reidmiller appeared relieved—in a disappointed but teddy-bear-like way. "No problem at all, Mrs. Ruskin. Leslie. I'll remind you about my invite in a few weeks. I think my cousin can hang on until then."

Amelia Westland, age thirteen years, six months
Butler County, Pennsylvania
December 14, 1875

> *He will regard the prayer of the destitute,*
> *and not despise their prayer.*
> —PSALM 102:17

It has been two months since coming to live with the Reverend Wilcox. I thank my God that he had taken pity on me—left without relative nor close friend to provide quarter, since three homes in the vicinity of our farm—those of the Stalls, Enquists, and Johnsons—also lost one or both parents due to the pox. I have stayed in an upper loft of the Reverend's small parsonage, a pallet with quilts on which to sleep. The weather had not yet turned bitterly cold, so it was tolerable.

It is great consolation that I have my books, which I have been allowed to keep, upon the petition made by the reverend, who prevailed upon officials on my behalf.

It was the reverend's sister who bid him find a suitable situation for me. "How shall it appear to your church," she demanded, "for a widower like you to have a budding young woman in your abode? They will think evil of you. She must go."

Reverend Wilcox has now made arrangements for me to enter the Butler Asylum for Orphans. "They will take care of your needs," he promised, then embraced me until I began to feel uncomfortable. I now await the conveyance they are sending for my few possessions and me.

I pray that God will go before me and find me there.

> *Blessed be God, even the Father of our Lord Jesus Christ,*
> *the Father of mercies, and the God of all comfort.*
> —2 CORINTHIANS 1:3

CHAPTER SIX

LESLIE WOKE THE NEXT MORNING to muted music. She sat up in bed and squinted at the clock. It was 7:00.

My heavens, we'll be late!

She jumped out of bed and tossed on a pair of jeans and a sweatshirt. She ran across the hall to Ava's room and swung the door open. "Ava! Get up ..."

There was no Ava! The bed was rumpled; pink pajamas were in a heap on the floor—but no Ava!

Leslie spun about and sprinted down the hall, racing toward the phone. Should she call 9-1-1? Her ex-husband?

Where could my baby girl have gone!?

Then she stopped dead in her tracks. Ava, wearing a mismatched shirt and pair of shorts, sat calmly at the kitchen table. A bowl of Cheerios, with several scoops of sugar slowly dissolving, was in front of her. There were two small puddles of milk—one on the table and one on the floor between the counter and table. Ava looked up at her mother, chewing most deliberately.

"Do you know what time it is?" Leslie asked, her voice wavering, higher than it should be, her attempt to control an implosion of nerves obvious to everyone but Ava.

Ava looked at her mother, over to the clock on the microwave, then back to her mother. "Nope. Mrs. DiGiulio hasn't taught us that yet." Then she dug into the Cheerios, making sure the spoonful was half cereal, half sugar, with a light sprinkling of milk.

Leslie let her mothering/homemaking autopilot kick in. She snapped two paper towels off the roll, wet them slightly, and bent first to the spilled milk on the table, carefully and completely wiping it up, then attending to the puddle on the floor. By the time she tossed the wet paper towels in the trash, she had regained control of her breathing but not her emotions. She pulled out a chair and sat down next to Ava.

"Sweetie," she said calmly, "the next time you wake up in the morning and Mommy's not awake, will you remember to come into my room and wake me up?"

Ava's brow almost furrowed. Then her face lightened as if she'd been calculating the cost or time of responding to this specific request. "Okay. I will. Even if it's like, real, real early?"

"Yep. Even if it's dark outside. This morning I went to your bedroom and it was empty. Mommy got scared."

Ava nodded … knowingly, Leslie thought.

Then, from somewhere, came a wisp of rock 'n' roll music. It was certainly not coming from the Stickles' apartment. Leslie had talked with them often and liked them, but they weren't the sort of people who would play '80s music in the morning.

Leslie leaned in to the sound. She recognized it as a hit by the band U2.

Ava chewed, swallowed, and wiped her mouth on her forearm. "It's Mr. Kenyon. He had a radio. I saw him … I like his music."

***

Jack did not pound a nail nor cut a board until well after 8:00. When he had applied for his contractor's license at city hall, he'd made sure he knew the codes regarding starting times: 8:00 for indoor work, 7:00 for work outside. But he knew that the squeal of a circular saw at 8:01 was not conducive to maintaining cordial relationships with neighbors. Instead of pounding and cutting, Jack planned to spend the first half hour reviewing what he would be tackling that day, taking measurements, jotting down notes, making sure his supplies matched his plan. There were few things more aggravating and frustrating than to be in the middle of something, only to find out that the one part, or the one piece of wood, or the one specific nail required to finish the job, was simply not there. If he had a crew, then the newest and lowest-paid man on the job would be sent out for supplies. Jack was both the highest and lowest man on his very small totem pole.

Jack carefully arranged what he needed for the day. He set up his new $29.95 radio on the counter in the kitchen, tuned it to WWSW—"All the Hits of Yesterday"—lowered the volume to middle-aged levels and started to nip away at the peeling wall in the front room of the apartment. He had brought a half-gallon of bleach with him, with an empty spray bottle, just in case there was mold behind the wall. He didn't smell a hint of it when he estimated the job, but you never knew with construction on old buildings.

With a pry bar, he began to pull away the flaking plasterboard; most of it came off in chunks. In less than an hour, he had the wall clean to the studs. Another thirty minutes and all the nails were removed from the studs.

No mold. That's good. Saves a lot of headaches. And all the wood is in good shape.

Jack packed the debris into large, sturdy contractor's trash bags. He was determined to be a different sort of contractor—one who cleaned as he went. And, well, he had to. There was no low-paid laborer to follow the crew around, picking up after them.

I can offer charm to my customers, but if I couple my charm with a clean job site, that's the stuff of good recommendations.

By noon, the new stack of drywall panels had been screwed into the studs, and the surface was nearly perfect. He had measured close, too close apparently, for he needed part of one more sheet to finish. Instead of having his ham-and-cheese sandwich on the balcony by himself, he planned on offering himself a treat: a real lunch, with real people. Since he had to go back to the lumberyard for drywall, he thought a quick stop at The Palm would be a nice reward. After all, he had a job—and a solid prospect for a second job. Things were definitely looking up for Kenyon Construction.

He pulled his truck around to the worn red-brick tavern and slipped out into the noon sun. Even though it was autumn, the sunshine was bright. Jack squinted as he made his way up the steps.

"Howdy, and welcome back," the bartender said.

The room was nearly empty. Two old men sat at the end of the bar, their faces a study in emptiness, their hands gently caressing the bottom half of a half-empty glass of draft beer.

"Thanks. A cheeseburger again today. American cheese. And a couple of bags of chips. No fries at lunch, right?"

"You got it," the bartender replied and made his way back toward the kitchen.

The television mounted above the bar was tuned in to some talk show unfamiliar to Jack. The audience hooted about something.

Jack nodded to the two old men who sat in shadows. They nodded back, then turned again to the TV, their watery eyes reflecting the blue light of the set.

The bartender came back with a big glass of Coke in his hand and carefully placed it in front of Jack. "A Coke is good, right?"

Jack nodded. He unwrapped a straw and folded the paper neatly.

The bartender leaned backward against the counter and placed his palms on the worn wooden trim.

"How long has it been?"

Jack glanced up from his Coke. He wasn't surprised by the question or that the bartender recognized the situation. Jack knew the two men at the end of the bar had given up. He knew the signs. He knew what the men were. He knew that they knew that he knew. Everything was brutally obvious to members of the club, even if it was a secret club, complete with secret looks and behaviors. And if anyone recognized the signs, it would be a man who worked tending bar.

"Thirteen months."

"Long time. Congratulations."

"I guess."

"For me, it's been fifteen years, three months ... and a week, I think. I haven't checked the calendar for a few days. By the way, my name is Earl. Earl Chapman."

Jack extended his hand. "Nice to meet you. I'm Jack Kenyon."

Before Jack could ask the question that immediately came to mind, the old bartender beat him to it.

"What am I doing here?" he said, sweeping the air with his arm. "You're thinking it, aren't you? Well, the truth of the matter is, I can't do anything else. I dropped out of high school a long time ago. My back ain't up to working in a mill. I like the people here. Most of the time, anyway. Once I stopped drinking, once I gave it up for good, it wasn't that hard anymore. Wasn't really tempted, I guess. I gotta work somewhere, and this place ain't that bad."

A rough female voice boomed out of the kitchen, which was hidden, except for a small window, "Burger's up!"

In a minute, a hot, greasy, delicious cheeseburger was in front of Jack, with two bags of Dan Dee potato chips, and a two-inch stack of paper napkins.

"Everything's a little greasy," Earl explained.

"No problem. A little grease won't hurt. Don't have to dress for my job," Jack said, taking a large bite out of the burger.

"What are you doing in Butler, Mr. Kenyon?"

"It's Jack."

Earl waved his hand in dismissal. "Everyone here is a mister. Only one name instead of two. Helps me remember. And it adds a little couth and dignity to the place, don't ya think?"

Jack smiled, not wanting to laugh with his mouth full. "I'm starting a construction business. I'm a carpenter."

"Are you good, Mr. Kenyon?"

Jack shrugged. "I think so. Spent the last year, a little over, actually, working up in Franklin on a big job—restoring an old mansion. Yeah, I think I'm pretty good."

"I saw a TV show about a mansion up that way ... Carlson, or Carson ..."

"Carter."

"Yeah, that's it. Big old place. By the river. Beautiful."

"It was the old Carter Mansion. They featured the place on a Pittsburgh cable station show named *Three Rivers Restorations*. Did a story on the renovation. It took a while to get done, but it turned out great. We finished it this past spring."

"And sober since then, right?"

Jack nodded. "All through the project. Nothing at all."

"Meetings?"

"Not for a while. Not since April."

"You should go. There's a couple of them in town."

Jack chewed, as if in thought. "Maybe I will."

"Where you working now? You said you had a project going on."

Jack spent a few minutes explaining what he was doing and where.

"Yeah, I know the building. It's a landmark. With the green screened balconies? I like that place. Somebody bought it?"

"A single mom … divorced. From Greensburg. She has a young daughter." As soon as he said it, Jack wondered if he'd said too much.

Jack saw Earl look at his left hand. There was no ring on that finger. There hadn't been a ring there for a few years. There was no longer even a hint of whiteness, where a thick gold wedding band had once protected the skin from the sun.

Jack looked up and saw the question in the old man's eyes. "I'm by myself too, now. Seems like ages ago."

Earl nodded, as if in sympathy.

"It's been a long time," Jack murmured. He took a deep breath, then added, even softer, "Feels like forever."

Earl let a moment pass, as if to allow air to come back into the room. "You should go to one of the meetings here. You really should."

Jack drank the last of his Coke, took a ten-dollar bill out of his pocket, and stood up. "Maybe I will. If I have the time. Maybe."

Amelia Westland, age thirteen years, six months
Butler Orphan Asylum
Butler County, Pennsylvania
January 5, 1876

I have a place to sleep, adequate food, and necessary work. My needs are met here. My first weeks, admittedly, were sad and confusing. Anxiousness came upon me whenever my thoughts would travel to our farm in Glade Mills, and to Mother and Father and Aunt Willa. Many others here were in worse states than I, but that knowledge has done little to curtail the great melancholy that threatens to steal over me at times.

There are many rules at the Asylum, but the Headmaster, Mr. Stevens, while stern, not smiling often, is fair, as is the Headmistress, who is more amiable. Breakfast is porridge with bread and blackberry preserves. After chapel, lessons are held in the morning; the boys' classroom is across the hall. And in the afternoon, we all work—the boys to the fields or barns, hauling water, logs, and large branches, tending animals; the girls to cleaning or cooking or sewing. Even the little ones are given small tasks. The work is less than I endured on the farm, but city girls complain much about soreness from cleaning and scrubbing, their more delicate constitutions demanding much rest. My life, I suspect, has toughened me, made me strong. I regard that as a blessing.

The same I must say about my faith. Despite my lamentable circumstances, these last months have been when God has been present most evidently, strengthening me and offering me peace in a sea of sorrow and despair and sadness. I pray, with diligence, in the morning and the evening, and God has placed His hand on my heart. And despite my surroundings, I strive to believe again that my future is without limits. I hear my father's voice, saying, "Be of good courage." I see my mother's smile, offering me encouragement of spirit.

I pledge to be joyful, more now, and in the future.

Now therefore ye are no more stranger and foreigners,
but fellowcitizens with the saints, and of the household of God.
—EPHESIANS 2:19

CHAPTER SEVEN

On Friday, Jack tapped at the door to Leslie Ruskin's apartment. He brushed whatever sawdust and dirt he could from his denim work shirt, wiped his hand on his blue jeans, and swept his hair away from his forehead.

Time for a haircut. I wonder where I should go.

Jack heard the metallic rustling of a chain being undone. The door opened halfway. Inviting, but cautious.

"Mr. Kenyon. What can I do for you? Do you need your check this morning?"

Jack had not forgotten about being paid, and he did need the money, but that was not why he was standing at her door this morning.

"This afternoon will be fine, Mrs. Ruskin ... or would you rather I call you Miss Ruskin?"

The question both disarmed and charmed the woman, Jack saw. Her smile was validation of his politeness.

"You know, Mr. Kenyon, I don't really have a preference," she said as she opened the door fully and stood just on one side of it, her left hand on the doorframe, as if to give balance, or for protection. "I guess Ms. Ruskin solves all the problems. I know lots of women like Ms. Mizzzz. But I don't like the way it sounds. You can call me Mrs. Ruskin. That was my name for a long time. I'm used to it." She paused, as if considering one more thing. "But Leslie is fine as well. In fact, call me Leslie. We don't need to stand on formality."

"Then call me Jack." He smiled. "I have a question for you, Leslie. It's about the trim in the bigger bedroom."

She stood and waited for his explanation.

"It would be easiest if I showed you," Jack said. "If you have the time, that is. I don't want to intrude."

"No, I can come. I'm just writing some letters. Job application letters."

Not knowing what to say, Jack remained silent and led the owner into the larger of the two bedrooms in the apartment on the west side of the building. He walked to the center of the room and turned, then pointed to the corner. "There's a problem with the trim."

Leslie looked in the corner, back to Jack, then back to the corner. "Problem?"

Jack picked up two short pieces of trim and held one against the corner of the door. "If I put the trim on the door, that doesn't leave enough space for the trim around the closet door. They're really too close together, but I know we don't have the budget to move either of the openings. My question is, do I leave the door trim full-size, and leave only a sliver of trim on the closet door, or do I split the difference and cut both trim pieces equally?"

Leslie cocked her head, as if deep in thought. She walked closer to Jack, who stood in the corner, holding both pieces of trim against the wall. He smelled something floral. Lavender, maybe. She smelled fresh and clean, and Jack was taken back, for an instant, to a time long, long ago. He felt that familiar lurch in his heart. It was a good feeling at first, until he began to remember what he had lost. Then it became painful.

"I … I don't know. What's more proper?" she asked.

Jack shook his head, as if clearing his thoughts. "What's more proper is not to build a closet so close to a door, but that's a boat that sailed long ago. I don't know what's proper in this situation. Where wrong things were done, sometimes there just isn't a right way to make them better."

Leslie crossed her arms, then looked from the trim pieces to Jack. "Why don't you do what's easiest—which means least expensive—and whatever won't be as noticeable? Wouldn't full trim on the door be easiest? You really won't see that the closet trim is thinner in that corner unless you close both doors."

Jack shrugged in agreement. "It will be easier that way. Thanks."

They walked back into the living room, and Leslie turned to the front of the apartment. "Oh, wow. You have the new wall up! It looks wonderful."

Jack had finished with the wallboard two days earlier and had put the tape and wallboard compound on the day prior. That alone made the room look fresh and clean.

Leslie walked over and let her fingertips glide over the new wall. Jack followed.

"This is so nice. You're making such fast progress," she said.

As she swept her hand over the sleek surface, her fingers ran into his fingers, just for an instant. It was the first time in so long that he'd felt the gentle touch of a woman's skin on his, even accidentally. When his heart lurched again, he vowed this was business, all business, and that any images in his head were officially banished.

She stepped back, smiling, almost beaming. "I'm so happy with the way this looks."

Jack smiled, and Leslie turned to leave.

As she had her hand on the door, she called back, "I'll have your check this afternoon. If I have to go out, I'll make sure to leave it for you."

"That works fine for me, Mrs. Ruskin ... I mean, Leslie."

He saw what he thought was a momentary slip of longing in her smile. Or was he simply projecting his own wants onto her? He watched the door close, then sniffed the air one more time before heading back into the bedroom to face the trim issue.

It was lavender; he was sure.

———

Mrs. Stickle took the kettle off the stove and carefully poured the boiling water into an old, nicked flowered teapot. She added in two large scoops of loose tea. "Teabags are just *terrible*," she had said. "No flavor. No ritual, either."

She covered the teapot with a tea towel to steep, then shuffled toward the kitchen table, her once-pink slippers making a sloopish sound with each sliding step.

"I'm so happy you stopped this morning, Leslie. I keep telling Arthur that we simply have to have you and your sweet daughter over for dinner, but Arthur can be a tad forgetful these days." Mrs. Stickle, broad shouldered, broad waisted, broad hipped, chuckled to herself. "I suspect he's only half of who's forgetting. By the time I think of inviting you over, you're gone. So, let's say that us having tea counts as at least a half of an invitation."

Leslie's grandmothers had both passed away when she was very young, so she'd never really had a relationship with them that she could remember, but Mrs. Stickle was Grandmother personified. Her teased white hair, done once a week at a salon, Leslie was sure, framed her gently wrinkled face, and she never went anywhere without wearing makeup and large clip-on earrings. Her spotless kitchen was scented with oranges and cinnamon, with a hint of chocolate chips and Vicks, and maybe a bit of cabbage. There were more doilies in her living room than any apartment had a right to have—each one white as blank stationery and primly protecting some surface from harm, as only a doily can do. Glass candy dishes on the coffee tables and end tables were always full. A calendar with a picture of a kitten in a basket hung on the side of a cabinet in the kitchen. Each day was marked off as it passed by, and in each square of that day was a reference to the weather, written in pencil, in a shaky hand—*cold, windy, sunny*—a daily weather report in retrospect, always perfect, without error. The small pocket of the calendar was stuffed with coupons. A Domino's Pizza ad dominated the thicket of money savers.

There was a flower arrangement on top of the refrigerator, with plastic tulips in harsh yet hopeful colors.

Mrs. Stickle brought out a small carton of cream, a small lemon, cut into slices, a china plate of gingersnaps, and two delicate bone china cups and saucers.

"Where is Mr. Stickle this morning?" Leslie asked.

"He's at church. That big old stone church on Diamond Square. Used to be the Second Presbyterian Church, but they changed the name. They have a seniors group three times a week. They wanted to call it a senior day-care program, and they did, for a while, but no one wanted to attend a day-care center at the age of eighty, so they changed it to Busy Hands.

To me, it still sounds childlike, but Mr. Stickle likes it better now, so I'm happy. It gives us both a break from each other for three mornings a week, and I don't have to worry about him for a few hours."

The tea came out, thick, dark, rich-looking. For tea, that was an accomplishment, Leslie thought. Mrs. Stickle loaded six sugar cubes into hers and snagged six gingersnaps. Leslie did the same, but with half the amount of her older neighbor of both sugar and cookies. She sipped, realizing this cup probably contained double the caffeine her morning coffee offered. The warmth—more hot than warm—unfolded in her stomach, like hands warmed against a blazing fireplace.

"So tell me, what are you having done in the empty apartment? I hear banging every now and then."

"It's not too loud, is it?" Leslie responded quickly.

"No, dear, it's fine. At my age there isn't much of anything that's too loud." Mrs. Stickle grabbed one of her gingersnaps.

"I'm having the place updated," Leslie explained. "The kitchen was so old. And the leak in the roof ruined one wall. He's patched that already. New fixtures in the bathroom. Then I'll paint and try to get it rented."

Mrs. Stickle waved her hand as if chasing a slow fly. "You'll have no trouble at all. The place is big and bright and clean and close to downtown—but I guess downtown is less important than it used to be. Seems as if everyone works somewhere else nowadays." She paused. "Who is doing the work? I've seen a very attractive young man come and go, but I don't recognize him."

"Jack Kenyon. Kenyon Construction."

Mrs. Stickle's brow furrowed, as if thinking caused contractions. "Is he from Butler?"

Leslie shrugged. "I don't think so. I haven't asked him. He's just starting out."

Leaning forward, the old woman patted Leslie's hand. "I saw on the news about how workmen can take all your money to do repairs that you don't need. Or was it that they take your money and then don't do the repairs? Well, either way is bad, I guess. He isn't one of those, is he?"

"I'm sure he's not. He always answers his phone. He's always at work early. He's very neat."

Mrs. Stickle had already eaten her six cookies and Leslie caught her sneaking a glance at the two remaining on Leslie's plate.

"Would you like these last two cookies, Mrs. Stickle? I had a very big breakfast."

"Well … only if they would be going to waste."

Leslie nodded. "Mrs. Stickle, you've lived here a long time, right?"

"All my life in Butler, that's right."

"Do you know a family by the name of Reidmiller?"

The old woman's brow furrowed again. "Yes, I know a Reidmiller family. Agnes and Merle. Live just up the hill by Ritts Park—or they used to. They might have moved out to that retirement place on Route 8. I could check my address book."

Leslie shook her head. "No, I just wanted to know if you knew them."

"If it's Agnes and Merle—well, they've been around for years and years. Nice people. They have a son, Mike."

Leslie brightened. "Yes, that must be them. I met Mike Reidmiller. He has a son in Ava's kindergarten class at school."

"That's him. Divorced, though. I guess that's pretty normal these days."

Leslie had never told Mrs. Stickle that she herself was divorced, though she was pretty certain that such news would have spread rapidly. She nodded. "He mentioned that."

"Did he mention that his wife was a witch, pardon my French? She was simply a horrible person. He is much better off without her. Much better off. No one was surprised when he got custody of his boy. No one."

Leslie could tell Mrs. Stickle knew more—much more—but Leslie didn't want to appear too inquisitive, or worse yet, a gossip, so she remained silent.

In good time.

"Mrs. Stickle," Leslie said, changing the subject completely, "do you know anyone in town who might be hiring? I need to find a job."

Jack switched the key in the ignition and the truck rumbled and jumped for a few seconds, as if it wasn't quite ready to stop moving. With a final hacking chug, it vibrated once more, then grew still. He reached for his clipboard and list of supplies.

Cook Brothers Brick may not have offered the absolute lowest prices in the area, but it was convenient, quick, and easy to get in and out of, and most important, the owner went out of his way to be pleasant and offer a warm greeting every time Jack shopped there.

And there was free coffee. Not great coffee, but free, offered from an old stained Mr. Coffee coffeemaker, with a stack of white Styrofoam cups, and a loose assortment of sugar packets, cream packets, and sugar substitute packets.

"Mr. Kenyon, how are you?" came the booming greeting from the back room. Burt Cook lumbered out from the small office. "Quiet morning today. Been looking forward to some company."

Jack waved as he poured a cup of coffee.

"You still working at the Midlands place?" Burt asked.

Jack nodded. "I figure maybe a month in the apartment. If I had a crew—a couple of weeks. The owner might want me to do some work on the downstairs. It's empty, but the space is really nice. It would make a great restaurant. Do you know anyone who wants to start a restaurant?"

Burt leaned on the counter, both him and the wood groaning slightly. "Does that place have brick arches in it? And a fireplace?"

"It does."

"I thought I remembered that. I did some work on that space. Remodeling. Back when I was still doing actual brickwork. When I was younger and everything didn't hurt so much."

Jack put his clipboard on the desk. Burt leaned sideways to look, then shouted toward the back. "Hey, Rudy! Come on out here. There's an order to fill."

Rudy, a short middle-aged man in a plaid flannel shirt and wearing a name badge more crooked than straight, came out with a wobbly cart and grabbed the clipboard, nodding, his lips moving, as he carefully read over the list.

"Burt, what was the Midlands Building?" Jack asked. "I mean, what was it when you worked on it? It's an interesting-looking place, but I can't figure out its history. Sometimes you can tell in old buildings. Sometimes it's a mystery."

Burt scowled, as if thinking was painful. "Well … it was empty when I worked on it. I think it was some sort of insurance agency before."

"Originally?"

"No. Not from the start. I think it was a variety store when it was first built. Maybe. Way back when … when they still had variety stores. After we did the brick repair work, a locksmith moved in."

"Big space for a locksmith."

"I think he only used half of it. It was there a long time, but I never saw much traffic there. Even back then, not much calling for a locksmith store."

Jack drained his coffee and dropped the cup into the trash can.

"You say a young woman bought it?"

"Yep," Jack said. "Divorced. With a young daughter. Real cute."

"Divorced, huh? And real cute? You have to be very careful around situations like that."

"I meant the little girl is cute," Jack said, then added, "well, they're both very cute. They're living in the middle apartment. It's really nice too. She wants to rent everything else. Know of anyone at all who might want to rent the ground floor—or the apartment?"

Burt shook his head. "Naw. But if I do, I'll let you know." He turned and headed for his office.

Rudy pushed the cart, now full, to the register, and Jack pulled out his wallet and took out a credit card. If Leslie paid him today, he would have more than enough for the next week. And the charge card bill wouldn't come for another two or three weeks. He signed the receipt, walked to the back, and leaned into Burt's office.

"Thanks again for the coffee."

He noticed, in a frame behind the desk, a picture of a thinner, younger Burt, standing next to a gleaming Harley-Davidson motorcycle. The face was leaner, but the smile just as expansive as it was today.

"You still have it?" Jack asked as he pointed to the picture.

"I do. I don't get to ride as often as I used to."

"Pretty bike."

"Do you ride?" Burt asked.

"I ... I used to. I had a big Electra Glide. '82. Deep blue. Lots of chrome."

"Used to? What happened? Everyone I know hangs onto those bikes forever."

"I would have too. But I sold it. Had to finance my truck and tools."

Burt looked both sad and impressed. "That must have been hard."

Jack wanted to nod, but didn't. "Well, it was no harder than all the rest."

And with that, Jack tapped on the doorframe with the tops of his fingers, as if signaling the conversation was over, waved good-bye, and walked to his truck to help Rudy load the supplies.

Mrs. DiGiulio looked up from her desk. She thought she heard a soft tapping, but no one at this school tapped so quietly. You tap that softly and no one would ever hear you over the hubbub of twenty-five small children— even if they had been told six times to be quiet. There was a shadow by the kindergarten door.

"If you're someone out there—come on in," she said in her best loud-but-not-angry schoolteacher voice.

"I'm not disturbing you, am I?" the shadow said as the door opened.

"No, not at all. A kindergarten teacher doesn't have a lot of papers to correct. I'm just getting things ready for tomorrow's lessons." She peered over her reading glasses, tilting her chin down toward the desk. "You're Trevor's father ... is it Michael?"

"It is. You have a good memory. At church, with people I've known for years and years, I still come up empty when I'm trying to remember their names."

Mrs. DiGiulio laid her pencil down. The pencil had hearts imprinted on it, along with her name in gold. Thirty of the exact same pencils rested in an apple-shaped cup at the far side of her desk.

"Remembering names comes with this job. You have to learn how to do it," she said firmly and clearly. "With kindergarten students, their names are critical. But then again, I have their names written in big bold letters and taped to their desks. That helps a lot."

Mike Reidmiller smiled in agreement. "That would make things easier. Maybe I'll suggest that at church." He walked carefully to her desk, as if unwilling to bump into something small and important.

"I know it's not time yet for parent conferences. But, well, I'm a single dad." He said the words without a trace of pity or sorrow but rather a statement of fact that might help explain things. "I guess when you have two parents, you get to talk about things together. And I guess that if I were a single woman, I might be more likely to talk to another mom about these things. But I guess I'm not either … a single mom or a married couple. I mean … you know what I mean. Men don't talk that much."

Mrs. DiGiulio looked up at him like a grandmother and offered an understanding expression. Not a smile, but something more knowing than that. "I'm pretty sure I do know what you mean. Your parents … Agnes—"

"And Merle. They're out at Sinclair House. North of Butler."

"Yes. Merle. I remember them. Your father was a councilman for a while."

"He was." Mrs. DiGiulio could hear the pride in the son's voice.

"Now they're both a little … lost. Some good days. But more bad days than good. So talking to them is out too."

"I'm sorry to hear that."

"But that's not why I'm here … to talk about my folks. I just want to know: How's my son doing?"

Mr. Reidmiller's words came as close to a plea as any words Mrs. DiGiulio had heard recently.

"Trevor? He's doing fine."

"No, I mean, *really*, how is he doing? Sometimes he doesn't follow directions so well. I'm used to repeating myself a dozen times to get his attention. But I was worried about how he would do on his own. Like, with strangers all around. Sometimes he gets real distracted."

Mrs. DiGiulio folded her hands on top of one another in a gesture so precise and perfect, it was like a pair of kittens coiling up for a nap. Doing so provided her a few extra seconds to think and respond.

"Yes. You are right. He can lose his focus at times. But in boys this age, there is nothing to worry about. Not yet, for certain."

"And that's the truth? No ADD or HDAD or whatever they call it nowadays?"

Mrs. DiGiulio remained firm. "No. No ADHD. He can get excited, but from what I have observed, he's just a regular boy."

Mrs. DiGiulio watched Mr. Reidmiller. He reacted as if a weight had been lifted or a veil removed or he'd found that his shoulders were suddenly now relaxed and limber.

"That's a relief. I couldn't tell if what Trev is—is normal."

"He's fine," Mrs. DiGiulio repeated. "Really he is. He can be a bit wound up at times, but we're working on that. And Ava seems to settle him down. Ava Ruskin. I'm sure you've met her mother by now. She's a single parent too. Ava sits behind him, you know." Mrs. DiGiulio gestured to the third row of desks. "Something about her, Ava, brings him back if he does get a little hyper. She never raises her voice with him. She never sounds upset. Her being in class really helps him."

Mr. Reidmiller nodded in a gracious, thankful manner.

A few seconds passed.

"I don't want to gossip," Mr. Reidmiller said, "because I'm not very good at it. I get lots of names wrong. But do you know anything about Mrs. Ruskin ... Leslie?"

It was gossip, Mrs. DiGiulio thought, but not that kind of bad gossip at all, not the prying kind. More like ... information.

"Well, Mr. Reidmiller, I don't know much. She's from Greensburg. From what Ava's said, I gather they lived in a big house before they moved here. And I know that she bought the old Midlands Building on North and Cedar. She's rehabbing one of the apartments. I run into Mrs. Stickle now and again—she's one of the tenants there—at Friedman's Market. She says that Leslie ... Mrs. Ruskin ... is a very wonderful person. Likes tea, she says. And cookies."

When he heard the word *tea*, his expression fell, but when he heard cookies, it brightened again.

"Thank you, Mrs. DiGiulio. Trevor loves this class and says he loves you. Thank you very much."

Mr. Reidmiller waved, and rather than walking out, shuffled backward to the door. He waved one more time as he closed the door after him.

No ... thank you, Mr. Reidmiller. Thank you.

Amelia Grace Westland, age thirteen years, eight months

Butler Orphan Asylum

Butler County, Pennsylvania

March 5, 1876

Catherine Sorenson has become my dearest friend. "You are so like my dear older sister whom I lost. In you, God has given her back to me," says she, upon which I reply, "God has surely given you to me as a little sister." She calls me "Mellie." She will be twelve years old upon her birthday in two months' time. She has the curliest mane of red hair I have ever seen, her skin almost as porcelain, as though lit from within. It is a chore to keep her tresses tame while working on certain tasks. When candles are snuffed out at night, she and I, in our iron beds with quilts piled high, whisper to each other, sometimes long into the night. We see our breath as small exhaled clouds in the darkness. Having such a friend makes my fears lessen and she helps me when I feel anxious about the morrow. Nor have I had any of the spells, which had prevented me from leaving my bed, since Catherine is by my side. The Headmistress noted the improvement in my outlook, and I give all the credit to Catherine, for she is calm and gay and pretty.

Even though I have prayed to our holy God to strengthen me, my weakness of spirit and my fears had bested me on many occasions, reducing me to near muteness. But increasingly, I have found the renewed assurance that God desires we all have. "And this is the confidence that we have in him, that, if we ask any thing according to his will, he heareth us ..." 1 John 5:14.

I take great comfort in the Sunday sermons, some given by great preachers who travel through the land, bringing God's Word to people without the blessing of a church nearby.

With God's provision, and because of His steadfast protection, my life shall surely have purpose and meaning.

I will be glad and rejoice in thy mercy:
for thou hast considered my trouble;
thou hast known my soul in adversities.
—PSALM 31:7

CHAPTER EIGHT

THE CELL PHONE ON JACK'S belt warbled. He could have changed the ringtone, or downloaded a more unique one, but he left the ring exactly as it was when the phone was first activated. To change the ringtone, he'd have to find the manual and read it—both chores he was pretty sure would never be accomplished.

He flipped it open. "Kenyon Construction."

He listened for a few moments.

"That's great. I'll be able to start at the end of the month, if that's okay with you. I'll call with the exact date when I know for sure."

He knew he wouldn't be completely done with the Midlands Building at the end of the month, but the overlap of a few days wouldn't be stretching his promise of "one-job-at-a-time" too much. Stretching just a little, maybe—but not breaking.

"Well, the kitchen I've just finished is almost exactly like your kitchen. If it's okay with the owner, I could show you what you could expect. Much easier than trying to draw it out, or show you in a store."

He waited a moment, then said, "I'll call you back if and when it would be okay to see the kitchen. And thanks a lot. I mean that."

He slipped the phone back in the holder, feeling a bit more secure. One job in progress, one more scheduled at the Pettigrews', and a few other estimates still pending.

Maybe I can make this work. No—I can *make this work. And I will. I will.*

Later that afternoon, after a full morning of hanging the final cabinets in the apartment kitchen at the Midlands Building, he brushed himself off, unfastened his tool belt, and tapped on the door that led to Leslie Ruskin's apartment. The door opened and Jack could hear the music for *Dora the Explorer* in the background.

"How's it going, Mr. Kenyon?" Leslie asked.

"Jack. If I get to call you Leslie, you have to call me Jack. That's the contractor's rule." He stood outside on the landing and explained that he'd landed another job and wanted to show the young couple the new kitchen in the empty apartment. "I'd never take anyone inside unless you said it was okay. After all, it is your place."

"Why sure, that would be perfectly okay with me," she said. "It's kind of a compliment, isn't it—that someone else wants to see how nice the kitchen turned out?"

Jack leaned his head just slightly. He caught Ava, sitting at the edge of the sofa in the living room, staring at the door. She ducked backward, out of sight, but a second later, she reappeared, and this time she waved.

"Dora's on," she called out, as if explaining her absence at the door with her mom.

"Her favorite show," Leslie said softly. A look passed over Leslie's face, indicating that perhaps she was considering something more complicated.

"Jack, would you like to come in for a cup of coffee? I was just about to make a fresh pot. Or do you have to run? Are you done with work for today?" Leslie asked as she glanced at her watch. "I heard you start early this morning."

Jack was never good at maintaining a poker face. In that split second, he wondered what emotion his face was showing. He was surprised, to be sure, that Leslie was inviting him in. Excitement? He couldn't tell exactly what he felt most. He was pleased, too. What she'd just said was a compliment, in a way, since she was obviously paying attention to his comings and goings on the job.

But maybe she's just making sure the job gets done on time. She probably wouldn't be watching me for any other reason … well, maybe there are other reasons …

He hoped he kept his voice in check. "Sure. If it's not too much trouble. Fresh-brewed coffee sounds good. I guess I'm still not used to instant. I mean, there's only one of me, so making a pot of real coffee seems like a big commitment."

Leslie laughed—a clear, crisp laugh, gentle, genuine, rich. "I know what you mean. It's the same debate I go through every day: *Now, how many cups am I going to drink? How many should I drink? Will I muster up the nerve to reheat it later?*"

Leslie closed the door behind him and led him through the living room and into the kitchen. They both hurried past Ava, not wanting to stand too long between her and the television. Ava bounced one way, then the other, not willing to miss a second of the show. But as Jack passed, she did stare at him, at least until he and her mother were in the kitchen.

Leslie measured out cold water into the carafe and poured it into the coffeemaker. Jack watched, trying not to stare, but it had been so long since he had been around a beautiful woman in a normal setting—a little family, a normal kitchen, an everyday activity like making coffee for two.

He took a seat at the table as politely as he could. He tried not to shed any sawdust.

It was a normal kitchen, with good light coming in through the dining area from the balcony facing the street out front. There was a vase of flowers on the table—not real flowers, but nicely done artificial flowers, in a simple glass vase. There was a stack of napkins in a metal holder, and on the front of the refrigerator, an explosion of papers and artwork, each signed in tiny block letters: AVA. Jack had a flash of the same melancholic mood that came over him whenever he was reminded of what he was missing … what he'd never have again. All the papers of his daughter's that he'd never see on a refrigerator door.

Leslie saw him looking. "They seem to do a lot of art projects at this age."

Jack nodded. Some papers were all but hidden by more recent acquisitions.

Leslie busied herself with cups and sugar and spoons. "Do you like milk with your coffee? Or I have cream. It's one of my few luxuries."

"Cream, if you don't mind. That would be great. I use the powdered white stuff when I'm by myself. It's nice when you can use the real thing."

She sat down, and they both watched and listened as the coffeemaker dripped and sputtered, the final elongated hiss indicating it was done with its brewing business. Neither of them moved for a moment. Jack didn't know why exactly, but he stood and reached for the coffeepot. It was not his job as host, but Leslie had hesitated.

"May I pour?" he asked.

Leslie, appearing grateful, smiled. "Why, thank you, Jack."

They both added in more than one serving of cream and sugar.

———

Leslie hoped Jack had not seen her hand shake as she reached for the container of cream in the refrigerator nor heard her take three deep breaths while standing behind the refrigerator door in an attempt to calm her pulse. She had turned away from him as she'd readied the cups and all the rest on a tray, delivering it to the kitchen table in a swift turn. She hoped he didn't know she was trying to make sure that the cups and spoons didn't rattle on their journey from the counter to the table.

"So, you have another job lined up. That's good, isn't it?" Leslie asked.

Inwardly she winced. The question sounded like one a girl asks on her first date with a boy she likes.

An image flashed into Leslie's mind—of an old etiquette column she'd read as a teenager. *You must get the boys to talk about themselves! They love talking about sports and cars. If you want date number two you must feign interest in all those topics.*

Jack didn't seem to mind being asked to talk about himself.

"It is. I knew it would be hard starting up in a place where I didn't know anyone, but I'll be busy for at least a couple of months."

"I really like the way the other apartment is shaping up. You've done a great job."

"Thanks. I'm sure you'll have no trouble renting it. I mean, *I* would rent it—if I could afford it."

For a moment Leslie felt a nervousness ... not the bad kind, but the giddy kind of nervousness.

"But it would be too big for me," Jack quickly continued. "I don't need all that space. And I want to find a small old house to renovate. Then sell it and find another to work on and sell."

Leslie did her best to hide her feelings, slowly turning her coffee cup, making small ceramic grating noises on the wooden table. "The ground floor looks great too. Just cleaning it up made a world of difference."

"Have you found any tenants?" Jack asked. "I let all my suppliers know about the space."

"Why, that's so sweet of you, Jack. I haven't started to advertise it yet. After we get the bathrooms finished, I'll put an ad in the paper."

"There is that one big wooden door in the back that I couldn't get into," he reminded her. "I can't tell if the lock is jammed, or if I don't have the right key for it."

"I'm pretty sure I gave you all the keys I had. But I'll double-check with the realtor at the bank."

———◦◦◦———

Jack finished his coffee well before Leslie. He wondered if he should stand up now and leave, or if he should wait for his host to finish. Too many years had passed since he'd had to worry about such things. He decided to wait.

Suddenly the noise from the television ceased. Ava walked into the kitchen with some deliberateness and stood close to her mother. Not very close, but closer to her than to Jack.

"Do we have any cookies? Or cupcakes? Trevor didn't bring any cupcakes with his lunch today."

Leslie stood and walked to the small pantry. "We have a few shortbread cookies left. You may have two of them."

"Can I have four?" Ava asked.

Jack could see that Leslie wanted to smile at the negotiations but didn't. "Three."

"Three is good." Ava extended her hand as her mother placed the three small cookies in her palm. "Thanks."

One cookie immediately disappeared into Ava's mouth as she headed out of the kitchen and down the hall to her room.

Both watched her leave.

"Such a cute girl," Jack said as he stood to leave.

"She is—and the trouble is that she knows it."

Jack wanted to say how true that was—to add something about his daughter that might connect him and Leslie—but he didn't. It had been too long, he told himself. He had terminated the ability to mention her in public. She existed only to him; she couldn't be shared with others … because of what happened.

He stood. "I should be going. You have things to do, I'm sure. Thanks so much for the coffee."

"Are you sure?" Leslie asked. "The pot's still half full. I'll never drink all of it. One more cup?"

Jack wanted to say yes, because he so badly wanted to spend the afternoon here in Leslie's kitchen, just talking and being with her. The whole night, in fact. There was something wonderful about how she spoke: her gentleness, the curve of her throat, and the way her eyes half-closed when she laughed. But he knew he couldn't—or shouldn't. Jack knew that if he asked, if he turned up the charm, even just a little, he could have a third and fourth cup, and more. He was that certain. But instead of asking for one more refill, he shook his head no.

Being here, being attracted to Leslie, being *very* attracted to Leslie, was more than he could deal with this day. "No. I'll take a rain check. Okay?"

"Sure," Leslie said. "That would be nice."

There was a tiny note of panic in her voice, he thought … as if she wondered if he somehow knew that this might be her first time with a man since her divorce.

He heard the door being latched as he walked down the steps to the street. He hurried to his truck, started the engine, flipped the visor down and paused for a long moment, then drove away, a few miles per hour faster than needed, a few miles per hour faster than he wanted.

Leslie kept her hand, white-knuckled, on the doorjamb a long time until her heart slowed to a normal rhythm. She gulped, drew her shoulders back, ran her hands through her hair, and drew in one last deep breath.

Okay. Okay. I feel fine. No problem. I'm fine. There's nothing to be worried about.

She called out, "Ava, let's go. Remember? We're shopping for furniture this afternoon."

She waited while her daughter, walking slowly and more carefully than necessary, came out into the living room, holding a picture book on dolphins in her hand.

"I don't want to go shopping. I don't like shopping."

Leslie refused to be drawn into the debate.

"I know, but we're going. We talked about this yesterday. We need a dresser for your room. We need a chair for the living room. And the whole apartment simply has to have some artwork on the walls."

"Like on the refrigerator?"

"No, sweetie. Like my grown-up posters. We'll need to get frames for them."

"Ohh," Ava replied, disappointed.

Five minutes later, the pair was in the minivan heading south on Route 356. Leslie had been told of a Catholic Charities resale shop near Saxonburg, a few miles south of town. Ava really did need a dresser; she had been using five cardboard boxes to hold her assortment of clothing, plus the dresses and sweaters that were hung in the closet. But cardboard boxes were depressing if used as furniture. Leslie was sure that some of her panic was caused by the image of her daughter rummaging through cardboard boxes when she got dressed in the morning.

A dresser will make things better, she told herself. *And it doesn't have to be a fancy dresser. Just a nice dresser. And a mirror above it. Every little girl deserves a dresser and a mirror—and maybe a little desk or dressing table.*

Glancing in the rearview mirror at her daughter, Leslie realized that Ava probably didn't care. Cardboard boxes were normal for her now, and until she had friends over, however she stored her clothes would be fine.

She needs a dresser.

Leslie navigated the minivan onto the gravel parking lot.

The place looks nice enough. Almost like a real store.

Ava unsnapped herself from her car seat and held out her arms for her mom to help her down and out. She reached up and took her mother's hand. Bells above the shop's door offered a cheerful little clatter when they walked in.

"Good afternoon. Glad to see you. Let me know if I can be of any help at all."

A woman of about sixty, maybe even a bit older than that, waved from behind a counter.

"I'd get up, but that takes a while and people don't want to be bothered when they shop, am I right? The big furniture is in the back room. That's where it gets delivered, and no one wants to haul it farther than they have to. Clothes are on that side—I guess you can see that. Smaller household things are out here."

Leslie kept nodding as the woman spoke.

"Now for prices. We put a price on everything here. And that's the price that you pay. The parish priest says some of us ladies are too easy and we'd be giving everything away. That would be me. 'Take it,' I'd say. 'Get it out of here and make use of it.' But Father Boyd says that's crazy. Well, maybe he didn't say 'crazy,' but that's what he meant. He says that we have to make a little money on this place to pay the rent and heat and all that. He says a charity like this takes money to run. I guess he's right. So the yellow tag on all the furniture has the price written on it. Father Boyd says to discourage any dickering because we're not allowed to take less than the tag. We keep the tag, and the tags and the money have to be even at the end of the day. And I guess God would be watching if we threw the tags away, now, wouldn't He? Besides, the prices are really cheap. I bought a great old bed here once and I'm still using it."

Ava was staring at the woman, perhaps because of her enthusiastic and animated monologue.

"And what's your name, sweetie?"

"Ava."

"Well, that's a real pretty name. Like Ava Gardner?"

Ava scrunched up her nose. "I dunno. Is it, Mommy?"

"No. I just liked the name. Ava Gardner was a little before my time."

"Gracious sakes, of course she was. But she was a very beautiful actress. Are you an actress, Ava?"

Ava shook her head emphatically. "Nope."

Leslie spoke up. "Do you know if you have any dressers? Ava needs a dresser for her room."

The older woman rubbed her forehead, pursing up her lips into a tight slit. "I think they brought in a whole bedroom set the other day," she said brightly. "I think it was for a little girl. It's in the back on the right. All white with pretty knobs and handles. It's real cute. You yell if you don't see it. I'll make my way back there if you don't."

Leslie took Ava's hand and wound their way through the cluttered room. The back room, nearly twice as large as the front, was crammed with all sorts of odd dressers and tables and chests and chairs and beds and sofas. They passed one chair, and Ava hopped up into it, kicked her feet, and said with some authority. "I like this chair, Mom. It's all cushy."

Leslie stepped back and looked. The chair, a fully upholstered one, was classic and pretty. The legs may not have been real mahogany, but they were solid and unscarred, the fabric clean, in a very rich medium shade of sage green. The tag read $10.

"That's cheap," Leslie said.

Ava turned her head to see the tag. "It says ten. I know that number. What's that squiggly thing?" she asked as she pointed to the tag.

"That's a dollar sign."

"Is ten dollars a lot?"

Leslie shook her head. "No. That's real cheap. I think this would be a great chair for our living room, for by the fireplace, don't you?"

Ava nodded with enthusiasm. "Are you going to buy this?" she asked, her feet still dangling and kicking in the air.

"I think so."

From the front of the store came the older woman's voice. "If you see something you like, tear off the bottom half of the tag. That means it's yours."

"Let's look around a bit more, Ava. There's no one else here. I think this chair is safe for now."

Ava hopped down and walked calmly through the narrow pathway between the furniture. As they came to the end of the aisle, Leslie caught sight of the white girls' bedroom set.

It is pretty, Leslie thought to herself. A double dresser, a small dressing table with a chair and mirror and a bed frame and headboard. It looked well made, almost hand-carved; though Leslie was pretty sure it was not. But it was delicate and definitely girl-like, yet simple. Ava walked over to it and touched the brass handles with some reserve.

"It's pretty, Mommy," she said very softly.

Leslie was certain it would be too expensive, even at bargain resale shop prices. She imagined a set like this, in a real store, would be close to two thousand dollars, so even a reduced price would be more than she could comfortably afford. Ava gently traced her finger along the scalloped edge of the table and stared at herself in the dainty, child-sized mirror.

Leslie looked for the tag, not wanting to hope too much to commit to anything. Her chest tightened, as if her heart was conditioned to respond to dashed dreams. Her breath grew a bit shorter, and sweat started to glisten on her forehead. She closed her eyes and willed it all to stop. She breathed in deeply and out slowly.

The moment passed.

Ava jumped to the left and pointed to a yellow tag. "There it is, Mommy. It says fifty and the squiggly thing means dollars. Is fifty dollars too much?"

Leslie was certain that it must have read $500, or that if it was $50, that was for one piece. She looked at the tag. Indeed, the tag read "$50 Set/5 pieces."

Leslie looked around quickly. There were no other tags.

The fifty dollars must be the real cost.

"Do you like it, Ava?"

Ava, who had never been the most feminine of little girls, who had never favored lace over blue jeans, who had never yet attempted to put on her mother's makeup and style her hair, touched the dresser again, smoothed her small hand along the satiny surface, and finally looked back at her mother.

"It's real pretty. Like a princess. Like that princess we saw on TV."

The bell in the front of the shop sounded.

Leslie didn't hesitate. She reached over and tore the yellow tag in two. "Then let's get this for you."

Ava, a child not given to spontaneous acts of affection—it wasn't that she was unaffectionate, but that her responses were most often considered and thought-out—jumped at her mother and embraced her fiercely. She waited a long moment until she whispered "Thanks" in her mother's ear.

When Ava released her mother, she stepped back, looked at everything again, then said calmly, "Will this fit in our car?"

It was a situation Leslie had not considered. She looked at all the pieces. They could tie the flat ones to the top of the minivan—there was a luggage rack that would hold them. The middle seats could be folded down to make space for the rest.

"I think so."

Ava didn't take her hands off the dressing table. "I bet Daddy could make it all fit."

Ava did not mention her father often. Neither did Leslie, for fear of sounding angry or hurt or saying something unwise.

"Maybe he could. But Daddy's not here right now."

Ava looked at herself in the small mirror with beveled sides. "I miss our old house."

Leslie's heart ached. "But our new house is nice. Isn't it? It will be nicer with this furniture, right?"

Ava sighed. "I guess."

Leslie could have let the discussion stop there, but she needed to explain. She had to. What happened wasn't her fault. Not at all. There *weren't* always two sides to every story. Sometimes there was only one. She bent down to Ava and took the child's hands in hers.

"We'll make it all fit, Ava. I know Daddy is not here, and Daddy could have done it. But Daddy had some problems and made his choice with his life. Sometimes men ... daddies ... just make bad choices. Maybe Daddy doesn't see it that way, but that's what happened. Mommy did her best, Ava, she really did. She did everything that Daddy wanted. She cooked and cleaned and tried to do everything Daddy needed. Mommy was there for him. I really, really tried. Then, out of the blue, there was someone else, and Daddy decided he didn't love me anymore. As if I had that choice. I don't understand how it all could change so quickly. I did everything he wanted. Anytime. Whatever it was he wanted. I tried."

Ava listened and nodded. Yet, even in the middle of this, Leslie realized she was saying too much. Ava had no business knowing what Daddy did or did not do. In fact, Leslie wasn't even certain Ava knew there was another woman involved in the divorce. Leslie had never mentioned her … until now. But maybe it was time for Ava to hear about it.

Ava's face was blank.

Leslie's heart rate sped up, unwanted and unexpected. "I'm sorry, Ava. I'm so sorry. It's okay. Really. We'll get it all in the van. We'll make two trips if we have to. It'll all be okay."

She went down on one knee and opened her arms. Ava slowly moved toward her, allowing herself to be hugged. There was a tension, a tightness in her daughter, that Leslie had not felt before. She held her for a long time.

"I'm not getting a new mommy, am I?" Ava finally asked. "Trevor said his daddy is looking for a new mommy. He says he wants a new mommy, but I don't think I do."

Then Leslie knew she had said too much. She stood up, and by sheer force of will, took Ava's hand and walked slowly toward the front, stopping to take the tag from the green upholstered chair.

"Mommy?" Ava said.

Through pursed lips, Leslie said, "What?"

"You said picture frames, too. Are you going to buy picture frames?"

Leslie shook her head. "Another day. The minivan will be filled anyhow. Is that okay?"

Ava nodded.

Leslie reached the counter and carefully laid the two tags flat. "It's fifty dollars for the whole set, right?" she asked, her words compressed.

"That's what the tag says. You got a deal on this one. Good for you. Let me call over to the church office. I'll get the custodian to help load your car. If you ask me, he loves it when I call him. Gets him out of the church. That's why he always runs over here. And he's got rope and all those sorts of packing things."

Leslie finished writing the check and slowly tore it out of the book.

"You pull around to the back, by the garage doors, and Freddie will take care of you. Thanks for shopping with us. Enjoy your new bedroom set, Ava."

Ava smiled happily and waved as her mother held the door open.

Amelia Westland, age fourteen years, four months
Butler Orphan Asylum
Butler County, Pennsylvania
November 25, 1876

Catherine considers me a giddy, silly schoolgirl. Perhaps I am. But I have made the acquaintance of a most agreeable young man, who is also residing at this Asylum. His name is Julian Beck. We have sat across the aisle in morning chapel and he glanced at me often, as I did at him. We have spoken on occasion, but for just a few moments, since prolonged association between the boys and girls at the Asylum is not encouraged. He appears to be pious, with a gift of oratory. He is agile and energetic. Catherine says she has heard tell he has been often in need of discipline. But his eyes are of the bluest color I have ever seen, and he has the most perfect of lips and beautiful blond hair, so to me, that is of no regard. I have taken a decided fancy to him, and I suspect his gaze might be enough to make many a woman swoon. His face fills my thoughts and dreams.

My voice shalt thou hear in the morning, O LORD;
in the morning will I direct my prayer unto thee, and will look up.
—PSALM 5:3

CHAPTER NINE

THERE WASN'T MUCH ROOM TO pace in Jack's small apartment. Five long steps took him from one end to the other. He walked to the windows, stared down at the street for a second, walked to the door, and then walked back. He grabbed at the television remote and snapped the power off. The electronic chatter had gotten on his nerves. He hadn't really been paying attention to whatever news program was on, but some noise was better than no noise at all—at least until it became aggravating.

He had finished work early today. Starting at 6:00 a.m., as quietly as possible, he had glued down the last of the countertops, and had put on new outlet covers throughout the apartment; most of the existing covers had been cracked and caked with paint. Starting early allowed him to leave the job site early without feeling guilty. He had a few estimates to do, and he never liked doing them after dinner. He would be too tired to concentrate. Earlier was better.

But now he felt distracted and disjointed. He wondered if he should head over to the Midlands Building, find some small project to fuss with, maybe tap at Leslie's door to ask her opinion.

That could be one way we could possibly have a little time together. I think she likes it as much as I do.

Instead he continued to work on his estimates until they grew more complex and frustrating. He pushed them aside, picked up a builders' magazine, and thumbed through it for a moment. He tossed it on the small end table, picked up a motorcycle magazine, and thumbed through that. In a moment, he tossed that aside as well.

I don't need to be reminded of what I don't have.

He thought of his daughter but forced her image away. He thought of his wife … the last time he saw her, the last time they spoke. He replayed that final scene until he could stand it no longer.

He thought about calling Ethan in Franklin, the only real friend he had in the world, but decided he had no good reason for the call.

And guys don't just call each other to chitchat, he thought. *Maybe I should go for a walk.*

He grabbed his keys, his wallet, and headed outside, into the warm autumn evening.

I could … walk past the Midlands Building. Would that be too desperate?

After five, downtown Butler became a quieter place. All the folks from the few banks, several office buildings, and other businesses went home to the suburbs and left the main street empty. Renovation work on the old Penn Theater came to a halt. The restaurant crowd wouldn't show up for a couple of hours.

Jack walked south instead of toward Leslie and stared in the windows of The Iron Works. Not many downtowns boasted of motorcycle shops housed in old department stores, but Butler did. While it was a far cry from selling linens and men's suits, the shop was neat and clean, and always had wonderful old bikes in the windows, their chrome catching the afternoon sun. Jack stared and wondered if he would ever be successful enough to buy one again. Working as a single contractor made the goal harder to achieve. One mistake could wipe out months of hard work. And there was only so much work a single person could produce in the course of eight hours—or ten—or twelve.

He began to think about Leslie again … the way she laughed, her hands as she had made coffee, how she'd touched him, the way that felt, and the scent she wore that day in the empty apartment.…

Jack shook his head and continued walking down Main Street, past the offices of the *Butler Eagle*, past the courthouse and around the historic Lowrie House. He strolled by the old Mansion House, where, according to its aged bronze plaque, the Marquis de Lafayette was entertained in 1825. He crossed Main and walked around Diamond Square, stopping to stare up at the tall Silent Defender statue in the square's center, past a big old stone church, then headed north and back toward home—toward his efficiency apartment that was barely big enough for one person, west of Main a couple of blocks off Jefferson Street.

His route passed by The Palm.

I'll stop in for a burger. I don't think I can eat any more ramen noodles this week.

He waited for a stoplight.

Just a burger. Nothing else.

He looked both ways and hurried across the street.

Only a burger.

He slipped into the cool dimness of The Palm. The tavern was fuller than at lunch—workers from the rolling mill down the street stopped off for a drink before heading home. The rumble of conversation and laughter were a comfort. Working alone, even with the radio on all the time, was hard.

Most of the afternoon patrons seemed to have edged farther inside, avoiding the half dozen seats near the front window with the flashing neon signs, and the afternoon sunlight. Jack slipped onto one of the stools, his back to the street. He nodded at the old-timers positioned at the end of the bar. He had seen them before. In fact, he had never *not* seen them when coming to The Palm.

Earl, the bartender, did not come up to him with his usual Coke. A new bartender with a very short crew cut and black plastic eyeglasses stood before Jack. A crisp, clean, tan apron was tied tightly around his waist and his white shirt was buttoned to the top button. He wore barely a hint of a welcoming smile.

"What can I do for you?"

Jack took a deep breath. He had expected to see Earl here. Earl understood him. Earl knew what Jack faced. Without speaking a word, Earl had known.

"A cheeseburger, I guess. Medium. With fries." Jack's mouth had gone dry. He knew why. He knew what to do. He *knew.*

"What to drink?"

He knew what to say. He knew what to answer. *He knew. He knew. He knew....*

"A draft. Iron City."

"Coming right up."

The words had been so easy. They had simply escaped from his mouth, and the draft poured, slowly, into a chilled mug, with the head foaming, reaching for the top.

The words were out, and there was nothing Jack could do to retrieve them. There the beer was, in front of him, on a crisp white coaster with graceful letters. The sweat of the ice on the outside of the frosted mug slid down the side, delicate and cooling and enticing.

Jack knew what he had to do.

He extended his hand and would have pushed the mug away, farther from his grasp. He would have done that. He would have. But the coaster must have been wet, and the mug stuck to the coaster and didn't slide at all.

A sip. A sip will not kill me. A sip never killed anyone. Just a sip. With the burger. Beer and burgers go together, right? Just a sip.

He tilted the mug ever so slightly, for just that sip, and there it was in his mouth. It went down his throat and felt ever so good. He allowed just a little more than a sip to pour from the glass and into his mouth. The yellowy punch, the familiar mellow caress filled his stomach, warming and cooling at the same time.

He put the mug down. Only an inch or two of the sparkly, wonderful beverage had been consumed. He would let it sit.

I'll wait for the burger, then maybe ... maybe I'll take one more sip. I'll ask the new bartender for a Coke ... or a glass of water. That's it. Just Coke with my food. I can't be hurt with a glass of Coke.

Then he forgot the Coke. He took one more sip, put the mug down, and stared at his hands, not knowing what he was going to do next, but knowing full well what he was going to do. He closed his eyes and, in that brief, incandescent moment, actually thought of offering up a prayer, but he didn't, because he didn't know what to say. The milk had been spilled. The door had been left open. The barn had been left unlocked.

There could be no recourse, Jack thought, no efficacy of prayer that would undo what had already been done. When he opened his eyes, he felt warm and whole again, for the first time in such a long time, like he had been welcomed back as an old friend. In just a few minutes, everything would be better again. He wouldn't be alone and lonely and down on his luck ... he would be okay again.

It's time. It's time.

The shadows were lengthening as Leslie and Ava watched. Freddie did his work well, with smiling enthusiasm, roping and tying and maneuvering and pushing every piece of furniture into the minivan and some on top of the roof—the flat pieces, headboard, and footboard. He snugged one last piece of rope and tied it tight.

"You got somebody on your end to help with all this? I ask, 'cause I'm not seeing a ring there on your hand. I pay attention to little things like that. Now if you need somebody at your end, you can tell me, and I'll come along and unload. I figure that's all part of my Christian service— you know what I mean, to help people who need help. That's why I like working at a church. I find all sorts of people who need help."

Freddie spoke slowly and plainly, as if words were not his native language. And Leslie wanted to cry after he finished; she wanted to thank him somehow. She never could have loaded the minivan by herself. She never would have been able to do this on her own.

"Thanks so much, Freddie. I have a man working on the apartment next to ours. He'll be able to help, I'm sure. He always works until five, so we'll be fine. But I really appreciate the offer."

Freddie bowed and nodded at the same time. "If you need me, I'm always at the church. You can call, and they always know where to find me."

Leslie was so touched, she had to hold back a sob getting into the minivan.

Ava had to sit in the front seat on the short trip home; the backseats had been folded down to allow for their new furniture. Ava worried the whole way about being stopped by the police and given a ticket for being allowed—being forced—to sit in the front.

Leslie dismissed her worries with a nervous laugh.

"You have to sit there, sweetie. What if the van were a pickup? There's only an up-front in a truck. Police couldn't arrest you for sitting up-front then."

Ava once again considered the jumble of furniture behind her. "I could get under the dressing table ... I think. There's almost enough room."

"But you wouldn't be able to use the seat belt, Ava. You are much safer up here. And I will drive extra carefully, all the way. It's not that far, sweetie."

With that Ava slumped down a bit in the seat, perhaps hiding herself from any police observation, and held tight to the seat belt with both hands. Her mother saw the gesture and wondered if it was just her way to feel more secure. Obviously, their lives had been anything but secure for the past few years. Perhaps Ava had always done that. Perhaps it was a more recent affectation.

Leslie pulled the minivan to the curb, just outside the door of their apartment building. Parking was seldom a problem, but she was happy the space right out front was open. She looked around and didn't see Jack's familiar silver pickup.

"Ava, could you run upstairs and ask Jack—Mr. Kenyon—if he could come down?"

"Which key is it?" Ava asked.

Leslie picked it out. "The one with the red dot on it. That's the key to the right door."

Ava took great care in inserting it and unlatching the lock, then took off at a run up the stairs. Leslie heard her knock on the second door. She waited. She heard Ava knock again.

"The door was locked and nobody answered," Ava said after running back down.

Leslie felt the panic rise again. *How am I going to do this? How am I going to get all of this upstairs? I can't leave it on the roof of the minivan overnight. Why isn't Jack working late like he always does? I need him now—to help with this, I mean.*

She grabbed her cell phone and dialed Jack's number. The call immediately went into voice mail. She left no message. Her heart began to beat fast, and sweat formed on her forehead.

What am I going to do now?

"You could call Trevor's daddy. Remember, Mommy? He said if you ever needed help with anything, he would help. Remember when he said that?"

Leslie did remember. Trevor had come over to watch *Dora the Explorer* after school one afternoon, and when Mike Reidmiller picked him up, he had made the offer.

Maybe …

Leslie wouldn't let the panic rise further. She'd have to ask for a favor. She didn't like asking for favors.

Upstairs, she opened up the kindergarten parents' directory and dialed the number. Ava waited at the bottom of the steps, inside the door, watching the minivan. Butler was not a high-crime city by any stretch of the imagination, but Leslie could be a worrier and did not want anyone to make off with the headboard and rails, tied to the vehicle's luggage rack.

Leslie watched her daughter, her little face pressed against the glass pane of the door. She spoke quickly once Mike Reidmiller answered.

"Trevor's father will be here in five minutes," Leslie said as she came down the stairs. "He said he'd bring Trevor along to help."

Four minutes later, a dark green car pulled up to the curb. Leslie was terrible at knowing which model of car, but it was very clean and the interior didn't have a jumble of bags and paper and wrappers that often inhabited Leslie's minivan.

"Looks like you bought out the store, Mrs. Ruskin. I hope you worked them down on the price," Mike said, smiling, as he began to unknot a fist-sized knot of rope.

"I didn't need to," she replied. "Sixty dollars for the entire load."

Mike Reidmiller nodded in appreciation of a good deal. "Well, we'll have this up in your place in a few minutes. It's all light stuff. No heavy sleeper sofas or entertainment centers."

Leslie helped as she could, and the four of them hustled every piece of furniture upstairs within the span of fifteen minutes. Mr. Reidmiller ("You have to call me Mike. You promised, remember?") insisted on setting up Ava's bed and placing the mattress and box springs on top.

"I'm not a man who leaves hard things for a woman to do," he said as he sweated, moving the furniture around, asking every minute or two, "Is this the right place for this?"

At the end of the move, Ava and Trevor sat on the sofa watching some chattery cartoon on television.

"Thanks, Mike, for your help. I didn't know what to do or who to call. I don't know many people in town yet."

Mike waved off her thanks. "It was nothing. A little bit of exercise is good for me." He wiped his forehead with his sleeve.

Leslie waited, wondering what to do next. She felt that familiar stab of tension in her chest. "Would you like some … tea? Coffee? Something cold?"

"Coffee for sure. Unless it's that flavored stuff. I don't like flavored stuff," he answered.

"It's just regular coffee."

"Then okay. Looks like the kids are busy for a while."

He followed Leslie into the kitchen and took a seat with ease, like he'd been there before and was comfortable in Leslie's presence—at home being in her home.

"This is a real nice place. You own the building, right? Trevor told me that … though, like I said, I'm never sure what to believe or not."

Measuring out the coffee and water, Leslie answered. "I do. I needed a place to live. I hope to rent out the bottom floor, as well as the one empty apartment. That would really help with the mortgage."

"Sounds like a smart move," Mike answered.

Fussing with the coffee and cream was just enough of a distraction. Whatever discomfort she was feeling, whatever unease was building inside her, was being kept at bay by the busyness of her hands, which were occupied just enough to keep her from thinking too much about what was happening.

He's a man, and he's already expressed an interest in dating me. I don't think I'm ready for this. Or am I? Am I being flirty with Jack … just because I'm ready? What about Mike? And what about Ava? Is she ready to see me with another man?

She placed the coffee and cream and a plate of Girl Scout Trefoil cookies on a tray and set it carefully on the table.

"Oh, boy—snacks," Mike said, grinning. "I would have done this for free, but cookies are one fine paycheck."

Later, Leslie couldn't recall what she and Mike had talked about as he ate seven of her shortbread cookies and drank two cups of her coffee. She must not have been too odd or disjointed in her conversation, though, for he laughed and slapped at his knee at least once. Maybe it was twice. She recalled him nodding and bobbing at the end, as if his body movements were a punctuation, a period of sorts, on their time together. He gathered up Trevor, ruffled Ava's hair in a good-bye, and at the bottom of the stairs, gave Leslie a modified, chaste, but enthusiastic hug of farewell.

"We hug a lot, our family," he said as he stepped out into the street, car keys in hand. "Call if you need anything else. Anytime."

Ava waved. Leslie almost waved. Their car sped off, Trevor leaning out the back window, yelling something neither Ava nor Leslie could understand.

Later that night, when Ava had been asleep for hours, Leslie sat on her new living room chair reading. She replayed the hug, the feeling of a man's larger arms around her, the masculine smell and bristly experience of it all. She shut her eyes hard, tight, breathing deeply.

Part of her loved being held tight and snug and encompassed. Part of her needed it, found it reassuring, like the purr of a cat … or like the sound of a lock being locked, like feeling warm and safe.

But there was another part of being held, when she felt unwelcome arms tighten around her and pin her arms to her side. It was claustrophobic, a feeling Leslie hated, dreaded, could not bear. There were other unpleasant memories. It was black and gray and loud and overwhelming, and it came in cycles. There was pain and panic, although Leslie hated the word *panic*. She never wanted to think of that word and tried to will it all to go away—all the years of trembling and fear—willed it all to simply disappear.

―――――――

Jack sat upright and squared his shoulders, inhaled deeply, and wondered if anyone around him had cigarettes. He would have liked to have a cigarette but knew they were bad for his health.

No sense in starting to smoke again. Nope. Expensive. No smoking.

He placed his hands on the bar. He had had enough. The cheeseburger and fries had been consumed a long time ago. Jack looked at his watch, squinted. It was darker now, and he couldn't quite make out where the small hands were positioned. He looked up and scouted the room.

Never a clock handy when you need one. Maybe they don't put 'em up 'cause then people will leave early or something.

"Hey, Sam, what time is it?"

The new bartender's name was Sam. At least Jack thought it was Sam. He'd said it once.

Sam looked at his watch. "12:30."

Jack had no idea it was that late. "Gotta go."

He pushed off the chair and felt the rubbery give of the wooden floor. At least it felt rubbery and unstable to him.

"I'm walking home! Don't worry about me!" Jack said.

Sam, the new bartender, hardly raised an eyebrow. He didn't seem to be the type that would insist on calling a cab.

Jack stepped out into the cooler air and carefully stepped down to the sidewalk, holding onto the railing around the entrance. He took several deep breaths. He tried not to think about what had just taken place over the last few hours. He knew what he should have done, and he knew, all too well, what he had done. Part of him felt sick, part of him felt well and complete for the first time in months. He liked that feeling of completeness, of being the master of his environment.

Carefully, he began walking and stumbled off the curb, his body not ready for the four-inch drop. He caught himself in midstumble and straightened up; he held his hands outright, like a tightrope walker for a few seconds, until he regained his balance.

He snorted out a laugh, a laugh at his own unsteadiness. He put his palms up and faced them out, like he was quieting a crowd who had gasped at his near fall. Then he held up one finger in the air, like he was readying the crowd for a new trick. He looked both ways, exaggerated the swiveling of his head, and crossed the street, making two course corrections along the way, keeping his arms outstretched to provide balance.

As he made it to the other side of the street, he looked around, blinking, as if he had entered some new and magical world. He shook his finger several times near his head, then pointed, as if he had suddenly discovered a passage to his home. He set off, walking stiff-legged, slowly, toward his goal.

Mike Reidmiller sat alone on the screened front porch of his home, alone in the darkness, with just one outdoor candle burning. Only the occasional sound of a car punctuated the silence, passing along on his street, just northeast of the elementary school and only eight blocks from where Leslie lived.

After coming back from helping Leslie unload her new furniture, Mike had busied himself around the house—cleaning, doing two loads of laundry, emptying the dishwasher, sorting mail, getting Trevor to bed on time for a change, and not letting him stay up to watch another jittery electronic cartoon from Japan.

When the wind was right, from the south, he could catch a snippet of the buzzers that rang with red lights in the downtown area. Even the buzzers were now silent for the evening. Mike sat in one of the all-weather wicker chairs he and his wife had purchased when they first bought the tidy white Cape Cod with dark green shutters on Butler's near northeast side.

All had been well for the first few years, Mike recalled. Maybe not perfect, but well enough. Then Trevor arrived, and everything changed. She had wanted children, but maybe not this child. Within a year, disagreements were common, her mood swings expected, sudden and unexplained departures the norm. Lost days and weekends were all part of their lives.

Mike always said that he could have lived with all of that, with all the anger and recriminations and dark times—but that she could not. When Trevor reached his second birthday, his mother had simply packed everything that she owned, loaded it all into their newest car, and drove away, claiming she would call when she "found herself," was settled, and was ready to start over.

She'd never called. Mike had tried to find her, and did, but she had refused to return, or even to talk. She'd found herself, he guessed.

He had imagined that she'd never contest the divorce, but she did and made it an expensive, painful process for all concerned. One thing was certain—she did not want custody of the child.

So, tonight, after a pleasant hour spent in pleasant conversation with an attractive woman, Mike felt sort of normal again, as if his bearings and compass were returning to some form of equilibrium. Leslie had laughed at his jokes, even if they had been corny. She had appeared grateful for his help, Trevor got along famously with her daughter, he thought, and she had allowed him to hug her in farewell. Maybe, he also imagined, she even encouraged the hug.

That's what he thought now, anyway. She was happy to see him. She did call him.

And in the warm darkness of this late autumn night, Mike sat in the dark, holding a warm, half-consumed can of cream soda, and grinned, though no one else could take notice of his happiness.

I'll call her next week. I'll ask her out to dinner. Nothing fancy, just a dinner between friends. We'll take it from there. I'm not in any hurry.

As he considered which restaurant would be most appropriate for casual friends and a casual dinner with no understated intentions, he wondered if Leslie would make a good mother for Trevor.

He needs a good mother, Mike thought, concluding his considerations for this event.

Amelia Westland, age fourteen years, nine months
Butler Orphan Asylum
Butler County, Pennsylvania
April 5, 1877

My delirious joy is soon tempered with melancholy. Julian has declared he shall be taking leave shortly. In six months' time, upon reaching his sixteenth year, he shall depart for the town of Butler to be indentured to a livery there, as he is skilled with horses. He is a strong young man, and I imagine his services are much in demand.

My days are filled with hope of even a fleeting glance from him, and I count the hours until it is the time for chapel services, where I am able to steal gazes at him for the better part of the hour, hoping they go unnoticed by Mr. Stevens and Headmistress. His return gazes cause stomach flutters, and I am scarce able to recount even a shred of any sermon or Scripture reading. It is as though some manner of spell has been placed upon my sensibilities. I then am compelled to repent, for I fear God's displeasure, but pray His forgiveness will cover such iniquities as I am prone to commit in regards to Mr. Beck.

Let love be without dissimulation.
Abhor that which is evil; cleave to that which is good.
—ROMANS 12:9

CHAPTER TEN

THE FLASHING LIGHTS, IRRITATING AND incessant, were not to be denied. Jack slapped at the air in front of his face, as if the lights were some sort of swarm of insects to be chased off with a swat of his hand.

The lights did not diminish.

He felt a dull prodding on his side, like having fallen asleep with his hammer still holstered in his tool belt.

"Hey! You! Get up!"

Blinking, Jack stared into the red and black darkness.

"Get up! You can't sleep in an alley."

He shook his head, trying to clear his vision and his thoughts. Neither became all that much clearer.

Jack felt hands grab at his shoulders and lift him upright.

"Come on, now, buddy. Take it easy. This way. Over here. Watch your step."

He felt a hand on the top of his head, pushing him down, and then he fell backward, onto something soft. He heard a door slam shut, then in a moment, another two doors slamming.

"Take him home?"

"No. Too far gone. We'll take him to the station. On a 42–29."

"But he wasn't creating a disturbance."

"No. But sleeping in an alley? What happens if a car runs him over?

Then who gets blamed? He can sleep it off in the holding cell. Maybe it'll just be a drunk in public charge."

Jack felt himself slip further down on the seat, then list over to one side. Thankfully, everything went black again.

———∞———

Leslie woke early that morning and slipped into Ava's bedroom, well before her daughter's normal time for waking. The little girl was asleep in the middle of the princess bed, with her arms out of the bedcovers, loose, at her sides. Her dark hair was spread out like a halo around her head.

The bedroom set was indeed perfect—feminine, sweet, and dainty. Ava and Leslie had spent two hours taking all of Ava's clothes from the cardboard boxes and organizing them, placing them, by category, into the dresser drawers. Leslie had used cleaning and disinfecting sprays on all the interiors, and had added sheets of drawer liner, scented with lavender, like her mom's. Ava had been so precise, placing her T-shirts just so, her socks all lined up heel to toe.

Before bed, she had sat at her small dressing table in her soft blue pajamas, on the small white slipper chair. Earlier they had discovered that the top of the tufted hassocklike chair folded open, disclosing a secret hiding place. Ava had been delighted, though she would not decide what items she would place there in secret. She had sat, staring at herself in the mirror, as if discovering her image in a new way, and for the first time.

Now, standing over her sleeping daughter, Leslie wanted to bend down to the bed, hug her little princess, and hold her close, but she did not.

She needs her rest. I would just wake her too early.

Instead, Leslie went into the kitchen, poured herself a cup of leftover coffee, and sat out on the balcony, listening to the town as it slowly came awake.

I wonder where Jack was yesterday. It's not like him to leave here early. I hope nothing happened to him.

———∞———

At first, Jack was certain that the pounding he heard and felt must be taking place outside.

Road construction? This early?

Then he realized the pounding was inside his head, and every pulse produced a new wave of pain and nausea. He held his eyes shut, hard and tight, then gingerly reached up with his hands and placed his fingers on his temples. He pressed ever so lightly and was rewarded with more and even heavier pounding. He opened his eyes. He was in a gray room with gray walls. One side of the room was bars.

He knew where he was.

Slowly he pushed himself into a sitting position. He looked at his watch. It was gone. He patted at his side. His cell phone was gone as well.

He knew who had them.

It may have taken him five minutes until his stomach settled and the pounding receded slightly. He pushed himself upright and walked to the bars. He reached out and held on, gingerly. The metal bars, painted with dozens of coats of dark gray paint, were cold and slick to the touch. He looked in both directions. At the end of the wide hall, beside a large gray desk, sitting in a large, tattered gray chair, was a massive policeman.

Jack croaked out a weak, "Sir?"

The mass of policeman did not move.

Jack tried again, as loud as his throat would tolerate. "Sir?"

The massive policeman slowly pivoted in his seat, the chair making unnatural squealing noises as he turned. "You up?"

Jack shrugged. "I guess."

"I'll call the arresting officer. He's still here. You wait there, okay?"

Jack was sure the massive policeman said that every time, amusing himself at the expense of the poor sap stuck in the locked holding cell.

If I have to make bail … I have a thousand dollars in my checking account. That should be enough for anything … unless it's disorderly conduct … then I'm screwed.

He rubbed his hands over his face, trying to think; trying to figure out what he should do—what he could do. He tried to remember what had happened last night, but his memory all but faded to black from the moment he stepped out of the bar. Even before that, details were sketchy.

If I have to make a larger bail … who would I call?

Jack's stomach again roiled silently.

A bail bondsman? But I bet they won't take a check from a new account. And they're so expensive …

I could call Ethan.

Jack winced at the thought.

I can't call him. I can't disappoint him like this.

He sat back on the hard cot, which was bolted down and chained to the wall.

I could call Leslie. I could … I don't know how, but I could. She would understand.

Jack held his head in his hands and tried not to think. He would have prayed, like they taught in the meetings, but he was too far gone, he was sure of that. Praying now would be a waste of time.

As if God would be listening to me now … after all this … again.

A few minutes later, a door clanged open and the massive policeman was followed by a policeman of normal size. He wasn't smiling, nor was he frowning. His face was a dead neutral.

"Jack Kenyon?"

Jack nodded.

"You have a rough night?"

Jack knew the answer and knew what the policeman was doing. He had heard it all before. He had heard it often.

"Yeah. From what I remember."

The police shook his head, scolding in a silent way. "We found you in the alley by the old bakery. What were you doing there? In Butler? Your driver's license says Franklin."

Jack knew nothing about an old bakery. He knew nothing about the alley. He could only shrug. "I was on my way home. I was walking. I live over on Jefferson Street. By the Chinese place."

The not-so-massive policeman nodded. "Used to be a bakery. You live there?"

"Upstairs. Apartment Three."

"You work around here? You have a job?"

"Construction. I'm working on an apartment in the Midlands Building."

The not-so-massive policeman brightened. "The building with the green screened balconies? What's that place like inside? It looks so interest-ing from the street."

Jack knew the morning could not get too much more surreal. "The apartments are real nice. Roomy. I'm rehabbing one for the woman who owns the building."

"That right, is it?"

Jack waited. If the not-so massive policeman mentioned misdemeanor, Jack's morning would slide from really, really bad, to downright horrible in an instant.

"Well, Mr. Kenyon, you were drunk in public last night. Can't say it was a disturbance, since you were passed out when we found you. You could be charged—"

Jack held his breath.

"—but I don't think it would be worth it. You're new here. You haven't been in trouble in Butler before. If you had, it would be a different story. But I want to impress on you that we don't take kindly to anyone being drunk and disorderly in town. You drink too much—your business, after all—you take a cab and get inside to sleep it off. You understand? I don't want to see you in here again, Mr. Kenyon. You got it?"

Jack nodded, grateful. Very, very grateful. "Yes sir. It has been a long time since I had my last drink. Sort of slipped this time. Won't happen again."

The not-so massive policeman started to smile, then didn't, as if he truly understood what Jack was admitting and promising at the same time. "Get to a meeting today. There's one over at the Knights of Columbus hall on Cunningham. By the old high school. At eight o'clock. You go. I don't want us to do this again." He drew in a large breath and held it awhile before exhaling. "See the property clerk when you go out. He has all your belongings."

Jack wanted to reach out his hand and offer it to the not-so-massive policeman, but he didn't. "Yes sir," he said instead. "I'll do that. At the Knights of Columbus hall, eight o'clock. I'll go. I promise."

But as he gathered up his belongings, the promise was already slipping from his thoughts.

I only fell once. I can handle this. I can do this on my own.

The cell phone was ringing as Leslie pulled out into traffic. Ava had just jumped quickly out from the minivan in front of the school and was running toward the kindergarten door. She hardly waved.

But she did wave a little, Leslie told herself.

Never good at doing the two things at once, Leslie pulled back over to the curb to answer the phone. She listened carefully.

"Certainly, Jack. If you don't feel well this morning, you can come later today. Or even tomorrow. We're a little ahead of schedule, aren't we?"

She waited. A vision of Jack tucked into bed, in need of some TLC, flashed into her mind. She pushed the thought away quickly. "Good. Then I will see you later."

Leslie flipped her phone closed, took a deep breath, then looked at herself in the rearview mirror. She wore her best blue blouse, with a dark blue blazer over top, and her most expensive, tailored khaki slacks. The dressing up was for the occasion of her first job interview.

Mrs. Stickle had a sister who lived next door to someone who worked in the Human Resources department at ARMCO, some sort of steel business, who said that one of the directors was looking for an administrative assistant. He didn't want some "kid right out of school," and Mrs. Stickle was sure that Leslie would be perfect for the job.

"Not that you're old, but you're not kid-young, so that's perfect," Mrs. Stickle explained.

ARMCO was "the producer of the finest flat-rolled carbon, stainless, and electrical steel products in the world." That was according to their Web site. Beyond that, not much of their process or product line made sense to Leslie. But she felt good knowing at least a little something about the company.

As she drove to Lyndora, five minutes south of downtown Butler, she mentally reviewed her qualifications for the job.

She had none.

Not none, exactly. But not all that many.

She had her résumé. She had gone to college—University of

Pennsylvania—and had graduated with a degree in art history. Every time she thought of that, she wondered what in the world she was thinking of back then. Teach art history? Work at a museum? Be a researcher? She really didn't know. Yet this is where the path of her life had led. She could type—not extremely fast, but fast enough, and she was a good writer. She could use a computer well. She knew a little bit about accounting. She thought of herself as an organized person. So she did have some experience.

Who am I kidding? I went to school, got married, and had a baby. What sort of experience is that?

ARMCO was much larger than Leslie imagined. She had to drive through a gate—two old brick towers, each holding a large ornamental ironwork gate, both sides folded back. There was no guard on duty, but there was a guardhouse. She parked in front of the main building and looked at her watch.

Twenty minutes early. Time to review the résumé.

She slipped it out of the leather folder and tried to stare at the words, tried to memorize the dates and accomplishments, in case someone inside the brick building quizzed her on the specifics. She had read recently—perhaps it had been in the career section of the Pittsburgh paper—that every job candidate had to know exactly what was on his or her résumé, backward and forward. "If you don't know it, what does that say about the quality of your work?"

She tried to read the words, but as soon as she tried to focus, the words began to swim on the page—not a lot, but they grew quivery and liquid. She shut her eyes and tried to take deep breaths, the classic response to the beginning of the familiar rising panic. She tried to remember what her yoga instructor had said. "Calm yourself. Stay centered. Take deep cleansing breaths while you keep your eyes closed. Concentrate on a peaceful image."

None of it ever seemed to work all that well.

Leslie simply shut her eyes, breathed, and prayed that this was simply a small shower of panic, not a deluge. She had no way of deciphering the severity at the outset of the event.

Not today. Not now.

If it happened now …

She glanced at her watch. Fifteen minutes.

It might pass.

It might not, just as easily. Her breaths grew shallower and faster. She felt the clamminess on her palms and her chest began to tighten.

No. Not here. Please, God, not now.

It was a familiar plea. It was a familiar prayer.

She jammed her eyes shut as tight as she could and imagined the panic in her palms, then unclenched her palms to keep the emotions under control and push the panic away.

It did not work. It had never worked, really. All of the self-help plans and advice had never done much good. Panic would flood her being, fill her to the core, and do with her what it would.

She managed to open her eyes to look at her watch. Five minutes left. She tried to reach for the leather folder to put her résumé away, but her arm wouldn't respond. All that she heard, all that she could hear, was a voice from somewhere inside yelling, pleading, screaming: *Get out of here! Get out of here! Get out. Get out.*

She could barely move her arm to find her keys. She turned them in the ignition. She knew she had to start the car. Her heart was beating fast, ready to leap from her chest, ready to burst from the pressure. Her vision clouded with an angry, dark fog. She jammed the minivan into reverse, and with as much control as she could possibly muster, edged back out of the parking lot. She drove back through the wrought-iron gates and back up the steep hill that led to Butler and back home, all the while, repeating, almost chanting, *Dear God, dear God, dear God….*

She parked the minivan at an awkward angle to the street, not far away enough to cause suspicion, but as close as she could. She bolted up the steps, slammed open the apartment door, and leaned back against it when it snapped shut. Trembling, she forced herself to the phone in the kitchen. She dialed the number. She prayed she would sound less frantic than she felt.

"I have an interview at 9:00 with Mr. Lytwak. My daughter's school called and said that she had … been hurt on the playground. It's not serious, but I have … have to take her home for the day. Would it be possible to reschedule the interview for tomorrow at the same time?"

She shut her eyes as she waited.

"Oh."

She listened.

"I understand. I understand. Maybe … maybe I could call him tomorrow? Maybe?"

She listened.

"Okay. I understand. Thank you."

She hung up the phone, scrabbling at the wall to find purchase, then ran down the hallway, into her bedroom, and slammed her door shut. Throwing herself on the bed, she pulled the pillow tightly over her head, not wanting to scream, not wanting to cry out in fear. She tried to breathe deeply to prevent the tears and the anguish, holding on to the pillowcase so tightly that the fabric almost began to tear.

Why now? Why are they coming back now? If he finds out, he'll take Ava for sure. He can't find out. He can't.

But if I can't get a job—he will find out. It's all starting again. Oh, God, it's starting all over again.

Amelia Westland, age fifteen years
Butler Orphan Asylum
Butler County, Pennsylvania
July 6, 1877

The idea has gotten possession of me to petition the Headmaster for the same manner of assignment as has been given to Julian Beck—not at the livery, of course, for that would be man's work, but perhaps as a domestic in the home of a Christian family in the town of Butler, so that I can remain nearby Julian. I pray that Mr. Stevens not ask my reason, for I am loathe to say a falsehood to him. Perhaps in that fashion we could continue to see each other on occasion. Meanwhile, my heart dares hope for any small time we may have to further our acquaintance here. I pray it shall come to pass.

Catherine, rather chagrined at my plan, has already begun to grieve my departure, though it is not at all certain as to if and when I shall be placed. She is such a dear. I should sorely miss her as well. I assure her that we will always be as sisters, as lifelong friends.

The LORD hath heard my supplication;
the LORD will receive my prayer.
—PSALM 6:9

CHAPTER ELEVEN

IF SOMEONE ASKED THE CASUAL observer—the average man or woman walking on any sidewalk in town—if Alice and Frank Adams were natives to Butler, odds are that the overwhelming majority would have said, "Absolutely not."

Perhaps none of them would be able to pinpoint the reason for their response. Perhaps it was Alice's fashion sense. Eclectic, to be sure, but expensive—or at any rate, exclusive. A style of skirt that never once appeared in any store out at the Butler mall. Her blouse—well, it just looked foreign. Maybe Japanese, maybe some other exotic Far Eastern designer brand that no one in Butler had heard of. And the shoes. Salon shoes, with some elegant-sounding Italian name printed on the inside, no doubt.

And Frank, even though he was most partial to jeans—expensive jeans, the kind you could only find in exclusive, hip, and trendy boutiques in London or New York or Pittsburgh; and even though he wore white shirts—almost always the kind of white shirt that famous people might wear; and even if he had been wearing Levi's and a T-shirt from Target, he still would have stood out. The shoes—Ermenegildo Zegna—worn without socks, of course. The color of his dark hair, and the cut, were clues. And the highlights. Everyone in Butler knows that most men do not highlight their hair, especially with light chestnut streaks, studied and practiced—almost natural, but not really.

Nothing they wore—or were—was by itself outrageous. But none of their apparel was from anywhere near Butler, either. They were simply cutting-edge stylish.

So when the tall pair entered the Main Street headquarters of the First Bank of Butler, tellers and personal bankers looked up. And while the bank employees didn't stare, exactly, the pair did garner more attention than the normal, average, everyday customer.

Being handsome, or striking, and not really acknowledging their good looks, added to their image. They stopped at the information desk.

"Who do we talk to concerning a property that you have for sale?" Frank asked.

The clerk, a Ms. Abigail Farkas, perhaps surprised by the question, looked around behind her, at the anonymous desks inhabited by equally anonymous personal bankers, as if one of them were about to raise their hand.

Actually, one of them did raise his hand.

"Lowell," she said, without much confidence, while pointing to a desk on the other side of the open space. "Lowell … something or other. He handles the commercial real estate for the bank."

Ms. Farkas scanned the list of employee names as she ran her finger down the paper. "Lowell … McDowell," the clerk added. "He *does* do the commercial real-estate stuff." She turned around, the other way, looking over her shoulder. "And he's here today. You're in luck, I guess."

Alice and Frank made their way down the long row of identical desks, with identical phones and computer terminals. Lowell stood to greet them and invited them to sit in the two matching identical guest chairs.

"You have an old building for sale. We want to buy it," Alice stated.

"You do?" Lowell replied, his voice rising in pitch. Lowell was new to the bank, and in his experience, few people—in fact, *no* people—ever just walked in and so stated their intentions.

"Yes. We do. It's a funny sort of corner three-flat and large retail space over on Cedar. We saw it before we left for Europe and we want to buy it. It has green balconies that have been screened in. What's it listed at?"

Alice and Frank sat down in the two matching chairs.

Again, Lowell was surprised. No one jumped to the price so quickly. He knew that he had not shown the building to them, but it was on the multiple listings sheet at one time, so perhaps it had been shown by another realtor in town. Lowell would have asked them, but then the honorable thing to do would be to instruct them that they should deal with the original showing agent if they wanted to buy it. But Lowell didn't, because unlike most of the other bankers here, he did get a commission on every piece of property that he sold for the bank. It wasn't as much as he could make as a *real* real-estate agent, but the bank offered a steadier income, with benefits, which is why Lowell was working for First Bank and not Century 21 or some other local firm.

"Yes … I remember that property …"

And all of a sudden, Lowell's heart sank, because he remembered that the property had sold several weeks earlier. After sitting on the bank's open listings for over a year, it had sold for much less than the original asking price, and now here were two customers who probably would have paid the full asking amount, which would have meant a bigger commission.

"But let me make sure …"

Lowell was actually sure—was now positive, in fact—that the closing had gone through without a hitch, but he didn't want to disappoint this nice, attractive couple. Maybe they would buy something else, some other run-down commercial property that had been sitting vacant for a year or two, and it would make Lowell's quarterly bonus bigger. That would be a good thing.

"I'm pretty sure it was just sold."

The couple appeared to deflate, ever so slightly.

"Sold? I knew we should have jumped on it before we left for Europe. I just knew it. Didn't I say that, Frank?" the woman said.

Lowell realized that he hadn't introduced himself, nor presented either of them with his business card, nor the specially designed real-estate brochure the bank had produced a few months earlier, the one with Lowell's picture showing a client in a business suit at a vacant warehouse. Lowell thought it was a pretty good photo of him, even if it had been windy that day and his hair seemed more than a bit mussed.

Lowell pulled out a folder from his desk drawer, flipped it open, and ran his finger down a long numbered list.

"Yes. The property did close … I guess it was nearly a month ago now.

A young woman from Greensburg purchased it," Lowell added, and then wondered if he had said too much. He wasn't always positive what was a matter of public record and what wasn't.

Frank leaned forward. He smiled in such a way that Lowell wanted to tell him more.

"Did she rent out the bottom of the building?"

Lowell was now more than flustered. He had no idea. And he had no idea if he had any further information on the building or the new owner, other than that the sale had closed properly, the bank had gotten its money, and Lowell would make his commission.

"I-I don't know. She didn't say anything about it. I think she is living there, in one of the apartments upstairs. At least that's what she told me she was thinking. That was her plan. She had her young daughter with her."

And again, Lowell remained unsure if the daughter was also a part of the public record or not.

"Well, then, there's still hope, Alice. If she hasn't made a deal with anyone, we can still do what we want to do—and we'll have no mortgage to worry about."

Alice stood up and smoothed out her Japanese skirt. "Thank you so much, Mr.—"

Lowell handed her a packet of business cards.

"—Mr. McDowell. You have been such a help."

Alice waited until Frank stood up, then they slowly walked out of the building.

Everyone in the bank did their best to not watch the couple as they went by.

* * *

Jack wanted coffee in the worst way but was fairly certain a cup of the brew would roil his stomach in a most wicked manner, so he ordered a large orange juice, without ice, along with two breakfast sandwiches at the drive-thru. It was a practiced meal, one he had downed perhaps a hundred times before—some protein, with enough liquid to offer some hydration. It was easy to eat as well.

He parked on a side street. There were fewer cars here and he would not have to parallel-park, because that would involve him pivoting his head back and forth and he was pretty sure that would bring on a ripple of nausea. Pulling to the curb, he slowly ate his breakfast in his truck. He had spent the morning in his apartment, doing his best not to be sick, and had succeeded. A handful of aspirin and two glasses of milk were all he could manage to get down. Now, with the egg sandwiches gone, and the aspirin taking effect, he felt almost normal.

Not normal at all, not really. But not sick, either. Just normal enough to do a little work.

He knew he didn't have the concentration to handle any complex tasks today—nothing with measuring or cutting or nailing. All of that required a steady hand.

He held his hand out in the cab of the truck. His fingers wavered like a leaf on a windy spring day.

No cutting. No power tools.

He stepped out onto the street and slammed the truck door behind him. He winced at the harsh metallic sound, gritted his teeth, and wondered if he was doing the right thing. He could have simply stayed home. Even Leslie said they were ahead of schedule. And he was— nearly a week ahead of where he had anticipated being. The work had gone smoothly.

He used his key to unlock the door to the first-floor retail space in the building, still empty and almost cavernous. Jack had spent a few weekends hauling away scores of large black contractor trash bags, filled with all manner of flotsam and jetsam, the odd debris empty buildings seem to attract—empty soda cans, wrappers from fast-food restaurants, old news-papers, empty boxes—nothing of value, but a lot of it.

He was unsure what he might tackle here this afternoon. Whatever it would be would need to be done slowly, gingerly, without any sudden moves, and without making a lot of noise. The tin ceiling needed attention. It was of the original stamped tin-plate squares, probably installed when the building was first built, which made perfect sense to Jack, because tin ceilings had reached the zenith of their popularity in the 1890s, and this building had been completed in 1897.

Jack had bought a fourteen-foot ladder for the job. All that the ceiling job entailed was screwing up loose corners. The finishing nails that had been used for repairs were not appropriate for the installation, and each of them had worked free from the ceiling over time. Jack selected three-inch stainless steel screws that would match the tin's appearance and hold tight for decades and never rust.

Working on the ceiling meant working above his head, which meant some internal pounding, just inside his temples, but it was bearable. The only noise he would have to endure was the quiet whirr of the cordless drill and the tinny squeal of the screw grabbing into the wood backing of the tin. He climbed the ladder slowly, as if he were climbing into a strong headwind, and his movements were exactingly deliberate, like a man nursing a critical headache.

If Leslie comes down, I'll just tell her I didn't feel up to working upstairs. I'm sure she won't give it a second thought.

Frank and Alice Adams pressed their attractive, tanned faces against the windows on the west side of the Midlands building.

"This would be absolutely *perfect*. Close to Main Street, but not right downtown. Parking wouldn't be a problem."

Alice stepped back on the wide sidewalk and looked up at the apartments on the second floor of the Midlands Building.

"What about zoning?" Frank asked.

She shook her head, indicating it was of no concern. "If the space was zoned retail once, that property almost always remains zoned retail. Grandfathered in. Unless there was an uprising among the neighbors. Or a massive neighborhood rezoning. And I cannot imagine either of those events occurring in Butler."

Frank stepped back from the glass. He watched Alice walk toward the main entrance, knowing her mind was working—redesigning, repainting, reconfiguring the old building on the corner, imagining how she might make it renewed and current and upscale and desirable.

"It's perfect, Frank. The arched windows. The original fireplace. Wonderful brickwork. Solid. But still … a bit quixotic and quirky. Perfect."

Hitching up his three-hundred-dollar True Religion jeans, Frank walked around the corner. He stopped suddenly. "There's someone inside. He's working on the ceiling."

Alice's voice dropped and tightened. "If someone else has rented this, I'm going to be *so* upset. Really, horribly, *totally* upset. I mean that in the worst way."

Frank knew that voice and knew the consequences. He walked to the front door, turned the gold signet ring on his right hand ever so slightly, and tapped at the door. He saw the man on the ladder jump and grab onto to the rungs, as if the sharp rapping had interrupted his balance.

The man slowly made his way down the ladder, set the drill on the ladder shelf, hitched his tool belt, walked to the front doors, and unlocked one.

———

The attractive, well-dressed man extended his hand as if he were in a receiving line at a wedding.

"I'm Frank Adams. This is Alice," he said with a tilt of his head backward. "We stopped at the bank earlier because … well, we wanted to buy this place. And now that we've learned that it's already been sold, we are most interested in renting out the first floor. Do you know if the owner is around, or if she has already rented the space?"

Jack, too nauseated to be too surprised, took Frank's hand and, surprised at his powerful grip, replied, "No, I don't think she's rented it. I don't think she's been actively advertising it yet."

The equally well-dressed and attractive woman, still standing outside, gave out a little, happy yelp. "I knew it! I could tell. This place told me 'I'm not rented!'"

Jack couldn't help but smile, even though it hurt to do so. "Come on in," he offered. "The owner is upstairs, I think, but I'm sure it would be all right if you looked around a bit."

Alice came in, like a breeze, Jack thought, and moved through the open space, with her arms partly extended, as if floating. She twirled around again. "Everything is simply perfect. Just *ideal*."

Jack gently tapped at the door at the top of the stairs.

"Her car is down on the street. That almost always means she's at home."

The three of them waited, silently, on the landing outside Leslie's apartment door. Jack leaned in closer.

"I don't hear anything. She might have walked over to her daughter's school. It's only a few blocks away."

Frank sort of issued a vague "harrumph," but Alice didn't seem to be upset in the least.

"Oh, that's all right, Mr. Kenyon. If it's not rented, I'm sure we'll be able to come to terms with Mrs. Ruskin. From what you've told us, she seems like a perfectly *marvelous* person. Now ... let's go back downstairs. I want to talk to you about what we want to do to the space. Maybe you can give us a quote on the work."

Despite the pounding at his temples, Jack smiled. It was turning out to be a fine, fine day—in spite of everything.

Leslie heard the tapping but didn't move from her bed. She heard the second set of tapping—louder, a little more insistent—and still remained immobile.

It will go away. It will go away.

The tapping did stop, and Leslie resumed a more normal breathing pattern. She knew she couldn't yet summon the power to stand and walk, unassisted, all the way to the apartment door and converse with whoever was doing the tapping.

After a long moment, she drew up the courage to roll onto her back. From there, she knew from experience, it was easier to sit upright, and from sitting, she would then be able to maneuver to putting her feet on the floor. And then it would be an almost simple matter to stand and eventually make her way to the door of her bedroom.

At least that is what she hoped the transition would be like.

She had yet to experience a full-blown attack here in her new home. In Greensburg, in the big home she once lived in, she knew the process. There, if the pressure grew too great, and too suddenly, she could retreat and eventually find her way back. But here, in Butler, everything was new, and she was not certain. Even that thought, that uncertainty, caused her chest to tighten.

But it slipped away, almost quickly, and that gave her a glimmer of hope.

She forced herself to sit up. That, in itself, was a victory. Now, it was only a matter of time.

But why did this happen now? Why are they coming back? If he finds out ... if I start doing this all over again ... he'll take her for sure. He will. He might even be watching me now.

She bunched a handful of bedspread in each hand, tightly, her knuckles almost white. She fought it, fought the beast inside of her, just like she had always fought it. And after some time, though she could not be certain how long, her hands relaxed and she opened her eyes again.

She didn't want to look at the clock, but she did. She took in a breath of relief. She had two hours until she would need to leave the apartment and meet Ava at school.

Two hours. That will be long enough. I can do that. I know I can.

She surprised herself by pivoting on the bed so her feet touched the floor.

I can do this. I will.

———◦◦◦◦———

She must have been a dancer, or is a dancer, Jack thought as he watched Alice glide about the open space.

"This is all *so* what I imagined," she was saying.

Frank grew serious. He started to measure the space by stepping one elegantly shoed foot in front of the other.

"It's eighty-five feet," Jack said. "And fifty wide. Plus the back section. Good-sized restrooms, plus a storage area, I think, which we can't get into until we find a key."

Frank stopped midstep. "Big space," he said with some degree of finality. Jack, had he not been almost sick most of the morning, would not have been so direct. "What are you planning to do? I mean … have you done it before? Whatever it is."

Alice's laughter trilled through the open space. "Why *of course* we have. Why would we want to do it again if we hadn't already done it? You, Jack, for a contractor, ask quite silly questions."

Frank, his hands on his hips, like a captain on a ship, replied for Alice.

"In Pittsburgh—Shadyside to be exact—Alice and I built and operated the most wonderful little restaurant-slash-coffee-shop-slash-bookstore-slash-gift-shop in an old renewed building. It was such a fun thing to do. And most successful. We sold it last year for a huge profit, took a few months off to travel through Europe. And now we're back. In the city of my birth. Alice was born in Saxonburg—if you can imagine. And we want to do it again."

Jack remained confused.

"No sense in explaining it all," Alice said. "We will just have to *do* it. Then he'll understand."

Jack waited a moment. "But … in Butler?"

Frank shrugged. "It's a stretch, I know. But it will work. We know it. The concept will work fine. We're from Butler, after all. And we think Butler is ready."

Alice stood in one of the window arches.

"Have you ever worked on a restaurant-coffee-shop-bookstore-gift-shop before, Mr. Kenyon?"

Jack blinked his eyes. "No … but I could…."

At the end of their meeting, such as it was, Jack watched the pair of them exit and walk toward downtown Butler. He had his third job, all but assured, and this project promised to be big, in a small sort of way, and had the potential to be most lucrative for the time invested, with good exposure and publicity. Walls, lighting, kitchen, restrooms, display area, storage, built-in seating, architectural enhancements—a bit of everything. And most of it Jack could handle on his own.

What was intriguing was that the Adamses didn't seem like the sort of folk who would argue over a few dollars. Jack could bid the job, not taking advantage of them, but not paring his costs down to the bone.

He opened a bottle of water he had brought with him. He was always thirsty after the sort of night he'd had the night before, when the alcohol burned off and called for more liquid. He sat in the archway, framed by rough-hewn bricks, feeling the afternoon sun warm his shoulders.

He felt good, or at least better, than he had all day.

Maybe last night was just an accident. I mean, I don't really want to start going to any meetings again. Everybody can slip up once in a while. I'm human. We all make a mistake now and then.

He sipped at the water and watched the street.

And things are going well now. Things are going good. Nothing to be worried about. I'll be fine. I'll be able to handle this. I'm sure of that.

Amelia Westland, age fifteen years, six months
Town of Butler, Pennsylvania
January 17, 1878

I am now in the employ of Dr. Richard Barry, Butler's most respected physician and surgeon, and his wife, Louisa. The Headmaster looked in favor upon my request, and because of my strong penmanship and academic standing, he allowed me to interview with Dr. Barry, and soon thereafter arrangements were made for my transference to his residence on Walnut Street. I am one of four servants at the good doctor's home, the youngest by far, but the only one with the ability to read and write and cipher with facility. The other two women servants, the Misses Burnett and Tollifer, share a small room on the third floor; the head butler, Mr. Sparks, has quarters above the stables; and I have a pleasant and commodious room with an agreeable bed and dresser in the attic of this fine house. It is warm and dry, and the food here, compared to that at the Asylum, is of outstanding quality and quantity.

Catherine wept for a fortnight prior to my departure from the Asylum, and I could provide her no solace. Perhaps in future I can suggest a place for her in the good doctor's home, when she is of proper age.

Owing to my skills with the pen and with numbers and correctness of my spelling, the doctor requested that I assist him with correspondence to patients, and to other physicians throughout Penna. On some occasions, I sit with him as he administers treatment to patients, and scribe his spoken notations onto charts. Though I am unsettled by the sights, I have been in observance of some of his medical procedures. Mrs. Barry, a beautiful but slight woman, retreats to the furthest reaches of this house when she hears a patient cry out in pain. Perhaps from my childhood on the farm, such is not as disturbing to me. Mrs. Barry treats us well, and seems to have taken a singular liking to me. She will oft instruct me as to how to comport myself in a more ladylike fashion. She has fine dresses from London and New York, but there is a haunted look in her eyes—as if the presence of the sick and ill might prove too great a strain for her most delicate constitution. I am sometimes called to help with her correspondence and diverse other things as well, as she wearies easily.

> *To every thing there is a season,*
> *and a time to every purpose under the heaven.*
> —ECCLESIASTES 3:1

CHAPTER TWELVE

LESLIE STOOD OUTSIDE THE SCHOOL, the sun dappling the sidewalk and playground. She was early this afternoon, a full quarter hour before school was out, hoping that being early would make it up to Ava for being late the day before.

Where were you, Mom?! I was all alone out here.

Leslie knew she could not tell her daughter that she was barely able to stand erect without fainting yesterday, let alone be exactly on time.

And Leslie assured herself that Ava had not been alone. There were a few students remaining on the playground when she had arrived, and there was always a teacher watching, making sure that every child would be matched up with a parent by 3:00. A child on the playground later than that would be ushered into the office and the secretary would call their home.

Leslie insisted that it had been at least twenty minutes before three when she had arrived, and Ava insisted that even though she couldn't tell time yet, it had been much later than that.

Today, Leslie checked her watch a dozen times during the afternoon, leaving the apartment at 2:05, to make sure she was outside well before the final bell sounded.

Ava came out of her classroom slowly, with a wary eye, and even though she saw her mother, she did not run to meet her like she had before. She strolled, as slowly and deliberately as a kindergarten student can stroll, and dropped her backpack at her mother's feet.

"Trevor wants to play with me. Wait here," she said, her words curt and final.

Leslie took the punishment without comment.

Okay, I was late ... almost ... yesterday. She has a right to be worried, or a little angry.

They both were well aware of what had happened in the past and Leslie wanted to assure her young daughter that being late one time was not the start of a downward spiral, a repetition of what was before.

Leslie picked up the backpack and hefted one of its straps up to her shoulder. It was surprising heavy.

They must have visited the library today.

Ava made a habit of selecting the maximum number of books allowed (five) and she worked under the assumption that a bigger book was a better book.

The door of the kindergarten opened, and a student shot out as if propelled by an unseen force, followed by Mrs. DiGiulio, shaking her head in mock surprise. She must have spotted Leslie in the shadows and waved to her, inviting her to come closer.

Something about a grade school teacher that makes you obey, Leslie thought as she walked closer. A few feet away, Mrs. DiGiulio used the whistle that was around her neck.

Every student on the playground stopped and turned.

"Well trained," Mrs. DiGiulio said under her breath, then shouted, "Ava Ruskin! Your mother will be in the classroom with me. Do you understand?"

Ava shouted out a "Yes!" almost like a little three-foot-tall Marine.

"Come on inside, Mrs. Ruskin. If you have a minute, that is."

"I do. I was going to let Ava play for a while."

Once inside, the teacher said, "Sit down. Take the big person's seat. Perching on these small chairs is for the small and the limber—and I am no longer part of either group."

Mrs. DiGiulio fussed with a pot on the counter behind her desk. "Would you like some tea? I just made a pot for myself, and I always make too much. It's my treat at the end of the day."

Leslie wondered if there were more tea drinkers in Butler than in

Greensburg. She never drank tea in Greensburg, and here, it seemed as if tea lovers surrounded her.

"Sure. That would be nice."

The teacher poured out two cups and handed one to Leslie.

"I already put sugar in the pot. And if caffeine bothers you, don't take more than a few sips. I buy this from a little coffee shop in Pittsburgh. It has the most curious mix of things, and they say this tea brews to twice the kick as Lipton's."

Mrs. DiGiulio swirled her tea, almost spilling it, and sat down at her desk. "Mrs. Ruskin, being a kindergarten teacher can sometimes be a handicap. I find that I have much less tact than other people. Children don't respond to tact, or veiled comments, and adults who are overly polite—or obtuse. Kindness, yes. Calmness, yes. But tact ... well, they get confused. They would much rather get to the point and deal with it. I've been a kindergarten teacher for nearly thirty years, so forgive me if I am too direct."

Leslie waved her hand, as if dismissing any concerns Mrs. DiGiulio might have—even if her confession brought a certain tightness to Leslie's chest. The kind she'd feel before her husband, or rather her *ex-husband,* in one of his cycles, would start his litany of all the things she had done wrong during the day, or week, or month, or year, and when she'd only be able to listen and never defend nor explain. Yet she smiled as bravely as she could, hoping Mrs. DiGiulio wouldn't start telling her what a bad parent she was, or what a bad job she had done raising little Ava.

"Do you feel all right, Mrs. Ruskin?"

Leslie felt a shimmer, like the ground quivering, just a bit. That is how her husband often started, by asking if she felt okay, if she felt normal, and then proceeded to tell her how foolish she was for thinking that she was normal and that she was far from normal and that normal wives and normal mothers do not go into a panic for running out of orange juice in the morning, although it was really obvious that she should have gone to the store the day before, or even gotten up a little early to run to the convenience store around the corner—even if they did charge too much, and a normal housewife would have planned ahead.

Leslie corralled her thoughts and attempted to smile. "I'm feeling fine, Mrs. DiGiulio ... why do you ask?"

She'd never have asked her ex-husband anything like that, unless she wanted to have a full evening's worth of being told exactly what was the matter with her.

Mrs. DiGiulio looked as if she were trying to evaluate, to temper her reply. Leslie knew, from experience, that hesitation meant bad things.

"I am not one to interfere, " Mrs. DiGiulio said kindly. "Oh, who am I kidding? I am one to interfere. But in a good way, Mrs. Ruskin." She laughed to herself. "In a good way, trust me on that."

She leaned forward. "In this classroom, we pray before lunch. I have always had the students pray before lunch. I know this is a public school and we're not supposed to do that, but I do. If they want to fire me for believing, then they should fire me. It's important that the children learn how to give thanks. A simple prayer is all it is. We have a big God, don't you think? But … that's not the reason for any of this. Today, at lunch, before we prayed, Ava raised her hand. And it was very simple. She asked me if I would pray for her mother as well as our lunch. And I said I would. I didn't ask what the problem was. I didn't ask if you were sick or anything. I figure that a child will tell me what he or she thinks I need to know."

Mrs. DiGiulio waited a long moment. "When a child does something like what Ava did—being worried about a parent, wanting to help, wanting me to pray about it—their request means it's something the child thinks they can't help with. I think they feel powerless. I think she's worried about something."

Mrs. DiGiulio smiled gently. "I told her we would pray for you, and I did, and then she looked a lot less worried, like she knew the prayer would fix things. So I knew I had to ask you if everything is all right. And if it isn't, is it something I can help you with?"

For the last minute or so of listening, Leslie had stared at her hands, now tightly folded and held in her lap.

No one must know.

"Sometimes people you think can't help, can," the teacher added.

Leslie remained silent.

No one must know.

"I want to help you. I want to help Ava. Let it go, Mrs. Ruskin. It's too hard to hold it all in."

Leslie continued her silence, then, after a long moment, looked up. Mrs. DiGiulio's face was kind, open, and caring.

The words came out on their own, almost with Leslie not saying them. "Panic attacks, Mrs. DiGiulio. I'm having panic attacks again. They're even worse than before."

She caught her breath, opened her hands, and placed them on the desk, flat, in submission. Mrs. DiGiulio simply listened, allowed her to talk, and didn't interrupt.

"If he knows ... if he finds out about them ... he'll blame me for ..."

"Your ex-husband?"

"He'll take Ava from me. I know he will."

Leslie drew in an uneven breath.

"And I can't let him do that. I just can't."

———

Jack switched out the lights and locked the front door.

The place must have been a locksmith shop. This is one huge and expensive deadbolt. And that locked door in the back. I suppose I could tear out the door-frame and saw around the door hinges. Wonder what's back there, behind that door? Must be something valuable ... or at least interesting.

He placed the brass key in the breast pocket of his worn denim jacket, and buttoned the snap, something he always did before ... well, before, when his life was much more episodic and dramatic and confused. He had gotten accustomed to waking up in strange places. Things in his pockets might be missing. He didn't want to lose this special key, so he added a small bit of insurance by buttoning it.

He was certain he wouldn't repeat himself again, never go back to that life he once led, even if he hit an occasional pothole or encountered the occasional accident.

Leslie hadn't returned yet to her apartment with Ava in tow, as she always did on school days, and Jack breathed a sigh of relief. He didn't want to further explain his absence from work that morning. He would have to lie, and he never liked lying—even if it was for the best. Despite what had occurred the night before, he'd accomplished a fair amount of work this afternoon. The ceiling was all but finished. There were only two missing tin squares, and Jack had managed to switch them, so the empty spaces were confined to the far corner of the room. He was certain he could find an acceptable replacement—maybe not a perfect match but close enough.

He drove back to his apartment and parked the truck in the alley where off-street parking was allowed overnight. He placed the truck keys in the other breast pocket and closed the snap as well, without thinking or considering what the gesture meant. He would have gone upstairs, would have taken his jacket off and sat on his Goodwill sofa and watched the early news, but he felt a certain restlessness, and knew he would not be able to concentrate nor sit still.

He walked instead. He walked toward the building that used to be the Post Office, with its massive granite columns, fluted and strong, like they could have been on the facade of some small Greek temple. The elegant building housed some anonymous state agency, and Jack grew dispirited every time he walked past. The lintel stone over the columns had the words United States Post Office carved in deep relief. These words were all but hidden behind a badly painted wooden sign, in faded red, blue, and white that announced it was the Regional Services Center/Mid-States Division/ H.U.D. The sign didn't fully span the carved words.

He tried not to get angry or indignant, but it was impossible. To Jack, such things seemed like a travesty against the historic integrity of a building.

Just cover all the words! Make it look like you planned ahead!

He walked past the old Post Office, down the street, toward the one supermarket in town. He stood outside the store and read off the weekly specials on cake mixes, eggs, ground chuck, and skim milk. Jack seldom, if ever, bought any of those items. He favored ramen noodles and canned meals that didn't need refrigeration, since his refrigerator was motel-sized and could hold little more than a carton of orange juice, a quart of whole milk, and a few bottles of water.

Instead of his typical miniaturized grocery shopping, Jack took a right turn and walked away from downtown, feeling like he needed to be somewhere other than right here, yet not certain where that other place was. He walked north along Main Street and headed up the hill. It was a steep hill. This was western Pennsylvania after all, and while there were no mountains, steep gradients abounded. He leaned into the hill and pushed his legs, hoping to clear whatever buildup had settled in his muscles and lungs and brain. Halfway up the hill, when he could see the crest when he straightened up, he stopped, breathing harder than he should.

To his left was a brick drive—not just a driveway, but a narrow road, curving into the hillside, cutting through a dense thicket of shrubs and trees and vines, like a lost road into a hidden jungle. Not a tropical jungle, but a western Pennsylvania jungle, with thorns and thistles and a tight culture of green leaf. At the edge of the nontropical jungle, on the south side of the brick road, was a sign. No one, Jack surmised, could see the sign while driving past, all but hidden by stray foliage and intrusive vinings: WELCOME TO NORTH SIDE CEMETERY.

Jack waited at the sidewalk. He knew there was a cemetery on this side of the street. He could see the waiting headstones, standing there patiently, he thought, as he crested the hill. But he had never been in the cemetery. He'd never had a reason to visit. But the air was warm, the sky pellucid, and Jack's head had only recently ceased throbbing.

Maybe the peace and quiet will do me good.

He stepped onto the brick pavement, its edges rounded, its channels made uneven by years of cars and hearses, and made his way, further inside and upward, heading to the crest of the hill, the high ground above the town of Butler.

———⊰∘⊱———

Mrs. DiGiulio wanted to come around the desk, put her arms around Leslie and hold her, like a mother comforting a child. But she didn't. Children were still milling about, in the halls outside were other teachers, adults, parents, who may read too much into any gesture of caring. And Mrs. DiGiulio knew enough about panic attacks to know that drawing attention to them was not a recommended course of treatment.

Instead, she leaned in closer and spoke with calm reassurance. "Mrs. Ruskin … I know it feels hopeless. But I'm sure it's not." She reached over and put her hand over one of Leslie's hands. "I know someone you can talk to."

"I've been to counselors. I've read books. Nothing helps."

Mrs. DiGiulio could tell that the panic in Mrs. Ruskin was rising. She could see the sinews in the young woman's neck tighten, drawn sharp in outline, pulsing.

"This person is different. He is."

Leslie shook her head. "I don't think anything would work."

Mrs. DiGiulio waved off her objection. "You have to be open. He's a pastor. Very nice. Tim Blake. I go to his church. The big stone church on Diamond Square. He talked about it."

"About what?"

"Panic attacks. He had them. He was open about the condition."

Leslie shook her head, as if to clear her thoughts. "Like in a sermon?"

Mrs. DiGiulio nodded. "He was really open about dealing with them. The congregation knew and was very supportive. If anyone would understand, he would."

"He's still preaching? They let him preach?"

"Of course, Mrs. Ruskin."

Leslie waited for a long moment.

"I'm sure he would love to help," Mrs. DiGiulio said with her most encouraging smile.

By the expression on Leslie's face, it was clear she had never been this open with anyone about her condition and was not certain if this openness was a good thing or a very troubling thing.

Mrs. DiGiulio saw Leslie look down at her hands as she spoke, her words quiet, almost without emotion.

"What's his name, again, Mrs. DiGiulio? I'm willing to try anything. I just can't lose Ava. I can't. I would die. I wouldn't be able to live anymore."

And as she heard that final sentence, Mrs. DiGiulio was quite certain that Ava's mom meant it.

North Side Cemetery proved to be a quiet place. The traffic noises retreated, held at bay by the thickness of trees and shrubs, held back by the rows of grave markers and headstones, some from the early 1800s, and silenced

by the sprinkling of small American flags, soft and still in the autumn
afternoon.

One of his first counselors, years ago, more than a decade ago, when
he was at the very beginning of his problems, once took him for a walk
in a cemetery, much like this one, asking him to imagine his name on a
headstone, the dates of his life, what it might say about him. Jack hated
the counselor for doing that, and now, he could not erase the man's image.
Every cemetery he passed, that counselor's smug and condescending face
popped into Jack's memory. He saw it today, briefly, and he pushed it
away.

*They'll say what they say. I'll be dead then and it won't matter to me. It
won't matter to them, either, I guess.*

He didn't like cemeteries for a hundred reasons. The quiet unsettled him,
unnerved him. It brought back memories. He didn't like those memories.

He arrived at the top of the hill, a little winded, and surprised that
the early settlers would use such scenic ground for a burial place. Standing
at the crest of the ridge, he could see down over Butler—the courthouse,
Diamond Square, the steel mills further south, the high, craggy ridge that
ran parallel to Route 8, south of the city, the creek as it became a river.
He would have sat down and enjoyed the view, but there were no park
benches in the area. After reflection, Jack tried to recall if he had ever seen
benches placed in a cemetery. He imagined that benches would be scarce,
so he kept walking, heading north, toward the end of Main Street, when
it stopped being Main Street and became Route 8 again. He knew there
was a small strip mall, a cluster of businesses, there. He thought there was
a restaurant in that mix. He was hungry now and did not want to go home
to yet another bowl of ramen noodles from his microwave.

His memory was correct. He took a window seat in the nondescript
eatery, in a small booth, facing the highway, and waited, his hands folded
politely, staring at the traffic.

"Need a menu?"

"Sure," Jack responded, though he was just as sure he would probably
order a cheeseburger and fries.

*These small places can fool you sometimes. Maybe they have something
exotic.*

They did not. Standard American fare dominated the short one-page menu. But the place looked clean and well cared for and that was enough for now.

The waitress brought silverware wrapped in a paper napkin, and a sturdy glass of water. The rim of the glass was nicked and scratched to a well-used patina, half full of ice, half full of water.

Jack didn't surprise himself. He ordered what he thought he would order.

The food came quickly. The cheeseburger was done correctly—a thick burger, medium, American cheese, with crispy fries, lettuce, and tomato on the side, everything hot, and just a little greasy.

As he ate, he noticed another table in the middle of the restaurant, occupied by a young family of three: a mother, father, and a small child, no more than three years old, in a high chair pulled close to the table. The father, maybe twenty-five years old, sat, leaning back, reading a newspaper, folded into quarters. Jack could see it was the sports page, the crammed text of a series of box scores to some contest. The mother and son sat together, the mother making sure that the child was eating some small chunks of something soft, both of them laughing, heads close, a child's arm in the air, a mother's hand cupping the back of a head. The child must have gotten hold of a packet of crackers, held it, flexed his arm, and sent it flying. It hit the newspaper directly.

The young father slapped the paper on the table, speaking quietly, but harshly; only shards of his words could be heard from where Jack sat. Both the mother and son cowered, just a bit, leaning away. The child looked surprised, then upset; the mother turned away from the father, her eyes locked on her son. The father sat still, his paper held like a weapon, then drew it back up again, shaking it once as if to clean whatever crumbs might have settled.

More memories. Another layer of sadness settled over Jack.

The waitress came to the table, picked up Jack's empty plate, and unasked, filled his water glass. Then, almost as she turned away, she asked, "Dessert? Cherry pie is homemade."

Jack shook his head, then reached for his water glass. He noticed the tremor in his hands as it moved. He wondered if the waitress noticed as well.

He knew the why and how and when of that tremor.

He knew it well.

After a long time to play on the playground, Ava seemed happy to take her mother's hand as they walked from the school. They crossed Main Street. Just to the north of them was a series of Victorian homes, most in immaculate condition, some needing a little care. And to the north of this small, exclusive enclave, was the entrance to the North Side Cemetery.

The light changed to green, and Ava took off with a skip.

"You're in a good mood. I take it school went well today?"

Ava nodded vigorously. "I got to be the milk person today. Chelsea was sick."

Leslie kept looking both ways as they crossed. It was a blind hill, after all. "What does the milk person do?"

Ava looked up, almost rolling her eyes. "Mom, I told you about this before. I was milk person already."

Leslie saw the near roll.

"I don't remember. Tell me again."

Ava offered a most dramatic sigh, her shoulder slumping. "Well … just before the clock's hands are together, Mrs. DiGiulio tells us when exactly, we get to leave class early and go to the lunchroom and pick up the milk cartons for lunch. We have to carry them on a big tray and they're real heavy so we carry it together. That's what a milk person does. If we didn't do it right, nobody would have anything to drink at lunch."

Ava stopped for a second. "Except for Jacob. He can't drink milk. He throws up if he does. He threw up the first week of school and made everybody sort of sick. They don't give him milk anymore."

She started walking again.

Leslie waited to speak. She knew she had to. She knew Ava was waiting for the question as well. Leslie could just tell.

"Mrs. DiGiulio said that you asked if the class could pray for me. That was very sweet of you."

Leslie looked down at her daughter, her Dora the Explorer backpack on her back, her dark hair glistening in the warm afternoon sun.

At one time, Leslie did go to church—the Congregational church where Ava went to preschool—at first with her husband. Randy had said he believed. But it had become clear that any faith he had was in himself and his ability to succeed, to control everything and everyone around him. Soon it was just she and her daughter who went to church. Until Randy decided that they shouldn't go either. Ava must have liked Sunday school. She asked about it now that they lived in Butler, but only occasionally, never insisting, just wondering if she could go once more, now that her daddy wasn't there. She once told Leslie that Trevor talks about Sunday school all the time.

"Mrs. DiGiulio says that God answers us when we pray. That's true, isn't it, Mommy?"

Leslie did not leap to answer. She had prayed. She had prayed a lot back then. She prayed to find a place where she'd no longer be terrified and shaking, with bands of fear gripping her chest so fiercely, like a giant snake squeezing the life and breath out of a poor, simpering creature, with her husband's … her ex-husband's … furious breath at her neck, his strong fingers tight on her arm, leaving an angry accordion of red marks on her white skin. She had prayed. She thought she had prayed to God. But her husband said that God doesn't answer stupid prayers. Maybe that's what they were. She wasn't sure then and wasn't sure now, what prayers might be considered foolish and what prayers God might listen to and actually answer.

She was as certain as she could be without really knowing, that He would listen to a child like Ava. Jesus liked children. She could remember, from the times she did go to church as a child, the brightly colored flannel pictures of Jesus on a black flannel board, with Him surrounded by children, holding them on His lap. He liked them a lot. Leslie knew that much about the Bible and Jesus.

I wonder if God listens to every prayer said by grown-ups? Gramma Mellie sure believed He does.

"It's true, Ava. I'm sure God heard your prayer."

Ava dropped her mother's hand and bent down to pick up a cluster of acorns, a triad of them, with leaves still attached. She stuffed it into her jacket pocket, the golden leaves sticking out like a small, rustling flag.

"Good. That's what Mrs. DiGiulio said." And with that, Ava skipped off in front of her mother.

This was a quiet block, filled with houses, and the corner, where their home was, was a quiet intersection, an intersection that Leslie did not worry too much about, though she still worried some. She let Ava skip, alone, to the corner.

"Don't cross without me."

Ava stopped skipping, but still swayed, left to right, as if she was listening to private music in her head, music that Leslie could not hear, music not loud enough yet to cancel out the voice of a concerned mother.

As Leslie closed the gap, she wondered again if she might find voice to a prayer that was not foolish, but actually heard, and perhaps, even answered.

———————

Jack was content with living in Butler. He liked it, for the most part, during the few months he had lived there. The town itself was small, compact, and close—at least the old part of the town. There were shopping malls and strips malls and clusters of restaurants, franchised businesses radiating out of the town, but the more charming old section of town and downtown itself was built on a human scale. Jack could walk from the south side to the north side in less than fifteen minutes. Even now, well on the north side of town, he was only a short stroll from the center of Butler. And this walk was all downhill, some of it steeply downhill, so the effort it would take to get home would be slight.

Having eaten an early dinner, he felt better, and the queasy blanket that had covered him since the morning was now gone, replaced by an emptier feeling in which sickness played no part.

He walked past the offices of the hometown radio station, a station he never listened to. He wasn't really sure why, but he thought it had to do with the fact that it featured an on-air swap meet every morning, and Jack couldn't tolerate that instead of music, or the sort of music that a swap-meet radio station might play.

He stood at the corner of North and Main, waiting for the light to change. The light snapped to green and Jack hesitated. Three blocks to the east was the Knights of Columbus hall. He knew that he should turn, but he hesitated.

He took a deep, deep breath, and instead of crossing the street, turned east, toward the old high school, past the Methodist Church, past a classically designed bank building, no longer a bank but an insurance agency.

Maybe … maybe I should go to that meeting.

The further east he walked, the slower his steps became, fear slowing each forward motion. Fear and embarrassment and anger.

He knew the building before he could see the address. Outside, in a large glass-enclosed structure, stood a statue of the Virgin, glossy with dime-store colors, the sort of statue that felt more at home in the 1950s than today—a female figure, close to life-size, with movie-star curls of plaster hair, and an ethereal heavenward stare.

Jack stared back for a long time, wondering where one would go to purchase a statue like that. *Is there a market for those anymore?*

He shook his head to clear his thoughts and walked to the front door, slowly, with hesitation and some level of dread.

I should go inside … I guess.

Once at the front door, he could see, on the side of the entryway mounted on the faux rock facade, a silver-framed, black announcement sign, with ridges running horizontally, holding individual white letters pressed into those ridges.

Times of meetings were posted, for the K of C clubs, youth meetings, special events and the like.

At the bottom was a simple listing: AA: Meetings—M, TU, TH, 8 pm.

Jack let out a sigh of relief. Today was Friday.

Well, I guess that's my answer then.

He turned quickly, as if he'd just remembered something in his car or house that needed urgent attention, and hurried away from the shadow of the entryway and from under the benevolent watch of the old Madonna.

Jack wouldn't admit to using circumstances as tests, but this afternoon, this attempt had been a test. The schedule had failed. The opportunity had passed. Jack was in the clear now. He had tried. It could no longer be his fault. He would have stepped through those doors; he thought he would have stepped through those doors, at any rate, had they been opened. But they were not. They were locked and Jack had no choice in the matter. He had to move on.

It had often been like this in the past. Jack had tried, but circumstances had prevented good things from happening. He had tried to be a good father. He had tried his best to be a good husband. But it was difficult. His job was difficult. Everyone had demands on his time. There had been stress, lots of stress, every day, on the job and at home. He had to deal with that stress somehow. If his wife had not understood, well, maybe it was that she never had to deal with such stress.

I did. I tried to be good enough for everyone.

So what if he stumbled once in a while?

Everyone makes mistakes. Everyone has a bad day now and again.

Familiar arguments brewed in Jack's thoughts. Familiar defenses, familiar offensives, familiar hurts and wounds were torn open, a little at a time.

As he crossed Main Street, as he waited for the light, a Butler police car slowly cruised past, the driver's window open, the driver's arm resting on the window frame. The officer, slow and steady, stared at Jack as he stood at the corner.

Jack's breath caught in his chest when the policeman stared at him like that, as if Jack had done something wrong or had something in his pocket that would cause trouble, something that if the policeman knew about, would bring about the flashing red lights.

But I didn't do anything wrong.

The squad car finished the corner, and made its way away from Jack. Even though the light had changed to green, Jack waited. He closed his eyes.

Nothing wrong at all.

He fought back the trembling in his hands. He fought back the anger in his throat.

Down at the end of the block, and just around the corner, right next to the old theater, was a small convenience store.

Jack crossed the street and walked inside. A bell jingled with an angel-like sound as he entered.

He knew what he wanted—and where it was. He picked it up, walked with great purpose to the counter, and laid his purchase and a ten-dollar bill into the metal tray. The clerk slid them both under the bullet-resistant glass, scanned the bottle, tapped at the register, tossed in the change, and pushed the tray back under the glass.

"You need a bag?"

"Nope," Jack said and slipped the pint bottle of vodka into his front jeans pocket.

He walked out, quickly, as if to distance himself from what he had just done.

Insurance, that's all. I won't even touch it. I'll just have it. In case. Insurance, that's all. The insurance will help. Steady my nerves. Just having it. Not drinking it. Holding it. That's all I'll do.

And he hurried toward his apartment and away from any intrusive eyes of who might be watching.

"Macaroni and cheese?"

Once upon a time, Leslie had enjoyed experimenting with recipes. Cooking and baking had always been so enjoyable. Now she considered dinnertime the most difficult period of her entire day. Deciding what to cook seemed like an insurmountable task at times, so most nights she stuck to a few traditional, tried-and-true favorites.

Ava screwed up her face, tight, like a pickle, or an olive in a jar. "What kind of mac and cheese?"

An unexpected response.

"What do you mean, what kind?"

"The kind in the blue box. I don't like the kind in the white box."

"The blue box?"

Ava set her jaw firm. "It's cheesier."

Leslie flipped open the pantry cabinet, hoping that there was a blue box in there.

There was.

She switched the burner on, added the water to the pan, and waited for the boiling to begin. This was the old-fashioned sort of mac and cheese, the kind where you actually had to cook the noodles and drain them, adding the butter and milk and cheesy orange powder at the end. The whole meal would only take a few minutes, but it gave Leslie something to do, something to accomplish.

She ladled the entire pot of yellowy noodles onto a plate, then called Ava to the table. Leslie planned on having a cup of coffee for dinner; her recent episodes seemed to strip away whatever appetite she may have had.

Ava sat, folded her hands on the table, and bowed her head.

The two of them seldom, if ever, prayed before meals.

"God is great, God is good, let us thank Him for our food."

Leslie looked up, but Ava's head was still bowed.

"And thanks for listening to me at lunch. Mrs. DiGiulio said You would listen. Amen."

Leslie added a soft amen of her own, led by her child's example.

Ava smiled, picked up a fork, and began to eat, bending her face to near plate level so she could easily shovel the noodles in without the possibility of dropping any or of wasting time in the process.

It reminded Leslie of a dog eating, and the practice would usually bring about a reprimand. But not this evening. There was too much on Leslie's mind to grow impatient over eating styles.

After observing half of the pile of noodles disappear into Ava's sidelong face, Leslie could hold back no longer.

"Ava, eat like a lady, please, and not a lady dog."

Ava poked upright, as if fully expecting her mother's request, almost as if she had been concerned that it had not been forthcoming sooner.

"What else did you ask God about?" Leslie asked, keeping her words just curious, not demanding. She turned her coffee cup, now half full of lukewarm coffee, moving the cup's handle to be perpendicular with the table's edge, making sure it was as perfect as it could be without measuring.

Ava chewed, perhaps thoughtfully, then swallowed large, making it appear that she was forcing a baseball-sized lump of yellow noodles down her throat.

"Things," she finally said.

"What sort of things?" Leslie asked, adjusting her cup again.

"Just things," Ava repeated, then speared another forkful of noodles.

Leslie, in most situations, would have left the subject lie, knowing her daughter could hold secrets completely. "That's all? Just things? You won't tell me?"

Ava looked at her mother's face, and the young girl's eyes caught Leslie's and held them there for a long time. There was a flicker of something— maybe it was hope, maybe it was resignation, maybe it was a sliver of maturity showing on the young child's face and in her eyes. Leslie wanted to believe that it was a glister of hope. Then Ava began to chew again, and the contact was broken.

And in that long moment, Leslie became, at the same time, both surer and uneasier, knowing that what Ava had prayed for seemed so very, very far away.

———————

Jack unlocked the door of his apartment and hurried inside, almost slamming the door after him, as if someone was pursuing him. He leaned against the closed door, breathing deeply, his eyes shut, feeling the pleasant outline of the bottle tucked into the front pocket of his jeans. The buzzer on the streetlight down at the corner sounded three times before Jack moved. Slowly, carefully, he extracted the small bottle of Russian vodka from his pocket. He made no attempt at opening it. He made no attempt to find a glass and something to mix with it.

Just insurance, that's all it is.

He placed the unopened bottle on a small shelf built into the wall, an alcove, most likely built to house an old-style rotary phone, as if this were the most natural place to secure such a bottle, not to be used, but simply to have; not to have access to it, just comfort coming from simple accessibility.

I'm not going to drink it.

He sat on the sofa heavily, grabbed the TV remote, hit the power button, then the mute button. The blue light of the screen flickered on. It did not matter what show was running. Jack did not want to watch or listen, yet the fluttering illumination felt right.

He hadn't yet taken off his jacket. He didn't think he could move easily, so he waited, eyes closed, arms folded across his chest, until the urges had diminished, became controllable. He waited and took shallow gulps of air, blocking out the images he'd once assumed were under control, or banished, or forgotten.

They weren't.

I'm not going to drink it.

He shouldn't have walked through that cemetery today. He should have remembered what headstones and epitaphs would do to him. It had been such a long time since he'd had to deal with all that. He thought of his daughter again and her mother.

I'm not going to drink it.

And then, from nowhere, from the darkness, came the image of the locked door in the back room of the Midlands Building.

Why am I thinking of that?

Jack let that thought take over. It was different than thinking about the closed bottle. But it was no safer. After a while, after the sky outside grew dark, Jack listed over to one side, found the small pillow at the edge of the sofa, placed it under his head, closed his eyes, folded his arms again over his chest, tucked his hands inside his coat, and prayed that sleep might come and free him.

I'm not going to drink it.

Just before sleep came to him, one thought rolled into his awareness: *I have made a wasteland of everything I've touched.*

Ava snuggled under her Pretty Princess blanket and smooshed up the pillows behind her. On her nightstand was an adult's thickness of books—books from the school library, as well as books Leslie bought at garage sales, at least twenty books in a teetering stack. Leslie watched as Ava removed one from the middle of the stack with great care and gently opened the cover.

The child smiled as she first encountered the first page. "This one looks real good, Mom."

For those few moments that she watched, Leslie felt at peace, but only for those few moments. That calm feeling, a stranger to her, disappeared as soon as she stepped out of her daughter's bedroom. It disappeared because ... well ... everything was tenuous; everything in Leslie's life precarious. Everything was at risk.

Am I ever going to be free of all this? Am I ever going to be safe?

She paced in the living room, between the kitchen and the french doors, finally sitting on the lawn chair on the balcony, watching the western sky grow gold, then darken. She pulled out the slip of paper in her breast pocket and stared at it. She looked at her watch again. She stood and walked to the phone in the kitchen.

She had found the strength, earlier in the day, to call the church where Tim Blake, the man Mrs. DiGiulio had mentioned, was senior pastor. Actually, he was one of only two pastors on staff. Grace @ Calvary was not an extremely large church, apparently. The tape message went on and on, giving times of services and meetings, a complicated message about the youth group, the times Pastor Blake would be in the office—and his home phone number as well. The tape claimed he'd be in his office Friday evening until 9:00.

She took a breath, then another, then took the phone off the receiver and dialed. The call must have been directed straight to the pastor's office phone after hours.

"This is Pastor Blake. May I help you?"

In that instant, Leslie froze, unable to make a sound.

"Hello? … Hello?"

Leslie felt a tremor in her hands. It was all she could do to return the phone to its cradle. It was all she could do to slump into a kitchen chair.

In the hall, near the bathroom, in the faint glow of the nightlight, she saw her daughter, standing there, almost in darkness. The young girl was staring intently.

"It was a tape machine, honey. That's all it was. I'll call later."

Ava stared at her mother for a long time, without saying a word, then shrugged and turned away.

Leslie knew what she was thinking.

She has seen this all before.

Amelia Westland, age fifteen years, nine months
Butler, Pennsylvania
April 10, 1878

I have not yet found a chance to seek out Mr. Beck, though I have discovered where the livery is located whilst on a rare afternoon ramble when the Barrys were on a short holiday. It is not a far distance, and my thoughts of him being nearby are constant. We have time to go to services, but it is plain Mr. Beck attends a different church than I. I am not perplexed, since our growing town boasts of six different Sunday meetings, ranging from Episcopalian to Methodist. I wonder, should our paths yet merge, if our faiths will meld without controversy.

I pray that we will see each other soon. God assures my heart that we will. I know God is with me, and I pray day and night that His will be shown to me. I do not wish to grow old alone and barren, like the Misses Burnett and Tollifer.

Perhaps, when it is summer, I might see Julian in the streets. As I grow mature, the doctor indicated that I will be allowed to visit the markets in town on his behalf, seeing as how the Misses Tollifer and Burnett find walking long distances troublesome and painful.

The LORD will command his lovingkindness in the day time,
and in the night his song shall be with me,
and my prayer unto the God of my life.
—PSALM 42:8

CHAPTER THIRTEEN

THE ONE TOOL JACK NEVER anticipated buying—or using—was a broom. In all his previous construction jobs, somebody else held the broom. No carpenter swept up. That was for whoever the new guy was.

Now Jack swept up. He had purchased two brooms: one wide brown industrial sort of push broom, and a more standard, residential model, made from artificial straw. And he had bought a large black metal dustpan. He would vacuum later. If you vacuum when there's too much dust, he'd learned, it spreads it around.

He started in the back rooms, the bedrooms, and worked forward, sweeping the room like a man cutting grass, making sure he was not stepping in debris already collected. He finished each room, deposited everything into a black trash bag, and worked his way up the hall, careful not to nick or bang the new quarter-round he'd installed throughout the apartment. The finishing trim was a small detail, one he hadn't quoted originally, but it made each room look finished and complete. Leslie had agreed wholeheartedly.

It took him nearly half an hour to sweep out the entire apartment. It looked so clean and renewed and updated, despite the age of the building and the architectural details.

There was only one task left for Jack to perform: installing the new tub. The bathroom was an odd size. A standard, in-stock tub would have fit easily, but there would be a large gap on each side, and Jack thought that a ledge around a tub of that size would invite water problems later on. So the tub that would fit just right was on order, and the order desk at Home Depot promised him it would arrive by the end of the week.

As he dumped the last dustpan full of dirt into the bag, he heard a soft knocking on the door. It was not Leslie, he was sure. Her knocks were solid and direct.

"Yes, can I help you?"

An elderly woman with large earrings stood there, peering inside, then eyeing him up and down.

"So you're Jack Kenyon," she said, making it both a pronouncement and an introduction. "I live on the other side of the building. Gladys. Just wanted to see what you did to the place. Leslie told me all about it."

She leaned in farther than Jack thought possible, without falling forward.

"Come on in, Gladys," Jack said, having no choice. "I'm sure Mrs. Ruskin would love to have you see the finished work—even if it's not totally done."

Mrs. Stickle shlupped inside, her rubber-soled cloth slippers making a grandmotherly, raspy noise on the bare floors.

"Beautiful, just beautiful," she said as she walked into the kitchen. She touched the countertops and cabinets gently, like she didn't want to disturb them, then carefully walked down the hall and peered into both bedrooms and the bathroom.

"Beautiful," she said as she looked at Jack.

"The bathroom isn't finished. Just waiting on the tub," Jack said, feeling as if he had to explain.

"Well, you've done a great job," Mrs. Stickle gushed. "I can see why Leslie really likes you and your work."

Jack, surprised that Leslie would be talking about him to her tenant, didn't know what to say.

"Well, I have a niece who's looking for a place to rent—her and her husband—who I never liked, but he does have a good job with the county," Mrs. Stickle said. "I'll tell Leslie about them. I bet they'll snap it up once they see it."

She headed to the door. Jack started to follow her.

"Thanks, but I can let myself out. This place is just like ours—except nicer, and it's the opposite sort of layout. Like a mirror image. Or is that a negative? Well, whatever."

The door snapped shut, almost in midsentence.

Mrs. Stickle carefully made her way down the steps, holding onto the handrail. Walking was not a problem for either her or Mr. Stickle, but neither of them liked navigating stairs. Mr. Stickle had a great aunt, Aunt Thelma, on his mother's side—the clumsy side of the family, Mrs. Stickle always said—who pitched herself down a steep set of stairs and broke both arms and a hip and was never the same after the accident. Mr. Stickle must have told that story a hundred times and often muttered, "Remember Aunt Thelma," just as Mrs. Stickle was about to ascend or descend any set of stairs, anywhere.

She made it to the ground floor without mishap.

I can see why Leslie finds that man attractive. Jack is one wickedly handsome fellow, she thought as she made her way onto the sidewalk, then scolded herself for thinking impure thoughts about the contractor she'd just met.

Maybe we should have some work done on our place. She grinned broadly, amusing herself.

Even though Leslie never really talked about him in that way, I could tell from her eyes. A woman can't hide when she's interested. You can always see it in the eyes. Now I recognize why. He is a beautiful man.

Back in her own kitchen, Mrs. Stickle tried to decide between iced tea and gingersnaps or hot tea and gingersnaps.

She decided on iced tea this time.

I need something to cool me off.

She did not stop grinning until she had consumed an entire plate of the crisp little cookies, then chided herself for her gluttony—and her lustfulness.

I guess there are worse things.

"Well, you should call. The loan has been preapproved. The contractor can do all the work. We need to act—especially now that we know the zoning is okay with the city."

Frank Adams sat behind his sleek desk, twirling his Mont Blanc pen, staring at the screen of his ultrathin laptop. His wife was sprawled in the black leather easy chair in the office, picking at the fringe of the Hermes scarf she'd purchased in that "absolute riot of a sale" in Paris on their trip.

They had gone to Europe with one suitcase each and came back with more than a dozen pieces, all jammed with indispensable items—all sample items that Alice was sure she could sell at more than twice their cost, providing they had a venue to sell them in.

Frank scrunched up his face. He had just lost at Solitaire for the third time in a row. Besides e-mails, accessing his favorite comic strips via the Internet, and occasionally writing a letter, Frank primarily used his multiple-thousand dollar, ultrafast, ultrathin, ultrachic Macintosh computer to play a simple card game.

"Alice, you have to make the call. She's a woman. I think a woman will respond better to another woman."

"And I think *you* should call. Men are better at getting what they want from a woman. Natural intimidation and all that."

Frank exhaled loudly and clicked to start a new game. "Well, we're more evolved than that, right? We don't want to perpetuate old stereotypes, do we? We want to break free from the sexist, patriarchal molds of the past."

Alice threw a wadded-up Post-it note at him. It bounced off the computer screen. "You just don't like to make phone calls, do you?"

Frank sighed theatrically. "And then there's that, too."

Alice reached over and snatched the card with Leslie's phone number scrawled on it. "Fine, fine. But now you *owe* me."

Alice flipped open her new iPhone—the kind that took pictures, videos, played music, sent text messages, and accessed the Internet—or would have if she had ever read through the manual to find out how to do all those things. Basically, she only made phone calls with the ultrachic phone.

"Mrs. Ruskin," Alice said, her voice louder than it might need to be, full of life, almost lilting, as it were, "how are *you* this morning?"

Frank played a red ten to a black jack.

"I mentioned to Mr. Lowell at the bank that I would be calling. We are quite interested in renting out the first floor of your building on North and Cedar."

Frank tried to play a red nine to the red ten and the card bounced itself back into place with what Frank saw as an angry, condescending snap.

"Yes, yes, we saw the interior a week or so ago. Your nice contractor was kind enough to let us in. We know it will be just the *perfect* space for us."

Frank appeared to be resigned to another loss as he flipped through the cards again.

"We checked with the city over zoning requirements and necessary permits and all that. We will have to file for a license, of course, but everyone told us that what we planned on doing with the space would be perfectly fine with the city. All we need to do now is to negotiate a lease."

Alice sprawled to a more prone position, nodding as she listened.

"Yes, we're planning to do what we did in Shadyside. Coffee, breakfast pastries, soups, sandwiches, salads, desserts, accessories and gifts, books—things that I find absolutely wonderful. No late-night hours. No horribly early morning hours. A sedate crowd that understands good taste. That's our market."

Alice listened and sat up. She grabbed for a pen and the yellow legal pad on the desk. She crawled out a number and added a lyrical dollar sign in front of it. She was smiling. Frank leaned over, read the number, and arched his eyebrows in surprise.

He mouthed the words: *That's cheap.*

Alice scowled and wrote: *Inexpensive!*

"Sure, that would be fine. The nice fellow at the bank said he would be able to help you draft a lease. I am simply *all thumbs* when it comes to legal mumbo jumbo."

Frank snorted as he started a new game. His losing streak now stood at seven.

"Yes, we do have a contractor in mind. We haven't signed anything yet, but he is the most *handsome* contractor in Butler—and most exclusive as well."

Alice laughed into the phone, louder than Frank liked, but that was his Alice.

"Of course you know him, Mrs. Ruskin. He's the gorgeous fellow who is doing the work on your vacant apartment."

Frank turned when he heard the word *gorgeous*.

"Oh yes, he *is* attractive, isn't he?"

Frank would have gotten upset, but he knew he was more attractive than any carpenter. And that was just how his Alice behaved.

"We will see you tomorrow morning at the bank. Ten a.m. would be just perfect."

Alice pushed at several buttons until she found the one that made the phone go quiet.

"Good negotiating," Frank said as he played a black queen to a red king.

"It takes skill," Alice replied. "And the rent will be cheaper by half than what we paid in Pittsburgh."

"You have to love Butler, don't you," Frank replied, snapping a jack to the open queen.

———

Jack was sitting alone in his apartment, the television humming quietly in the background. A pot of water was slowly coming to a boil on his small stove, a crinkled square of ramen noodles waiting on the counter. Normally, Jack did not return home for lunch, but today he had slept later than anticipated and had rushed out of the house without packing any food. Ramen noodles were not his first dining choice, but they were the least costly. There was a foot-high stack of the square noodle packages on Jack's kitchen shelf.

His phone warbled.

"Kenyon Construction."

Jack stared at the tiny bubbles in the water and delicately slipped the noodles into the pot, using a wooden spoon to stir.

"Of course I remember showing the space to you and your wife. Have you decided to rent it, then?"

Jack stirred the mix, not that it was necessary, but it felt more like actual cooking when he did.

"Alice and Frank's? No, I don't think I've heard of that place. But

I haven't been in Pittsburgh for a year or so. And I seldom made it to Shadyside."

He tapped at the seasoning packet, balancing the phone between his shoulder and his ear. He wanted to make sure he used the entire packet. The noodles were bland enough without shortchanging on the seasoning.

"Sure. I could do that. Will you need a full commercial kitchen?"

He tapped out the seasoning into the pot and took it off the heat.

"What about display cases? I could do that—but I'm not really set up for fine cabinetmaking."

He stirred the noodles.

"Okay. That I can do. When do you need an estimate?"

He kept stirring and reached for his one clean bowl.

"I can meet you there this afternoon. I'm still finishing up at Mrs. Ruskin's vacant apartment."

He took a soupspoon out of the canister that held all his silverware.

"Three o'clock would be fine. I'm looking forward to it."

He took the bowl and spoon and sat on the sofa.

I should have gone for a real meal—this time to celebrate. It looks like I have another great job.

Leslie wondered how many more days she might be able to comfortably walk to Ava's school. The air carried more of a chill now, or more like a sharpness to it, as if gently warning of the weather to come. But for now, with the sun out, and the wind slight, walking the few blocks was a pleasant interlude.

Caring for Ava, finding a job, making wisest use of her limited financial resources were a constant worry for Leslie. She knew there were services for working parents that picked children up at school and then took them to an after-school center. Leslie saw the vans every day, parked at the end of the block, waiting for their small customers. It might be necessary, Leslie thought, but it was also expensive. The increase in childcare costs would eat up much of whatever salary Leslie could hope to earn. And she hated the thought of Ava having to go from school to day care.

If only my parents were close.

They weren't. A number of years earlier, her mother and stepfather had moved to North Carolina—to escape the cold, they said. Leslie never understood the reason. It might not get as cold in North Carolina as it did in Pennsylvania, but it still grew chilly and damp, a most miserable combination.

Leslie had talked with her mother about her predicament, and while her mother sympathized, she'd made it clear that Leslie could expect no financial help from them.

"Your stepfather isn't made of money, you know. A postmaster doesn't get a huge pension. You'll have to handle this on your own. No one forced you to get divorced, Leslie."

Leslie had grown weary of such conversations.

Maybe I can trade babysitting with another mother in class, Leslie thought. *Even Mrs. Stickle said she would help out. Maybe for a day or two a week …*

Leslie's thoughts were interrupted when she stopped at the corner of North and Main Street. Regardless of what the crossing guard indicated with her stop sign, Leslie always stared hard up the steep hill that made up North Main.

One of these days there's going to be a runaway truck. There will be.

Today was not that day.

Leslie waited at the corner of the playground at Ava's school, where she always waited, her hands in her coat pockets. The playground had gotten a new coating of wood chips and Leslie sniffed the air, thinking that it now smelled like a pet store or a huge hamster cage, filled with cedar shavings.

She smiled at the thought.

Across the street, she saw Mike Reidmiller, waving enthusiastically.

He is a nice guy, she told herself. *I should try my best to be pleasant.*

She smiled as broadly as she could and waved back.

Mike Reidmiller almost jogged across the street. He didn't appear to be the sort who jogged very often. Not that he was heavy, but he had more the physique of a football player—not one of those sleek players who catch passes but one of the fellows in the middle of things, who fall down on every play, buried underneath other players in a big jumbled pile of arms and legs.

"Leslie, how are you?" he said, not out of breath, but on his way to being a little winded.

"I'm doing very well, Mike," she said. She would not have used his first name, but he had scolded her, or at least mock-scolded her, for using "mister" too often. She went on to tell him that the ground floor of the building would soon be rented, which was going to be a great relief.

"Well, that makes it perfect."

"Makes what perfect?" she asked.

"A perfect opportunity to celebrate."

Leslie wasn't sure what he meant.

"I always take Trevor out for ice cream on Friday afternoons. You know, celebrate one more successful week of kindergarten. For Trevor, that's a big accomplishment."

Leslie wanted to say that Trevor was a much better student than his father gave him credit for, but didn't. Ava said Trevor was so smart and nice, but sometimes got "squirrelly, like somebody poked him with a pin or something." She knew Mike was concerned and let him have his concern without diminishing it.

"So, we're going out for ice cream. At my cousin's place. I told you about my cousin's place, didn't I? Cunningham's? On Main Street?"

"You did."

"And remember when you promised to think about going out for coffee with me? No time like the present, I always say. Well, I never say that, actually, but come and join us—you and Ava. We can walk there. What do you say? Okay? A good time to celebrate, right? Okay? Then you'll be off the hook—coffee-wise, that is."

Leslie wanted to say no. She didn't want to start something that might not be right—not right just now, anyhow. Mike was a sweetheart—so pleasant. A nice man most women would really appreciate being next to. A sweet, pleasant, nice man who would make a great …

"Sure. We can go with you. Ava would love it."

Mike beamed, like a small puppy that has just been presented with a Milk-Bone dog biscuit.

Both Trevor and Ava screeched when Mr. Reidmiller told them the news, screeched like only small children can do—a mix of joy and happiness in a teeth-grinding squeal.

The four of them set out for Cunningham's, only a few blocks south on Main Street. It would be a short walk home for Leslie and Ava afterward.

"Have you ever been here before?" Mike asked. The children had run ahead a half block, which allowed for adult conversation.

"No, I haven't," Leslie answered. "Isn't that terrible? I love good coffee and it's so close to home."

"He does a good job. I stop here a lot. I think I would stop a lot even if my cousin didn't own the place. Maybe if he didn't, it wouldn't be so good. But it is. So I am one of his most loyal customers, I guess."

The north side of downtown appeared to be regentrifying at a faster pace than the blocks south of Jefferson Street. Two new restaurants had opened within the last few months, and another entire building was being renovated and turned into condominiums.

"I figure if he can hold on for a few more months, he should have all the customers he wants from the new residential building."

They stopped for just a moment by the sign offering the condominiums for sale.

"Starts at $295,000? Isn't that a lot of money for an apartment?" Leslie asked.

"It would be for me," Mike answered. "But my cousin says the workers stop in at his place all the time. He says the new places are really big, and have granite everywhere, and marble, and all sorts of snazzy features. I guess you need to do that if you're charging so much."

Mike called out to Ava and Trevor, "You wait at the corner. Don't you dare try to cross the street without us."

The children turned back to their parents. Trevor shouted back, "Then hurry up. Why do you walk so slow?"

Leslie laughed. "Ava says the same thing to me—all the time."

Mike held the door of the coffee shop open, allowing everyone to enter.

Leslie stopped and stared. The interior was straight out of a 1890 postcard: dark, high-backed wooden booths, with carved swirls on the outside faces, frosted glass on the walls, the old sort of mirrors with the silvering slowly fading off, resulting in mottled reflections, tin ceilings, old-style ceiling fans, display cases with curved glass, an old-style fountain, with dark wood counters. Here and there were modern touches—a very sleek, brass Italian espresso machine with chrome dials and fittings, stylish menu signs, hand-painted on chalkboard, and a case filled with all sorts of pastries and cookies, all upscale and chic and trendy.

"I had no idea," Leslie said softly, not sure what idea she might have had originally.

"My cousin is pretty creative," Mike said, almost apologizing.

Trevor was well aware of the drill.

"Strawberry sundae. Strawberry sundae," he said, his choice obviously made well in advance. "Whipped cream. Whipped cream. No nuts. No nuts."

"Me too, me too," Ava echoed, surprising her mother. Up until this moment, Ava had never once uttered the words "strawberry sundae."

"My treat," Mike said, then quickly added, "if it's okay with you that Ava gets a sundae. I mean, some kids have allergies and all that. Or it wrecks their appetite or something."

"No, it's fine. Thank you, Mike."

"Two lattes for the adults? And a couple of those frosted biscotti? I love those frosted ones. The regular ones are okay, but the frosted ones are really, really good."

"Sure," Leslie agreed. "They do look good."

The two children took a front booth, looking over the street. Right above their booth, on a sturdy shelf, were two aquariums, filled with all sorts of colorful, darting exotic fish.

"My cousin likes fish. He has, like, twenty tanks at home," Mike explained.

The barista placed the two biscotti in a silky waxed bag and the two thick lattes in mugs on a tray, which Mike took. Then he escorted Leslie to a booth a bit further back in the store.

"Let the kids eat and talk by themselves. The fish will keep them amused. Trevor can sit for hours watching them. Makes me want to get a fish tank at home. But I figure, with my luck, all the goldfish will die and I'll have to try to explain the death thing to Trevor. Better that he comes here to watch. Safer. And less expensive."

Leslie took her seat opposite Mike. As he sat down, she felt his knees bump into hers.

"Sorry. I usually have Trevor across from me. He's smaller."

"That's okay," Leslie said. "I'm not used to being with other adults either. Takes a bit of getting used to again."

Mike took his biscotti from the bag, snapped it in half and popped one half into his mouth, grinning. "I love these things."

Leslie nibbled on hers. "You're right. They are good."

From where Leslie sat, she could see the reflection of Ava and Trevor in the mirror beside her. The two of them were kneeling on the benches of their booth, leaning forward, carefully scooping out the ice cream, and looking as if they were savoring every bite, chatting away as only kindergartners can do.

Mike chewed, swallowed, and took a drink. "Well, this is nice."

At that moment, a door behind them banged, in a friendly way, and a short, barrel-chested man approached, wearing an apron over his T-shirt and jeans and a baseball hat.

"Hey, cousin, how are you?"

Mike stuck out his hand.

"Ernie, this is Leslie."

Ernie grabbed Leslie's hand and pumped it enthusiastically. "So this is the woman you've been telling me about. Nice. Real nice." Ernie's eyes traveled up and down, twice.

Leslie wondered if Mike was blushing more than she was.

Ernie offered a wide grin, not leering, but close—more like a happy-that-you're-here grin. "How's the coffee? How're the cookies? You like 'em? I have an aunt who makes 'em fresh every day. I guess, it's really *we* have an aunt. She's a saint, that woman. Let me give you some to go. I bet your little girl will love 'em. I'll fix you up. Okay?"

Leslie managed to croak out, "Okay."

Ernie barreled away, toward the front of the store, calling out to other customers.

"Sorry about that. He can be sort of loud and … loud," Mike apologized.

"It's okay, Mike … he seems very nice."

She looked down at her hands. *He's telling his cousin about me?*

"And sorry about … you know … talking to him about you," Mike added to his apology.

"That's okay," Leslie answered, unsure of her response.

"I mean, you're an unusual woman. He asked. You're a single mom. You bought a building. You're fixing it up. That's pretty unusual—at least it would be for our family. I give you a lot of credit for taking that sort of risk. I don't know if I would do it. That's what I told Ernie about. I didn't say anything about you being … you know … nice. I mean, well, you are nice. I mean that in the pretty way. Not in the way that Ernie said it. You know."

Mike slapped his palm against his forehead. "I don't know what I mean. I get in front of a beautiful woman and my tongue gets all tangled. Well, not really my tongue—it's my brain. There are so many things I want to say, but I usually manage to get everything flummoxed up."

Leslie wanted to take his hefty hand in hers and pat it, saying everything was okay and that she wasn't mad or upset or offended. "It's okay, Mike," she wound up saying instead. "I understand."

"Sometimes I get so nervous. Especially when I'm around someone I like. You know what I mean. Like a woman. Not that I've been around women all that much. I get nervous and my heart starts to pound and I get all flustered."

"It's okay, Mike. It really is."

His honesty and transparency was so sweet and childlike and endearing that this time Leslie did reach over and patted at his hand, flat on the table. Her smaller hand only covered a third of his.

She saw his eyes snap to her hand as it rested on his, even for those brief few seconds. His eyes snapped back up to hers, as if trying to read something in her eyes, trying to ascertain what it was that she was trying to say, trying to say without words.

"Do you really?" he said, soft as a whisper. "I mean, do you really understand?"

"I think I do."

She saw his hand move, just a little, the one that she had just touched. But then he stopped. She could see that he was considering something, calculating some odds, perhaps, or trying to decipher what she had meant by touching his hand and whether or not she wanted him to touch her hand in return, or if he were merely inventing all this because it was something that he wanted. She could see all this in his face. He was that sweet and honest.

Ava ran back first and slid into the booth next to her mother. Leslie watched her look first at Mike ... Mr. Reidmiller ... then back to her mother, as if inspecting the remnants of their conversation.

Trevor bounced up. "Can I have a second sundae?"

"You most certainly cannot," Mike answered. "You never have two sundaes."

Trevor's face tightened, as if he were reviewing every desert he ever ate, checking to see if there had ever been a day with a double desert. It didn't take all that long. "Okay. Can we go home now?"

"Attention span of a gnat, I always say," Mike whispered, smiling. "Shall we? We'll walk you home."

Leslie was about to protest, about to say that she and Ava could easily walk home by themselves, that it was only a few blocks, but she looked at Mike's ever-hopeful face, his eager smile, and she nodded.

"That would be nice of you ... Mr. Reidmiller."

Leslie was sure Mike was about to correct her but saw his eyes dart to her daughter. He said nothing except, "My pleasure, Mrs. Ruskin."

On the way out, Ernie presented Leslie with a large bag filled with cookies and treats—far too many for the two of them, perhaps as an apology.

"You enjoy, Mrs. Ruskin. You enjoy 'em, okay?"

Leslie promised she would.

"Okra?"

"Bland."

"Butternut Squash?"

"Maybe. A little too much gray in that one."

"Even with the Eggplant?"

"Might be okay. If we use Eggplant on the back wall."

"Is there one that's called Zucchini? For the fireplace wall. Or the entry wall. Calming. Green."

Frank rustled through a stack, a pile, of paint chips, strewn haphazardly on their work desk. "I thought I saw one called Zucchini."

Alice held a dealer's hand of paint chips, casting one off after another, like a poker player discarding useless cards. Baxter, the cat, sat to one side, on the desk, batting chips that came too close. The elegant feline was much too lazy to get up and give chase, but all chips that came within paw's reach were quickly dispatched to the floor. And under the desk sat Worthless, the couple's other equally elegant cat, their first cat, older by a few years, barely raising a cat eyebrow over the storm of big fluttery multicolored snowflakes.

"There was a Zucchini—and a Sage—but all those food colors made me hungry. Remember that wonderful vegetable omelet we had in Paris? Was it in Paris or Brussels? That little restaurant where no one understood us," Frank said.

"No one understood us in any restaurant in all of France or Belgium, Frank. We just pointed, remember, and were always happily surprised at what came out of the kitchen."

Frank appeared hurt. "I know French, *pardon*. I took French in high school. They understood me. It's just that they were being arrogant and did not want to admit it, that's all. Those French."

Alice smiled as she flipped away nearly identical colors: Eggshell and Cream Cheese—neither of which she planned on using. Baxter clawed both of them to the floor. "Well, whatever your skill in French is, or *was*, we still have to pick the color scheme for our new place. And we simply *must* plan for our coming-home party. We've been home for nearly three weeks and have not done a party yet. That's simply too long to wait. People are *talking*. I ran into Milly …"

"Molly."

"Molly? Who's Molly?"

"Milly is the one you always call Molly. It's Milly."

"Milly. Molly. Whatever. Anyway, she says we must get together. It's been *ages*. I think she and her husband are just adorable. He's an architect or something, isn't he?"

"Engineer."

"Whatever. A party would be a wonderful way to see everyone again. And announce our new venture. Start the buzz. *And* it would be a business deduction."

Frank stood up, brushed off the chips that had hidden on his chest and lap, and stretched. "Sure. I like parties. But that doesn't change the fact that I'm still hungry. I would love to go out for some interesting food. Butler simply does not have interesting food. Cheap housing. Close to Pittsburgh. Small pool. Easy to be big fish, cutting-edge. But no interesting food."

Alice replied, nodding. "Well, there is that small place over in Lyndora, but it's closed at lunch."

Frank rubbed his stomach theatrically. "Maybe I'll be forced to cook something."

He stepped to the doorway of their studio/office/workroom. They lived in a comfortable bungalow on the north side of Butler, just at the edge of the really expensive properties. Years ago, when they first purchased it, they had torn out most of the interior walls on the first floor, replacing them with movable partitions—all heavily laden now with artwork and collages and wire/textile assemblages and other collections that Alice was noted for. The front room was a sort of studio/office/workroom. In the rest of the space, a few sleek black leather sofas floated, intermixed with the artwork and panels. A modest-sized kitchen—efficient and terribly modern—lay in the back of the house. The entire second floor was an expansive master bedroom suite, with two huge closets, and one large spa-like bathroom.

"An un-loft," was how Alice described it.

Frank, uninterested in labels, just said it was "organic." He was not sure what that meant, but it sounded artistic and avant-garde—at least for Butler.

When they had operated their store in Pittsburgh, they had rented a large apartment in an historic building in nearby Shadyside and returned to Butler on their days off.

"So what would you like to eat? A panini? A frittata? Stir-fry? A couple of frozen White Castle hamburgers?" Frank attempted to remember what their refrigerator held without actually going back there to do an inventory.

"White Castle!" Alice all but shouted. "Yes! White Castle! How many do we have left in the freezer? I need at least six of them."

Frank scratched his head. "An entire box of fifty, I believe. Remember when you ordered it online when we arrived home? You said you would never be left without a White Castle ever again."

Alice had been despondent when she found out that Paris did not have a single White Castle hamburger franchise.

"Well, then, White Castle it is. And could you do them in that little stainless steel oven on the counter with the cute little door on it? It tastes *so* much better that way. You're *so* good at that," Alice said, knowing that boasting on her husband was a surefire method of getting him to do something for her.

Frank *pshawed* in reply. "To make it taste just like in the restaurant, I would need a huge, greasy griddle with steam vents in it and a swarthy, underpaid immigrant to do the grilling. But yes, I will use the convection oven."

He padded down the hall, or at least where the hall used to be until they tore out the walls, whistling to himself, happy to be cooking, or at least reheating, in a creative fashion.

As he busied himself in the kitchen, Alice discarded a few more paint chips onto the desk, but there was no longer a cat there to help. Baxter and Worthless both had grown instantly alert when Frank made his way to the kitchen, charging along the wooden floors just in case he would mistakenly open a can of tuna and drop it.

He turned the key in the door, pocketed it, and hurried down the steps of the Midlands Building. Jack whistled as he hurried to his truck, being in a very good mood. There were now two jobs penciled in on his calendar— two good jobs.

The kitchen and bathroom job for the young couple over on Brady Street might take four weeks, but if Jack pushed, three. And Frank had intimated that plans, permits, loans, and the like remained a bit nebulous, but on schedule. They would want to start the renewal of the interior soon.

"The city said everything would be fine, but I don't want any additional problems. We'll wait until we have all the little bits of paper in hand to start. That's fair, isn't it?"

Jack assured him that it was totally fair.

"And we have an architect to draft up everything so the city people will be satisfied."

Jack said that sort of arrangement was typical and would be fine with him. He would review the plans and put together a bid.

Now Friday night had arrived, and Jack felt more than a bit expansive.

It would be so nice to have someone to share this with.

But that remained impossible, he told himself. Instead, he got into his truck, and headed toward The Palm.

Earl will be happy to hear.

He pulled along the side street by the tavern, switched off the engine, and stopped. He could get out, have a meal, drink a few Cokes, and talk a bit with Earl, as he waited on other customers. That might take an hour, tops.

Then what?

Jack imagined himself driving home, back to his small apartment, and channel-surfing until he dozed off sitting on the depressing sofa. The triumphant evening was not so much of a triumph when reduced to such stark and dismal terms.

I don't want to go in there. I don't. Not with Earl there.

He put the key back in the ignition, started the engine, put the transmission in gear, and started to drive. He did not have a destination in mind, that's what he told himself, but he really did. He simply did not admit it to himself.

He crossed the bridge south of town and made the sharp right turn, following Route 8, out of town, toward Pittsburgh. He had traveled this route several times; he knew what businesses existed along the road. One of his lumber suppliers was down this stretch of road.

That was not his destination.

The road cut through some surprisingly empty stretches, bordered by thick stands of trees and greenery, now glistering with the dying reds and golds of autumn. He did not pay attention to the color nor the restaurants he passed. Some seven miles south of town, he saw his destination.

He had not really intended on heading here. But here he was. He pulled his truck around the back. He always pulled his truck around to the back of places. He told himself that he didn't know why, but he really did.

For a long moment, he sat there, in the quiet of the cab of his truck, the engine clicking as it cooled. He closed his eyes because of the struggle.

At last he opened his eyes, took the keys from the ignition, slipped them into the breast pocket of his jacket, and carefully buttoned the pocket shut.

The four headed back toward Leslie's place. Ava and Trevor were animated, jumping up and down off the curbs, turning every handle on every parking meter as if expecting loose coins to pour out. Mike and Leslie walked slowly, side by side, not touching, but together, Mike commenting on the chill in the air, the coming of winter, being prepared with storm windows, putting bags of rock salt in the trunk.

Leslie knew he was that sort of man—a man who prepared ahead, looked ahead, making sure there would be no surprises, making sure all the bases were covered, and the gutters cleaned out for the cold rains of October.

"Are you looking for a job?" Mike asked. "I mean, not that I need to know …"

Leslie smiled. "Mike, it's okay. You can ask me questions. I won't break."

He slapped at his forehead again, as if it had been a practiced move. "Sorry. I'm never too sure."

"I *am* looking for a job. I was supposed to have an interview at ARMCO. But something … came up and I had to cancel. Now I'm back to square one."

"Well, I know a few people in town. I'm not sure if anyone is hiring right now, but I'll ask around."

Leslie wanted to tell him that it wasn't necessary, that she didn't want any special favors. But if he asked around and that helped land a job, so much the better, she told herself.

In a few minutes, they were at the Midlands Building. Leslie unlocked the street door. Ava asked for the key for the upstairs door and she and Trevor took off like monkeys climbing a tree after bananas, leaving Mike and Leslie alone in the small vestibule. Leslie thought Mike had hesitated a moment, allowing the children to charge ahead.

When the upstairs door clamped shut, Mike turned to Leslie. "This has been nice, real nice. I'm glad you two came with us. It was fun."

"It was fun," Leslie agreed.

Mike hesitated, then spread his arms and hugged Leslie. Leslie had seldom, if ever, felt so engulfed, so protected, as in his thick arms. He hugged like she was fragile, not wanting to break something in the process.

"This was nice," he repeated, talking toward the wall.

Leslie nodded against his chest.

Then he leaned back and bent down a lot to kiss her ever so lightly on the lips. He let the kiss linger longer than Leslie thought he ever would when he began the kiss.

He leaned back, flushed, and perhaps embarrassed, and repeated, one more time, "This was real, real nice."

Leslie nodded.

"I should go," Mike said. "Trevor has had enough sugar for a while and the walk home will help."

They both walked upstairs, Leslie going first. Then Mike gathered his son, and the two departed in a chorus of good-byes, clicking the door shut behind them.

Ava stared at the closed door. "That was nice," she said.

Leslie would have agreed with her, except she was waiting for the familiar bands of constriction in her chest, precursors to panic, begin to form around her heart, leaving her mute. Yet the panic did not start, and Leslie was unsure how to stop her preparations, her bracing for the storm, if the storm never appeared.

Alice swept every paint chip off her desk, or what was her section of the large work surface. Worthless, after assessing his chances of finding that errant open can of tuna on the kitchen floor were nil, had wandered back underneath the desk. The deluge surprised him, but it was not enough of a surprise to get him to move.

Alice flipped open her worn red leather address book, with numbers crossed out, names crossed out, Wite-Out frequently used, to add yet one more entry. She resisted going digital, though everyone encouraged her in that direction, and her phone had the capability. Alice had refused all entreaties, claiming that written numbers were much more secure than some wired piece of plastic that could be rendered useless by a dead battery.

She ran her index finger down a long list and settled on one number. She picked up the phone from the desk, a landline, "just in case that wireless system shuts down some day," she'd explained, defending the dinosaur. She tapped at the numbers, then leaned back in her chair, crossing her legs, nearly taking off the ear of Worthless, who still had not budged an inch.

"How *are* you?" Alice all but shrieked, in a pleasant shriek sort of way.

She waited a long time to reply.

"No! *Really*? That's wonderful. How are you feeling? You can still travel, right?"

Alice tapped at the piles of paper, looking for a pen.

"Well, I know how busy you are, but you simply *must* come down to Butler."

She nodded as she listened.

"I know it is nowhere near as cosmopolitan as Franklin, but Frank and I have found a new place to start Alice and Frank's Take Two. A *wonderful* old building with *oodles* of character and charm. We are just about to start work on it. You *must* come and document the renewal process. I know that you love taking the 'before' pictures. That's the start of the drama, right? This is such a wonderful project, Cameron. It would be just *so perfect* for you."

She began to jot down names and numbers.

"I will call him immediately. But you can do it, right? You're the star, right? You have pull, my dear. You *must* learn to exercise it properly. You must."

Alice sat up, laughing at whatever had been said in reply.

"I will call you tomorrow, then. You will make plans to come down. Remember your promise."

Alice nodded one last time, then replied.

"We miss you, too. Frank sends his love."

She took a pen, and flipped open her calendar, and wrote "Three Rivers/Cameron" on an open square for the correct day, then drew an arrow to the following week, with a question mark, then another arrow to in between the two dates, and wrote "Confirm/Callback/Cameron."

Amelia Westland, age seventeen years
Butler, Pennsylvania
July 10, 1879

Julian Beck has twice called upon me here at the Barry residence. We have taken tea in the parlor. Dr. Barry has expressed his concern, in his kindly way. He did not say so in so many words, however, I have had the disquieting feeling that, at first impression, he does not approve of my Mr. Beck. Mrs. Barry has also inquired as to my perceptions of various aspects of Mr. Beck's character, not showing outright disapproval, perhaps, since she has but briefly met Julian, but from her manner I discern she also is showing her concern. I am sure that it is only in the interest of my well-being that she and the good doctor have done so. I do not wish to be unwise in my affections toward Julian, but such feelings as I have in my heart for my "beau ideal," do I pray they be banished if he is not who God desires for me?

> *For thou art my rock and my fortress;*
> *therefore for thy name's sake lead me, and guide me.*
> —Psalm 31:3

CHAPTER FOURTEEN

IT WAS SO QUIET IN Leslie's apartment. As part of her sixth birthday celebration, Ava was spending the night with the Stickles, her new de facto grandparents. Both sides all but begged to allow the sleepover. Mrs. Stickle said that they would make sugar cookies and have chocolate-chip pancakes for breakfast. Ava had been too excited to deny Ava such an innocent pleasure.

But that left Leslie alone, an occasion that had seldom occurred in the last six years. In fact, Leslie could not recall the last time she had been off "mom duty" at night. With the sole custody of a child, that was nearly impossible.

Leslie had gotten a small bundle of firewood, sold for a few dollars outside the convenience store, and had arranged the logs in the fireplace. Once the fire was started, she sat down and tried to read. But sometime after 11:00, she slipped out of the french doors and walked out onto the balcony, decided it was too chilly to sit there, and returned to the kitchen to make a cup of instant coffee. So far today, this cup would be, perhaps, her tenth cup of coffee. She knew it was too much caffeine, but she didn't have any soda in the house and had always resisted resorting to wine on these occasions. So coffee it would be—regardless of the total daily consumption. And the ritual of making coffee had become a soothing activity: routine, easy, and mind occupying … for a little while, at least.

She had tried her best not to think of Mike and his embrace and all the rest of it, the totally unexpected part of it, until this moment. She wondered if Ava, who was very intuitive and perceptive, had noticed anything different. If she had, she'd made no reference to anything out of the ordinary. This evening, she had given her mother a hug, a peck on the cheek, found her teddy and blanket, and had taken Mrs. Stickle's hand.

Leslie poured the hot water onto the spoonful of coffee. She sipped at it, disliking the taste, disliking the acrid sensation on her tongue at the end of the day, yet knowing she would drink the entire cup because she'd made it and didn't waste things in a cavalier fashion.

What was he thinking?

She turned her cup around so that the handle pointed away from her.

Did I encourage him? Did I lead him on?

She turned the handle around again.

And ... did I like it? It has been a really, really long time since I've been ... you know ... kissed by a man. I like him. I guess I like him. He's a nice guy. He seems to be normal. He seems to be a decent person.

She breathed in deeply, waiting for that unsettled feeling again.

But there was none. Maybe what she had felt earlier was simple excitement, an expected response from an unexpected kiss.

Maybe I did encourage him. Maybe touching his hand like that and being nice because he was being so kind and sweet was the encouragement.

She picked up her coffee cup, now cool enough to carry and half-consumed so spills wouldn't be a problem, and walked to the french doors of the balcony.

Maybe I wanted him to do that. Maybe Ava needs a strong man in her life. Maybe it's already time to start thinking about making a more stable home for her—with a mother and a father. Maybe it is time. And Mike is very easy to be with.

I guess ...

She looked down at her cup.

I could do a lot worse.

Then she looked up at the moon, just rising, almost hidden by the streetlight at the end of the block, and thought about Jack.

I wonder what he's doing tonight.

Jack waited in his truck a long time, watching the moonrise, deciding a thousand times. He wondered why his life so often careened from rock-solid good to horrifyingly bad. He wondered why God would let his life spiral, sometimes out of control, and never bring him back from the edge.

A long time ago Jack had decided that God was in the lifeguard business. But Jack was also convinced God must just have been paying attention elsewhere when he was pulled into deep waters.

Or maybe He doesn't care. Just as likely He doesn't care about someone like me.

After he'd taken the keys out of the ignition and buttoned them into his coat pocket, he stepped out onto the gravel parking lot. Slowly he made his way around to the front and into the familiar darkness that enveloped and welcomed in such a wonderful way, making Jack feel, at least at that moment, like the right decision had been reached.

Celebration. Release.

The next time Jack looked at his watch, he could barely make out the small numbers and arrows, but correlating his watch to the NASCAR-themed clock behind the bar, he determined it was a few minutes past 11:00.

That's not so late. Only a couple of hours. Well, maybe a few more than a couple.

He scooped the small pile of bills and coins from his pocket. He fished out a five-dollar bill and smacked it onto the bar. He nodded to the bartender, who smiled back at him. Jack wondered as he snaked his way back to the front door if the bartender's smile was a five-dollar smile or an accidental ten- or twenty-dollar smile. Jack had made miscalculations like that before. It was not the sort of mistake he could go back and examine. If he overtipped, so be it.

Glad that the front door was a push door and not a doorknob door, he made his way outside. Now that late night had come, the temperatures had dropped, and Jack could see his breath in the air—little clouds of alcohol-fueled breath, dissipating into the darkness.

He sat in the cab of his truck for a long time, breathing in deeply, hating himself for what he had done, blaming it on what had happened to him, blaming it on the fact that he was alone tonight, every night, blaming it on....

"I'm not going to drink anymore," he said out loud, emphatically, and thumped his palm on the dashboard, as if adding an exclamation point. "I'm not. This time I mean it. Sober. Sober from here on out."

He felt fine. He felt in control now, now that he had promised all this manner of self-destructive behavior was behind him, and that a new start had begun, right here, right behind the tavern on Route 8.

He jammed the key into the ignition, started the truck, and carefully pulled out of the parking lot and onto the highway.

I'm okay. Really. It was only a few drinks, anyhow.

He drove slowly, or what he thought was slowly. He had trouble focusing on the road as well as the speedometer. But he was dead certain he was traveling within the speed limits, although he wasn't sure what the speed limit was on this specific stretch of Route 8.

Probably forty-five or fifty. And no way I'm going that fast.

He was sure that he was in his lane and remained in his lane. He was being so very careful that when the sharp turn in the road appeared all of a sudden, not marked at all, he cursed, and swore it was not a turn he recalled negotiating on his earlier trips. It threw him, confused him, and he twisted at the steering wheel, feeling the front tires catch the softer dirt and gravel of the shoulder at the side of the road.

The truck barked and shifted as he fought the wheel, the tires squealing, trying to regain purchase on the smooth asphalt, the gravel and dirt of the shoulder clutching at them.

He wrenched the wheel again, and the truck bounced, then veered farther off the road. As Jack slammed on the brakes, the passenger side crunched against a stand of trees. As if in slow motion, Jack watched as the sideview mirror snapped off like the head of a dandelion in the wind. He could hear the mirror's glass explode, spreading like a small comet.

In a matter of seconds it was all over.

The truck stopped moving. Jack unclenched his right hand from the steering wheel and threw the transmission into park, the terror rising in his chest like a tsunami.

After a long moment he stepped out of the truck. The vehicle had wound up several feet off the road, well out of traffic, the front tires deeply mired in mud. As carefully as he could, he stepped around to the passenger side. Mirror gone. Supporting arm gone. Clean little holes in the sheet metal where the mirror had been ripped from the car. Some scrapes and scratches on the door and front fender, but some of them might have been there from before.

Not that bad, Jack reassured himself.

He slapped at his hip. His cell phone was still there. He grabbed it, and his hands shook so that he struggled several times to flip the slim unit open.

If a police car sees me here, they'll get me on a DUI for sure. They will. And if they do that, I'm in jail. Everything will be gone. I can't let that happen. I can't. Not for just one screwup. I promised to go sober now. I made that promise. If they find me here, I'll be in big trouble.

He took off, almost at a jog, toward the city, wanting to get some distance between himself and the truck.

If the police come, they'll chalk it up to me running off the road and getting stuck in the mud, and that I had to go for help.

That'll work. I can get the truck in the morning.

After a few minutes of jogging, he realized that walking the eight or nine miles back to town might take him most of the night. And he was certain that if a passing patrol car spotted him wandering along Route 8 in the middle of the night, far from anywhere, they would stop him, eventually put two and two together, and arrest him for drunk driving and leaving the scene of an accident. Besides, the wind had begun to pick up and it felt like rain.

I have to call somebody. I have to call somebody to get me. That's what I have to do. They'll come get me and then I won't have to worry about the police.

He stopped in front of a closed tire repair shop, under the glare of a sodium vapor light, flipped open his phone, dialed a number, and dialed it without hesitation—just as the first drops of rain began to fall.

———≫⊶≪———

Leslie, startled by the electronic warbling, lurched for her purse, not wanting to wake Ava, then remembered that Ava was not there. She grabbed the phone and snapped it open. "Hello?"

Her heart began to beat fast. No one called close to midnight. It might be the Stickles. Or her ex-husband. Both scenarios, however briefly considered, scared Leslie more than any horror she could imagine.

She repeated, "Hello?"

"Mrs. Ruskin? Leslie? This is Jack. Jack Kenyon."

His words sounded precise, as if he were trying hard to pronounce every single letter.

"Yes?"

What could he want? Why would he call this late?

"Mrs. Leslie, I didn't want to bother you and all, but I'm sort of in a pickle."

She heard what she thought was a muffled laugh, but it might have been Jack coughing.

"I need your help."

"What sort of help, Jack?"

She heard him cough again, this time a bit longer.

"Jack? Are you okay?"

There was another spasm of muted coughing, then the rustle of something, as if he was holding the phone against his clothing. She waited.

"I need your help."

Then Leslie knew he had been drinking. She was well aware of the signs.

"You said that, Jack. What do you need?"

Jack coughed again. "I got my truck stuck in the mud. On Route 8. There shouldn't be any mud there. Too far to walk home. It's raining. I need a ride. Can you run down to get me?"

For a moment, Leslie was dumbfounded.

Why would he be calling me? Couldn't he call a taxi?

As if hearing her thoughts, Jack said, "No money for a taxi. I looked. I have three dollars."

He sounds lost and like he really needs my help. Ava's next door. I could slip out for a half hour.

"Where are you?"

Jack's command of precise English began to break down and he slurred the name of the tire repair place.

"On the west side. Not too far. Be here in ten minutes, I bet."

Leslie stood up, grabbed her purse, and a jacket since it was now spattering rain, and said into the cell phone, "Wait there, Jack. I'll be there in ten minutes. You just wait there."

And with that, she hurried down the steps and tried to be as quiet as possible as she started her minivan and headed south along Main Street, then south on Route 8.

———

Leslie snapped on the lights, tossed her jacket onto the sofa, grabbed the electric kettle, filled it with water, grabbed two cups and the canister half-filled with instant coffee. In the time it took her to do that, Jack had removed his coat, let it drop where he stood, then had slumped, heavily, into a kitchen chair.

"Thanks again, Mrs. Leslie," he said, repeating himself in his thanks. He had not said much during the ride back to Butler. Leslie made the impetuous decision to bring him upstairs and attempt to sober him up—at least a little—before she took him home. She knew that people who drank too much often hurt themselves or caused fires trying to make coffee.

He seems harmless enough now, she assured herself. *Just too much alcohol. That's all. He is still a decent person.*

"Thanks. I was in a real pickle, you know. Saved my life, you know."

Leslie had not spoken much. She set the hot cup on the table, retrieved the cream from the refrigerator and the sugar bowl from the counter.

She sat a distance away from him. She didn't like the smell of alcohol as it worked its way out of a person. That sickly aroma brought bad memories.

"Jack …"

"You saved my life."

"What happened, Jack? What were you doing out there? Why did you try to drive home in your condition?"

Jack looked up at her, and despite his haggard look, despite suffering the ravages of too much drink, he was still a very striking man: face cut just so, his chin, his eyes, his mouth, all formed in that perfect way that looked both gentle and dangerous at the same time. Leslie knew, in another time or place, those looks really would be really hazardous.

"Wasn't that bad. Didn't drink that much. Not nearly as much as I used to. I guess I'm out of practice. A couple of years and … you get weak, I guess. You lose concentration," he said, grinning at his own words, then hiding the grin as he saw Leslie's stern expression.

Leslie was intuitive, at least when it came to reading others. *He had a problem with drinking, I bet. That's why he's starting over here. Maybe he's running from something. Maybe his past.*

She watched him drink his coffee. She watched him hold the mug with both hands. *Just like Ava and me. Running from something.*

"More?"

Jack nodded and pushed the mug closer to her.

She made him another cup, knowing it would not bring him sobriety but would at least keep him awake, allowing nature and time to do their work. Already, he seemed a bit more in control than when she'd found him, standing alone, in the rain, lit by the garish glare of the security floodlight.

He poured in cream and added three spoonfuls of sugar.

"Jack …"

He looked up, and directly at her.

"Jack, you have to get help if this is a problem. You could have killed yourself, or someone else."

He nodded. She watched his eyes. He had heard the same speech many times before, she knew. She knew how ineffectual repeated speeches were. Her ex-husband could have taped his speeches. It would have saved him a lot of energy. He could simply have referred to them by number: #1—The Unfit Mother; #2—The Unfit Wife; #3—The Crazy Woman; #4—The Woman Who Was Beyond Help; #5—The Loser Who

Had No Business Thinking She Was Worth Anything. She knew the speeches all right.

"I know. I know," he finally said. "I should go back to the meetings."

"Meetings?"

"AA. Meetings. I used to go. I was better."

"You should. It would help. Wouldn't it help?"

He shrugged. A wave of … sadness passed over his eyes. "Since my wife … since my little girl … I don't know. Nothing matters. If I got killed, it wouldn't matter. No one would care. Nothing matters."

She could tell from his voice, from the teary warble in his words, that he was near the edge.

"Jack, it can't be all that bad. There is always hope. You have to stay well. For them. Stay well for them."

He put his head in his hands and choked back an anguished cry. "You don't know …"

She pulled her chair closer to his, almost right next to his. "Jack, you have to try to get better for them."

He kept his face hidden. His shoulders shook silently. Leslie couldn't help herself. She reached out and put her arm around him. A moment later, she put both of her arms around him.

"It's okay, Jack. It will be all right."

And despite all the red flags and all the warning bells and all the signs—yes, she could see and hear every single one of them—she found herself intensely drawn to this man, drawn to help him—to ease his pain, to make it all better, to bring some light to his darkness.

I can make this better for him. I want to.

After a few minutes of holding Jack in her arms, she released him and he sat straight in his chair, not looking at anything, trying not to look at her. But, for an instant, her eyes found his. She could tell he felt better. It had felt so good to hold him, to feel him in her arms. Protective, secure.

Yes, I know this would be crazy. Get involved with this person? It would be crazy … foolish.

He did not look at her as he finished his second cup of coffee.

Crazy. Yes. And what would my ex-husband say about it?

She sat up straight as well.

And he is married. Isn't he? Or is he divorced too?

"Do you want any more?" she asked.

He shook his head. "No. I'll be okay now. I'll be fine."

He has to be divorced.

"Do you want me to drive you to your apartment?"

Jack stood, perhaps still a bit unsteady, but steady enough.

"No, I can walk. I think it's stopped raining. The air will do me good."

"What about your truck?"

He waved his hand in polite dismissal.

"My landlord can take me out there. He owes me a favor. No one is going to steal it between then and now."

"Are you sure?"

"Yes. And thanks. I don't know what I would have done without your help tonight. I'm sorry for bothering you like this."

"Don't worry about it."

He stood by the front door. He just stood there, holding the doorknob, and he looked back at Leslie. She stood a few feet away in her running sweats, her hair held back by a headband, feeling anything but feminine or attractive. He stood and stared, hard. She didn't move and met his gaze head-on.

He let his hand drop, then walked the two steps to her, and put his arms around her. He held her, not tight, but neither was his embrace loose and unfeeling; it was tight enough that she could feel the firm muscles of his arms. She only hesitated a moment, then wrapped her arms around him, despite the scent of alcohol, despite all the warning bells that had gone off and all the red flags she saw, and embraced him back, her head on his shoulder.

After they held each other for a long time, she released him. Looking straight into his eyes, she said, "You get better, Jack Kenyon. You have to get better."

He nodded, reached over to her, and put a single finger softly on her lips. Then he opened the door. Before he slipped out, he said quietly, but with conviction, as if he had not said the words recently, "I will. I promise."

The door closed, and Leslie listened to his footsteps on the stairs and the opening and closing of the downstairs door. She hurried to the french doors and saw him walk—with purpose, she decided—toward downtown and toward his apartment.

He meant it. I could tell. God, I pray he meant it.

And then Leslie wondered to herself why she mentioned this to God, after so long of a silence between them.

Amelia Westland, age eighteen years
Butler, Pennsylvania
July 5, 1880

Such serendipities! I could scarce have imagined this day when I first became acquainted
with Dr. Barry. Despite my fears and paralyzing nervousness, which still visit me from time
to time, the good and gentle doctor has surprised me with an action that goes far beyond
the realm of any woman's expectations. For payment of our services, he has given each of
his servants a coin every week to hold in saving, a substantial amount to me, who has never
seen that sort of money. Other than purchasing necessities and a few frocks and items of
accessory, I have retained all the extra monies I have received.

I have discovered that God has other plans for my life. Dr. Barry, on the date of my
birthday, summoned me into his office and presented me with a paper. He spoke as I read:
"You are too skilled a young woman to remain here and without benefit of further education. I have made inquiries and procured you a position in the fall class at the Indiana Normal
School where you shall be trained as a schoolteacher." Even before I could ask, he added, "And
I have secured a scholarship for your tuition and board." I later discovered that Dr. Barry
has done this twice prior, yet I have not heard him breathe a word of this generosity toward
those in his previous employ before this very day.

I threw my arms around him with abandon and embraced him fiercely (forward, I know,
yet he is as a father to me) until he became embarrassed by my gratitude. I will depart in a
month's time. Me ... an orphan without resource or advantage ... to become a schoolteacher!
Such a dream come true! What protection God has given me. How He looked upon me, so
undeserving of His grace, with His glorious favor, for I know it is because of nothing I have
done that such blessing has come to me.

During my time thus far in the good Dr. Barry's employ, I have had but a half dozen
opportunities to enjoy a visit with Mr. Julian Beck. Neither of us stated our romantic inclinations toward each other, but I have dreamed that such inclinations simply went unsaid

but, nonetheless, are present in both him and me ... and will soon be made evident. From my countenance when we are together, it is difficult to imagine that he could be ignorant that this girlish heart is beating for him alone. Dr. and Mrs. Barry have not encouraged our society; however, they have been kind to allow Julian chaperoned calls. I shall dearly miss his calls when I am away.

> *With men it is impossible, but not with God:*
> *for with God all things are possible.*
> —MARK 10:27

CHAPTER FIFTEEN

THE RAIN HAD STOPPED. It was well before dawn and Jack was walking. His landlord didn't owe him any favors. He wasn't even sure if the man even owned a vehicle. He had lied to Leslie and he remained unsure why.

It just seemed appropriate.

The truck was not that far from town. If he walked fast, an hour or two, he'd be there. The walk would give him a chance to think, to burn off the alcohol that was left in his system, a chance to be by himself. He seldom felt alone, even in his solitude.

Ghosts. Too many ghosts.

He strode with purpose along Route 8, nearly oblivious to the passing traffic. He recounted his steps last evening; he recounted the actions that led him to where he was this morning. He knew what Leslie said was true. He could have killed himself. Or worse yet, he could have killed someone else. The vision of that—of him careening into a car filled with innocent victims—so terrified him that he had to stop and breathe deeply. The vision caused him to nearly become sick—not just spiritually sick, but physically sick. He saw images swirling of him plowing into a family car. He saw faces of small children, their eyes lit in terror at the galloping head-lights aimed at them, their little hands held up in an attempt to protect themselves from the carnage.

He began to run, began to run from the image, running fast for a mile, maybe two, then slowing to a jog, then a quick walk, his sides hurting, his shins burning, his lungs tight. But he had escaped the visions, he had outrun the terrifying images and thoughts and the might-have-beens and the there-but-for-the-grace-of-God scenarios.

Now he was just a tired, hungover man on the way to rescue his truck, stuck lightly in the mud.

He crested a small hill, and there it was, his battered truck, parked well off the side of the road, as if parked there on purpose. He squinted, hoping to determine if the police had placed a ticket on the windshield. He squinted and walked with a quicker step.

There was no ticket.

He breathed a sigh of relief.

He looked again at the damage. It was not severe at all. The mirror was gone, but the door was only slightly scratched. It would be no problem to get a replacement mirror and the scratch buffed out. Or he could leave them as they were.

He unlocked his door and climbed in. The cab stunk of liquor, a sour, decaying smell, tinted with an acrid cigarette odor. He didn't think he had smoked last night, but he might have, in an effort to drive sober. It had never worked in the past, but the past was so difficult to outrun.

He turned the key. The engine started right up. He put it into reverse gear and gingerly applied the gas. The truck lurched a bit; the tires scrabbled to catch purchase in the moist dirt and gravel. A spray of stones splattered the undercarriage, then the truck bumped and rose up and backward. He was not as stuck as he'd feared. He stopped the truck on a piece of drier ground, still well off the road, and put the transmission in neutral.

He took his cell phone from the holster on his belt. He knew the number. He'd known it all the time. He was good with numbers. And this one, he remembered.

He dialed it and waited.

"Yes ... when is the next meeting? In Butler. Downtown is best."

He listened and heard a page being turned.

"Grace at Calvary? Grace Street at Calvary Street? I don't know where that is at."

He listened a long moment, his eyes watching the morning traffic speed by.

"Oh … a church. The big old stone one on the square? That's Grace at Calvary?"

He nodded.

"An 'at' sign. Yeah. I know where the church is. What time? Okay. Good. It's not a closed meeting, is it? That's good. Great."

He closed the phone, slipped it back into the holster.

He put on his seat belt, looked over his shoulder behind him, and pulled out, a thin spray of stones shooting off his rear tires. He settled down as he drove, making plans for this morning, making plans to stop at McDonald's for breakfast, then on to work, then tonight, at six, he knew where he must go.

And maybe, during the day, he might see Leslie.

He had absolutely no idea of what he might say to her, other than assuring her that her faith in him was not unfounded.

Even if such faith in him, by and from others, always had been unfounded and undeserved in the past.

———————

Leslie had fallen asleep late, well after 1:00, maybe closer to 2:00 a.m. She rose early and forced herself to be wide awake before Ava was up. Then she remembered. Ava was at the Stickles'. She would not be home until lunch.

It felt strange to have a morning by herself, without her daughter. She padded into the kitchen in her pajamas, walked to the french doors, and looked outside. She walked back to the kitchen. Then she went into the living room, where the smell of last night's fire still lingered, and sat on the sofa, switched on the television, switched it off, and went back into the kitchen.

The buzzer rang, making her jump and turn as if being attacked. It buzzed again, and she ran to the french doors, peering down, hoping to see who was ringing her bell that early in the morning. Outside, double-parked, was a white-paneled truck with *The Bloomery* painted in fancy scrolled letters. She opened the french door and shouted down, "Who is the delivery for?"

The deliveryman, holding a wrapped package, stepped backward toward the curb and then looked up. "Leslie Ruskin."

"That's me. You can leave them on the stoop. Or wait. I'll be right down."

She ran to her bedroom, found the nice robe that she rarely wore, and hurried downstairs, with two dollars to tip the driver. Wrapped in gossamer paper was a lovely bouquet of flowers. She could tell that the arrangement had been selected from the florist's autumn collection.

Back upstairs, she unwrapped it carefully and breathed deeply. The scents were wonderful. She took the small envelope attached to the bouquet and opened it slowly, not sure why she was hesitant.

> Thanks for last night. Sorry for moving too fast, but I liked the end of the evening the best. You are wonderful.   Mike

His handwriting grew smaller and smaller and tighter and tighter as he got to the end of his message. She could barely make out the "Mike."

Who else could it be—really?

She took the artificial flowers out of the glass vase on the kitchen table and primped at the fragrant flowers and the ferns as she placed them just so in the vase, turning it one way, then the other, and stepping back to admire them. It had been a long time since anyone had sent her flowers.

And as she looked at them, standing in the kitchen in her robe and pajamas, she felt it. The tight bands. The constriction. The sense of dread and doom. The panic slowly rising. She tightened her hands into fists, her knuckles turning white.

She retreated a half step at a time, until she bumped into the far corner of the kitchen. Her shoulders wedged against both walls, she let her body slide down until she was on the floor. Her legs splayed out beneath her, her arms tightly folded across her chest. Her eyes shut, and her mouth softly formed the word *no* over and over again.

Not now. Not today. NO!

But today, something unexpected happened. She summoned all of her strength in an effort that surprised her—in fact, amazed and shocked her. She placed her palms flat on the floor and pushed herself back up first to a kneeling position, then a standing one. She felt tears and pushed them back, at least for now.

I will not cry now. No tears.

She looked at the clock on the microwave in the kitchen. It was always five minutes fast.

At 9:10. I will call. I have to. Now. Today.

She stumbled to her purse and tried to control her hands as she removed the phone from its base. Her eyes all but refused to focus as she punched in the number.

She listened to the recorded message. There was always a recorded message. A woman with a pleasant voice listed the worship times and the evening prayer and fellowship hour, and the sign-up dates for the senior high spring break trip to Williamsburg.

"If you want to leave a message for Miss Whiting, please press 2. If you want to leave a message for the senior pastor, please press 3. For the associate pastor, press 4."

Leslie jabbed at the number three. Expecting to hear a tinny recorded voice, she was surprised, almost to the point of dropping her phone, to hear a real person pick up on the other end.

"Pastor Blake here."

In that instant, Leslie all but forgot why she had called.

"Uh—hello?" She forced herself to think, to focus, to force herself to remain in the moment. "Pastor Blake?"

"Yes, this is Pastor Blake."

"Pastor Blake. Good. I got your name from … well, I guess it doesn't matter where I got your name."

Why can't I remember Ava's teacher's name? Why in heavens did I forget that now?

"No … it probably doesn't. How can I help?"

He sounds so kind.

"This person … she said that you had suffered from panic attacks."

There was a moment of silence.

"I did. I suppose I still do. Or could. I haven't for quite some time."

"Pastor Blake, I need help. I can't function anymore. I don't know what to do."

"Have you been treated for them in the past?"

"No. I don't want to take medicine. That makes people like zombies. I mean … if *you* take it … well, maybe it isn't that bad."

She waited until he replied. "No. I don't take the medication. Although I have seen people who have been helped by it. But I didn't go that route."

Okay. Maybe he does understand.

"Then what can I do? How do I get out of this?"

"There are ways to treat the condition. There are behaviors that will help you cope—help you and those around you deal with the attacks. But you know … the most important thing you have to do is to find a center, find that peaceful place inside of yourself. I know of only one way to really find peace."

"That's what I want. Peace. Can you help me?"

She waited.

"Yes. I think I can. Well, I sure can try. We can both try, right? Can you come and see me? This morning?"

———

Leslie walked away from the church, feeling lighter than she had in months and months, and stronger, more like she was before, before she had been beaten down and nearly destroyed. That destruction, that deadly erosion of her soul, of her confidence, had taken years. She realized now that it had started even before Randy. Looking back at her tumultuous years as a teen, and even as far back as her childhood, she couldn't think of a single person in her life who had ever really believed in her. It had taken years, but she had even stopped believing in herself.

Maybe getting better would take less time.

I am a well person. At least I was. I was. And I can get there again.

Pastor Blake had promised Leslie nothing—no miracles, no "turn to Jesus and be instantly cured." He had not merely recited words written in one of his dusty theological tomes. But he had given her hope. He had listened to her story and, with compassion, had given her reassurance that she wasn't going crazy, that her problem was not a matter of human willpower, nor the lack of it. That it was often caused by stress, loss, or separation. He had told her that people who sought treatment for panic attacks often got better. That they could lead normal lives. He had shared his own experience, and told her how the peace of God had changed his life. He had asked her if he could pray for her, and she'd agreed. After the prayer, he had said, "Leslie, I believe in you."

He had also given her a book to read that had helped him, and a Bible that was called a recovery Bible. There were pages of verses that spoke of God's promise to help a believer desiring help.

"They are both important," he had said, as he walked her out through the silent sanctuary, with its magnificent golden stained-glass windows, to the front doors of the church. "But this one—" he'd pointed at the Bible "—is the most important."

Before she had left, Pastor Blake had said, "As you read, I want you to think about where you are with God, Leslie. Next time, maybe we can talk about that, okay?"

Now Leslie held the books to her chest. Those last words kept echoing in her mind.

Where are you with God? Where are you with God?

She looked at her watch. It was only 11:00. She hurried her steps. She stopped at Friedman's for milk and cupcakes on her way home. Even though she imagined Ava would be chock-full of forbidden treats at the Stickles', Leslie could not help herself and wanted to offer her daughter one more birthday treat—a little celebration with candles for just the two of them. She asked for a half dozen cupcakes this time—an indulgence for both herself and her Ava.

Whistling, she put the cupcakes on a plate, put six small candles on one of the cupcakes, put the other groceries away, and placed the book and Bible from Pastor Blake on the kitchen table. She was ready to spend the next thirty minutes or so reading and thinking about what the pastor had said. And waiting, anxious for Ava's return.

Leslie sat down and opened the Bible. It was something she had never done in the past. Her parents were not really churchgoing people, except for Christmas and Easter, perhaps. She had gone to summer church camp and a few other events for kids, and she remembered kind people telling stories about Jesus and other Bible characters. As a child she always knew God was there. While majoring in art history in college, studying in detail the intricacies of the most beautiful, remarkable, diverse works of art ever made by humans throughout the world, over the course of their time on planet Earth, she had become completely convinced that the creative impulse, the passion of artists and artisans to express themselves, had to have been placed inside their souls by an incredibly creative God. But things of faith were never really discussed or practiced in her home. She thought about Grandma Amelia: with all that had happened in her lifetime, and despite her own shortcomings, she had great faith, a steadfast belief in God that was so integrated into her life. Leslie wondered what had happened in her family between the time of her Grandma Amelia, and her grandparents' and mother's time. Such faith—or even a little—apparently hadn't been passed to them. Or perhaps it had been, and they had chosen to walk away from it.

Now she had drifted as well. She and Ava had stopped going to church when Randy had given her so much flak about it, and it seemed like a lifetime since she'd even thought about it.

Where are you *with God?*

Her phone rang. Leslie did not recognize the number on the caller ID.

"Hello?"

"Hello, Les. Long time, no see. How's tricks?"

She did not want to recognize the voice, but she did—sweet and almost oily, with just a sprinkling of malice to it.

"Hello, Randy."

She debated on what to say next. She had had imaginary conversations with him every day, conversations where she would get angry, or grow quiet, or tell him of her successes with the building, or that other men had found her attractive, or that Ava was blossoming without his darker presence. But she said none of that. Now that her ex-husband was really on the phone, none of her rehearsed speeches felt right.

"How are you?" was all Leslie said in reply.

"Well, I would think you might have more to tell me. You never were at a loss for words before. Things not quite as rosy in Butler as you imagined? Is that it? You have nothing good to say to me? From what I read in the papers, Butler is the new up-and-coming place. Lots of pleasant opportunities. You're not letting them slip by, are you?"

Leslie felt the hairs on the back of her neck stand up, bristling at his happy, confrontational style. "No. We're fine, Randy. Ava and I are doing just fine."

She thought she heard a laugh of derision, but it could have been Randy clearing his throat. He often said he was just clearing his throat when he was laughing at her.

"Well, isn't that great. I am glad to hear that."

There was silence for a moment. Leslie was not providing any cues, not speaking any more than required.

"And things are going well for me … and Lisa. She's a great gal. Keeps the house just perfect. Cooks something new every night. Things couldn't be more wonderful."

Leslie nodded and did not speak.

"She says she wants kids. I told her we need to wait awhile. You know what I mean. Get used to each other. Not like we did it. Or you did it, I guess."

He had always accused her of getting pregnant with Ava in an effort to further tie him down.

"Anyhow, Les, I'm calling because … well, I know that the judge you finagled to get on our case did not want to hear anything of the truth. Hey, and that's okay. You have Ava. He said sole custody, and I can deal with that. Even if I have every right to an appeal. My lawyer said so. That judge was nuts. But you remember that he allowed for visits. And you know I haven't insisted on those visits. I mean—you had to move the whole way to Butler, just so I couldn't see my daughter every day. And I want to see her. I want her to get to know Lisa. They'll have a ball together. Lisa is real nice, a real normal gal, if you know what I mean. So … it'll be okay, right?"

Leslie could hardly catch her breath to speak.

Okay? For what? For you to come here? Invade my life? For you to take my little girl? To have her meet your new wife—the wife who isn't crazy like me?

"Come on, Leslie, don't make me spend my hard-earned money getting some expensive lawyer to demand what the judge said were my rights. I get to see Ava. And I want to see her. I want to make sure that she has everything she needs. I want to make sure she's safe—you know what I mean? A visit. That's all. A visit. I'll take her out to get ice cream or something. Maybe Lisa can buy her some clothes, okay? She does need new clothes, doesn't she? I mean, just because you never bought yourself anything cool to wear doesn't mean my daughter has to look like a poor person. I'm thinking of next weekend. On Saturday. I'll have to get up early on my day off so I can drive the whole way from Greensburg."

Leslie could not bear to remain silent. "Butler is less than two hours away from you, Randy. The way you drive, it's less than an hour."

"Hey!" he shouted into the phone. "Don't you go poisoning our little girl's mind like that! Saying I'm some sort of maniac driver. I'm not. She loves her daddy. Maybe you don't—or can't. But Ava does. Don't go telling lies about me to her—you hear? If you do, the judge is going to hear about it."

She did not reply.

Neither did Randy.

"Ten o'clock on Saturday?" she finally suggested. Her words were as void of emotion as she could render them. He hadn't even remembered it was Ava's birthday.

"Fine. I have the address. Ten."

The connection broke.

And the words on the pages of the Bible began to waver and swim.

He's going to take her from me. He is going to try and take my sweet Ava away from me.

———◆———

"He's going to come and take her away. Or at least try to. I know he is. I just know it!" Each word of Leslie's on the phone became tighter, higher pitched, more clenched.

"Leslie, listen to me," Pastor Blake said, calm, measured, knowing that any other tone simply would add fuel to Leslie's fire. "All will be well. With God's help, you are in control now. Randy is not. You remember what we talked about last time, don't you?"

"I do. I think I do. But I don't know anymore. All I can see is him coming here and taking her from me. Finding some reason that she has to go home with him. I'm worried, Pastor Blake. I'm really, really worried."

Pastor Blake's small office was barely able to provide enough distance for a proper pacing as he talked to her. The church, built over one hundred years ago, originally the Second Presbyterian Church, was a wonderfully brooding Romanesque stone castle on the southeast corner of Diamond Square. Butler dropped off at the southeast corner of the square—or at least the geography did. A steep valley, train tracks, and a smallish creek that would go a ways and soon become the Connoquenessing River all lay before him, spread out like a relief map in a museum. He never tired of the view, watching the cars wind around the sharp corners and struggle up the tight, steep Kittanning Street hill.

He always wished he could expand his space—just a little—but he knew that would be difficult. Any sort of renovating of the old structure took a team of stonemasons to accomplish—and Pastor Blake's church was not that flush with excess cash.

I can make do with small, he told himself often. If he were working on a difficult sermon, he would pace in the sanctuary instead, up and down the aisles, until his theological problem had been solved.

Today, the problem facing him was not theological in nature but by no means less thorny.

"Leslie, you know I can't speak to the legal issues here. But I am sure that if it ever came to that, the courts would be fair. No one is taking anyone."

"But the panic attacks. If he knows I'm still having them, and that they have gotten worse, he can find some smart lawyer to find that I'm unfit. Then she's gone."

Pastor Blake knew that a large part of his counseling job was simply calming people down, helping them to see the facts of a situation, and to deal with the reality at hand—rather than an array of terrible "could-bes" or worst-case scenarios.

Some people automatically think of the worst thing that might occur and then treat that like it is going to happen.

He had expected Leslie to be like that, and she was. It did not surprise Pastor Blake, nor did he think ill of her; it was just so very typical of her condition. And he understood—completely.

"Leslie, we have to take this one step at a time. He can't just come and take her away. That would be kidnapping, since you have sole custody. He won't and can't do that. So you have to stop going to that place in your mind. Stop going there. Focus on your response—not on what might happen, but on what has happened."

He heard her take a few deep breaths.

"That's good, Leslie. Slow, rhythmic breathing. Helps you stay centered." As he listened to her breathe, Pastor Blake was praying under his own breath.

"So what I am going to do now?" she asked, her voice still troubled.

"Well, I can't see you today. I have several back-to-back meetings and appointments." As soon as the words were out, he knew it was the wrong thing to say to the wrong person.

"Oh, I am so sorry, Pastor Blake. I know you're very busy. I have no right to think you can drop everything for my stupid problems. I'll … I'll be fine. Really."

Pastor Blake sat down, gently, not wanting to make his office chair creak more loudly than it did. For some reason, he never wanted a caller to know when he sat down.

I need to get a new chair, too.

It was a thought that often crossed his mind.

"Leslie, that's not what I meant. Tomorrow is simply a better day. Can you come over at six? Can your neighbors watch Ava for you? We can talk. And then, if you want, you can stay for our prayer meeting later."

He waited for her reply.

"Prayer meeting?"

"It's not scary, Leslie."

"Do I have to pray? I mean, does everyone have to pray? Out loud? In front of everyone? Or can I listen and pray silently?"

Pastor Blake would have chuckled, but he knew that to Leslie, it was not a chuckling issue.

"No, Leslie, you do not have to pray out loud or in front of people. You can just listen, if you'd like. Or you can be prayed for by others. Prayer helps. It's vital, you might say."

"Okay, then, tomorrow at six," she said.

"Tomorrow at six."

And when he put the phone back on the base, he offered a silent prayer to God, praying that He would reveal Himself to Leslie; reveal His love in some fashion, in some way, so she might know the truth. The truth that would set her free.

When he opened his eyes, a lumbering UPS truck was wheezing up Kittanning Street, politely elbowing oncoming traffic out of its way.

Amelia Westland, age nineteen years, three months
Indiana Normal School
Indiana, Indiana County, Pennsylvania
October 21, 1881

I can scarce believe it has been nearly two months time since my arrival here in the hills of western Pennsylvania. Fall has painted the landscape with a colorful palette of reds, oranges, and golds. The days fly by with exceedingly great speed as I diligently apply myself to learning. My mind is filled with wonder at the fullness of knowledge possessed by my professors.

My first weeks I experienced periods of melancholy and loneliness, whereupon the Preceptress, perceiving my disposition, has graciously taken me under her wing, as if God had sent a guardian angel to me. I am day by day taking an increasing part in the society of my fellow students, yet I sorely miss Catherine. I have received letters from her, as well as from Dr. and Mrs. Barry, who are making plans for my return to their home for the Christmas holiday.

I have taken it upon myself, much too forward for a genteel woman, I am sure, to, unsolicited, write to Mr. Beck during my tenure here at the Normal School. He has not answered every correspondence, but he has written in return on occasion, his hand less sure than mine, for his gift is in speaking rather than writing. But his few words cause my heart to stir. He works still at the livery, much to my happiness, and has recently stated that he is anxious to hear of the location of my posting as a teacher when I am graduated. If it is in Butler proper, I am praying that he will yet be in residence there and soon thereafter seek me out. I also pray I may have the happiness of seeing him over the Christmas holiday should it indeed be possible for me to return to Butler for the span of but ten days.

> *For it is written, He shall give his angels charge over thee, to keep thee:*
> *And in their hands they shall bear thee up, lest at any time*
> *thou dash thy foot against a stone.*
> —LUKE 4:10–11

CHAPTER SIXTEEN

WEDNESDAY EVENING CAME TO DOWNTOWN Butler. Long shadows cut across Diamond Square, and the daytime traffic, a constant rumble, gave way to a more sporadic grumble—a few cars now, then a truck, a couple of well-insulated motorcycle riders, followed by long breaks of silence. From its spot at the center of the square, the Silent Defender statue looked down on the city as it stretched and got ready for the night.

Jack left his truck at the apartment and set off on foot. He didn't want to drive. Being behind the wheel provided him with too many options. It was too easy to stop and turn around, or simply keep driving. He could play the parking place game; he'd played it before.

If there isn't a place to park, I'm not driving around for hours looking for an empty spot. I'll go home and come back tomorrow.

He would not have wanted to count the times he participated in the game. He not only thought of God as a lifeguard but also as a parking attendant at times.

If He wanted me to be here, there would be a place to park nearby.

He knew such a thought was heretical—not really knowing fully what heresy it suggested—but he assumed that it was bad and that only heretics would fully believe it.

As he came closer to Diamond Square, he realized Butler was much different than most places: There was a plethora of empty spaces nearby.

Diagonal spots all around the square were vacant, plus a nearly empty lot full of parking spots.

Maybe God does want me here tonight. Jack quickly pushed the thought away, assuming that if there was an all-knowing deity, a "Higher Power" as he'd heard in previous AA meetings, that He wasn't paying attention at this one specific moment.

Grace @ Calvary was a beautiful church, Jack thought, as he walked closer. Rough-hewn granite blocks, each block the size of a small oven, were stacked in perfect symmetry, with arches and keystones over the front doors, and golden windows deeply recessed into the stone, walls tilting inward slightly, pushing one's eye to the heavens. The roof was done in slate—dark, heavy, leaden gray.

No one builds this way anymore.

The doors were dark walnut in color, thick, planked, and with curved tops to fit in the massive archway. A small sign, with adjustable letters under a glass cover, listed the service times. Near the bottom were the two letters: *AA,* with an arrow pointing away from the main entrance. Underneath the *AA,* the sign read: *Use Side Entrance. Room 102.*

Jack looked into the front doors and saw the main sanctuary, with a white dome, and heard the sounds of a piano and a guitar filled in with voices—younger rather than older voices, Jack thought. They were singing—not a hymn he'd never heard, but an upbeat version of one he had: "Amazing Grace." Their voices were rather good, Jack decided. He climbed the few steps into the narthex, then stood in the doorway to the sanctuary and listened. In between the familiar verses, sung with a decidedly contemporary beat, they began singing an unfamiliar chorus:

> *My chains are gone, I've been set free.*
> *My God, my Savior has ransomed me.*
> *And like a flood His mercy reigns.*
> *Unending love. Amazing grace.*

As the song went on, Jack could not have moved from that place had there been an earthquake. All alone and unnoticed in the darkened narthex, as the words of the song washed over him, his throat tightened, and tears formed. Because it was a rehearsal, the musicians went through the song a second time. He listened again, until the end, and it was only then, because the group began to break up, that he could bring himself to leave.

He turned and headed outside, wiped at his face, and took a couple of deep breaths.

It must have been the part about the chains that got to me.

He walked to the side door. Once inside, he faced two stairways—one up, one down. He imagined that the meeting room was downstairs.

He was correct.

A brown-topped folding table stood in the hallway, and a near-commercial-grade coffeepot—a big stainless steel West Bend sixty-cup model—squatted in the middle. There were Styrofoam cups, plastic wicker baskets filled with sugar packets and cream packets, and a plastic cup filled with brown stirrers. At the far end was a clipboard, with a sign-up sheet attached under the metal clip.

Mailing List Sign-up! was written in thick letters at the top.

Next to it was a tented sign that said, *Tonight: Step 3—Made a decision to turn our lives over to the care of God as we understood Him.*

Jack poured a cup of coffee, added sugar, tasted, added cream, tasted, and added another sugar. He looked at his watch. The meeting should have started five minutes ago. His heart was beating faster than it should. He didn't want to walk into the room alone, and unknown. He wanted to gently, carefully, place his coffee cup on the table, then sprint down the hallway, up the few steps, and run until he could not run any longer. That's what he wanted to do.

But he did not. He could not.

He drew in a breath. And another. Then he walked to the door of room 102, put his hand on the doorknob, and opened it. He stepped inside and felt the eyes of a dozen other men snap to him as he found an empty chair.

He sipped at the coffee, now tasting like a bitter poison, but he maintained his normal face, tried his best to maintain his normal breathing, looked up, and listened.

"My name is Brad, and I'm an alcoholic...."

One hour and twenty minutes later, Jack stood up from his chair, shook a few hands, nodded to others, and tossed his empty cup in the trash can overflowing with empty coffee cups.

The man who had loosely led the meeting—tall, forty-something, with a warm smile—introduced himself to Jack. "I'm Bob McNeil. I'm the associate pastor here."

He shook Jack's hand and told him he was always available should Jack need any help, or if he was interested in a sponsor. Jack thanked him, then walked down the hall, up the steps, and into a chilly dark autumn evening.

He zipped his coat up to his chin. He set off walking toward his truck.

Relieve me of the bondage of self, that I may better do Thy will.

The words of the ending prayer Bob had read kept echoing in his mind, along with the words of the song he'd heard earlier, with a similar theme.

My chains are gone, I've been set free.

Jack jumped into his truck, and a few minutes later found himself in front of The Palm, debating with himself, debating whether he should risk entering to find Earl, and what his odds were of not finding Earl, and what might happen if he entered and there was no one to help stop him from doing what he so desperately wanted to do.

Bondage … chains …

As Jack walked out of his meeting, Leslie was walking into the prayer meeting, held upstairs in the sanctuary, held every Wednesday evening at 7:30, right after worship-team practice. Had she hurried up the steps, they would have run into each other. Had Jack stopped to chat for even thirty more seconds, he would have seen her walk into the church, unbuttoning her coat, putting the keys to her minivan into her purse.

Jack gambled. He gambled big. If Earl was there, if Earl was behind the bar, Jack would have a cheeseburger and a Coke. Maybe two Cokes.

If Earl was not there, Jack would walk in, slap a twenty-dollar bill on the bar and ask for a double Jack Daniels and Coke.

It could have gone either way. Jack remembered what he had told the group this night, about his past experiences. "I would go to a meeting," he had said, in a quiet, almost guilty voice, "then I would go out and get loaded. Like I owed it to myself—for an hour of being honest. If I was honest with somebody, even for a little while, I could drink. It hurt being honest, so I drank more."

Several men tonight had nodded in agreement.

Jack flipped the coin, high into the air, and did not wait until it spanked off the pavement. He stepped inside. He did not breathe until he sat down at the bar, in his spot, in his now-comfortable place at the first turn of the bar by the window.

"Good evening, Mr. Kenyon," came the greeting.

It was Earl.

Jack finally allowed himself to relax. "I just came from a meeting," he said, as if admitting something dark or onerous.

Earl knew what to say and what not to say. "Good. Burger and a Coke?"

Jack nodded, then quickly added, "Wait, with cheese."

Earl tilted his head just so, as if his wry smile was all the validation Jack required or needed this one chilly autumn evening. "Good meeting?"

Shrugging, Jack replied, "I still want a drink. That's not changed."

Earl leaned in close. "That'll never change completely, my friend. You always want to get off the train. With time, the station gets a little further away. Take heart."

And Jack sat there, in the dim light, amidst the smoke, the pool-table chatter, the drone of the television overhead, the sloppy bravado of the old men at the other end of the bar, the clatter and swish of glasses, and the pungent odor of beer and highballs. He ate his burger and drank his two Cokes, thinking about the prayer and the song about the chains.

He didn't say another word until he stood, slipped a ten-dollar bill on the bar, waved to Earl, saying, "See you later."

Leslie drove the few blocks home.

I could have easily walked there. I don't know why I thought it was so far.

But then she realized she would have to walk past two bars on her way home, and though neither place was disreputable, a single woman, regardless of the city, had to be cautious.

I really liked tonight.

Leslie didn't pray out loud this evening. Pastor Blake had been true to his word. No one pressured anyone to pray out loud. A number of people did. Maybe not everyone, but most of the twenty or so people of all ages made Leslie feel right at home. Pastor Blake did her a great favor and introduced her to the rest of the prayer group and mentioned that she was new to town, owned the Midlands Building, and had a daughter at the Brittian Elementary School.

No one pressed her on marital status. No one pressed her on how and why she knew Pastor Blake. No one had pressed her on anything.

But they had prayed for her. She had mentioned renting out the bottom half of the building and her concern that everything would go well with her new tenants. Also that she needed to find a job.

People prayed for her, her tenants, the contractors, her employment, and her daughter. She was touched by their openness, their care, and their willingness to pray for a complete stranger.

Then Pastor Blake prayed. He didn't mention her name. But she knew it was she he was praying for. And that was okay. It felt good that he prayed for her.

"We pray for all of those who are facing trials. We pray that they will find the strength and perfect peace that comes only from complete surrender to You, Lord. For Christ is our peace. We pray, Lord, that You would draw them to Your love. We pray that Your will be done. We pray for people who have hurt us at one time, that we can forgive them, that they, too, will be changed. And we pray for the safety of our children."

He prayed about a lot of other things, but that is what Leslie remembered. And as he had prayed, the older woman sitting next to her had reached over and taken Leslie's hand in hers and squeezed it, just for a moment. To her, it felt like the hand of God Himself, reaching out to her. That's when the tears behind her eyes—tears held back for so long—began to silently flow. That one simple caring touch from a total stranger had the power to cause Leslie to open her heart, closed for so long, just enough to allow the peace she so desperately needed to begin flowing in.

Now, as she drove home, she had to admit to herself that she felt even more hopeful than she had when she'd first talked to Pastor Blake, and even more than she'd felt after they had met—before the prayer meeting.

Gramma Mellie believed in the power of prayer. Maybe Gramma Mellie was right.

Amelia Westland, age twenty years, eleven months
Indiana Normal School
Indiana, Indiana County, Pennsylvania
June 10, 1883

My time at Indiana Normal is now at an end. I have studied diligently, as I promised Dr. Barry. By God's grace I have received my diploma and certificate from the State of Penna., that allows me to seek out teaching situations within the Commonwealth. I have written letters to the persons in charge of the schooling in Butler County, inquiring as to open positions for this imminent school year. I pray God's will be done.

Catherine is now in the employ of Dr. Barry. Perhaps he plans the same path for her as was mine. I am in hopes that the days until the time I shall see her again will be short.

So shalt thou find favour and good understanding
in the sight of God and man. Trust in the LORD with all thine heart;
and lean not unto thine own understanding.
In all thy ways acknowledge him, and he shall direct thy paths.
—Proverbs 3:4–6

CHAPTER SEVENTEEN

ALICE HELD A QUART CAN in front of her like it was some dead animal she'd discovered living under her bed. Her other hand held a paintbrush, which she treated much the same.

"I can't tell from paint chips. Unless I was as small as a Barbie doll, which I am not. I need to see this on a wall. And not only in the morning light, but all through the day and at night, too."

Frank sat on a folding chair in the midst of the clutter of their new venture. He was flipping pages on a clipboard, apparently deep in thought, a pencil tucked behind his ear at an absolutely rakish angle. He was wearing his two-hundred-dollar workshirt, custom-made, with his monogram on the cuff, made of very fine Egyptian cotton denim. He wasn't sure whether denim was made in Egypt or not, but the tailor had said it was, and Frank had no good reason to doubt him. And the shirt was stunning. Even Alice admitted that.

Alice did not like to paint walls.

"I see a freshly painted wall and I get vertigo, and I wind up falling against it. Why is that?" she had remarked.

She dipped the brush and carefully stroked the paint onto a rear wall, creating a big square of color.

"I can't paint," she said emphatically, hoping Frank would take the hint and take the paint and the job from her. He did not.

"Frank," she said, with some expectation in her voice.

"Alice," Frank responded, attempting to match her tone, but his attempt was totally contrived.

"Frank, can *you* paint? I'm no good at this."

He looked up. "Weren't you a fine arts major in college? Of course you know how to paint."

She would have stomped her foot, in an Ethel Merman sort of theatrical move, but was afraid if she had, the paint would somehow slop out of the can and spill all over her leopard-skin flats.

"I used teeny, tiny brushes. I can't use these big clodhopper brushes."

Frank stood up, put the clipboard on the chair, and stepped to his wife's side. "I'm not painting a thing—but that color is superb. That is one terrific choice. You have remarkable color sense."

Alice beamed. "You think so?"

"Oh, I do. No need to go any further."

And with that, he walked off, tape measure in hand, leaving Alice to wonder if he had agreed so quickly just to get out of painting.

The more she pondered, the more positive she became that Frank had done just that.

Yet … the color was really smashing on the wall, and she didn't want to be bothered anymore with the decision.

She put the paint can down, as if it were still that dead, unattractive animal, and stepped back.

We are on our way. The focal-point paint color is the first step. Once that's done, everything else falls into place.

She squinted.

And the paint color is just so perfect.

She opened her eyes wide, and knew for a fact, just then, that Alice and Frank's Take Two was going to be a smash hit as soon as it opened.

———

Totally surprised, Jack tapped at the glass window of the Midlands Building and smiled. The cool morning had left pockets of condensation at the top and bottom corners of the large display window.

"What are you doing here so early?"

Frank and Alice sat together at a folding table, with white tablecloth, candle, cups, and a plateful of what Jack surmised to be croissants. There was a blazing fire going in the fireplace.

Where do you get croissants in Butler?

Alice beamed and waved him inside, taking his arm, pulling him to the table. Before he had a chance to decline, she poured him a cup of coffee.

"We couldn't wait to try out the fireplace," Frank explained. "As you can see, it still works great."

"Have a croissant," Alice said. "And a scone. You simply must try a scone. We found a *wonderful* little bakery—Dominique's. French. They are simply delightful. We now have our pastry source for the store. Croissants are an indispensable part of Alice and Frank's."

Frank pulled up another folding chair to the table—all matched items, of course—and insisted that Jack join them.

"We have coffee—good, solid, Eight O'Clock French roast coffee," Frank said. "We don't believe in fancy. Just excellent quality."

Then Alice stared at him, and they both burst out laughing.

"Who am I trying to kid? I love fancy things. But I also love Eight O'Clock coffee. French roast. Ground this morning. Another perfect taste."

Jack felt more than a bit overwhelmed. He never had this much conversation in the morning. Never. But, in spite of what he was most used to, he found himself enjoying it.

"The croissant is delicious. I don't think I've ever eaten a fresh, authentic French one before," Jack said, talking as he chewed, as politely as he could. He felt he needed to hold up his end of the conversation.

Alice swung her hand out and clasped it over her heart, as if about to swoon. Jack figured this wasn't an unpracticed gesture. Alice would be the sort of woman who managed to pretend to swoon often.

"Never have eaten a real French croissant? Where were you raised? Barbarian Land? Egg McMuffin Acres? Good *heavens*. No croissants?"

Frank apparently enjoyed the show as much as Jack did. "Ask him, my sweet, when he had his first latte?"

Alice narrowed her eyes in mock suspicion. "Don't tell me …"

Jack shrugged. "I don't drink lattes. I've never had a latte."

Alice pretended to collapse on the table. "No lattes! No croissants! I'll bet you've never had a scone, either. We have hired Cro-Magnum

Contractor, Frank. We *must* bring him into the twenty-first century."
Alice's hand stopped in midswoop. "We *are* in the twenty-first century,
aren't we? Somehow that sounds so … futuristic."

Alice adjusted her Bulgari scarf, broke off a large corner of her
croissant, and popped it into her mouth. "Frank, my dear, please,
walk Jack around the store. Ask him about our plans. See if he agrees
with what we have envisioned. Our last contractor, that *horrible* little
man in Shadyside, had absolute *tremors* when we asked for nontra-
ditional furnishings. So *outré*. He simply did not understand our
ethos. You understand our ethos, don't you, Jack? Please say that you
understand?"

Frank pulled Jack to the far corner, where he grabbed his clipboard.
"Pay no attention to the woman behind the curtain. She is a highly frus-
trated theater double major."

Frank took the pencil from behind his ear, carefully, as not to disturb
his morning hair. "This is my rough sketch. I will have the architect *du
jour* draft the final plans, but I would like your opinion on the viability of
what I'm suggesting."

For the next half hour, Frank lead Jack around the room, pointing
out where display cases would go, where moveable tables would be placed,
where seating nooks and window seats would be built in, where the ceiling
would be dropped to afford intimacy, and where lighting would be the
most dramatic.

Jack nodded throughout the walk.

"I can see that.

"I could build that.

"That would be an easy construction.

"That makes sense."

At the end, Frank said, "That's about it. What do you think?"

"Wonderful. It will be a really neat place when we're done."

Frank beamed.

"Neat. You hear that, Alice? 'Neat.' We have 'neat' ideas."

Alice looked up from a catalog, written in French. "Neat. I guess neat
is one step closer to nifty. Our goal. Neat and nifty. Sounds like a law firm
from the fifties."

"One thing, though," Frank said. "That door on the back wall. The old carved one with the huge deadbolt on it. What's behind that?"

Jack turned to look. He knew the door Frank mentioned. The door was huge, nine feet tall, done in solid walnut, Jack thought, with hand-carved panels—a vine and floral motif, almost like a border on an illuminated manuscript, or a motif of William Morris, Jack thought, cut into the dark, dense wood. It was both an antique and a work of rare craftsmanship, of fine artistry.

Jack walked to it, to examine it one more time. "It's a wonderful old door. Amazing carvings. I looked at it before. Asked Mrs. Ruskin about a key, and she said she didn't have one. Neither did the bank who sold it to her."

Frank tried the doorknob, an ornate brass one, as if no one had ever tried simply opening it. Of course, the door did not budge.

Jack pointed to the opposite edge of the door. "Now, here's where it gets interesting. Ninety-nine doors like this out of a hundred, maybe nine hundred ninety-nine out of a thousand, have hinges on the outside, so the door can easily open outward. If it's for storage, you don't want the door opening into the inside. Takes up all the storage area with the swing. But there are no hinges out here. The hinges are inside. That's unusual. Like they didn't want anyone to be able to pull the hinge pins out to get inside."

"Well," Frank said, "you can just cut around it, right?"

Jack made a *sweesh* sound by breathing in over clenched teeth. "Maybe. But see down there by the floor? I cut into the plaster—to see what I might be up against. Two four-by-four posts stacked against each other, I think, surround the whole door. There would be a whole lot of demolition to this wall to get it out. And there's a second lock at the bottom of the door," Jack said pointing. "Almost as big as the main deadbolt. There's no key for that either."

Frank rubbed his hands together. "A mystery. I love old mysteries. What do you think is back there? Al Capone's treasure?"

Jack had to laugh.

Frank's voice now had an excited edge to it. "Diamond Jim Brady's lost diamond stickpin collection? He was from Butler, you know. There is a rumor that he had dozens of dazzling diamond stickpins—three-carat monsters. That's where he got his name, you know. When he died, there was only one single stickpin found. Maybe the rest are in there. This building is from the right time frame."

Jack shrugged and held his palms up. "Maybe. But I wouldn't take a loan out on the possibility."

"Wait until I tell Alice. She will be so excited about finding a hidden fortune."

And with that, Frank hurried to his wife, who was still seated at the table, flipping through her French catalog.

Jack turned to the door once more, and wondered how he was going to get this door open without destroying it in the process.

Sometimes things have to be broken in order to be made whole.

That night, Jack lay in his bed, hoping sleep would come and free him. His workday had gone fine. He had successfully battled his urges one more day. He had talked for an hour with Earl over his dinner. He had walked the streets until it became dark. He'd showered and now lay in the stillness, the traffic light buzzers now silent.

He dozed off.

He awoke with a start, sitting up in bed, just like in the movies, he thought. He blinked, trying to focus.

3:00 a.m.

He covered his eyes with his hands and tried to remember.

It was a dream about that door. I managed to get to the hinges somehow and slipped the hinge pins out and pushed the door open the wrong way.

He tried to focus on the images of the dream.

There was something inside … perfect … some perfect thing.

It allowed me to forget. It erased the memories.

He felt like crying.

If I could just forget.

He opened his eyes to the darkness and everything that he lost was right there, in the darkness, just past the reach of his fingertips, waiting for him, waiting to ruin whatever he had ever hoped to become.

It was all so real.

Amelia Westland, age twenty-one years, one month
Lyndora
Butler County, Pennsylvania
August 5, 1883

God is good, and faithful and just. I have always held that to be certain, regardless of my circumstances. He has been steadfast in His care of me, allowing me to be interviewed for a position to teach in the town of Lyndora, just to the south of Butler proper. The schoolhouse, in good repair and of modern design, features a sizeable classroom with stove, and all necessary books and materials, plus a teacherage at the back, consisting of a pair of small rooms, which features a small fireplace, furnishings, and a closet for the teacher's personal effects. The school committee has informed me that a winter's supply of coal and wood is included in the stipend, plus some free time in the summer in which one may seek other employment to augment one's salary.

The position was extended to me, and after much prayer, I accepted the kind and generous offer. In the interim I have been again housed in the home of the generous Dr. and Mrs. Barry, a godsend in my life, who have been so keenly interested in my studies and pleased with my successes. The staff was likewise kind to me, and precious hours in Catherine's company brought me much joy. On one lovely day, I strolled down to Cliff Street to Harton's Livery, the establishment that now employs Mr. Beck, who is no longer indentured, but fully and gainfully employed.

We enjoyed a polite meeting, restrained and cordial. There was much to speak of, but he had scarce a half hour for his midday meal, and since I cannot be seen without chaperone after hours with any man, we made the best of our time. He inquired as to my recurring spells of nervousness, and I truthfully told him that I appear to no longer be vexed with such a condition.

Since I brought all my possessions with me to Butler, I will be allowed to occupy the quarters in the schoolhouse prior to the commencement of classes and prepare for the term ahead, which begins in three weeks' time.

But my God shall supply all your need
according to his riches in glory by Christ Jesus.
—PHILIPPIANS 4:19

CHAPTER EIGHTEEN

"I HATE THIS SCARF, MOMMY," Ava said, her voice muffled by the muffler. "It's not even cold outside."

Leslie had bundled Ava up, with a thicker scarf than necessary and a heavier coat than the season warranted. She took no chances with colds and flu, and Ava was either the beneficiary or the victim, depending whether one was mother or daughter, of a relatively illness-free childhood.

"The weatherman said it is only 38 degrees this morning. That's almost the temperature of ice cubes. You don't want to be an ice cube, do you?" Leslie asked.

Ava glared at her mother, not really angry, but not thrilled with the overdressing either.

"We won't be able to walk to school much longer. It will be too cold."

"Good," Ava said, emphatic. "Then I can wear my Dora coat instead of this dorky jacket."

"Ava!" Leslie responded with a hint of exasperation.

"Well, it is dorky. Everyone thinks so. Even Trevor, and Trevor doesn't think anything is dorky."

"Well, we will just have to be dorky and healthy and warm, I guess," Leslie said, putting an end to the conversation.

She waved as Ava walked inside the school. This time, Leslie was certain Ava didn't wave back, or even look back.

Today was Wednesday. Three more days until Randy showed up. Leslie dreaded every moment as the weekend drew closer.

Pastor Blake was helping her walk her through her emotional gauntlet, her minefield of anxiety. While she wasn't happy about it, she now accepted that the situation with Randy would eventually occur. She also realized that no one was stealing anyone—at least not just yet. She did not confide in Pastor Blake that her ex-husband was capable of some evil, horrid actions—and he very well might try some legal maneuver. Maybe not this weekend, but sometime.

Mike Reidmiller waved to her from his car as he slowly drove down the street from school. He pulled close to the curb and rolled down the window.

"Hi. We ran late, so I had to drive," he said, smiling.

"And it's getting colder. I may have to start driving as well," Leslie answered.

Mike offered a wave of dismissal. "Cold doesn't bother me. Trevor either. I guess we're built more for the cold than the hot."

Leslie had no good reply, so she remained silent.

"Listen, Leslie …"

It was obvious that Mike was trying to say something but seemed at odds with language.

"Leslie—" Mike made a noise in his throat, then hurried to add—"are you going to be home this morning? I have to … I have to go now … but can I … will you be home? Can I call you later?"

"Sure. I'm home all morning. Jack is putting in the tub today. I'll be home."

Mike appeared to be in a hurry, rolling up his window while calling out, "Then I'll call you later, okay?"

<hr />

Leslie walked up her staircase and found a note slipped under the number 2 on the door.

> Tub delivery delayed until tomorrow. I'm at the
> Pettigrews'. Call cell if needed.   —Jack

She took the note and carefully folded it. She admired the way he formed his letters, like an architect, she thought—angular and precise.

After her failure at ARMCO (although it was not a failure, per se, just that she never got a chance to interview, she told herself), she had despaired over her future. It was Mrs. Stickle who raised her hopes again.

"That museum around the corner and down the street—" she had said, leaving the rest of the sentence unspoken.

"There's a museum around the corner?" Leslie had asked.

"Well, a few blocks away. The Maridon Museum. It's filled with Oriental porcelain and painted plates and fancy Chinese statues and all that sort of stuff. Makes Mr. Stickle's skin crawl, he says. I think it's all very beautiful. Anyway, my beautician at the Cut 'n' Curl Beauty Shop said that they're looking for an assistant docent. Or assistant curator? Which one was it? It's not the volunteer one … it's the one they pay a salary to. An assistant curator. Yes, that's it. I have no idea of what a curator does with a building full of Chinese tschochkes, but it might be something you could be good at. You went to college for that, right? Art history?"

Leslie had replied that she did indeed study art history, and that same day, she had quickly gone to the museum's Web site:

The Maridon Museum is the only museum in the western Pennsylvania region with a focus on Chinese and Japanese art and culture. The Pittsburgh Post-Gazette pronounced the Maridon, "a gleaming little gem of a museum." The museum—both the objects and the buildings that house them—is the gift of Mary Hulton Phillips, a lifelong resident of Butler, PA. The museum is her legacy to this small town.

Leslie also learned that the Maridon had a permanent collection of over eight hundred Asian objects—some dating back to the second and third century BC—plus three hundred pieces of Meissen porcelain. She had gotten the address on McKean Street and walked the few blocks to the museum, amazed that she'd never seen it.

I never come this way. All my destinations are in other directions, she thought as she looked up at the building, now closed.

She sent off a résumé and a cover letter to the head curator, whose name was listed on the contacts page of the Web site. She made a note to call in a few days.

I have an art history degree, after all. Although I'm not sure if that quali-fies me for this job. It sounds interesting, though. Bless Mrs. Stickle, and her beautician, for the lead.

Leslie chuckled to herself at the old-fashioned word Mrs. Stickle had used for hair stylist, and at the picture she conjured in her imagination of the Cut 'n' Curl Beauty Shop her neighbor frequented.

And then, for the two-thousandth time, she berated herself for major-ing in art history, which she loved, instead of something practical, like nursing. And every time she thought this way, she quickly realized that the sight of blood made her squeamish and that she knew she could never go around poking poor people with needles.

Maybe I should have gone for something like accounting, then.

It was a familiar circuit in her mind.

Like I can even balance my own checkbook.

The phone rang and she remembered that Mike was going to call about something—all very mysterious.

"Leslie, it's Mike. Mike Reidmiller."

"Of course, Mike. I knew it was you."

"Well, I like to be careful. Maybe you know a couple of Mikes and you don't like one of them. What if you thought I was the Mike you didn't like? That would be bad."

This is one very sweet man, she thought. *And sensitive.*

"So anyhow. I'm the good Mike … that is, if you do know more than one."

"We have established that, Mike," Leslie replied, happy to be talking to him.

"I wanted to ask you earlier, but I was leaning out of my car window, and all of a sudden, I thought that was just the wrong way to go about it. Like I was sixteen and didn't know anything about women. Well, I'm older than that now, and I guess I don't know a lot more about women now, either, but I'm pretty sure that asking a woman out while leaning out of your car window is not the proper thing to do, is it?"

Leslie, swept up in his explanation, hadn't realized he was asking her a question. "Yes. I mean no. I mean … it would have been okay. I think."

She laughed as she found herself stumbling as badly as Mike.

"Listen, Leslie, I want to ask you out to dinner. Not just you, but you and Ava. For tomorrow. That's Thursday. So it's not like it's a big date night or anything—just a normal, regular dinner, that's all. Do you think you would want to go? Or come to dinner? I have it all planned. I mean, it's not cooked yet or anything like that. What do you say? You and Ava up for a meal?"

Leslie debated with herself.

A sweet guy. A really nice man. I could learn to … Would I be settling …?

She mentally shook her own shoulders.

It is only a dinner. How many nice men have asked you out recently?

"I would like that, Mike. That is very sweet of you."

"Well, that's just swell. How about I pick you and Ava up at six tomorrow night. It's a school night and all that. So we could eat and talk or whatever and the kids could get to bed at their normal time. Would that be okay? Six?"

"Sure, Mike, six is fine with us. We'll be waiting."

"Thanks, Leslie. You won't regret it."

She wanted to laugh again, his closing line was that funny, but she didn't because she was sure he would obsess about the cause of her laughter for the rest of the day.

———

At 5:55 p.m. on Thursday, Mike pulled to the curb. Leslie had been waiting by the french doors since 5:45, sure that Mike was the arriving-early type. He literally jumped out of the car. He was wearing what looked to be a new sweater. It had sharp creases on the arms, something that occurred only upon purchase or on fresh dry cleaning perhaps, and Mike did not appear to be much of a dry-cleaner sort of man.

She opened the door before he got to the street entrance.

"We'll be right down."

He held the car door for her, all the while Ava regarding him with a suspicious look. She clambered into the backseat. Trevor was buckled tight in a booster seat.

"Okay that Ava doesn't have a booster seat? I didn't have an extra one. We could get one out of your car."

"It's only a few blocks, Mike. Just promise not to crash."

"Okeydokey. No crashes."

Mike's green car, a Chevrolet, Leslie thought, even though she was not good at car identification, was sort of beige on the inside, with cloth seats. There was a hint of aftershave in the car and Leslie couldn't tell if it appeared just this evening or was a permanent scent. The cup holder held a battered thermal cup; one that probably once bore a Dunkin' Donuts logo, but that was long faded. A thicket of maps nested above the passenger side visor. Leslie noticed, with some satisfaction, that the floor was spotless, as if it had just been vacuumed.

"I hope you like home-cooked food," Mike said as he crossed Main Street, without looking twice for runaway cement trucks. "We could have gone to a restaurant, but I thought, well, the kids eat in five minutes and Trevor has all the game systems and videos and stuff—that's if it's okay that Ava plays them, or watches a video."

"I'm sure it will be fine, won't it, Ava?"

"I'm not watching anything scary. I have nightmares."

"Nothing scary," Mike said in his best dad voice. "I promise."

Ava wasn't used to hearing a dad sort of voice, and Leslie was sure she was busy processing the different tone.

Mike pulled up to a very nicely kept Cape Cod on a quiet street of attractive homes, several blocks northeast of the downtown, with white stucco and siding, dark green shutters, and neatly trimmed evergreens surrounding the front of the house and lining the walk. A swing hung from a low branch of a large oak tree in the front yard. A small porch adorned by several large clay pots with autumn flowers in them. Leslie wondered if they were real or artificial. If they were artificial, they were good artificial. There was a white screen door in the front. Mike pulled up close, turned off the engine, and almost tripped trying to get around the car fast enough to open Leslie's door.

"Sorry," he said, almost out of breath. "Out of practice."

She smiled.

He is sweet.

They entered a very neat, very clean, very precise home, with everything just so.

"It's not always exactly like this," Mike said. "I tidied up a bit."

"It's just lovely," Leslie said and meant it.

The living room furniture, not outright stylish, was not dowdy either—just pleasing and comfortable. Not bachelor furniture, but not grandmother furniture. Tweeds, soothing blues and browns, with throw pillows, in the right accenting colors. A few nice lithographs on the wall. The paint color was some soft taupe shade, a nice complement to the furniture. A low fire in the fireplace warmed the room.

"This is very nice," Leslie said, repeating herself. "I guess I'm a little surprised."

"By the design or by the cleanliness?"

Leslie had to laugh. "Both I guess."

"Well, thanks," Mike said, smiling in satisfaction. "Let's go into the kitchen. I thought that rather than eat in the formal dining room, we'll have dinner in the eating area off the kitchen."

He had the table set with two plastic plates and two plastic tumblers, and a kid's set of silverware by each place.

"I made macaroni and cheese and chicken fingers. I thought I could feed the kids first. Trevor eats everything in about five minutes and then wants to run from the table. Does Ava eat slow or fast?"

Ava spoke up. "I eat normal."

"Well, the two of you will eat normal, then you can go play games or watch a video."

Mike had been correct. Trevor was done in five minutes. Ava took a few minutes longer. Then they both ran upstairs.

"One of the bedrooms is used as the TV room," Mike explained.

He then cleared the table and reset it with a crisp white tablecloth, simple china plates, almost-crystal glasses, nice silverware, and matching cloth napkins.

"Whatever you're making, it smells absolutely delicious," Leslie said.

"It's nothing fancy, I assure you," Mike said, as he bent to peer into the glass front of the oven. The oven was stainless steel, like the refrigerator and dishwasher and microwave.

Leslie was surprised. She had thought Mike to be a Kenmore sort of guy—white appliances from Sears.

"I saw the recipe in the Sunday paper and it sounded good. I know they say that you should never try things out for the first time on guests, but this sounded pretty safe. I'm not a very inventive cook. With Trevor, all I need to know how to cook are grilled cheese sandwiches. And mac and cheese. And chicken fingers. Maybe a hot dog occasionally, when I let him have one. None of that is too taxing."

Leslie sat at the table and watched him work. He took a covered bowl, filled with fresh green beans, and placed it in the microwave. He reached down and took out of the oven three baked potatoes, wrapped in aluminum foil.

"I know," she replied. "Cooking for Ava doesn't get too far afield. If I want grown-up food—and I'm not even sure what that is anymore—I wait until we go out to a restaurant."

Mike took a vase off the counter, in which he'd arranged a bouquet of fall flowers, and placed it on the table.

"A little bit of elegance," he said as if feeling a need to explain the flowers' presence.

The microwave beeped three times. Mike donned oven mitts and carried the bowl to the table, then retrieved the tray from the oven. He set the tray on a trivet.

"The recipe title was 'Downhome Meat Loaf.' I don't what made it 'downhome,' but it sure does smell great. Would you like me to serve some to you?"

Leslie nodded.

This is one sweet man.

He laid a thick slice of meat loaf on her plate, and some green beans, complete with butter and slivered almonds, and placed a foil-wrapped potato on one side of the plate. A simple salad completed the meal.

"Would you like ketchup with this? Some people swear by it. But I do have some brown gravy. Would you like some for your meat and potato?"

The gravy, smooth and tasty, was in an actual gravy boat, one that matched the plates on the table.

For a time, everything was quiet. Mike carefully and methodically prepared his own food—pouring gravy, adding a little bit of salt, adding a dash of pepper to everything, like he was trying to give each condiment the same attention. He had taken two bites when he set his fork down and declared, "Well, this is actually pretty good."

Leslie agreed at once. "Mike, you're a good cook. Everything tastes delicious. I am so impressed."

He waved off her compliments, though it was obvious he liked receiving them. "It wasn't all that hard. I mean, cooking is easy if you have a recipe to follow. And it helps if you have company that you really like."

He's trying his best to impress me ... but in a sweet way.

They chatted about Mrs. DiGiulio's kindergarten class and how both Ava and Trevor just adored her, and that Mike was still concerned that Trevor would have "issues" as he grew older. Learning issues, Mike said.

"When his mom left, he was real young, but it hit him hard. He still doesn't understand. To be honest, I still don't either. I'm just afraid that not having a mom will affect him somehow. Make him more squirrelly than he already is. Make it hard for him to concentrate or something. You read magazines nowadays and everyone is telling you how hard it is for a child to grow up in a single-parent home. Even my pastor last Sunday was talking about it, and how the men of the church should seek out the families without a dad and help be a father figure. Well, that's true, but no one ever talks about providing a mother figure for the kids without a mom. I mean ... I know there are fewer of us, but Trevor really wants a mom. I can see it in his eyes."

Leslie felt his eyes on her as he spoke. She was certain that he did not mean to be as direct as he sounded, but she was also sure that Mike would love it if Leslie could provide that mother figure.

"It's hard. I know all about it," Leslie said, commiserating. "People forget how much work there is and how hard it is and how lonely it gets sometimes."

Mike's eyes seemed to light when he heard her agreeing with him.

"It can get lonely. And this house ... I mean, it isn't all that big, but it's big enough for four people, for sure. Maybe even more."

Mike's eyes met Leslie's and for a moment, seemed to link, then there was something in the exchange that shifted, and Leslie looked away. When she looked back, she was all but sure that Mike saw the gesture as one of flirtation. He was smiling, smiling in a self-satisfied way, as if discovering the solution to a very difficult problem. Then he reached over the table and took Leslie's right hand and held it, even squeezed it a bit.

"It's big enough for four. It really is."

And Leslie remained silent, not sure if it were simply a statement of fact, or if Mike intended it to be an invitation or a proposal, or something else all together.

Whatever the intent behind his hand-holding and dinner and smile, Leslie remained unsure of the proper response, the sort of response that might have made sense to her.

I know ... I know ... I know what he's asking.

She closed her eyes.

Am I ready to answer that question? Maybe not just yet. But ...

Later that evening, Leslie sat in her bed, without the light, just sitting in the dark, reviewing the evening. Mike, of course, had driven them both home early, since it was a school night.

Ava had not run up the steps as she had before but had waited with her mother at the bottom of the steps. There would be no good-night kiss with sons and daughters so close.

Mike had looked about and had given Leslie a quick hug instead, and even that got the close eye of Ava, who had nearly squinted as she watched.

As Ava had gotten ready for bed, she'd told her mother that she'd had a good time, and that Trevor sure had a lot of video games and DVDs for a little kid, and maybe that's why he was so jumpy in school.

"I tried one game and I couldn't figure out when to make the little man jump on time. Trevor was real good at it."

The entire evening spoke of Mike's tenderness, his thoughtfulness, and his careful preparation.

He really tried hard. No one has ever done anything like that for me. Certainly not Randy. I'm not even sure he knows how to work a stove or oven. Mike thought of everything. And the meat loaf was really good. He did a good job with the whole thing.

She fluffed her pillow and lay down.

She waited for the panic to set in. She had waited for the panic all night. She had almost called him to cancel earlier in the day—not because she felt panicked, but because she was terrified of becoming so during their meal. Instead, she had begun to pray, and did so silently through the entire night, uncertain at first, with simple words from her heart—just as Pastor Blake suggested.

She waited even now for the chest tightness to begin, the sweating, the shallow, urgent breathing. But nothing had happened. None of her usual triggers had started anything. She remained … normal.

Having an un-date with Mike, having Mike talk about … marriage, she thought, would have been perfect triggers before. But not tonight.

I wonder if that means I'm comfortable with him.

She turned to her left side.

I am comfortable with him. He's easy to be with. He is a gentleman.

She turned to her right side, trying to compress the pillow to the exact thickness required.

I like him. I really do.

She flipped onto her back, feeling as if the comforter was attempting to tangle her legs in a knot. She tossed the comforter to the side and made sure the thin thermal blanket was in place.

But do I like him enough?

The thought stayed with her, even as she drifted off to an almost restful sleep.

Amelia Westland, age twenty-one years, six months
Lyndora
Butler County, Pennsylvania
January 27, 1884

Standing before a room of students perplexes me at times, occasionally frightens me still, yet at the close of the day, when the disappearing sun colors the sky scarlet, the process of passing on knowledge to children invigorates me and passion floods my veins. It is as if God has ordained me to teach, for there is much joy in the work set before me. I do not know, and am hesitant to ask my students, if they share such an evaluation of my abilities. If they were to respond in the negative, I am sure my enthusiasm would suffer a serious blow. (Yet I think, and pray, that they would find me earnest, and our days filled with a desire to learn and grow.)

There are presently twenty students in the class: four in first, four in second, three in third, five in fourth, two in fifth, and two in the last grade, six. Some allow the lessons to soak into their souls; others fight and stammer on occasion. I have noted some students' anxieties, much like my own, and therefore I am able to offer counsel and comfort.

The director of schools for the entire county, a Mr. William Styles, a refined gentleman of much breeding and education, sat in on my class last week, and presented me with a good recommendation and praised much of what he had observed that day. Such reviews are rare, I am told. In this, God continues to show Himself faithful; for it is only in His power I am able to flourish.

> *The LORD is my strength and my shield; my heart trusted in him,*
> *and I am helped: therefore my heart greatly rejoiceth;*
> *and with my song will I praise him.*
> —Psalm 28:7

CHAPTER NINETEEN

LESLIE SAT IN CUNNINGHAM'S ICE-CREAM/COFFEE shop, hoping she would not run into anyone she knew. Mike would be at work, so he most likely would not stop here. His cousin seemed only to be around in the afternoon. She had not made that many friends in Butler yet, so she felt safe making a cell phone call from her booth.

The number now was familiar to her.

"Pastor Blake? I hate to always bother you."

"Leslie, it's no bother. Trust me. I get paid for this, remember? And if I didn't want to take your calls, I could let them go into voice mail, right?"

"I know you're being kind to me. And I appreciate that."

Leslie allowed the barista to add coffee to her three-quarters-filled mug. The dilutions of sugar and cream had been perfect, and now the ratios were all different. She would have waved the pleasant young man off, but this way, she bought herself a bit more privacy since he would not be around for a while. She sprinkled in a hazing of sugar and a dribble of cream.

"What can I do for you this morning?"

Leslie quickly related the story of last night's dinner, leaving out some of it, but claiming a small victory.

"An evening like this would have been sure to trigger panic in the past."

"That's wonderful, Leslie. There is hope, right?"

"I'm doing what you told me to do. It works. Or is working."

The pastor let a moment of silence form.

"Pastor, I have a question. Nothing about panic attacks."

"Go ahead."

"Should you be with someone … allow yourself to be with someone … just because it's safe?"

"Safe? You mean, like 'not dangerous'? Or like 'just good enough'?"

Leslie nodded, even knowing the pastor couldn't see her.

"Yes. No. Not safe from danger, but just safe. Like you said: just good enough. No fireworks. No stirring desire. You know, like between a man and a woman."

Leslie hoped he couldn't tell she was blushing—keenly embarrassed by what her question implied.

"No need to be embarrassed, Leslie. Pastors get to deal with the whole body—not just the mind and soul."

This brought silence to her side of the conversation.

Does he get questions like this often?

"It's not an everyday question," he replied, causing Leslie to be surprised again. "But if you want my personal opinion—the answer is yes. You know, back in the times of Jesus, and when the Bible was written, there was not a lot said about romantic love. Sacrifice and commitment—yes. Lust—yes, like in David's life—but not love as we talk about it today."

"So … is it okay?"

"Leslie, here's my pulled-punch counselor's response: Only you can decide that. I just read an article on the Web …"

He goes on the Internet? A pastor?

"… about some book a woman wrote on 'settling.' Her premise was that a lot of modern women wait their whole lives for a perfect man who will fit every preconception they have. And they reject a lot of men who are pretty good, even very good, but not perfect. Is there a perfect mate for all of us? I'm not sure. Does God have one and only one person out there that we have to find or else He will be unhappy with our choice? We will be unhappy? I hope not. What would happen if I were sick the day I was supposed to meet that person? I think our task is to find somebody we respect, enjoy being with, who shares our values, understands us, perhaps—someone with whom we experience a deep friendship, perhaps. And if they don't set off Roman candles, so be it. That part of love fades quickly for most couples."

"So … is it okay?"

Pastor Blake sighed. "Have you found someone? Is Mike Reidmiller the person you're talking about?"

I keep forgetting that Butler is really a small town.

"Maybe. I don't know. He could be. I mean … yes, it's Mike, but I don't know where things are. Maybe that's what is making the panic attacks go away."

The voice of the pastor grew firm, and he quickly responded.

"Leslie—do not confuse the two issues. The panic attacks are a separate thing. Mike has nothing to do with them. If you like him, fine. If you really like him, go with it. But go slow. You're not a teenager anymore. Romantic love changes when you're older. You're a mother, too. You have to consider your daughter. Everything changes. So my advice is to go slow."

Leslie was nodding the whole time.

"And pray about it," the pastor continued. "God has promised to guide those who ask for His help."

"You're right. You're right. I'll pray. And go slow. And I won't expect fireworks."

Like the ones I feel with Jack …

She slipped the phone back into her purse. The barista, probably bored that there were only a few customers in the store, stopped at the table again, with a coffeepot in one hand and a hopeful smile on his face, eyebrows arched in supplication.

"Sure, a little more would be fine," Leslie said, lying, knowing that this new coffee would disrupt her perfect arrangement of coffee, cream, and sugar once again.

Grandma Amelia prayed about such things. I guess I could too …

Saturday came, and Leslie had spent the previous twenty-four hours in a state of dread. The panic—well, the panic was not entirely out of the equation that was her life, but it had diminished. Whatever Pastor Blake had said or done, or what he'd encouraged her to do—pray—had helped. And perhaps, Leslie thought, it was the mere fact of sharing it, opening up about her situation that was working to diffuse it.

But yet, as the visit from her ex-husband neared, she grew closer and closer to the edge of that familiar panic. The anxiety was fueled by the terror she felt—the terror that she might lose her one and only daughter.

She prayed the only prayer that she knew how to pray.

Oh, God. Help me. Help me … give me peace.

He had said he would be there at 10:00 in the morning on Saturday. He had never been a man whose word she could depend on, so Leslie had told Ava he would be there by lunch. If he arrived early, it would simply be a surprise to her, rather than her being crushed at waiting for hours in anticipation.

Leslie couldn't help it. She paced back and forth in the apartment, even though she knew her pacing set Ava off in a bad way. Ava would see the pacing and worry that her mother was falling into a self-destructive pattern. So instead of pacing in front of Ava, Leslie left the girl watching Saturday-morning cartoons, a rare treat, for Leslie did not appreciate the content of most of those programs, and walked downstairs, so she could pace outside in the chilly morning air. She told Ava she was stepping outdoors for a breath of fresh air and would be on the sidewalk in front of the building.

She only took a sweater, so Ava wouldn't think she was set on intercepting her father before he came upstairs, but it was enough. She checked her wristwatch every few minutes, starting at 9:30.

She waved through the front display windows to Alice and Frank, who were explaining something to each other, in loud animated voices, their arms swinging and gesturing. They both stopped when they saw her and stared at her, their faces both a large question mark.

"I'm waiting for someone," she said, loudly, to carry through the thick glass.

"You can wait in here," Alice shouted back, then mimed being frozen, wrapping her arms around herself.

"Thank you, but I'm fine. Where's Jack?"

Both of them, as if on cue, spun around, looking for him, as if they expected him to be there. They both thought each other's actions hilarious, and Frank finally shouted back, "He's working on the Pettigrews' place. We're waiting on some permits. But that doesn't stop either of us from obsessing about things. I hope you don't mind us being here."

Leslie thought about miming back, but couldn't think of anything specific, so she simply said loudly, "It's fine. You go back to work. Don't let me bother you."

She turned back to the street, feeling empowered, to a degree. She was now a businesswoman of sorts, or at least a landlord, and that felt good. She paced from the Stickles' door, marked with a skewed plastic name-plate, and a smiling stained-glass angelic cherub, held on the window glass with a suction cup, then back to the front door of the Midlands Building, soon to be the home of Alice and Frank's. Leslie considered it an odd name, until Mrs. Stickle told her that the couple had "made millions" with their store of the same name in Shadyside. Leslie doubted that they had made millions, but she was fairly certain the store had been profitable.

They dress better than anyone I've seen in Butler—or anywhere, bar none.

Then she turned and walked back, a half-block circuit.

She did not see his car, but she saw him. He must have parked around the corner. She glanced at her watch. It was 10:30. Her heart started to beat fast, not yet panic—fast, but fast like that moment in class when the teacher angrily announces a pop quiz—on the only day that you hadn't done the required reading.

He did not wave, or acknowledge her, until a few feet away. Then he stopped and eyed her critically.

He's gained weight. And his hair is thinner. Maybe it's the cut.

"Hello, Leslie. I'll have you know it took me two hours to get here. And I stayed at the speed limit the whole time. Two hours. That's not just a trip around the block. Two full hours."

She knew he was lying but would not belabor the point. The first time she and Ava drove from Greensburg, when Leslie was not sure of the route, and half afraid to be on her own, it took one hour and twenty minutes, including two potty breaks for Ava.

"This doesn't make a father's visitation an easy task, Leslie. I want to go on record as telling you that."

The judge had allowed her to move within the state.

"If you leave Pennsylvania, if you plan on relocating, you must alert the clerk of the court of that decision. I will decide if parties need to gather to adjudicate the matter. Is that understood?" he had said.

Leslie had agreed and asked if relocating to Butler fit into the custody guidelines. It did.

"You packed on a few pounds. You been eating fast-food trash again? Are you cooking for Ava at all?"

I've lost weight. From stress … because of what you …

She stopped herself.

I will not go to that place. God, help me not to go there.

He folded his arms across his chest. He was wearing the khaki jacket that she had purchased for him for his birthday. He had claimed that the style was wrong and that she had no idea of what he wanted—or looked good in—and that only a blind man would be caught wearing it. He had tossed it into the corner of the closet and left it there, until he demanded that she clean things up. She had put it on a hanger and didn't touch it ever again.

"Are you dating? You are seeing men, now, aren't you? Someone like you can't do without, can you? Or do all the men in Butler already know how crazy you are?" He grinned at her. "No. I shouldn't say crazy. Lisa always reminds me of that. She says I should say 'mentally unbalanced.'"

Lisa? Giving him advice on what to say about me?

"So you have nothing to say to me? It's been a long time, Leslie. You've done nothing I would find interesting? Figures. You haven't changed a bit. You're as worthless as you've always been. I should go to court for custody of Ava so she'll at least have a better chance with her life."

The front door opened and Ava tore past her mother, her arms outstretched, her hair streaming behind her.

"Daddy! Daddy!" she shouted, glee obvious in her voice. He bent down and scooped her up and spun her around two times, then set her down and knelt in front of her.

"You are getting so big, Ava. I hardly recognize you. Like a weed, you're growing so fast. Is your mother feeding you too many fast-food hamburgers with all those bad growth hormones in them?"

Ava leaned back and turned to her mother, with a most curious look, like she wasn't sure if her father were kidding, or if her mother was trying to make her grow up faster. "Nooo, Daddy. We hardly ever eat out."

Randy looked up at his ex-wife. "Well, Ava, Daddy will take you out to a real restaurant for a change. Get you out of that cramped old apartment, what do you say about that? And ice cream, too. I bet you don't get a lot of ice cream, either, do you?"

Ava turned to her mother again. "Do I get enough ice cream, Mommy?"

Leslie wanted to scream. "I think you do fine, Ava."

Randy stood up, took his daughter's hand, and stage-whispered to Leslie, "We'll be back by five, maybe sooner, so don't go anywhere. Wait here for us. You got that?"

Leslie fought the old feelings, stirred up this morning, as best she could, until she felt things crumble, just a bit. "I'll be here."

Ava didn't look back as they walked away, almost breaking Leslie's heart. But she'd known somehow, even before this morning, that Ava wouldn't look back, and had tried to steel herself to the fact when it happened. They turned the corner, walking away from downtown.

She looked down at her right hand. It was responding like the proverbial leaf in the wind. She quickly grabbed it with her left hand, to stop it, to stop the actions of her body, to try and prevent their betrayal, to force herself to stand up, to stand up for herself, to respect her own self.

She tried, she really, really tried, but he knew her too well. He knew where to attack, at her meager resources, at her awakening desire, at her lack of worth. He knew. And if he could do all that damage with a few words …

Leslie wasn't sure if she could be strong enough to face him and stare him down.

Let God fight for you, Pastor Blake had said.

As Ava and her father slipped around the corner, the front door to the Stickles' opened. Mrs. Stickle peered out, grabbed the newspaper that was on the step, clutching at the robe she had draped over her normal house-dress. She was wearing her once-fuzzy slippers.

"Leslie, dear, it's cold out here. What are doing standing there in only a sweater? I saw you from the window. Get inside before you catch your death."

Leslie didn't move, not right away.

"Leslie? Are you okay?" Mrs. Stickle asked in her most grandmotherly voice. "Would you like some tea?"

It was then that Leslie turned, the anguish obvious on her face. "Yes, Mrs. Stickle, some tea would be great."

In minutes, the teakettle began to whistle, and Mrs. Stickle began her tea-making ceremony. This time there were no gingersnaps, but a plate of Lorna Doones instead.

"Where is Mr. Stickle?" Leslie asked, just to make conversation.

The older woman shrugged. "Who knows?"

Then she laughed, picked up the teapot, and sat down at their kitchen table. "His nephew picked him up to go to some car show in Pittsburgh. He has always loved cars, but neither of us drives anymore, so I don't see the purpose in it. I suppose it's like going to a movie with handsome men in it. They'll never be calling me to ask for a date, but I still enjoy looking at them."

Leslie nearly laughed aloud.

"Was that your ex I saw with Ava?"

Leslie nodded.

"I have to ask. I mean, these days, I guess it doesn't matter. Ex-husband or ex-boyfriend?"

"Ex-husband. We were divorced over a year ago. This is really the first time he has come to Butler to see his daughter. We lived closer before. Even then he didn't come around that often."

Mrs. Stickle chewed her second cookie thoughtfully. "Does Ava know anything about it? She's such a sweet little girl. But she's never mentioned anything about the divorce. Not that I asked her or anything."

"She knows we have to live apart. She accepts it, I think. But she misses having a father. She talks about Trevor Reidmiller and how it's so sad that he doesn't have a mommy...."

"That's Agnes and Merle's grandson, right? Mike's son?"

"That's what you said."

"Well, that woman Mike married was a tramp. A tramp, I tell you. In the worst sense of the word. I remember that Agnes told her son not to go through with the wedding, but Michael was older, a little bit older, and I think he thought he would never have another chance. Such a shame. Then her getting pregnant. I'm glad that the little boy looks like his father. I mean ... with that woman, you would never know for sure."

Leslie listened, almost glad there was another story being told—a story that didn't involve her and her pain.

"But ... that's a whole different ball of wax," Mrs. Stickle said, as if recognizing her landlord's discomfort. "Though I don't know what balls of wax have to do with it."

Leslie picked up a cookie and nibbled at it. It tasted like cardboard in her mouth. "He shows up, and I immediately think he wants to have custody of Ava. I get so scared about it. I couldn't live without Ava."

Mrs. Stickle did what any proper grandmother would do in this situation. She shuffled her chair close to Leslie and put her frail arms around her. "Not to worry, Leslie. God wouldn't let that happen. You're a good mom. I see that. Everything will work out fine."

A month ago, Leslie would have gone into panic mode. But not today. A month ago, she would have started to hyperventilate, sweat, and tremble. All of those conditions were not far from the surface, but none of them manifested themselves. Instead she relaxed, thankful for the simple peace and security that Mrs. Stickle offered to her. She sat, comforted—not happy, but not desperate or terrified.

"You let God take care of things, dear. He will make it right. You have to trust. Just like that preacher on TV says. You know—the one with the curly hair—the one from Pittsburgh."

Leslie had no idea who she meant, but nodded anyhow.

"He says that God loves us and has a plan for our lives. I believe that. I do. He does love us. You have to let Him love you, Leslie. Open your heart. You have to trust."

Is that why I've changed, God? Are You why I'm not panicking?

Leslie sat back up as Mrs. Stickle shuffled her chair back into position, and took a second cookie.

This time it tasted better, almost as if a Lorna Doone was the perfect cookie to eat after your ex-husband has just taken your most precious thing in the entire world with him, and you do not have any idea where they are.

Open my heart? Trust? Can I do that?

<hr />

The downstairs buzzer rang and Leslie jumped to the entry to unlock the downstairs front door with her buzzer. Randy said five o'clock, and it was only two in the afternoon. She pressed it for five seconds, then swung open her door and hurried to the second-floor landing.

Ava came running up the stairs, her little feet clad in plaid sneakers, thumping like a horse.

Randy, remaining downstairs, made no move to step into the building. He just leaned in. "I have to go. It's a long drive home. But then, you're well aware of that. And Ava had a wonderful time. We all did. Be prepared for me to call you this week."

He stepped out and the door latched behind him.

Leslie remained, staring at the door, until she heard the electronic chatter from the television behind her. She walked back into the living room, not wanting to interrogate her daughter, but keenly interested in what had transpired. Ava had not seen her father for months and had spent only a few hours with him—when he had claimed they would be together all day.

"You have fun, sweetie?"

Ava shrugged, not turning her attention from the cartoon on the screen. "I dunno. I guess."

Leslie promised herself, over and over, that she would remain calm and settled. "What did you do? Your father said something about shopping."

Ava turned to her mother, a quizzical look on her face. "We didn't shop. He drove around a lot. He talked to that new lady."

"Lisa?"

"I guess. He doesn't like Butler. He said it stinks."

Leslie waited.

"Does it stink, Mommy?"

"No, sweetie, it doesn't. It's a perfectly nice town. Did you and Lisa talk?"

Ava didn't appear upset or troubled. Leslie was happy she had that kind of child who accepted things as they were and never became agitated over the way things should be.

"Maybe. A little. She asked if I was hungry."

"Were you?"

"No. But we ate at the funny restaurant. The one at the top of the hill."

"Which one?"

"The one with the funny name."

"Dingbats?" They had eaten there once. Leslie thought the food was good but the environment frantic.

"Yeah. That one. I had chicken fingers."

"Did you go for ice cream?"

"Daddy said it was too cold for ice cream. He said you only eat ice cream in the summer."

Leslie waited.

"Can I still eat ice cream when it's cold, Mommy? I like ice cream a lot."

"Of course you can, sweetie."

Leslie waited. "Anything else? You do anything else?"

Ava shrugged again. "I don't think so. We drove around. It was okay."

Leslie waited. "Your daddy said he might come back to see you in a little while. Would that be okay with you?"

"I guess. Sure. Maybe."

Leslie stood up and walked into the kitchen, away from Ava's sight. She lifted her hand to reach for a coffee cup and could barely garner the strength to pick it up.

Leslie couldn't tell if it was from relief or anxiety, or maybe both.

Amelia Westland

Lyndora

Butler County, Pennsylvania

July 4, 1884

I have ceased marking each entry with my age. It seems a childish affectation, yet I am loath to cease it, since it has marked every entry in this diary to date. But when one becomes an adult, one must put away childish things.

I find the greatest pleasure in having a dwelling place of my own, my own private quarters in the teacherage. No one enters it, save me. Yet I am not lonely, for the children fill my days until dusk, and the peaceful nights are most welcome. The bed is fine, and most comfortable. The mothers of the children are exceedingly appreciative of my attentions to their offspring. Many have given me bread, or eggs, or quilts they no longer have use for. The space that was once sparse is now flush with many beautiful objects. I have gotten a few new skirts and blouses made up, of a simple and serviceable style and of durable fabric, such as are appropriate for a woman in my position. I have enjoyed frequent visits here from Catherine.

I find myself in such a wonderful mood. I have met with my Julian again. He could not come here, not by himself, for if he were observed visiting a single female schoolteacher alone ... why, there might be serious repercussions for us both. No, we met at a picnic sponsored by his church, a well-respected Lutheran church, to which I was invited by Julian. Since there were crowds of people in attendance, there was no need to worry about neither chaperones nor gossip. He managed to procure a seat at my table, where we partook of refreshment together.

The weather was perfect: not overly warm, with some clouds and sun. He inquired as to my days and how I have gotten on in Butler. We chatted as comfortable as any couple might—conversing, laughing, posing questions, positing opinions on some town matters and diverse other topics.

Oh ... but evening was drawing our time together to a close. I dearly wished to linger, however, I stood and thought to excuse myself, for I had a walk of thirty minutes to my home. The pastor of this Lutheran church, a most agreeable man, bid me farewell, but refused to let me, a single woman, walk all that way alone. Since no mode of conveyance nor chaperone could be offered, he assigned a young man to provide me escort, one in whom his implicit trust resides—a certain Mr. Julian Beck. I was in heaven.

Once out of sight of the crowds, in the growing darkness, Julian took my hand and I near swooned. What else might have been discussed between us from that point on, I have no recollection. I am assuming that Mr. Beck will call on me again, owing to his most forward nature.

> *I will praise thee, O LORD, with my whole heart;*
> *I will shew forth all thy marvellous works.*
> *I will be glad and rejoice in thee:*
> *I will sing praise to thy name, O thou most High.*
> —PSALM 9:1–2

CHAPTER TWENTY

IN THE PAST, JACK USED to enjoy watching college football games on television. He would get a six-pack of beer, a big bag of chips, maybe some dip, and while away a pleasant Saturday afternoon. But he could no longer do that. He could no longer drink a six-pack of beer or *any* amount of beer. And he found that, without the beer, the games did not interest him as much as he thought. The beer had been the real attraction.

He had stopped at Alice and Frank's—not to work, but to ask if they had any blueprints yet from their architect.

"If I have to draw up a firm quote, I have to see what sort of materials he is specifying," Jack had said.

Frank had all but waved him off. "What about just doing time and materials?" Frank suggested. "Isn't that what you contractor folks are always asking for? So you never have to worry about underbidding a job?"

Jack had to agree. This job was made for time and materials. He imagined that Alice might be inclined to change her mind when the actual work was being performed.

"Then we'll do time and materials," Frank had stated again. "You work fast. We'll be here all the time, so I doubt you'll be sleeping on the job too often."

So instead of having preliminary plans to start working on a quote, he had nothing to do. None of the three games that he could get on his tiny television had any personal interest for him—no alma maters, no schools he wished he could have gone to—just big Midwestern schools that had teams that rivaled the professionalism of professional football teams.

He thought about going for a drive, but he didn't want to be stuck in his truck for an afternoon—especially since he wasn't in an exploring mood.

Maybe I'll just go for a walk. Maybe get lunch.

He grabbed his coat and headed out, straight for The Palm. He debated, on the several-block walk, if this was a wise choice.

What if Earl is not there? What if I don't recognize the bartender? What happens if I ask for a beer?

He told himself that this trip would be fine, that he would simply get lunch, then walk back to his apartment. Maybe he would drive out to the truck dealership and finally get a replacement mirror for the one that had been torn off.

It would just be lunch. A burger. Nothing else. A Coke. That's it.

He slowed as he approached the tavern, knowing that this sort of brinksmanship could prove dangerous. He had come too close to the edge before … and fallen.

This time is different. This time I mean it.

He had told himself those same words before, maybe those exact words.

He walked in, took his seat at the bar, and waited, tapping his fingers on the polished surface of the wooden bar.

I will only order a burger. I have a meeting to go to tonight, and I'm not going in drunk.

He waited, and the bartender with the heavy plastic glasses and a tight white shirt buttoned to the neck, sidled up.

"Yes?"

Jack looked up. "Where's Earl?"

"Earl?"

"The other bartender. The one that's usually here."

"Earl?"

"Yes, Earl. He's a friend of mine. Where is he today?"

"Oh … Earl. He's not here."

Jack spread his hands on the bar, palms down. "And do you know where he is?"

"In the hospital."

To say Jack was surprised would be an understatement. "Hospital? What hospital? Why?"

The other bartender shrugged. "Don't know why. The owner called me this morning to work for him. Said he was in Butler Memorial—the one on Brady Street."

Jack jumped off the stool.

It would be as quick to walk there—or jog—as it would be to run back and get my truck.

Jack didn't jog, but he walked as fast as he could. If he had tried to run, he would have arrived sweating and out of breath, looking more like a patient than a visitor.

———

Earl was in room 407. Jack stood in the doorway, trying to get a look inside without being noticed.

A nurse slipped up beside him. "You can go in. He's by himself. And he was awake five minutes ago."

The television bolted to the wall played softly, as if background music. There was some monitoring device on a stand that beeped every so often. Jack shuffled in, making sure he wouldn't cause any undue noise.

"Hey, Earl," he called out softly.

Earl, lying flat and faceup, rolled to his left slightly and raised his head off the pillow. "Mr. Kenyon. Nice to see you. How are you doing?"

Jack moved more quickly to the chair by the side of the bed. He sat down. "I'm okay, Earl. How are you?"

Earl pursed his lips, as if he were considering his answer. "Well, Mr. Kenyon, nice of you to ask. I'm dying. I don't know the fancy doctor term for it, but 'dying' works okay for me."

Jack looked around, as if someone might come out from behind the curtain and yell, "Surprise!" But there was no shout. It was simply Earl, lying in a stark hospital bed, with white sheets, a television with bad reception, a curtain dividing the room, the scent of alcohol and disinfectant, and blurred, garbled announcements, repeated again and again out in the hall, over the hospital's public address system.

"What do you mean, dying? Doctors can fix things, Earl."

Earl blinked at him, as if trying to focus.

I don't know why I'm so … worried about this. I've only known this man for a couple of months.

"Doctors can't fix everything. Cirrhosis is something that they can't fix. Slow it down some, I guess. But fix it? Nope. Can't do that."

Jack wanted to reach out and take him by the hand or hug him or something but did not. "But you looked healthy. You were working last week. You looked fine."

Earl coughed a little and maneuvered himself to almost a sitting position. He was wearing faded green hospital pajamas, with a laundry number written on the hem of the collar. The skin below his neck was white, almost garish yellowish-white, lined deeply, mottled.

"'It is better to look good than to feel good,'" Earl said, smiling. "Wasn't that a line from a TV show?"

"It was, Earl. From *Saturday Night Live.* Billy Crystal."

"Yeah. Little things went bad. Then big things went bad. Like an old car that nickel-and-dimes you to death, until the engine block cracks and then there ain't anything anyone can do to fix it."

"Are they sure? I mean … what about other doctors, or better hospitals?" Jack asked in a whisper, as if the doctors would take offense at his suggestion.

"Yeah. Everybody is sure. Second and third opinions. And this is a pretty good place, as hospitals go."

Jack rubbed his hands over his face.

"A couple of months."

"What?" Jack replied, not having asked any question.

"I got a couple of months. I know you didn't ask, but people want to know. If you have a couple of years, then people go back to being normal and treating you like they've always treated you. A couple of years is a long time to be real nice to someone. But a couple of months … people treat you real good, 'cause they know it won't be long."

"Earl, that isn't true. People are nicer than that. You have to give them credit."

Earl turned his head and squinted at Jack, as if trying to draw the truth out of him.

Jack finally said, "Well … maybe you're right. Or partly right."

A nurse bustled into the room, went to the far side of the bed, grabbed Earl's arm, slapped a blood pressure cuff on his upper arm, pumped almost furiously for a moment, then grabbed his wrist and watched the large clock on the wall of the room. She dropped his arm, clicked a pen from her coat, made a notation on the chart, and then marched out of the room, all without uttering a single word.

"And she's the nice one," Earl said when he was sure she was out of earshot.

Jack had to laugh at that but held his laughter quiet—out of respect, he guessed, or guilt. "Earl, do you have any family? I could call them. Or has someone done that for you?"

Earl slipped down a bit against his pillow. "No. No family. Nobody to call."

Jack didn't believe him. "Everybody has some family. Aunts? Uncles? Cousins? Somebody."

Earl closed his eyes. "Nope."

Jack waited. He knew what lies were. He had been the master of deception for so long that he was able to spot a falsehood as soon as it was uttered. He knew Earl wasn't telling the truth. His words, his tone, reminded Jack of … of Jack, a few years ago, when if he said that the sun rose in the east, you would wake up and check it out for yourself.

He waited. He knew that lies had a short shelf life.

"Do you want coffee? Something from downstairs? I saw a snack bar or cafeteria there. Can I get you anything?"

He waited.

"A coffee. The stuff I get here is weak and cold and decaf. So try for hot and strong and regular."

Before getting the coffee, Jack sat for a moment by himself and wondered how he would feel if the situation had been reversed and he were lying in the hospital bed with a few months left to live. Who would be there for him?

My parents … but I'm not sure they would care. My brother. But it's been a long time since we've talked. Aunts and uncles—but my parents—somebody would let them know. They'd want to know … even after all that's happened.

He didn't find it curious that he thought of his wife and daughter. It was never curious. It was something else all together—but not curious.

Maybe I'm as alone as Earl is.

He purchased three cups of coffee and tossed in a handful of plastic creamers and a dozen packets of sugar—one cup for himself, and the other two for Earl. One cup was often not enough, so the second cup was insurance.

He came back into the room. Earl had gotten himself into a sitting position and was staring intently at the television.

"I brought cream and sugar."

"Black is fine for me."

Jack took off the plastic lid and placed the cup on the small nightstand. They both watched five minutes of national headlines.

"Are you sure there is no one to call?" Jack asked.

Earl set the half-full coffee cup back on the nightstand. "Listen. Mr. Kenyon. You're prying now, you know that? You think I'm lying to you. You think because you're a good liar, or used to be a good liar, that you know how to spot a lie. Well, maybe you do. I was right where you're sitting, so I know how you feel."

Earl spoke more harshly than Jack expected. He was almost angry. "I was married once. Who wasn't? I drank a lot. Got arrested a few times. Got into fights. My wife—my ex-wife—gave as good as she got … maybe better. But that's all water under the bridge. She left, said she never wanted to have anything to do with me—ever."

"I'm sorry to hear that."

I've heard the same story a hundred times in a hundred AA meetings.

"I had a son. Have a son."

The disclosure wasn't a shocking revelation to Jack.

"I wrote to him a lot. Maybe his mother threw the letters away. I never heard from him. I don't even know if either of them is alive or dead. Being sober for all these years didn't amount to much, you know what I mean, Jack? Sober, drunk—they are all gone, the years. Maybe I should have stayed a drunk for all the good being sober did for me."

"Earl, you know that's not true."

"Bull. I could've stayed drunk, died early, avoided a whole lot of heartache in the process. I don't know. Maybe it was worth it. But maybe it wasn't."

Jack sat quietly. He would have protested loudly, and heartily, but he knew what Earl meant. He knew what Earl was feeling.

You stop feeling bad when you stop drinking. But your problems don't go away. All the crap you did in your past doesn't get erased. It's still crap. Sometimes I wonder if it might not be easier to just let go. Who's going to care, anyhow?

Jack sipped at his coffee and did not say another word for a long time. Earl had slipped down in his bed and the drone of the TV went on. The announcements in the hall continued, and the nurses and the trays and the carts clattered by in a river of muted noise. Afternoon sun filled the room and Earl slipped into a sleep. Jack watched his new friend's chest rise and fall and stared at the dips and beeps on the screen on the monitor by the bed. He wondered what it was monitoring.

Jack had a pen and a small notepad in his pocket. Since starting his business, he always had a pen and pad in his pocket; there were always notes to be taken, reminders to be written, lists to be compiled.

He flipped a few pages to an empty sheet.

He wrote:

> Earl,
> It's worth it. It has to be. If you want me to try and find them, I will. But I won't mention it again, unless you ask. I will visit you tomorrow, right after my meeting.
> Jack

He slipped out of the room and down the busy hall, through the lobby filled with groups and families, almost all with GET WELL SOON helium balloons in tow. He walked onto the street, into the autumn chill, and headed back to The Palm. He still wanted a burger for lunch.

───◦◦◦───

Two weeks after mailing her résumé to the Maridon Museum, the one that Leslie had no idea was only blocks from her home, the curator had called. Mrs. Jewell Pindler spoke with a clipped, almost British accent, which

Leslie thought might be an affectation. And if it was, it was done very well, she'd thought.

"She wants me to interview," Leslie said into the phone. "She said I sounded perfect for the position. What do you think I should do?"

"Just be yourself," Pastor Blake urged, "and relax. If you get the job, fine. If not, you will move on to other opportunities. It's all in God's hands, and He knows what's best. Pray for peace. That's critical."

Of course, she agreed with him. But she'd never fully felt that way. She liked to please people, she knew, and that could sometimes be part of her undoing.

She did pray, though, which was unusual for her, never wanting to bother God with her small problems. But it was feeling more natural. And every time she prayed, God felt closer.

And I should brush up on my Asian art history before the interview, she thought, smiling to herself. *As Gramma Mellie said, "Put wings on your prayers."*

<hr>

The interview went better than Leslie could have hoped. Mrs. Pindler was warm, funny, and actually British.

"How I landed in Butler, of all places, is such a tale. Almost amusing, in a sordid way."

Mrs. Pindler was impressed that Leslie had done an international studies semester in England while in college. And Mrs. Pindler knew Alice.

"I love that woman," Mrs. Pindler nearly shrieked when Leslie told her about their plans for a new café/bistro. "She is the most wickedly stylish, most creative person in all of Butler County. And you have her for a tenant! How deliciously lovely. And her husband, Frank—what a nice chap. They are regular contributors to the museum's endowment fund."

Leslie determined early into the interview that she could do the job, that it sounded like fun, with a variety of responsibilities, including organizing special exhibits, classes, and docent tours. It didn't pay as well as she'd hoped, but the hours would be flexible and the work interesting.

Mrs. Pindler walked her through the four galleries of the main building, all subtly lit to effectively showcase the exquisite details of each work of art. In the first two, ornate jade and ivory sculptures, some as large as four feet tall, sat among delicate Chinese paintings—one of which was a landscape on silk made in the midseventeenth century. Exquisitely decorated Mandarin scrolls filled a third gallery. The fourth gallery displayed the famous collection of Meissen porcelain figures. Leslie was surprised by the whimsy of some of the pieces.

"Well, my dear, I am delighted to have met you," Mrs. Pindler said as they completed their tour. "Our museum board meets in a month." She leaned close and whispered, "A bunch of stuffed shirts, but they do need to be in on this decision. As soon as I can, I will call you."

Leslie left the museum in perhaps the best spirits she'd been in since arriving in Butler.

She and Mrs. Pindler had really hit it off.

Amelia Westland
Lyndora
Butler County, Pennsylvania
August 9, 1884

My Julian is indeed a daring young man. A sealed note was delivered to me in the noon posting.

Stay awake. At moonrise, wait for a sign.

All so enigmatic. At moonrise, some few moments past ten, when all was still and dark, I heard small pebbles raining on my window. I cracked open the door and peered into the moonlight. A figure in dark clothing stole to my door and silently entered my rooms, without being bid to enter.

It was Julian, of course, and when I closed the door, making sure no one had observed his coming, he turned me about, facing him, and embraced me, only stopping the embrace to kiss me in short duration. Then he stepped back, as if waiting for me to object.

I did not.

Behind drawn curtains, we sat in my two chairs, in the dark, side by side, and spoke in near whispers into the wee hours. He told of his dream to leave the livery and travel the west—as an itinerant preacher. His pastor, the same Lutheran pastor who assigned him as my escort—stated that Julian was ready to do just that. He has been fervently studying the Scriptures and has prepared a number of sermons on various passages of Scripture.

When I heard this, I was exceedingly chagrined, but then my Julian again kissed my pouting lips and posed: "Come with me, Amelia. We can travel the west together."

How I will manage to teach on the morrow is beyond my power to imagine.

Create in me a clean heart, O God;
and renew a right spirit within me.
—PSALM 51:10

CHAPTER TWENTY-ONE

JACK PUT HIS EAR TO the door. He heard rustling from inside the vacant apartment. He was certain Leslie hadn't yet rented it out, so it couldn't be new tenants. He carefully inserted his key and, as silently as he could, turned the lock and opened the door just an inch. If there were burglars—though there was nothing in the empty apartment to steal—Jack wanted to make sure Leslie and Ava were safe.

He could see one side of a ladder.

Burglars don't bring ladders into a building, do they?

He leaned in farther.

Leslie was on the ladder, holding a paint roller, attached to an extension, and she was rolling paint on the section of the wall Jack had replaced. She had not heard him.

Silent, he watched her work. She was wearing shorts—cutoff jeans—and an old black T-shirt. He could see the muscles in her arms and legs flex as she moved the roller up and down the wall, applying a coat of primer over the wallboard. Her hair was held back with a bandana, exposing her long neck. A few flecks of white paint were spattered on her cheeks and arms, but a drop cloth carefully lay on the newly sanded floor. He could see the concentration on her face and the tip of her tongue between her closed lips, just a hint, as she worked.

Even with paint on her face, she's so beautiful, Jack thought.

He coughed a little, not wanting to scare her.

She turned toward the noise, and when she saw him, she grinned sheepishly, as if she were caught intruding on his domain, his workspace.

"You do good work, Leslie. You're a good painter."

She laughed. "It's out of necessity. Painters are expensive. I want to save where I can."

She descended the ladder slowly; Jack tried not to stare. She leaned her roller against the middle step, careful not to let any paint drip.

He swallowed hard. "I don't want to interrupt you. I just came back to get a measurement for the lights in the bathroom. I want to make sure the bases will cover the holes I cut."

Leslie took a rag and wiped her hands and tried to get some of the paint spots off her arm. They had already dried.

"I'm a mess."

"No. Real painters always look that way," Jack said. "I mean, not as nice as you, but they do get paint all over themselves."

Leslie smiled. "We're almost done here, aren't we? I could put an ad in the newspaper for this place, couldn't I?"

"You could. You should. A few small things to finish. Having a renter will make things easier, won't it?"

She nodded. "Still no job. So rent money would help a lot."

They looked at each other. The room was still, but it was obvious neither of them were made nervous by that silence.

"I would offer you something to drink, but I know there's nothing in this refrigerator. And there is no place to sit, even if I had something to offer you."

Jack waved her off, even though he wanted an excuse to stay there, to talk with her, to be with her. "That's okay. We could get some coffee or something if you wanted to take a break."

Leslie looked back at the wet wall. "Well, I'm almost done. You could—"

"What?"

"You could get us something to drink and bring it back. I need five or ten minutes more to finish this wall. Then I could take a break without feeling guilty."

With how he was feeling, looking at her in her cutoffs, Jack might have come up with a hundred reasons why this wasn't a good idea, but he didn't want to think about any of those reasons.

"Sure. I can do that. I'll be back in five or ten minutes … with something. Okay? You wait here."

And he slipped out, closed the door, leaving Leslie alone with the paint roller and ladder.

———◦∞◦———

She waited only a heartbeat or two, dipped the roller in the paint tray, and finished the last few feet of the unpainted wall, hoping she didn't look so horrible without makeup and wearing the worst clothing she had found in her closet that morning. With rising excitement, she hoped she could finish and get cleaned up, at least a little, before Jack returned with … whatever.

———◦∞◦———

He had two coffees and two pink cold drinks in a cardboard carrier, with a small bag of cookies, most likely purchased at Cunningham's on Main Street. The silky bag was hard to mistake.

"I didn't know if you wanted hot or cold. I should have asked. So I had to get both. And some cookies. You can't take a break without cookies. If you don't want cold, we can put these in the refrigerator for later."

He handed the carrier to her, then said, "Wait. I'll get chairs."

He returned with two battered lawn chairs that had been floating around the building and had found their way to the first-floor space. Jack set them up—not close together, but not far apart either. He offered her a choice, then took the empty chair.

"This is nice," Leslie said. "Very nice."

Jack nodded, almost happy for the first time in a long time. He was not sure what it was about Leslie, but he found himself pleased to be in her presence, content to just talk with her, about anything. Jack believed in chemistry. Maybe believing in chemistry was part of his undoing. It had been in the past.

He was out of practice, knowing what a woman might be thinking, but he was pretty sure that she enjoyed this small connection—this brief sharing of lives—too.

Jack asked her about Ava and her school and how she was faring, being new in town. Leslie chattered away about Mrs. DiGiulio, and what a fantastic teacher she was and how much her daughter was enjoying the experience.

After a few moments, they both stopped talking. Jack watched her hands, the way they moved, the way she held her cup—not delicately, but with purpose and style. He looked at her soft throat, not wanting to stare, not wanting to be obvious. He watched her eyes, her beautiful mouth.

Later, as he remembered this little slice of an afternoon, he would recall being at peace with her and almost being at peace with himself. At the same time, he could feel his heart … *dance is the word, I guess. She makes my heart dance.*

He knew then, for certain, that this was the woman who was meant to be in his life. He didn't allow himself to believe, totally, that she was thinking the same thing he was thinking, but he hoped she was. *Is that what I read in her eyes? That she feels the same way?*

He had almost convinced himself that she no longer saw him as the drunk who called her in desperation in the dark of the night.

Jack had completed the vacant apartment and had done a very good job. The tub held up the completion for more than a week, but now it was installed, and Leslie had repainted the whole apartment by herself, working for a few hours a day while Ava was in school. She had done a thorough job on painting—not exceptional, but far from amateurish. Jack had complimented her on the final inspection, and even Alice and Frank added their approval.

She knew he had another job to do before he started on the downstairs restaurant, and that was why she never saw him. She would have called, she would have sought him out, but with everything else going on in her life, she knew that one thing she didn't need was additional drama.

Not that she thought Jack was bad drama, but he had demons in his life, she knew, and, at the moment, Leslie was reluctant to take on any additional worries.

But I still think about him—a lot of the time. I still think he needs someone. And he is … so handsome. Maybe that's why I'm thinking about him. Not that Mike isn't handsome, in his own way. But when I was painting, and we sat and talked, there was something amazing there. Demons or not, there was definitely something there. Something very, very special.

Now, turning the corner with an armful of groceries, Leslie almost ran into Jack as he ducked out of the first-floor space.

"I haven't seen you in a while," Leslie said as she regained her grip on the two paper bags. She always answered the question "Paper or plastic?" with "Paper," since that could be recycled, even though she had recently read an article that said paper bags used more energy to produce.

She could see that Jack was doing his best to hide the fact that he was uncomfortable. At least, that is what she saw—his eyes averted, his shoulders slumped a bit, maybe carrying a bit of guilt.

"I guess I've just been busy, Leslie. Busier than I thought. I started that other job—a kitchen and bath. You met the couple, remember? The Pettigrews?"

"I do," Leslie said, shifting the bags in her arms. "They seemed nice. Very excited with their new house."

"Let me help you with those," Jack said, taking both bags from her. "I'll take them upstairs."

"You don't have to do that."

"Least I can do. No bother at all."

He followed her upstairs and set the bags carefully on the kitchen counter. He leaned his back against it and crossed his arms, the muscles in them flexing. Leslie tried not to think about his muscular forearms or how it would feel to touch them.…

"Do you have the vacant apartment rented?" Jack asked. "Mrs. Stickle said that she had a nephew or niece or someone who was looking."

"A niece—and I guess that makes her husband a nephew-in-law to Mrs. Stickle. They looked at the place, and loved it. They would have rented it, but they have three months to go on their current lease. I told them if it's still not rented by then, I'll let them know. A few other lookers, but no one's signed anything yet."

"Someone will soon enough. It's such a nice unit." Jack stepped backward toward the front door.

Leslie saw the move and reacted with her emotions this time, not thinking it through, not debating, just acting. She hardly ever followed her emotions. Her father always said that emotions couldn't be trusted. "Be safe. Think things through" was his motto.

"Do you have to take off right away?" Leslie said as friendly as she could. "I was about to make coffee. Or maybe lemonade. Stay for one of those. I owe you, since you bought the last time, remember? Tell me all about the plans for downstairs. I see Alice and Frank coming and going all the time, always in a whirl. You do have time, don't you? For just a cup of coffee?"

She could tell that Jack was debating whether to stay with her or go back to work.

Contractors set their own hours, she thought. *Fifteen minutes here can be added on at the end of his day.... Guess it's not just lost time he's considering.*

"Well ... I guess a coffee sounds good. I still haven't progressed from instant. I keep thinking that one of these days I'll break down and buy a coffeemaker."

Leslie measured coffee and water, wondering if he could sense what she was feeling.

She brought the coffees to the table and sat facing him. She studied his face for a moment, then spoke. "Jack, how have you been? Really. I've been worried about you since ... that night out on Route 8 ..."

Jack looked down at his feet, a small scowl passing over his mouth. "I haven't touched anything since that night. I'm going to meetings." His words were soft, almost whispered.

"That's good. I am really glad for you." Leslie's words were cautious, but she wanted so badly to affirm him, support him as best she could.

Jack looked up, his eyes still pained. "Did I ever tell you about Earl ... Earl from The Palm?"

Leslie shook her head no.

"He's dying. And I don't know what I should do for him."

"Dying? Is he an old friend?"

"No. Not really. I met him at the bar. He works there. Or worked there. He's a recovered alcoholic."

"At a bar?"

Jack opened his hands. "I know. I asked him about that too. He said he wasn't tempted anymore. And he had to work somewhere."

"And he's dying?"

"Said a couple of months. Doctors say anything sometimes. I don't think he sees much hope. And I don't know what to say to him."

Leslie wanted to say something to draw out the pain but didn't know the words to use. She wanted to do something to make it better for Jack, remembering all the times people in her life had done nothing, leaving her alone and adrift with her pain.

"You could talk to Pastor Blake. Of all the people I know, he would have good advice. He is really good at knowing what people need. He could help."

"Pastor Blake? From Grace @ Calvary Church. With the symbol instead of the 'at'?"

"That's the one. Do you know him?"

"No. But ..." Jack looked hard at Leslie, as if confirming something in his thoughts. "That's where I go for meetings. I know the church. A beautiful old stone building. Such a perfect example of Romanesque architecture. I looked it up in one of my books. What's the pastor like?"

"He's young. Well, younger than an old pastor. You know ... all pastors used to be old and gray. At least they were all older than me. Pastor Blake is just a little older than me, but not by a lot. Easy to talk to. Smart."

Jack drained his coffee.

"More?"

He answered without hesitation. "Please."

She poured, and as she poured, she looked at Jack. She had seen him a hundred times before and found him very attractive, but seldom had she paused to *really* look at him, as she did now—his intense eyes, his cheekbones, his chin, his nose, the way he held his head. His sensitive eyes. Sensitive lips.

She looked at his hands. They were rough and calloused, but she saw sensitivity there as well.

A witch's breeze of red flags snapped and rippled in the air of the kitchen, and Leslie ignored them all. She saw them, she knew why they were there, and she chose to completely disregard them.

"You should talk to him. The pastor. About Earl. He would have advice. Good advice. Nothing pie-in-the-sky, just solid stuff. I'm sure he's had experience with that sort of thing."

Jack didn't add cream or sugar to this cup.

"The thing of it is," Jack said, as if relating an often-told story, "is that Earl had been sober for a long time. And now he's dying. Alone. And he said he didn't think giving it up was worth it. He would have died alone back then—when he was still drinking. And now, he's dying alone, sober and alone after all those years. He asked me what the difference would be in his life—with alcohol and without it. And I didn't have a good answer for him."

Leslie waited. She resisted the urge to talk, to offer a simple reply, an easy path to grace and forgiveness with hasty assurances that everything was going to be all right. Sometimes life wasn't all right. Leslie was beginning to understand just how difficult life could be. She thought about her great-great-great grandmother's diary. Life could be very difficult, indeed. It took work and courage and risks, but the payoff was worth it. It made your life full and satisfying, or at least, with God's help, allowed the chance for it to be full and satisfying.

Too many people offered quick solutions to me—and I hated them for doing that.

"Have you always been a carpenter?" Leslie asked, not sure why that question came now.

Jack looked surprised. "Why?"

Leslie leaned toward him. "I don't know. You don't sound like a carpenter."

"What's a carpenter supposed to sound like?"

She put up her hands partway, as if in surrender. "I'm not sure. But they don't sound like you. You sound … like more than a carpenter, that's all."

Jack slipped down in his chair just a bit. He appeared deflated, resigned, like he'd wanted to stop battling for a long time and this was a perfect time to stop, to lower his guard, to end the resisting, and simply be honest.

"No. My father was a carpenter. A great builder. He built beautiful houses. I learned from him. You know, growing up, in high school, working summers during college."

"What did you study?"

"Law. I'm an attorney. Was. Corporate law. I was a corporate attorney."

Leslie could see him in a three-piece suit, starched shirt, with a different haircut, polished shoes, carrying a briefcase, attending trials. She could see him doing that. It fit him perfectly.

"I was almost disbarred. Put on extended probation. It was a long time ago. It seems like it was a long time ago."

She had not asked for more details. He looked up, as if to see if there was any shock or revulsion or pity in her eyes.

She tried to keep herself blank, open, just listening, not judgmental.

"I was drinking. Partying. I lost it all. The job. The big house. The expensive cars. The luxury vacations. My wife. My daughter … It seems like a lifetime ago. It seems like … a different person was in my life then."

Leslie wanted to slide her chair closer and ask him to share more. She wanted to touch his hand and tell him that she wanted to hear everything, and that whatever he said, she would not be taken aback or scandalized. It wouldn't change her feelings for him. After all, she had problems too. She knew what it was like—to lose just about everything.

She wanted to say all that, but she couldn't. She couldn't even move her chair. So she just let the words stay out there, in the air, by themselves, without her response, and she let his statements just … be, for a moment.

Maybe then, after the silence, she would slide her chair closer and take his hand. She would let her emotions out.

And she would have—would have moved closer, would have taken his hand—except his cell phone, clipped to his belt, silent for all this time, picked that specific moment to chatter alive, crying out for his attention.

At that moment, Leslie decided that she hated all forms of new technology.

———

"Well, Mr. Kenyon," Alice said, her voice chipper and vibrant, "are you sitting down? You don't have to be sitting down, but if someone gave *me* this news, and I knew what the news was, I would want to be sitting. But I guess if I *knew* the news, then it wouldn't be news and I wouldn't have to be sitting after all."

Alice often talked this way. Jack was becoming used to it, like getting used to a person who spoke with a thick French accent.

"Mrs. Adams, I am sitting. Feel free to share whatever news you have. It sounds like good news, from your tone."

Jack could almost hear her twirling about whatever room she was in, filling that space with flowing dresses or scarves or boas. Alice was known to wear boas at times.

"Well, the news, Mr. Kenyon, is that the most popular television show on cable—at least the most popular cable show in western Pennsylvania— *Three Rivers Restorations*—has selected *our humble project* to be featured in an upcoming show."

She let the news sink in. "Isn't that the most delicious news you have heard recently? Cameron Dane Willis just got off the phone with me and she was *so* excited by our project. She is absolutely *smitten* with what we plan on doing. She and her entire crew will be down at Alice and Frank's *next weekend*. Isn't that so wonderfully … wonderful? She wants to spend time documenting what the place looks like now. The 'before,' you know? Show the viewers how an ugly duckling will be transformed into an elegant swan. I am simply *beside* myself with anticipation."

It sounded to Jack like he was listening to the first stages of Alice hyperventilating.

"Maybe *you* should sit down, Mrs. Adams," Jack said, pretty much in all seriousness.

"Don't be a silly," she replied. "Now the question is, can you be at the store next Saturday? That's when they would like to do the filming. It won't take more than a few hours of your time, she said. Of course, this will be on the clock for you … even though it will be a *tremendous* boost for your construction firm. *Lots* of publicity. People will hear your name and tell themselves that if Alice and Frank are using you, then you *must* be good."

"No, Mrs. Adams, no payment required," Jack said firmly. "Cameron is an old friend. It would be like me asking to get paid for a social call. I would be honored to be there with you and help out any way I could."

"Well, that's so nice of you. And Cameron did say that the two of you knew each other in Franklin. How perfectly serendipitous all of this is, don't you agree?"

Jack became more aware that Leslie was hearing only one side of this curious conversation. It was apparent that she was trying to avoid looking like she was eavesdropping but couldn't be totally unaware that something was going on.

"Mrs. Adams, rest assured that I'll be there on Saturday, although I don't think Ms. Dane … Mrs. Willis, that is … really thinks I will be the star of the show. You're going to be the star." Jack could almost see Alice Adams waving off her well-deserved compliment. Then he added, "Have you cleared this with the owner of the building? Don't you think that she'll need to know what's happening? I mean, would you like to wake up with a truckload of cameras and lights on your doorstep?"

There was a painful silence on the other end. "Why … why, Mr. Kenyon, I never considered I might need to … or even think I would … but you're absolutely right. I will have to talk to her. She's a reasonable woman, isn't she? She would have no reason to refuse this … don't you think?"

Jack could note the tint of panic in Alice's voice.

"We've rented the space. We have a lease. But could she refuse this?"

Jack let her go on long enough, then stepped in. "I'm sure she'll be fine with this," he said, fairly certain Leslie would welcome the chance to make her property a little famous. "Would you like to talk to her, right now?"

"Whatever do you mean, Mr. Kenyon?"

"I'm sitting with Mrs. Ruskin at the moment, having a cup of coffee. Would you like me to hand her the phone?"

Jack could hear Alice start to smile—a wry smile, he imagined.

"Why, Mr. Kenyon, you are simply *filled* with surprises, are you not? A man filled with surprises."

And with that, Jack handed the phone to Leslie.

Amelia Westland
Lyndora, Butler County, Penna.
August 13, 1884

All life is complicated. My life is perhaps more complicated than most.

Two days prior to this posting, I received two callers on a Saturday morning. I was occupied with the cleaning and tidying of the classroom, when Dr. Barry tapped at the window, grinning, and holding a bouquet of fine flowers. Despite my rather disheveled appearance, how delightful it was to see him. We chatted for just a moment, when I observed a second gentleman there in the Dr.'s buggy.

Dr. Barry introduced me to a Mr. Samuel Middelstadt. Mr. Middelstadt is a recent widower—within the last twelve months—and has two small daughters that need care. Mr. Middelstadt is a businessman, though I am not sure what sort of business he might be in. But he is a well-bred man, prepossessing in appearance, whose clothing was most smart and clean, and his shoes were of a high polish. He became most amiable, and we repaired to the teacherage for a slight refreshment.

Before leaving, Mr. Middelstadt stated that he would have sent to me in a few days a correspondence, indicating when perhaps he might escort me to dinner at the Willard Hotel, which is quite possibly the most elegant establishment in all of Butler County. I am told dinners there cost as much as three dollars per person.

After pondering this, I can only assume that the good doctor wished Mr. Middelstadt to meet me in hopes of promoting our affiliation.

My head spins. Mr. Middelstadt is a most agreeable man. Would I ever have imagined that such a predicament could happen to me? And whatever does one consider proper attire for an evening at the Willard Hotel?

Shew me thy ways, O LORD; teach me thy paths. Lead me in thy truth,
and teach me: for thou art the God of my salvation;
on thee do I wait all the day.
—PSALM 25:4–5

CHAPTER TWENTY-TWO

MRS. DIGIULIO STOOD ON THE playground, clutching her thick sweater around her throat, and waved to Leslie, like she called to her students, a wide swooping arm movement, like a mama duck using her wing to cluster her recent hatchlings to her side.

Leslie hurried over to the teacher.

"Just a moment of your time, Mrs. Ruskin," she said as she shepherded her inside. "I don't know why this chill doesn't seem to affect my students. If I didn't insist, they would all go out to recess without coats on. I don't see how they do it."

Leslie bustled in, her own coat zipped tight to her throat.

As if forgetting something, Mrs. DiGiulio pushed the door open, again used her whistle, and called loudly to Ava, telling her that her mother was inside with her.

"Don't want to make any child upset."

A sprinkling of fall leaves were hung from the ceiling, twirling on thin strings, hanging down from the metal grid work that held the acoustical tiles in place. A student's name was written on each leaf, in bold, dark letters—some handwriting clean and clear, other names scrawled and nearly illegible.

Leslie looked for her daughter's leaf. Ava's handwriting, for a girl, was terrible. Girls were supposed to be neat and precise, developing hand-eye skills early. Yet Ava was anything but that. She tended to be wildly dramatic with letters, or tight and miserly.

"I hope this doesn't have anything to do with Ava's writing technique," Leslie said anxiously. "I keep on her about being neat, but none of it makes any difference to her."

Mrs. DiGiulio, letting go of the collar of her sweater now that she was inside, dismissed Leslie's fears with a little wave. "Kindergarten students can be neat. And they can be sloppy. Has nothing to do with intelligence or ability or common sense. Ava is a smart little girl. Don't worry about it."

Mrs. DiGiulio took Leslie's right hand in her own. "That's not why I asked you in. I wanted to know how you're doing. Ava seems to be more … more secure right now. I don't know what makes me say that specifically, but it's the feeling I get. And that makes me want to ask: How have you been, Mrs. Ruskin? Did you talk to Pastor Blake?"

Leslie nodded enthusiastically. "I have. I am, I should say. He's such a nice man. And … well, he's helped me a great deal. We talk. He listens to me. He suggested a few books. He has given me some techniques to use. He prays for me. There is a group of women in the church that meets for prayer, and I'm always on their list."

Mrs. DiGiulio could hear the waver in Leslie's voice. She squeezed her hand, a squeeze of reassurance.

"It's all little things, Mrs. DiGiulio. This is the first time I've talked about it with anyone. Maybe that helped too."

Mrs. DiGiulio leaned very close to Leslie. "Prayer, my child, is not a little thing. I know you know that. It's a quiet thing. It's not a pill or a treatment, or some sort of expensive therapy. But I am telling you—prayer is the biggest and most powerful thing you can do. I know how effective it is."

Leslie was that close to tears—not anxious tears, or fearful tears, but tears of gratitude. "I haven't had an attack for weeks. I can still feel them threaten. I can still tell that they are close. But … maybe it is the prayers. I haven't had one come to the surface. Even when my ex-husband came down last week to take Ava for the day. In the past, that sort of situation would induce an immediate attack. But not this time. I keep reading my great-great-great-grandmother's diary and I see the struggles that she went through. They didn't call them panic attacks back then, in the late 1800s, but she suffered from severe anxiety attacks. There was loss and separation in her life too. And, well, in the past, reading her words depressed me— seeing how hard life was for her. But now, I see all her little victories. She used Bible verses and prayer. And I think her example has helped me figure out a lot of things. I don't know why I didn't see it before."

Mrs. DiGiulio put her arm around Leslie's shoulder, just like Ava said the teacher did all the time in class with her students. "You know, Mrs. Ruskin, God provides us the grace and the knowledge to deal with things just when we need them the most. Maybe He sees that you needed that clarity now, and that's what He has given you."

"Maybe you're right. I do feel clearer about a lot of things. Not everything. But many things."

Mrs. DiGiulio began walking her back to the door. "We'll never have it all figured out, Mrs. Ruskin. That much we can be assured of. Life is a journey, and we just keep walking, by faith, one foot in front of the other, one step at a time. And trust God to guide our steps."

Just like Gramma Mellie said …

"Now get back out to Ava before she thinks I've kidnapped you."

"So—how do I look?"

Trevor peered at his father. Then he squinted and craned his head forward, then sideways, all without moving his feet. He twisted his mouth into a weird upside-down grimace. "I dunno. How are you supposed to look?"

Mike Reidmiller smiled, knowing his son was all but oblivious to apparel, regardless of the style. Mike had put on his best shirt—the one he bought at a factory outlet store in Hershey when he and Trevor went to Hersheypark last summer. The shirt was advertised at the original cost of $130. That was an extraordinary amount that Mike would never, ever spend on a shirt, but since it was only $40 at the outlet store, he thought it a fine, practical purchase. He liked the little contrasting horse embroidered on the shirt, where a pocket should be, and hoped that it wouldn't look like he was showing off.

"I don't know. Dressed up a little. I don't wear this shirt very often."

Trevor shrugged and would have said "Whatever" had his father not scolded him often for always saying the word.

Mike's khaki pants claimed never to need ironing—but they still did.

"Your aunt will be here in a few minutes. You'll be okay with Aunt Denise?"

Trevor looked at his dad with an odd stare. "Why? What's she going to do with me?"

Mike sighed. Trevor had an oddly tilted view of reality, he thought. "Nothing. She'll cook dinner. I'll be home soon. So ... I just couldn't leave you by yourself, could I?"

Trevor shook his head. "Where you going?"

Mike hated to lie to his son, but if he had said he was going to drop by Mrs. Ruskin's place, unannounced, Trevor would have pleaded to take him along.

Mike couldn't do that, not this time.

"I have to go to the store to try on clothes," he said instead, knowing that other than getting shots at the doctor's office, the thing Trevor hated most was trying on clothes.

———

Ava danced from the living room to the kitchen, her little arms in motion, her feet, not matching her upper body, moving to a music all their own. Leslie watched the performance, and when her daughter stopped, perhaps from a degree of self-consciousness, she applauded, politely, like a mother not wanting to embarrass a child further. Ava didn't appear to suffer from any inhibition, though, and smiled up at Leslie, then took a deep theatrical bow.

"Don't you hear the music, Mommy?" Ava asked.

"Music? Where?"

"Just listen," Ava insisted and put a finger behind her ear and pushed it out farther, as if to scoop up the notes.

Leslie tilted her head. Then all of a sudden, she did hear music, music that sounded like it was from an old French movie. Leslie didn't recall any French movies she may have seen specifically, but there were accordions with strings and a warbled soprano voice accompanying it—all of which added up to French in Leslie's mind—and all coming from downstairs, she realized, ebbing through the floorboards and joists, not really loud, but definitely there. Ava's dance had been in harmony with the music, after all.

"That's Mrs. Alice's music," Ava declared. "She dances to it. That makes Mr. Frank laugh. Then she laughs too, and sometimes they both dance."

Ava had been given permission to visit the Adamses—only if she asked her mother and asked them if it was okay. Alice, not yet a mother, delighted in the small child. Ava occasionally returned with a feather boa wrapped dramatically over her shoulders, dragging the ends on the floor, looking like a glamorous urchin.

"Can I go down and see if I can visit?" Ava asked, almost pleading.

"Sure," Leslie said. She had made Alice promise to be honest and send Ava back upstairs if ever they were involved in something important or if Ava would prove a nuisance. She made her *promise*-promise, and Alice did so, crossing her heart with her finger, making an X.

Just as Leslie was ready to close the door, she heard Ava say in her best grown-up voice, the voice Leslie had been working with her to use with all adults, "Hello, Mr. Reidmiller."

Leslie held the door open and looked out. Mike Reidmiller was at the bottom of the stairs. He offered a slightly self-conscious wave.

"I would have called, but I'm not so good on the phone. Can I come in for a few minutes?"

"Of course," she replied, holding the door open wider, inviting him inside. There was a hint of a man's cologne in the air. "That's a nice shirt, Mike."

He tried his best not to look smug. "I know no one drops in on anyone without asking nowadays, but I'm just so bad at calling, and the small-talk thing. I thought I would just give this a shot. I really hope you don't mind. I'm not interrupting anything, am I? Are you in the middle of cooking dinner or something?"

"No. Ava's downstairs for a while. She loves the new tenants, Mr. and Mrs. Adams. Mrs. Adams is like a big child, I guess."

Mike nodded, knowingly. "I know. I went to high school with Alice. Alice Barret. She was a real cutup back then. We figured she'd move to

Pittsburgh or Philadelphia and not come back to Butler, ever. You know—the bright lights and the big social scene and all that. But now she's back."

"I could make coffee," Leslie volunteered. She felt like she'd been making a lot of coffee in recent days.

"No. I need to be honest. I'm trying to cut down on coffee. It gives me gas."

She saw a very pained look on Mike's face and wanted to smile, but did not, knowing he was kicking himself for bringing up an awkward topic. At least, she hoped that was why he was grimacing.

"Maybe a glass of water. Or soda, if you have one?" he asked.

"Sure. I was at the warehouse club this week, and I sometimes treat Ava and myself to some sodas. I know they're probably no good for you, but for a treat, sometimes it's okay."

Refusing the offer of a glass with ice, Mike popped the top of the can and took a long swallow, as if composing himself. "Leslie, I've been wanting to talk to you … ever since that night … when I, when we … you know. And there was that dinner thing, too, which was also … nice."

"I remember, Mike," she replied. "I remember both events very clearly."

He smiled at that. Leslie hoped she hadn't replied with too much enthusiasm. She had enjoyed that moment. She liked being found attractive by a man, and she enjoyed that small thrill of an unexpected kiss, but she wasn't sure where it would lead. She didn't even want to think about it—not all that much.

"Well, I've been thinking about it a lot. It keeps me up at night. Sometimes, anyhow. I really enjoy being with you, Leslie. I'm enjoying this, even though I'm as nervous as a cat in a room full of rocking chairs."

Leslie felt sorry for him. "Don't be nervous, Mike. We're friends, aren't we?"

Mike nodded earnestly. "I hope so. But … I want to be more than friends."

It was a statement Leslie had anticipated—almost since that one evening that made Mike so nervous.

"I know what an attractive woman you are, Leslie. I know you could have any man you wanted. I know I'm not on the top of anyone's 'Most Handsome' or 'Most Eligible Bachelor' list. But I want to move to the head of the line. I don't know how you feel about all this … but … have you thought about remarriage? I know you've been divorced for a short while, just like me. At first, I didn't want to hear anything about it. It hurt. I was hurt. I hated what happened, and I didn't ever want to risk having to go through that sort of hurt again. But over time, I got over it. I bet the same thing has happened to you. Time fixes things."

Mike waited for Leslie to say something. It was obvious that he wouldn't wait long, that he'd rehearsed his words—maybe not the exact words, but the basic content, the progression, the tone.

"I've thought a lot about remarriage," he continued. "I know Trevor really needs a mom. He's different now than he was. Less tender, maybe. He needs a woman in his life. And so do I."

Mike must have read something in Leslie's face. *Shock* wasn't the word, exactly. *Panic* wasn't the word, either. Maybe *unease*, or *concern*, or *confusion* as to what to say and how to reply—she could see him assessing her expression.

"Leslie, I'm not asking for an answer now. Good heavens, not just like that, out of the blue. But, hey, we're both older. Neither of us has a lot of time to waste … not that being with you is a waste, don't get me wrong. But if marriage to someone—me or anyone else—is out of the question, then I wondered if you could tell me that. So our time isn't … used up. So … we could move on to other people."

Mike took a handkerchief out of his pocket and mopped it across his forehead. "I'm really nervous, Leslie. I'm doing all the talking and you're sitting there, looking so beautiful, and I don't know what else to say."

Leslie knew she had to say something. All the inner dialogue flew past in a rush: *Is safe okay? Is looking for security okay? How much does Ava yearn for a father? How much do I want to have a man hold me and love me and make me feel wanted again? Do I wait for my heart or do I listen to my head? Do I accept "good enough" and try to make it better?*

"Mike …"

He leaned forward, took a long drink from his can of soda, wiped his forehead again, and waited.

"Mike, I know how hard it is being a single parent. I don't know who has the harder job—a single mother or a single father. It's hard not having an adult to share life with. I'm lonely lots of times. I'm never alone, but I am lonely."

"Exactly," Mike replied.

"You are a very sweet man, Mike. I am so blessed to have you in my life. But I would be lying if I said that I was ready. I'm dealing with a lot right now. And I'm just beginning to see the light at the end of the tunnel. I like being with you, Mike. Ava likes you and Trevor. I like Trevor too. I know we're older and we can't pretend we're in our twenties again and footloose."

Mike placed the empty can on the table, as if fearing the worst and that he would have to leave in a hurry.

"I can tell you this: I would like to continue to see you. As a friend. Friendship can deepen. Let's see what happens. And I promise you, Mike: If I change my mind, if I see that we're not to be—you know, a couple … a couple with a future—then I'll tell you right away. But, for now, let's be friends. Let's see what happens, okay?"

Mike didn't appear to be crestfallen, nor did he appear to be overjoyed. His expression was somewhere in the middle of that range. "Okay. Sure. I can do that, Leslie. But you have promised to tell me, all right?"

"I have, Mike. And I also promise that it won't take … I don't know … more than—a year? Does that sound unreasonable?"

"Okay. A year. We decide … you decide in a year. I can live with that."

"Good."

Mike stood up. Leslie could see where Mike had darkened his shirt with perspiration. He had been that nervous. She realized what he'd just done was incredibly brave.

"Did you know that *Three Rivers Restorations* is doing a show on the downstairs space?" Leslie said, as much to lighten the atmosphere as anything else.

"What?" Mike's eyes were wide. "Really? *Three Rivers Restorations?* That's like my most favorite show ever. I mean, of shows like that. On cable. I always watch it. I love that Cameron woman. She is so funny."

"I guess she'll be here this Saturday."

Mike's jaw all but dropped.

"Really. Honestly? Can I … no, that sounds forward, even for me."

"No, what?" Leslie replied.

"Well … could I come and watch? Maybe I could get her autograph. Would that be okay? I don't want to be a pest."

At this moment, had Mike asked if Leslie cared for him, she would have said yes, so sweet and considerate was his asking.

"I expect you to be here, Mike. The crew gets here at the crack of dawn, but she's supposed to arrive at 9:00. I want you here to watch—and help. Okay? Bring Trevor so Ava will have someone to play with."

"That is great, Leslie. That is so great. Trevor will be so excited."

After he'd left, she watched through the french doors as Mike walked down the street with almost a bounce in his step, as if the excitement of the show wiped clean any disappointment he may have experienced in the minutes earlier.

In spite of what she'd just said, and in spite of her own reservations, she grew fonder of him with every passing moment.

Amelia Westland

Lyndora, Butler County, Penna.

September 12, 1884

A note, a time, darkness, and more pebbles on the window.

Julian takes me in his strong arms and places a hundred sweet kisses on my lips amidst his caresses, holding me tight, so tight that I can feel his heartbeat. I blush, yet I do not protest.

He tells me his plans to commence his travels are nearing completion. He has saved some monies, enough to take two people on horseback to Ohio and down along the Ohio River, where itinerant preachers have prior traveled, he claims, and have met with good and enthusiastic response, providing support, and won souls.

Julian, in between kisses, tells me, much to my surprise, that we could travel together as brother and sister, so no suspicions would be aroused. I assumed that such an arrangement would be completed with a quiet marriage; yet Julian says nothing of such a union.

And in the midst of his kisses, and more, I forget to press him on the issue, yet I remain confident that his intentions toward me are noble. Nor do I converse of my affiliation with Mr. Middelstadt, who seemingly has taken a decided fancy to me.

> *Restore unto me the joy of thy salvation;*
> *and uphold me with thy free spirit.*
> *Then will I teach transgressors thy ways;*
> *and sinners shall be converted unto thee.*
> —PSALM 51:12–13

CHAPTER TWENTY-THREE

CAMERON DANE WILLIS, THE HOST of *Three Rivers Restorations—"Showing the Best of Restoration in Western Pennsylvania"*—reached up, grabbed the top of the door and the frame of the car above her head, and hoisted herself out of her seat. She had been overjoyed that Ethan, her husband, had offered to drive her to Butler. He did not always enjoy her shoots.

"A whole lot of standing around in between scenes, listening to the crew gripe about the director and the director gripe about the talent and the talent gripe about the homeowner and the homeowner running around trying to get everyone to wear those stupid booties on their shoes—and they never fit."

Cameron forgave her husband often and seldom insisted on him accompanying her. But this was different.

"I can't even see the pedals in the car anymore," she moaned. "And I hardly even fit behind the steering wheel. And it's Alice and Frank's."

Ethan had taken pity on his very pregnant wife and had driven the two hours south to Butler that morning with her in the car, turning and twisting in her seat, attempting to find a comfortable position for her growing body.

Chance, Cameron's stepson, had spent the previous night with his best friend, Elliot, and the two of them would amuse themselves at the Hewitts' until Ethan and Cameron drove back home to Franklin on Saturday evening.

As Cameron exited the car, Alice Adams ran to greet her. She had been waiting by the door since 8:00, wanting to make sure that she was the first person Cameron saw. Alice embraced her as best she could, trying to wrap her arms around her, avoiding the swell of her stomach.

"I am so pregnant," Cameron said, as if needing to explain. "It feels like I have been the size of an elephant for months now."

"But you are glowing, just glowing. I am so happy for you. Frank is so happy."

Cameron smiled. She was aware that pregnancy suited her. It rounded her face, it toned her skin. All of the horrible things that some pregnant women complained about seemed to happen in reverse to Cameron.

"Thanks, but now I need a bathroom. That's the downside of pregnancy."

Alice took her by the arm and led her toward the front door of the store. She waved to Ethan. "Hello, Ethan. I'll be back for you later."

Ethan waved back and leaned against the car, as if he was accustomed to leaning against the car in these sorts of situations.

Cameron slipped in and out, looking refreshed.

Alice drew her close. "What does Chance think about this—getting a baby brother or sister?"

Cameron shook her head. "He thinks the whole thing is 'pretty icky.' That's what he told his friend Elliot, who told his mother, who told me. But I know he also is excited to get to be an older brother. He's been lonely."

Alice whispered the next question. "Is it a boy or a girl?"

Cameron pretended to be shocked, then quickly relented. "Ethan will kill me if he knew that I knew. And he would kill you if he knew that I knew and told you. He refused to have the doctor tell us when we were there together for the ultrasound. So I called the doctor later to find out myself and swore everyone to secrecy."

"So what will it be?" Alice was atremble.

Cameron whispered, "You can't breathe a word of this, but buy a pink baby outfit."

"Ah! Italians make the most divine baby clothes and shoes you've ever seen," Alice answered, elated, and hugged her again. It was obvious that Cameron was used to getting hugged by now.

As the two of them untangled, Cameron looked around the mostly empty first floor.

"So tell me, Alice, what's the plan for this space?"

———

Amidst the crew setting up lights in the still almost-empty space, Alice and Cameron walked—well, Alice walked, and Cameron mostly waddled—through the space, Alice declaring in a loud voice what she planned to do here and there and what colors they might use and what finishes she'd selected, and what lighting types, and where the seating areas would be and the table placements and the kitchen layout. Everything was on paper, and nothing was built, but everything "would be fantastic," Alice declared.

"I loved the pictures of this place you sent me," Cameron said as she settled down into a folding chair. "It looked old and quirky."

Alice hovered around Cameron, pointing and directing. "Everyone loved our place in Pittsburgh. I loved it and was sorry to sell. Everyone said we should franchise. I don't know about that, but after our trip, even before our trip, I knew I couldn't stay away from the restaurant-slash-retail business. It is just too much of an adventure. You never know who's going to walk through the front door."

"Speaking of not knowing who is coming through the front door ..." Cameron said as she struggled to get up.

"Sit down, stay down," Jack scolded in a most solicitous manner. "I can come to you."

He bent to her, and his embrace was tender. "You look great. How do you feel?" he asked as he pulled up a chair next to her.

"Like a great big balloon. Other than that, fine." Cameron was telling the truth, but she was still beaming.

"Well, I'm so excited for you and Ethan. You'll be wonderful parents."

She took his hand and held it tight. "I hope so. It's such an unknown. I know Ethan has gone through it before—but I haven't. Sometimes I worry a bit."

Jack squeezed her hand in return. "You'll do fine."

"It's so nice that we get to see each other again. I can't say I ever thought this would happen," Cameron said.

"Small world," Jack replied, then remained silent.

A member of the crew called out, "Mrs. Adams? We're ready for you in makeup."

Alice arose in a twirl, adjusting her Burberry scarf, grinning and patting at her hair. "That's something I never thought I'd ever hear," she said as she was escorted to the crew's makeup department—a canvas director's chair, a woman with a large tackle box filled with cosmetics, a stool, a standup mirror, and a light on a pole.

Jack watched with bemusement. The process made him think of a child's make-believe play.

Cameron pulled his hand closer to her. "Tell me, Jack, how are you—really?"

Cameron knew some of Jack's story. He had shared most of it with Ethan. He'd had to tell him the truth of his addiction and his recovery. But neither of them knew his detailed history.

"I'm okay. Really."

She waited, looking at him, her eyes asking for the truth.

"I'm going to meetings. Now. There have been a couple of times when I fell. It was hard. But now I'm better. Really."

Cameron held his hand tight, as if she could tell that something was wrong, that something was left unfixed in Jack's life, as if he were still hiding something. "You know, Jack, Ethan had a lot of secrets. You can talk to him anytime. You know that. He found God, Jack. He found peace in letting go of the past, just like I did. You should talk to him. We've both found peace. We are finding our pleasure in God."

Jack nodded. He tried to smile, tried to reassure her that he would talk to Ethan, but it was clear that both of them knew Jack wouldn't talk about anything of substance this day. Jack might ask about construction or estimating or historical authenticity in working on the building, but that's as far as their conversation would go. It would have nothing to do with spiritual matters and nothing to do with finding peace.

Cameron, most often, had the gift of knowing the right words to say at the exact right moment. But on this morning, that gift had failed her.

The director called for Jack as well. "Everyone on camera this morning needs makeup. Otherwise you'll all look like zombies. And George Romero already made that movie."

Jack gave Cameron an overly enthusiastic smile. "My fans need me," he said, then stood and walked away.

What right does she have to give me instructions? I don't want to be told what my life needs, what to find pleasure in. Maybe I don't have a perfect mate and a perfect house and a perfect son, but that doesn't give anyone the right to tell me what to do or to tell me what I need. Finding peace? That's easy for her to say. That's easy for Ethan to say. Yeah, his wife died, but that has nothing on me. Nothing. People think that because they "found the way," everyone else wants what they have. Well, they don't. I'm fine where I am. And I don't need a Mrs. Perfect to tell me that I'm a loser.

Jack sat in the canvas chair, closed his eyes, and let Lois, the makeup technician, apply base and color to his cheeks, without making any snarky comments, without pretending if he hated it or loved it.

He just sat there, silent, with eyes shut, waiting for his turn to stand in front of the lights and have Cameron ask him questions, carefully written on a large white clipboard, and hoping he could answer them without disclosing what was going on inside his thoughts.

———

As Cameron looked over at Jack in the canvas makeup chair, she wondered how she could have better handled her conversation with him. It was obvious he had wanted to answer her. It was obvious he'd been holding his tongue. Cameron knew, from the look on his face, as soon as she said the words, that they may not have been the right words.

I think I may have sounded as though I was scolding Jack, rather than just being excited—scolding him for not being at peace, even though that isn't what I meant.

Cameron bit her lip, then closed her eyes and said a silent, earnest prayer for Jack.

Paul Drake parked his perfectly polished black Lexus at an odd angle in the street, the oddness saying, very clearly, that the driver was an important person who could not be bothered with the subtleties of parking in parallel. A uniformed policeman began walking up to the car, apparently to instruct the driver to move the vehicle, but Paul stepped out into the chilly air, his hair done exactly right, his skin kissed by the sun, with a deep tan camel hair jacket and a silk tie that appeared to cost two hundred dollars, even if you saw it from across the street.

"Sir?" Paul said, speaking first, "Paul Drake. I am the producer of this humble little television show and I would so greatly appreciate if you could keep an eye on my car there. No need for it to be scratched while you're on duty, is there?"

The policeman stopped in his tracks and appeared to be formulating a reply.

"I'll have your name listed in the credits as providing security for us. You and all your fellow officers on duty this morning. We at *Three Rivers* so appreciate your service."

As Paul spoke, the police officer actually began to enlarge in size, inflating as it were, from the praise and the potential mention on a television show.

Paul Drake, the producer, walked with an air of confidence into the restaurant space, as if he had been there a hundred times. "Cameron? Where are you, Cameron?" he called out while adjusting his shirtsleeves and jacket.

Cameron came walking up slowly, with Alice and Frank in tow, looking eager to introduce them to the real owner of *Three Rivers Restorations.*

Paul held up his hand to stop any conversation. He tilted his head and stared at Alice. He pointed at her feet. "Are those Christian Louboutins?"

It was Alice's turn to swell with pride. "Oh, yes they are. You are the first person to recognize them. How *fabulous.*"

Paul was obviously impressed. "Where did you get them?"

Alice waved her hand as if it were no big thing. "In Paris, of course. We were there for a few months recently. They were *such* a bargain at only seven hundred Euros. I am sure that is much less than you could find them here—*if* you could find them."

Frank stood at her side, not willing to tell her how much a Euro actually was in comparison to the American dollar, not willing to diminish her triumphant moment of style.

Paul made some sort of elaborate gesture, with both hands. "Anyone who wears Louboutins," he answered, saying the shoe brand in a very correct French accent, "will no doubt succeed. Good heavens. Culture! Style! In Butler, of all places. How perfectly amazing."

Mike stood next to Leslie. He wanted to take her hand or put his arm around her waist, but after her decision to be "just friends—for now," he thought it might be too bold and rash a move. Instead he stood there, next to her, in the crisp autumn air, in the brilliant fall sunshine, among a small crowd of people who had gathered on the wide sidewalk opposite the Midlands Building, watching the crew of *Three Rivers Restorations* at work.

A television crew of any size would have been big news in Butler, and this was a big crew by comparison. *Three Rivers Restorations* maintained a programming crew of five, and a filming crew of fourteen. Lighting a building in the midst of renovation took a lot of people—preparing it for sound, making sure that wires and cables were properly strung.

And since the production had become popular, that meant it was now profitable—more profitable than any other show in Drake Cable Productions history. They could afford a bigger crew.

Two reporters and a photographer from the *Butler Eagle* were on hand to document the initial phase of the show. Being on television added an immediate sense of viability to Alice and Frank's venture.

"Why would a TV show do a show on something that was going to fail?" people asked themselves.

Even the local radio station, WBUT, had an on-air personality roaming the sidewalk, getting some man-in-the-street interviews.

"This is so exciting," Mike said. "Cameron Dane is really pregnant, isn't she? Do you think they'll show that on camera?"

Leslie pondered for a second. "I don't know. Probably. Or maybe they'll just show her from the shoulders up."

Mike nodded as if he had not considered that option.

On the other side of the street, Alice stood on her tiptoes, scanning the crowd, waving to familiar faces. Once she saw Leslie, she nearly sprinted across the street. She didn't worry about cars, since the police department in Butler was kind enough to block off traffic on this small stretch of pavement. A cluster of uniformed officers stood nearby, watching, making sure crowd control would not become an issue, laughing among themselves.

Alice got to Leslie, out of breath, obviously excited. "They need to talk to you, Leslie. Once Cameron heard that the building was owned by a single woman who was rehabbing it—well, there was no stopping them from demanding that you appear for a short interview. You simply must say yes, Leslie. Please? For your new tenants?"

Mike was thunderstruck, just being close to someone who might appear on his favorite local cable television show. "You have to do it, Leslie. You have to," he insisted.

Leslie allowed herself to be nearly dragged across the street and thrust down into the makeup chair. All the while Alice hovered about, calling for more color to be put on the poor child's pale cheeks.

———※———

"And what led you to buy this building, Leslie?"

Cameron Dane Willis stood next to her, in front of the corner doors of the building, with the carved stone lintel and brick framing as a backdrop to the shot. Cameron had that ability to be friends with people right away, making them feel as if she had known them for years, and with Leslie, that ability was more than evident.

Even though she was trying to avoid looking into the camera, as instructed, Leslie saw it from the corner of her eyes.

And there is no panic, she thought to herself as the soundman adjusted the boom microphone over their heads. *I am so thankful for the prayers of all those wonderful ladies at church. Mrs. DiGiulio and Grandma Amelia were right.*

"Well, Cameron, my daughter and I needed a place to live. I wanted a property that would also produce some income. My great-great-great-grandparents lived in Butler, so I was somehow drawn to the area. When I saw this building, I just knew it was the one. Something compelled me to buy it."

Cameron's smile encouraged her, as if saying without speaking, *You're doing well. Good answer!*

"And you're planning to rehab the upstairs apartments?"

For just a second, Leslie appeared confused. "There are three apartments upstairs. One is rented. One is where my daughter and I live. The other has just been renovated. I'm trying to rent the empty one."

Cameron's face showed her excitement. "May we see that empty apartment, Mrs. Ruskin? Our viewers would love to see what you've done to it."

Leslie debated, silently, quickly. "Sure. That would be fine. It's not furnished, but that will show you the real architectural beauty of the building."

"Then let's go."

Cameron waited, then the director called out, "Cut!"

And a whirl of technicians and camera people began disassembling equipment, asking where the stairs were for the second-floor location.

As Leslie followed the crew upstairs, she caught sight of Mike's face, brimming over with excitement. She looked around for Jack but couldn't find him in all the activity.

Paul Drake hovered behind the crew as they made their way upstairs to the empty apartment. "This isn't going to cost me overtime, is it?"

Bruce, the location director, shook his head. "No. This place is a paradise compared to most of the places we film. Clean. The electricity works. We're way ahead of schedule."

Paul stood in the background, allowing his crew to do what they do. He knew that intruding in the process by asking questions simply cost him money. He walked through the rooms where the crew was not working, nodding to himself.

This is a very interesting building and a very nice apartment—with the original fireplace, no less. Everything is done just right. Updated, yet they respected the historic attitude of the place. If I had reason to be in Butler ... more than hardly ever ... I would think about renting this apartment. It is just so, so charming. And that little screened-in balcony is simply to die for.

He heard the owner, that cute Leslie something, talking to Cameron about the reasons for using the materials they did.

I would swap out the counters for thick granite. And get a Viking stove.

And as the next shot was being filmed, Paul made a note in his little electronic notebook: *Have assistant call Butler re: rental.*

He smiled to himself.

It would be nice to have another private getaway, now, wouldn't it?

‑‑‑‑‑‑

While Alice and Frank finalized their floor plans for the Midlands Building, gathering permits, selecting colors and fabrics and finishes, specifying lighting, Jack continued his work at the Pettigrews' house. Theirs was a much simpler project—new cabinets in the kitchen, new countertops, new bathroom fixtures, new tile, new lighting. Jack was happy that he hadn't run into any snags on the job, unforeseen handicaps and problems that would eat up profits and chew up time.

So far, there was nothing uncovered that had caused any headaches. The new cabinets had been installed without a hitch, and the three-man counter crew was due in the next day to install the granite tops. Once the Pettigrews had seen the stone samples and realized the affordable difference in cost, they'd jumped at the opportunity.

Jack was packing up his tool chest for the day, having swept the kitchen floor, and tidying up the area.

They have to live here. And nothing aggravates a customer more than always cleaning up behind a contractor.

Jack rationalized the time spent as a wise investment. It seldom took more than fifteen minutes and was sure to get him a more positive referral later.

Melanie Pettigrew peeked into the kitchen as Jack latched his toolbox closed. "Hello, Jack," she said, "or should I call you Mr. Kenyon, now that you're a famous television star?"

Jack shook his head. "How did you find out?"

"Butler is a pretty small town. Word travels quickly. What was the host like? She always seems so well prepared—and so pretty."

Melanie leaned against the center island, or what would soon be the center island with the addition of the countertop. Now it was more like a cabinet skeleton.

"She's very nice. I knew her before she became famous—up in Franklin."

"Really?" Mrs. Pettigrew said, obviously fascinated and more than a little starstruck. Mrs. Pettigrew was not much older than twenty-five, Jack surmised. There was a very wholesome but naive beauty about her, as if she were unaware of how pretty she was. And from that naive attitude, Jack guessed she hadn't often ventured far from Butler.

"Is she rich from doing that show?"

Jack shook his head. "I don't think so. It pays well, I think, but she's not rich."

"Alice from across the street said she was pregnant. Is she?"

Jack nodded.

"Can you do that? I mean, be pregnant and still host a TV show like that?"

"I guess so. Nobody looked all that surprised when we were filming."

"Did they pay you for being on the show?"

"I wish they had—but no, I think everyone does it so they can be a little famous for a while. It was my fifteen minutes of fame."

Melanie took on a sudden, starry look. "Do you think she would pick our house for a show? I mean, we're having an entire kitchen and bathroom replaced. What do you think? Would she?"

Jack knew that *Three Rivers Restorations* looked for big, interesting historic projects, and a simple kitchen and bath was none of those. But Mrs. Pettigrew was so excited that he didn't want to crush her enthusiasm.

"Well, I don't know, but the next time I see Cameron, I will definitely ask her."

"You will?" Mrs. Pettigrew squealed, jumping up and down just a little and grabbing Jack's arm in her excitement. "That would be so awesome."

———

As the week wound down, Jack felt the energy drain from his body. His work at Alice and Frank's wouldn't take off for a few weeks from now. His work with the Pettigrews was all but completed. He had enough money in the bank to weather several weeks of idleness.

It was not the lack of income that scared him. It was the lack of having something to do, something to fill his days, something to tire him out, something to help him fall asleep when darkness arrived.

Without work, he worried about what he might find to occupy his hands and his thoughts.

There are only so many walks I can take. There are only so many books I can read.

Friday would be his last day with the Pettigrews. He could have been done today, he told himself, but he wanted to do a final cleanup; he had a few switchplates and wall-outlet covers to put on, and one last wall sconce in the bathroom to install.

An hour. Two at the very most.

Then what?

He sat in the living room of his small apartment.

Maybe I could go look at houses for sale. Maybe I could find a good fixer-upper in town.

He dismissed the thought.

You need to be sharp when you do that. You need to really pay attention.

He felt anything but sharp.

He looked over to the alcove in the wall. The pint of vodka remained in the same spot where he'd placed it, in its little home near the door, where it greeted him each time he came in. He stared at it. He wondered if he had any mixer, any soda, in the refrigerator.

Vodka tastes terrible plain. Maybe it's good I don't have anything to mix with it.

He sat and stared at that bottle for a long, long time, until he no longer heard the buzzers on the Main Street stoplights. He kicked off his shoes and laid on his bed, still fully clothed, on his back, with his hands folded across his chest, his head on the pillow, and waited, once again, for sleep to free him.

God, where are You?

Amelia Westland

Lyndora

Butler County, Pennsylvania

October 6, 1884

Mr. Middelstadt has called on me now five times, in one of his stylish conveyances, apparently with the blessings of the good doctor and the superintendent of schools, for both have sent correspondence asking how our society is progressing, and telling me what a fine gentleman is to be found in Mr. Middelstadt, what a pillar of the community he is becoming, how much his children are in need of a mother, and various and sundry other encouragements—some subtle, some less so.

I think him indeed a fine gentleman, most courteous and polite, with impeccable table manners. I bless my Aunt Willa, and Mrs. Barry, too, for instructing me in the proper ways a lady must behave. Mrs. Barry provided me with a few lovely dresses and accessories which she no longer had need of, that I might be presentably attired on my engagements with Mr. Middelstadt. (I have no idea how dear dinner was at the Willard Hotel, for my menu was without prices printed on the selections.) He indeed is a fine gentleman and treats me like a lady. I have met his children, on two occasions now, two very pretty little girls of six and eight years who behaved quite well and were most respectful to me. I have seen his house—rather like a mansion, truth be told. Three stories, more rooms than I could count, gaslights, several servants, fine wood and upholstered furniture with embroidered fabric, elaborate silk drapery, lavish wallpapers and sparkling chandeliers, delicate China, silver service, crystal glassware.

I fail to imagine how I would act in such a place—and as lady of the house. The very idea has caused the spells of anxiety to return a time or two, but I managed, through prayer, to settle my nervousness and stave off a lengthy episode.

Hear my cry, O God; attend unto my prayer.
From the end of the earth will I cry unto thee,

when my heart is overwhelmed: lead me to
the rock that is higher than I.
—PSALM 61:1–2

I sought the LORD, and he heard me,
and delivered me from all my fears.
—PSALM 34:4

CHAPTER TWENTY-FOUR

SATURDAY MORNING WAS ONE OF those perfect, pellucid mornings, when you could see all the way into space through the cloudless blue sky, when your breath had just a puff of frozen vapor as you exhaled. Not truly cold, but bracing. A day perfect for football and wearing a sweater under a houndstooth sport coat, with thin leather driving gloves, a scarf around your neck, and your best girl, wearing a fur-collared jacket, hanging on your arm and smiling up at you.

Jack had none of those things.

He zipped up his black sweatshirt, the one with only a small tear on the elbow. He put on his regular jeans and his regular work boots. He found a black knitted wool hat and pulled it down over his head.

He stopped before he reached his door. He looked over at the small bottle of vodka, sitting there in its little home.

Small, but enough.

He walked slowly to the alcove and picked up the bottle. Surprised at the coldness of the glass, he slipped it into the pocket of his sweatshirt and snugged it down, deep inside, so it wouldn't tip out, fall, and break.

He made his way down the steps and walked down the alley, down to where he had parked his truck.

He had nothing to do this day. Nothing at all.

He didn't walk slowly because he was hesitating for any specific reason. He walked slowly because any action this morning felt like he was walking with weights attached to his feet through some invisible, thick, viscous liquid, like heavy water, each step more agonizing than the one before.

Jack knew the symptoms. He had done all the reading. He had seen the magazine articles.

A doctor once told him that alcoholism and depression often went hand in hand. Some people drank to self-medicate, to mask the pain, to hide from some crushing reality. That doctor had wanted to prescribe anti-depressants for Jack. He had not wanted the prescription.

It wouldn't cure it. It would just be another crutch, another mask. That's not what I need.

Jack knew the symptoms well.

He got into his truck and turned the key. Nearly a full tank of gas remained. Jack considered that a good sign. He backed up, drove down the short alley, turned left, then made a right and was on Route 8. The weather was clear, the traffic was light, and Jack knew exactly where he must go.

―――――

Leslie awoke that morning to the buzzer for their front door. She blinked to clear her eyes, fumbling for her robe.

It's before eight o'clock. Who would come this early?

She tied the robe around her waist and cinched the collar closed. She wished she had enough money to install a closed-circuit video-camera system.

Maybe after a few months more rent from the Adamses.

She opened the door, with some caution, and peered down the steps. The light was so bright that all she could see was a silhouette—a man's silhouette. It was not Mike—much too small. Not Frank—much too short. And not Jack—not athletic enough. The shadow turned, and Randy almost pressed his face against the glass, offering a thin, insincere-looking smile.

"Buzz me in. It's freezing out here," he called.

Leslie reached around the door for the buzzer, then hesitated.

What does he want? Why so early? Should I tell him to come back later?

She quickly decided that if she sent him away, he would simply threaten to use that as her refusal to allow him access to his daughter. And maybe the courts might believe him.

She hit the buzzer and the downstairs door clacked open.

Randy blew on his hands as he entered her apartment, eyes looking about, looking for something—something incriminating, perhaps.

"Listen, I know it's early, but I want to take my kid out to breakfast. Lisa had some stupid scrapbooking thing to go to today up in Saxonburg. I dropped her off and have nothing to do for the morning. So I thought I could see my kid for a change. She up?"

Leslie felt pummeled. This was not on the court-approved schedule, but since he had missed so many, she doubted whether he even considered that schedule when making plans.

"I'll take her to breakfast. Then I got to get the oil changed in the car, and then a carwash. Maybe she'll enjoy that. Can you get her up … or are you hungover or something? You're not moving too fast, you know that?"

He sat on the sofa and waited, as if he were accustomed to her jumping when he told her to—which he was.

Leslie could not think clearly enough to argue. Instead she padded down the hall, into Ava's room, and tried to wake her daughter as gently as she could.

She put her hand on Ava's small shoulder and shook it just a little. Ava was not always gracious upon waking, and she liked to sleep later on the days when school wasn't in session.

"It's Saturday, Mommy. I sleep in on Saturday," Ava said with a groggy voice.

"I know, sweetie," she said softly into her ear. "But your father is here. He wants to take you to breakfast."

Ava rolled onto her back. She squinted at her mother. "Why?"

"I'm not sure. But he's here, and he wants to have breakfast with you."

Ava tried to roll onto her side. "Can't he just eat here?"

"I don't think he wants to do that, Ava. You have to get up."

Ava grumbled and, with her mother's prodding, sat up. Leslie went to the dresser and got out a pair of jeans and a pink sweatshirt. "Put this on, okay?"

Ava stumbled into her jeans and pulled on the sweatshirt without complaint, even though she had recently started to have an opinion about her clothes.

It's early. If she were fully awake, she wouldn't have wanted to wear either.

Randy stood by the door, waiting. "Hey, Ava. How are you?"

Ava hardly acknowledged him as she made her way to the steps.

"She just woke up, Randy."

"Yeah, sure. Like you aren't telling her things about me. We'll be back by noon. You better be here 'cause I have to pick up Lisa at 12:30. Got it?"

He didn't wait for a reply—simply pulled the door shut after him.

———◦∞◦———

Jack rolled his window down a few inches. It was too cold for an open window, but nice enough, with enough sun, that a small breeze felt good, refreshing. He was headed down Route 8, toward Pittsburgh.

His parents no longer lived in Pennsylvania. A number of years ago, when Jack was mired in his problems, they had moved, his father recently retired, to Arizona. He received Christmas and birthday cards from them, and that alone was their connection.

He did not blame them.

Addiction can be expensive and emotionally devastating, Jack knew. He realized that his parents could not be blamed for turning away from him. He might have done the exact same thing.

He drove farther into the city, crossed the Allegheny River at the 62nd Street Bridge, and headed south, along Butler Street.

He knew where he was going. This was familiar ground to him. He had grown up here.

He turned south, into Schenley Heights, situated between the ultra-fashionable Shadyside and the sprawling campus of the University of Pittsburgh. Not every house was huge, but many were. Not every house was architecturally significant or interesting, but many were.

Jack slowed down and turned onto Webster Avenue. The block had not changed much since he had been gone. Some houses had been repainted—some with historic colors Jack liked, some he didn't. A few older and smaller houses were gone, replaced by large new houses, built in a not-quite-historically-correct style, that hulked on the small lots—expensive, impressive, and attempting to fit into the neighborhood when everyone knew that they couldn't, wouldn't, and shouldn't. Jack paused at a stop sign, and then proceeded more slowly. He pulled over to the curb halfway down the block. He looked to his right, through the passenger side window at a house.

He had once owned that house, a sort of Spanish/Moorish-style home, with a tile roof and twisted terra cotta columns flanking the front door. It was authentically and significantly historic, one of the first houses built on that block, filled with all sorts of quirky delights.

Jack stared without expression, memorizing the lines and the colors and the details once again. After perhaps ten minutes, he put the truck back into gear and headed east on Baum Boulevard, then north on South Negley Avenue, then west on Penn Avenue.

He slowed and entered through the tall brick columns. The wrought-iron gates were folded back, unlocked during the day, during visiting hours.

He grabbed at the wheel tighter with his right hand to stop the tremor that seemed to have possessed his entire arm.

Several years had passed since he had last been here, yet the route was indelibly etched into his memory.

Only a small number of people were out today. Sunday would draw more crowds. The Pittsburgh Panthers would not be playing tomorrow; people would leave themselves time to remember.

At the crest of a small rise, he turned, pulled to the side of the road, and switched the engine off. The ticking of the motor, as it cooled, grew loud in the silence of the day.

Jack didn't want to leave the truck. He would rather have stayed inside. He would rather have started the engine again and driven off, never to return.

But he knew he had to be there … and he had to do what he was about to do.

He pulled his cap on, zipped up his sweatshirt, and stepped out into the brilliant sunshine and the biting, chilly air.

He stepped onto the grass and began to walk. He counted as he went. They were twenty-five steps from the road. He had that number memorized. It may have taken a minute to get to them; it may have taken an hour. Jack was not aware of time.

He turned, closed his eyes, and waited.

Then, after his heart slowed, after the trembling in his hands abated a little, he opened his eyes once again.

He faced two tombstones—plain granite, simple, unpolished, rough-hewn edges, as if they had just been carved from a quarry—the grass neatly trimmed, the world around them stretching away forever.

Jack felt his left hand shake, even though he had put it in his pocket.

He wanted to run.

Instead he sat down.

He sat down on the grass and stared and tried not to remember.

The buzzer sounded angry, impatient. Leslie ran to the door, hit the buzzer in return, and quickly opened the door to the apartment.

"Hi, Mommy!" Ava shouted from the bottom of the steps, then ran up as fast her legs could carry her, her hair bouncing with each step.

"You have a good time?"

"Yeah, but Dora's on," she said as she hurried to the sofa and scrabbled for the remote.

Randy kept the downstairs door half open. "Come here," he commanded. "We need to talk."

Leslie closed the upstairs door and slowly walked down to meet her ex-husband.

"Listen, we need to talk."

"You said that, Randy. But here? It's cold outside."

"I don't want the kid to hear us," Randy replied.

"So … go ahead."

"Listen, I want Ava. I'm going to go back to court. I want custody of Ava. I thought I'd do the right thing and let you know."

Of all the things she had imagined Randy asking for today, custody would not have been first on that list.

"What?" Leslie could think of no other word that would express her incredulity.

"You heard me. I'm going to go back to court to get custody. Lisa wants kids, but she found out that she can't have any. Something about her tubes being too narrow. I don't know. Woman's stuff. But then I thought—hey!—I already have a kid."

"What? You have to be joking. Say that you're joking."

There was a slow burn evident in Randy's eyes. "I am not joking, Leslie. And don't think I don't mean it. I can make your silly little panic attacks look like a Sunday school picnic, once I'm done with you."

"You have to be joking," Leslie said, her voice starting to waver, ever so slightly.

Randy pushed his face closer to hers. "I said, I am not joking. So you get ready, Miss Crazy Lady. I'll have Ava sooner than you can say, 'I'm nuts.'"

Leslie, back on her heels, the fingers in her hands clenching into fists, waited, and wondered what to say in reply.

Jack stared at the two tombstones.

ELIZABETH WILLIAMS KENYON
1969–1999

EMMA ELIZABETH KENYON
1994–1999

A familiar pain formed in his heart and a lump in his throat. Guilt elevated his pulse, making his eyes water.

He waited. He knew it would come. He knew what to expect. The past would soon roar out at him like an avenging lion and devour another piece of him. He knew it was coming and he wouldn't move.

It wasn't my fault.

That day in 1999 had begun like any other day, with one major exception. Often, on a Saturday—well, more than often ... nearly always—to relieve the tension from a hellish workweek, Jack would mix a pitcher of Bloody Marys, heavy on the Tabasco sauce, and would have most of the pitcher gone by the time the college ball games started on TV. Elizabeth was on him again—about his drinking, about all the late nights, at work, at play, and his other habits he thought he'd kept secret from her.

But this Saturday, Jack had made her a promise. "No drinks until dinner, if that will make you happy."

"It will," she had replied coolly.

So he had knocked back a few Cokes—only Cokes, no hidden rum spikes, just ice—and had puttered about the house. Early that day, he'd taken Emma for her ballet lesson. Jack had loved watching her dance, her wispy blond hair bouncing to her steps in her little pink tutu and tights, even though she didn't appear to have a natural knack for it. She'd loved it, Jack had loved it, and it gave his wife an hour to herself.

By early afternoon, Elizabeth had claimed there was no food in the house worth eating and that she wanted to go out for a nice meal.

"We could go to the club, or eat at the Schenley Marriott. They have such a nice spread."

Jack had said he didn't care, that she could pick, and the three of them had all climbed into his Jaguar. Elizabeth didn't like his car but tolerated his affectation.

They headed down Butler Street. Jack remembered it well, a day much like this day—chilly, clear, bright sun, no reason for worry on the roads, a sober driver, and dry pavement. What could go wrong?

It was not my fault.

Jack had brought his car, under the speed limit, under control, to the crest of the small hill by Arsenal Park. The red light had turned to green....

The light was green! It had turned green!

From the north, from narrow 39th Street, most of the oncoming traffic was hidden by the diner on the corner. It had come in a blur, a dark blue blur like a shot, like the driver hadn't seen the light at all, like the sun was in his eyes and blinded him, or like Jack should have stopped instead. In that second, in that split fraction of a second, he'd heard Elizabeth scream and saw her hand fly up …

She was wearing her favorite red coat.

… as if her arm might provide protection from what was to come. Then the splintering of glass, the rumbling, twisting, wrenching, tossing, screeching, and rending of metal and glass … the sliding and turning in the air, falling and being slapped one way and then another … a long hiss, silence, and more silence … wet and being on the pavement, not being able to move … then a scream, a long time, a siren … and nothing at all.

The driver of the old blue Chevy Impala had been drunk—more than twice the legal limit in the state of Pennsylvania. They had discovered that during the autopsy.

Elizabeth had died instantly. She didn't have her seat belt on. She always complained that the seat belt wrinkled her blouse.

A massive collision like that wrenches the internal organs from their moorings.

Emma had died on the way to the hospital.

Jack had suffered a broken ankle. When the car had tipped, he was on the pavement. One open door caught the ankle just so, and had cracked two small bones. He was bruised. He was cut.

He was alive.

They were dead.

It was not my fault.

If he had been more observant, he would have seen that car. He could have swerved. Maybe all his drinking the week before had dulled his reaction time. Who could tell? Maybe if he had never touched alcohol, he would have snapped the wheel quickly and allowed the Chevy to miss them completely.

If only he had been looking.

Jack didn't cry. He never cried at the cemetery. Too public. Never in public.

Maybe it was my fault. I could have prevented it. I could have done something to save them.

He stared at their names.

It was all my fault.

And then he tapped at his pocket and slowly withdrew the pint bottle of vodka he'd brought with him.

It seemed only fitting, he thought, to do what he was about to do.

———◦∞∞◦———

Leslie unclenched her fists. She tried to remember what Pastor Blake had said about confronting the demons in her life.

"We all have demons," he'd said. "Some are big. Some aren't. And God is ready to help, with His awesome power. But you have to ask for strength. He wants us to ask."

Dear God, please give me what I don't have.

"So, you get ready for a fight, Leslie, because I'm bringing it," Randy all but spat, his face close to hers.

Leslie would not recall until much later, when her blood pressure had returned to normal, and only after Alice told her that she was inside her soon-to-be-restaurant and had witnessed the whole thing, but when Randy finished making his threat, Leslie—all 128 pounds of her—grabbed Randy by the lapels of his jacket and actually hoisted him, for a second or two, right off the ground.

She had read somewhere about a mother who had lifted an entire car after it had fallen on her child. *That must have felt like this,* she thought to herself, almost detached from the reality of it all.

She dropped him, unceremoniously, but kept hold of his jacket and said in an icy, stone-cold voice, "You try that, Randy, and I will fight you forever."

Randy's eyes had widened.

"You can have visitation. You can see her when the judge says you can see her. But—listen to me, Randy—you will *never, ever* get custody of Ava. Do you hear me? NEVER!"

Leslie looked at his eyes. Where there was once bravado and bluster, where there had always been bullying and intimidation, there was something else. Leslie had never, in their entire marriage, seen it in Randy's eyes. It was fear.

"You are nothing but a bully. I'm sorry that your wife can't have children. But don't think that you're going to hand Ava to her as some sort of possession that you have to give away. You don't. You haven't seen her in all this time and now you come back and try to assert your rights as a father?

You're a big bully, Randy, and I'm not going to tolerate it anymore. DO YOU HEAR ME?!"

Randy nodded.

She let go of his coat, and he shook his arms and patted down the ruffled fabric, as if being hoisted off the ground was a normal occurrence, as if he was used to being manhandled by a woman half his size.

Leslie had nothing else to say, partly because she had shocked herself nearly speechless. She never once imagined that she would stand up to Randy—stand up to him and make him back down. She was not the sort of person who would do that.

But she had done it.

There was a large crack, she realized, in who and what Randy had pretended to be all these years—a big, gaping crack Leslie could now see through. She might even be able to drive a car through it.

Randy couldn't clamber into his car fast enough. He gunned the engine, rolled down the window, and shouted back at her, "I'll see you in court!" Then he sped away, his tires screeching at the stop sign at Main Street.

Leslie wondered, as she watched him drive off, if her heartbeat would ever return to normal.

Jack stood and held the bottle in his right hand. He grasped the top with his left and he twisted it slowly, the bottom of the metal top breaking with the smallest grating noise.

Jack unscrewed the bottle top. He could smell the whiff of alcohol, even outdoors, even with a breeze; he could smell it and almost taste it again. It had been his favorite drink at one point, being clear and nearly odorless. He'd assumed that since it didn't have a telling odor, like whiskey, no one would smell it on his breath. Of course, he was totally wrong. The alcohol, as it burned off, left a sweetly sour smell to the breath of those who indulged. It was like the smell of decay, or decomposition, like the smell of a swamp on a humid day.

He held the open bottle in his hand and slowly dropped to his knees. His hand trembled more than it had ever trembled. The liquid danced in the neck of the bottle.

He looked at the gravestones, refusing to let his vision cloud with tears.

"I can't bring you back. I know I can't bring either of you back. I would have changed places with you that day. But I can't change what happened. I'm sorry. I lost both of you and I am so very, very sorry. My heart breaks every time I think of you and what I have lost."

He looked at the liquid, wavering in the bottle, anxious to exit, anxious to be inside him, to be doing its work. The tremor in his hand did not stop.

He turned his wrist, ever so slightly, his arm extended, and the clear liquid, the giver of warmth, began to spill and splash on the dying grass.

"I can't bring you back," Jack said, his voice only a raspy whisper. "But I can live a life that is worth something. I could throw away what little I have, but that would be of no honor to you. I can make something of what I have—as a testament to both of you—as a sacrifice to you."

He waited. There was the faint sound of traffic, carried by the slight breeze.

"This is my sacrifice."

He dropped the bottle, now empty, and raised his head to the sky. "God, I know You probably can't hear me after all I've done … but I need You."

There, on his knees, he bowed his head. "Please hear me. Please help me. Please let my life be a testament to these two."

And Jack remained where he was, for a long time, until his knees grew stiff and cold.

He stood up. He picked up the empty bottle. He walked back to his truck. He started the engine and began to drive home, to his life, begun anew once again.

Amelia Westland

Lyndora

Butler County, Pennsylvania

March 8, 1885

Mr. Middelstadt—Samuel—has proposed marriage to me. He did not bend on knee as is imagined in stage plays and theatrical performances, but sat beside me in his carriage and took my hands and said it would be a good thing for the two of us to be so united, that it would bring him great pleasure. He has needs only a wife can meet, and he offers such a fine existence, with a good house, stability and money and prestige.

It was scarcely unexpected, owing to his most attentive behavior, his generosity toward me, with lovely gifts and a delightful courtship, but is nearly overwhelming for a poor orphan girl from a tiny farm in Butler County.

I must pray and ponder my decision. I am fond of Samuel. If my answer to his proposal is yes, then I must bid Julian and his passionate kisses farewell. Yet Julian has not offered me an honest relationship nor a solid future. Perhaps our passion is amplified in the illicitness of it all, with my willing complicity.

Yet, despite the shortcomings of Julian and what he proposes, it is such a temptation. The life he offers is one of uncertainty, yet letting him go is unimaginable. His eyes devour me and I am swept away with ardent desire by his words of love. Pray, what do I do? Follow my heart or choose the safe and proper path?

Or do I remain steadfast, singular, stay as a teacher, inhabiting the life God has given me to lead and such gifts with which to serve Him?

How I wish that God had provided some sort of tablet, visible to His children, on which He would scribe His will or desires. But alas, there is no such thing.

(I have read what I have written and have come to the realization that I must hide this diary, for if anyone were to find these words, other than myself, I might be scandalized. I shall endeavor for this to remain hidden from human eyes forever.)

Call unto me, and I will answer thee,
and show thee great and mighty things, which thou knowest not.
—JEREMIAH 33:3

CHAPTER TWENTY-FIVE

JACK WENT BACK TO WORK the following Monday, not sad, but sober, and determined to stay that way. He made no proclamations, no fancy speeches, to friends or to Earl or to Leslie.

Jack had disappointed too many people in the past.

For a long time, people had excused him. "It was such a tragedy," they'd say. "I can't blame him for wanting to forget."

But after all the missed court dates, after failing to complete assignments, the dropped cases, after becoming abusive at work—people had had enough, had given him enough sympathy. He had driven drunk. He had gotten arrested several times, and had shouted and thrown punches. His parents had provided bail money. He had borrowed mortgage payments. He had acted inappropriately with other men's wives. He had wrecked two more expensive cars, those times all his fault. He had lost good friends and had made new ones—new friends who hastened his descent.

Jack had found it easy to slide downhill. And in the careening downward, he had hurt everyone who tried to slow his slide.

He hadn't wanted to stop.

But now he did.

He saw himself standing in front of two doors: one leading to life, and one leading to destruction. He desperately wanted to choose life.

This morning he stood in the rear of Frank and Alice's, staring at another door, the massive door, the valuable antique door, the beautifully carved wooden door with hidden hinges and two hardened deadbolts.

He had called in a locksmith, who had spent only a few minutes looking at both locks before making his recommendation.

"Tear the door down," he'd said bluntly.

"You can't open an old lock?" Jack had asked. "Your Web site said, 'We can open *any* lock.'"

The locksmith had gathered up his tools, slowly slipping them back into a black leather satchel. "Oh, these locks aren't that hard to break. Both are good ones, but not terribly sophisticated, compared to today's models."

"Then why can't you open them?"

The locksmith had motioned Jack to come closer. He'd pulled a small flashlight from his pocket and had focused it on the keyholes, first the bottom one, and then the top.

"What am I looking at?" Jack had asked.

"You're looking at the work of a person who really wanted to keep people out of this space. See that sort of puttylike stuff?"

"Yes. I saw that before. I thought it might be … just old putty."

"It's not. Someone used a torch, probably an acetylene torch. I think they had them back then, or some sort of hot welding equipment. Anyhow, they welded the keyholes shut. I don't think Houdini could get these open. So … my advice to you—tear the door down. Although it is a very pretty door."

Jack had ignored the door for several days, but felt drawn to it, as if there were some sort of wonderful secret behind it. Alice had suggested leaving it just as it is. "Some hidden treasure perhaps? Our customers will love the mystery. It could be like a carnival sideshow," she'd said.

Frank wanted the door saved. "If we break it, we pay for it—and that old door has to be worth several thousand dollars. I say leave it. Alice will love you for it. She adores mysteries."

Mike Reidmiller had stopped in one afternoon, and when Frank again suggested that it might indeed be some loot from the treasures of Diamond Jim Brady, one of Butler's most flamboyant and rich philanthropists and investors, Mike had gotten excited.

"He loved diamonds," Mike had said. "I did a paper on him in high school. They said he had more than two million dollars' worth of diamonds when he died. In today's money, that would be like fifty million dollars. And after his death, they only found a few of his diamonds—a couple of rings and stickpins. The rest of it—all those diamonds—vanished. This building is the right age. He died in 1912, I think. They looked in all the banks in town and didn't find a thing. Maybe that's what's back there."

Jack had dismissed that as implausible … but the idea had begun to grow on him.

Maybe there are diamonds there. Maybe he had his workers lock up his valuables, thinking he would be back to claim them. Maybe the room is stacked high with diamonds.

Then he'd dismissed it all again, attributing it to false hope and wishful thinking.

But standing in front of the door, locked tight like it was, made opening it all that much more tantalizing to Jack.

There has to be a way to do it that doesn't involve major construction.

Getting into that space would be easy, if you didn't mind a little demolition. Jack knew he could cut through the thick four-by-four timbers, the two of them guarding each side of the door. But he might have to add extra bracing and supports for the wall, since the interior wall, he determined, was load-bearing. He could cut a narrow opening beside the timbers, cut just one of two studs, and squeeze through. That would not be difficult, but no one wanted to pay for the demolition and the repair work. And what made that option more complicated was that on one side of the door, there was electrical service. On the other side of the door, was plumbing— one of the main waste water pipes for the building. That meant rerouting either or both, neither offering an easy, inexpensive job.

So now Jack simply stood and stared.

What if I make small cuts … here … on this wall and on the opposite wall inside the storage room … just big enough for my hand to get through? Those holes could be patched easily. Then I could reach around with a pry bar and lift out the hinge pins. If they aren't painted over. If I can get leverage on them. If they haven't a locked bottom ring. If I can twist just so and work without seeing what I'm working on.

He rubbed the side of his face with his hand.

A lot of ifs and maybes.

He put his hand on his tool belt.

Kind of like my life so far.

He was off the clock now, so staring and thinking were not draining anyone's bank account. He walked over to the wall, put his palm against it, and pressed. No give, no slack. He moved six inches farther. He pressed again. There was a slight sway. No stud. Finding studs with electronic stud-finders was made difficult because of all the lath and small nails used in the era of construction of the building.

Today builders like me would simply install wallboard sheets—plaster between two sheets of thick paper covering—in four-feet-by-eight-feet lengths. Back then, builders would nail in thousands of strips of wood, called lath, at right angles to the studs, and apply wet plaster over the lath. Tedious work, solid construction, hidden studs.

Jack got a very long screwdriver from his tool kit. He placed the tip of it on the wall and pounded. It easily penetrated the plaster, nicked a lath strip, and was soon against the opposite wall in the storage room. Jack pushed harder and the screwdriver went through easily. He pulled it out halfway and maneuvered it around. There were no obstructions in the space between the walls.

If he figured right, six inches to the right of the hole that he just made would be where the door hinge would be.

Tomorrow, I'll bring my hole saw. If I can't get to the hinges, then there's only one hole to repair.

"Pastor Blake, I need a lawyer."

Leslie sat in her usual chair in the pastor's office, her hands folded, a brown cardigan sweater over her shoulders, her purse at her feet. Sunlight was streaming in through the golden stained-glass windows, casting diamond-shaped patterns on the floor. She could hear a train rumble past on the tracks in the valley below.

She had just recounted the episode with her ex-husband to the pastor, trying to make her manhandling of Randy seem less dramatic that it was.

"I only sort of picked him up."

Pastor Blake let out a chuckle. "But you stood up for yourself, Leslie. That's huge. That's a big step. And no panic?"

She shook her head no. "Some hyperventilating afterward. But everything else—all my typical symptoms—stayed away."

Now Leslie returned to her real worry concerning that incident. "He'll get a lawyer. He is good friends with several attorneys. He called them ambulance chasers. I thought they were mean-spirited, but they won most of their cases. He'll get one of them to represent him. Probably for free. They all went to school together. And if he says he's going to do something, he'll do it."

"But he has no legal basis to seek custody, does he?" Pastor Blake asked, obviously knowing that Randy did not.

"No. But … there is my past. You know, with my medical issues. My emotional issues. The panic attacks happened all the time when we were still married. He could make a case just on that, I'm sure. I read about these things all the time. Judges do crazy things. And he's very well known. He grew up in the town of Greensburg and his father was some sort of long-term councilman. He has friends all over."

"Then you'll need good representation."

Leslie appeared pained. "I know. But I can't afford it. What's a retainer of a good lawyer for something like this? Five thousand, at least, I bet—for this type of case. More? I don't have that sort of extra money around. I went out on a limb to buy the Midlands Building."

It was apparent to Leslie that Pastor Blake sympathized with her and recognized the seriousness of her dilemma.

"I'm better now. Much better," she continued. "But he'll make an issue over what happened in the past."

"You do need an attorney, Leslie. I wish these sorts of things could be handled outside of the courtroom, but they can't. You'll need an attorney, if he tries what he threatened. Perhaps you could qualify for free legal aid from the county or state."

Leslie shifted in her chair. "Maybe. But my father always said that you get what you pay for. I know that I might find some help, but I can't risk losing Ava by using free legal aid. I just can't risk it. Would you risk your daughter to save money?"

Leslie knew Pastor Blake would agree with her.

"Well, I'll pray for a solution," the pastor answered. "And there is a lawyer in the church. I can ask him for advice—with your permission."

Leslie agreed.

"All I know is that I need a good attorney. Now my biggest problem is finding the money to pay for him."

———————

Jack hefted the biggest drill he had, placed a circular cutting saw, a round cup with sharp cutting teeth, and placed that saw on the small hole he had made the day before. He called back over his shoulder.

"I'm cutting now. No one get jumpy."

Alice and Frank were both in the store, moving large cardboard templates around on the floor. "I don't believe in feng shui, but furniture is either put in the right place or it isn't," Alice was saying.

Jack did not work on Saturdays—unless he had to—and he explained that what he was doing was at no charge to the job.

Often, when Jack started a saw or a drill, or his pneumatic nail gun, Alice would shriek. "You have to warn me when you're going to make a racket," she'd told him.

So Jack issued his standard warning, and Alice made a theatrical move to cover her ears.

The hole saw whirred silently until it bit into the plaster. Little clouds of white dust erupted and the teeth of the saw gnashed and growled as they sliced through the lath. Jack pulled it out, undid the saw, added an extension to the saw bit, and slipped the saw back into the hole, to cut through the other side of the wall. He was finished in only a few minutes.

He tried his arm through the hole. It fit easily, though it grew more and more snug as he reached in farther. But he was through, into the mysterious storage room. He pulled the flashlight off his belt and placed it at the hole. He could see the circle of light on the far wall—some sort of dark green wallpaper, and nothing else. He could not get enough of an angle to see anything else.

He had come prepared, bringing a small mirror mounted on a

telescoping pole. He threaded that through and shined the light off of that, off of a corner of the mirror. He could just make out the hinge.

But how am I going to get to the hinge? My arm won't bend that way. I should have thought of that at the beginning.

The hinge and hinge pin were easily visible—large, no rust, unpainted. It would be easy to remove, if he could just reach it.

But how am I going to reach it?

He sat back down on the folding chair by the door and tried to think of what might work.

———※———

Leslie and Ava walked back to their apartment after visiting the grocery store. Ava had fallen in love with the cupcakes from the bakery. She was not a child who demanded much, never had tantrums solely over the purchase of one thing or another—but her desire for these cupcakes came close to triggering all those childish reactions.

"I love them, Mom. You have to buy them for me. You do."

Normally, Leslie resisted giving in to such demands, but Ava used the ploy so seldom. So today, there was a box with a half dozen assorted cupcakes at the top of one of the bags.

"How come we can't drive to the store, Mom?" Ava asked. "Everybody else drives."

Leslie had answered the same question before and wondered if this was Ava being six or Ava being absentminded.

"Because we only live a few blocks from the store. Because this saves gas. Because it's a nice day. Because this is good exercise. Because Grandma Amelia walked two miles just to go to school—after she did all her chores for the morning."

Leslie added up all the reasons into one superdefense of walking to the store. The sheer volume of answers silenced her daughter for an entire block.

And every little bit helps. If I'm going to have to come up with five thousand dollars or so, I'll have to start somewhere. I save on gas and I buy less since we have to carry it home.

While waiting to hear about the museum position, she had kept sending out résumés and answering ads, making phone calls, searching for a job that would allow her to work the hours that Ava was in school. Mrs. Pindler had called from the museum to let her know that the board had met but hadn't had time to consider her application. She had assured Leslie that everything was fine, and that she would force them into a decision when they met the following month.

Ava stopped at the corner and turned back, holding a paper bag filled with bread, hamburger buns, lettuce, and a bag of Goldfish, and gave her mother that look—that six-year-old look of impatience for "Let's hurry it up."

I need to save up money—and fast. A free attorney might be fine, if I didn't really care about the outcome. But I cannot risk that with Ava. What if they don't get the right medical records? What if they think that panic attacks can't be cured?

She finally made it to Ava's side. "Look both ways—twice," Leslie reminded.

Ava did that, sweeping her head back and forth, back and forth. "No runaway trucks, Mom. Let's cross."

Maybe Jack knows a good attorney....

———⚬⚬⚬———

Jack thought he had his dilemma figured out. He stared and thought and poked around, until he came up with a solution that just might work. Using clamps, he fixed the mirror to the wall, so he could see the reflection of the middle hinge. He then drilled a hole through the thick beams surrounding the door, several inches above the hinge and almost parallel to it. He took his fishing wire—the cable used to thread new wires through conduit—and attached a smaller wire noose to the end. He fed that wire through the second hole and, twisting it just so, managed to get that small wire loop over the head of the hinge pin.

It only took a hundred tries and a full hour—but I got it.

He pulled the wire tight, watching his progress on the small mirror, twisting his body this way and that, as if to help guide the wire to its goal. It snugged fast around the rounded head of the hinge pin. Jack pulled slowly and steadily. The hinge hesitated at first, then began to slide up and out. When he had the pin removed from the hinge, Jack let out a small whoop of pleasure.

He was sweating, his arms hurt from the prolonged tension, and his back was killing him from assuming an unnatural position for so long—but he had one hinge free.

Only two more to go.

———⊙⊙———

Back at the apartment, Leslie put away the groceries, her mind in turmoil.

Maybe I could ... just take Ava, pack our things, and take off and hide somewhere out west. Some remote town. Wyoming, maybe. Make a new start. Go somewhere where he'll never find us.

Even though she knew it was a foolish, and probably illegal, plan, the prospect of never having to deal with this worry was so very, very attractive that she often considered it—even though she knew she would never do it.

I'm stronger than that. I'm the great-great-great granddaughter of a very strong woman.

But where am I going to come up with five thousand dollars?

———⊙⊙———

Jack leaned back and heard the muscles and bones in his back crackle and pop in protest. It was now five in the afternoon. Following the same process as he had used on the first door hinge, he had the second one removed. The middle and the top hinges were free.

Now he was on his stomach, trying to get at hinge number three—the one closest to the floor. He feared that the last would be the hardest. It often happened that way in construction: The last of anything was the most problematic. Things broke, tools didn't seem to work the way they worked at the beginning, and workmen grew tired and sloppy.

He checked his watch. It was a little after six, and his wire noose was around the head of hinge number three. He pulled. Nothing moved. He tugged again, wrapping the wire twice around his hand. Nothing moved.

He sat up, put his feet flat against the wall, leaned in, took up all the slack he could, and methodically pulled back hard, using his legs as leverage.

The pin squealed—he could hear it through the thick door—and moved a hair. Jack redoubled his efforts and pulled again, and the pin popped free.

Jack had done it—without destroying the door or creating a huge repair bill.

It had taken most of the afternoon and part of the evening, but he had done it.

Now all he had to do was push against the hinged side of the door. The deadbolts wouldn't like it, and he knew that the doorjamb may suffer some damage, but it would be minor. It would be easy to replace a cracked doorjamb once the door was off—even if he did have to use a piece of expensive walnut or mahogany.

He stood up, anxious, excited. He looked back into the room. Frank and Alice had gone. He hadn't noticed their departure and wondered if he should call them back for this moment.

But whatever is in this room doesn't belong to them. I should call Leslie.
He considered it.
Maybe the room is filled with dead mice.
He decided not to call anyone.

Placing his shoulder against the left side of the door, opposite the doorknob, he pushed, steady, and the door gave way, with some squealing of hinges and wood. He heard some splintering from the strike pocket—the part of the door that the lock fit into—as it broke.

He forced the door open twelve inches or so, enough to get his torso into the room. He held a flashlight in one hand and clicked it on.

The room wasn't large—perhaps ten feet by ten feet, about double the size of a standard walk-in closet.

No shelves. No hidden doorways. But against the far wall stood a dark object, tall as a man's chest, perched on four legs the size of a man's fist. Jack focused the light.

The object was a safe. A brooding, hulking, black safe, with a large numbered dial and a thick handle and some sort of faded painting on the front, perhaps an eagle and a sun.

The door of the safe was closed tight.

Jack squeezed back out the heavy door of the storage room and pulled it shut. He glanced out the windows. The sky was dark and the streetlights had just come on. The black fingers of the trees scratched out menacing shadows on the windows and floor.

It's time to call it a day. I'll come back tomorrow and get the door open properly.

Amelia Westland Middelstadt
Butler, Pennsylvania
May 21, 1887

Not a full year has passed since we were wed, and I am with child … great with child, and scarce can walk another step. I have been ill for much of my confinement and have taken to complete bed rest these last three months. Dizziness plagues me, and I find it difficult to discover a solid food that might take purchase in my stomach.

Yet I feel this life growing inside, turning, moving, kicking, and when such things occur, my spirit soars, and I endure in spite of the illness. I am filled with wonder at the miracle of it all.

As I near my travail, I am exceedingly fearful, and pray unceasingly. O God, please bless me with a child of my own. This I vow, on this page, and on this date, that this shall be the last request I should ever trouble Thee with, O Great Creator—just one small child brought safe and well into my arms. May this stepmother live to be a mother, I pray.

Dear God, hear me, listen to my plea, have mercy upon me a sinner.

Catherine is ever by my side. I am overjoyed by her marriage to Henry Albertson, who is now in Samuel's employ. I have told Catherine that if I were to pass on during my travail, she is to tell the child, if the child survives me, that I expect him or her to follow God, to pray always, to live a holy life, to follow one's heart.

Thou shalt keep therefore his statutes, and his commandments,
which I command thee this day, that it may go well with thee, and
with thy children after thee, and that thou mayest prolong thy days
upon the earth, which the Lord thy God giveth thee, for ever.
—DEUTERONOMY 4:40

CHAPTER TWENTY-SIX

LESLIE AND AVA STOOD TO one side. Frank and Alice were on the other side of the door. Even Mike and Trevor were in attendance—all anxious, all excited, all ready to see the big unveiling.

Jack, once again, pushed on the left side of the door of the storage room. This time he was wearing his full tool belt. His big drill and reciprocating saw were at his feet—just in case he needed them. The door gave way, and Jack slid sideways into the dark space. Instead of a flashlight, he carried a battery-powered lantern for better illumination.

The door closed behind Jack as he wedged into the darkness. From inside the storage space came the sound of a drill, then tapping, and then the drill again. Jack had told everyone when he called him or her Sunday morning that he should be able to make short work of the locks, and perhaps he wouldn't even have to loosen them—just slide the door out of the way.

Now they had all gathered to see what was behind the big old door.

Less than five minutes passed and the door rocked a bit, then began to slide away from the opening. Jack had his hand at the top and the side. The door backed away and he hefted it sideways, out of the opening, and into the empty store.

Everyone crowded around to get a look at the now-open storage area.

"It's a safe," Alice said.

"That is exactly what Jack said was in there," Frank answered. "How perceptive you are, Mrs. Adams."

She gave him a playful but almost powerful sock on his shoulder. "But it's a big safe. A huge safe. I was expecting something smaller."

"Have you tried opening it?" Leslie asked Jack.

"No. Not yet. I wanted witnesses, in case there's nothing—or something—inside."

The room, wallpapered in a dark green William Morris pattern similar to the pattern carved on the door, was devoid of any other items—just the safe, which stood flat against the rear wall. No pictures, no papers, no shelves, no lamps—just the safe. The very large safe.

They all crowded into the small room as best they could, watching intently, hoping for some absolutely fabulous treasure hidden all these years.

Leslie had confided in Jack, when he had called earlier in the morning, that if the safe were full of diamonds, all her worries would be behind her.

"But I don't have my hopes up," she had added.

Jack knelt at the safe. He tried the handle first. It moved up and down. He turned to look at the chorus of hopeful, excited faces. He pulled the handle ... and the door opened almost effortlessly.

The chorus all but gasped in unison.

Jack grabbed his flashlight and focused it on the safe's interior.

There was another gasp from the audience, this time, subdued, softer.

The interior was completely empty. There was a small niche in the upper right-hand corner of the safe, with a separate door. That was already open and the interior of the small cubbyhole was also empty.

There was nothing inside.

Nothing at all.

The chorus groaned a sigh of regret and disappointment.

Leslie elbowed her way to the safe. "Nothing at all?" The disappointment was obvious in her voice. "Nothing? Not even an old newspaper? Or a few dollar bills? Nothing?"

Jack appeared confused. "Why go to all that trouble—for an empty safe? I don't get it."

Leslie stood up from the safe and edged back out of the storage room. *I was so ready for some good news. For some jewels or something of value. Now … I'm back at square one.*

She sat on the folding chair outside the little room and wished things had been different.

From the front of the building, Alice ran back to the safe in the storage room. A few seconds later, she ran out again, hurried to her laptop, tapped the keys, waited, then let out a whoop.

"It's a Diebold Bankers Safe! With original paint. And the combination was written in pencil on the inside of the door."

Excited, she hurried back to Leslie and said, "You hit the jackpot!"

"What do you mean? It's just an old, worthless safe with nothing in it."

"Oh be still, my heart. You, Mrs. Ruskin, are a rube. A nice rube, but still … I know that might hurt, but you are one. The two words that never go together are *old* and *worthless.*"

Alice grabbed Leslie's hand and pulled her into the storage room. "See the painting on the front door of the safe—the eagle and the sun? See the gold striping along the edge? See the decal of the company who made it: Diebold Banking Systems, Inc.? You have one rare safe on your hands."

Alice kept hold of Leslie's hand and pulled her toward the front of the building, to her laptop computer. On the screen was a picture of Leslie's empty safe—only it was a picture of a more dinged and dented example of the Diebold Banker's Safe. Leslie's safe was pristine, showroom quality by comparison.

Alice hit the mouse and the page scrolled up. The copy under the last picture of the safe read: *Extremely Rare.*

In smaller print below, it said:

> One of the few known surviving models of the
> Diebold Banker's Safe in existence. Paint: Good
> Condition. Company decal: 75% Intact. No
> Combination. Pick-up price: $5,700. Firm. Delivery
> available, quotes on request.

Leslie stared at the computer screen, then at Alice.

"You, my dear, have a very expensive, old, empty safe in your back room."

———❦———

Jack hired three finish carpenters for three weeks to finish up Alice and Frank's job. Jack could do built-in furniture like they had requested—window seats and the like—but he was not set up to do cabinetmaking. The three brothers were between jobs and were excellent finish carpenters with a shop nearby. They agreed to work for less than they normally charged. In those three weeks, Alice and Frank's place was transformed from a bare shell with interesting architectural details into a whimsical and fascinating bistro/bookstore/café with perfectly fascinating architectural details, some exposed bare brick walls, some plastered walls in rich colors, exposed beams, quirky little nooks, wonderful natural light during the day, and a plethora of odd lamps, track lights, spots, and recessed lighting, mixing old and new, hip and traditional, funky and … not funky.

Alice had selected an explosion of colors for the interior—greens, the color of moss or spring leaves on some walls, and an eggplant shade on others, with accents of a red the color of Mexico. The palette was an unexpected combination of colors—contrasting yet unified, like music of different strains, all melding together into perfect harmony.

At least that's what Alice said.

If Jack didn't understand it completely, he didn't let on. But he always claimed that he was just the simple carpenter and would do anything the customer wanted.

Alice used the same abandon in selecting the fabric for the chairs and sofas and window seats—a quirky but pleasing mix of vintage French prints.

In the back corner, Jack installed a small but very serviceable kitchen. Two bathrooms, per code, were just beyond that, and a small storage area lay behind the kitchen. A very sleek, European refrigerated display case had been imported from France, or Italy, or some place that wasn't America.

Jack said he didn't like foreign things as a rule, except for french fries and French cars, but he really liked the display case.

"It looks like a Ferrari," he said.

Stock began to arrive: books, handmade jewelry and luxurious scarves, accessories from the Adamses' buying trip in Paris, a mix of art objects from Alice and Frank's house—contemporary, vintage, and antique—and all manner of fascinating things, from very small and affordable to very large and expensive. When Leslie saw the array of things for sale, and how Alice and Frank's was coming together, she was amazed. She could see that the very artistic Alice knew what she was doing. The woman obviously had a flair for the unique, and a real sense of how to merchandise it.

The one thing that Jack had not yet completed was the removal of the wonderfully old and supremely heavy Diebold Banker's Safe from the storage room.

To Leslie's absolute amazement, the safe sold within five days of her posting it on the Antiquesafes.com Web site, for only a few hundred dollars less than the eight thousand she was asking for it.

The buyer had contracted with a local firm to have it moved. And now the five burly men were there, with a floor lift jack, sheets of plywood to protect the floor, prebuilt inclines for steps and curbs, and a large truck with a heavy-duty, reinforced-lift tail gate.

They spent an hour preparing for the move, laying down the plywood, figuring out which ramps were needed, measuring doorways and steps.

Leslie came down to watch the move. She had already received a check for half the sale amount, and the movers were to bring the second payment—a cashier's check—when they moved the safe out of her building and to its new home.

Disappointed as she was for not finding treasure, the safe was a rare stroke of good fortune in her life, she told herself.

If Randy does go to court over custody, I can fight him now.

Two of the burly movers carefully threaded the floor lift along the plywood path. They gently maneuvered the lift under the safe and started pumping the handle, gradually bringing the weight off the floor.

"No more than an inch," one of them called out. "More than that can tip it over if it gets wobbly."

Jack was in the storage room as they maneuvered it, watching their work. He wasn't concerned about anything specific. He simply wanted to see how they accomplished moving such a huge and heavy object.

The arms of the lift caught the underside of the safe, and a few seconds later, after resting on that one spot of real estate for almost a century, the safe was airborne—an inch or two off the base. Both men grabbed the handle, released the brake, and began to strain at the weight. The safe seemed to groan, wobbled a fraction, and moved forward.

As it came away from the wall, everyone heard it: a shuffling, sliding sound. And as the safe moved farther away from the wall, something fell, with a papery thump to the floor—released, as it were, from being held captive behind the safe for an unknown term.

"What's that?" Jack asked, knowing that no one had the answer.

He waited until the safe was out of the room to retrieve the object. It was dusty, for certain, and held closed with a moss green ribbon, tied around it—not as a decorative wrapping, or ornament, but simply securing the pages closed. As soon as he picked it up, he knew what it was.

There was no other object, no other book, with the same sort of heft, or feel, or tactile sense.

It was a Bible.

———

Jack carried it out, tenderly, like he was carrying a wounded puppy, and presented it to Leslie.

Alice hurried over. "Another eBay item?" She laughed. "There is no one else I know who can get rich from an empty storage room."

"I don't know," Leslie said, running her hand over the dusty cover. "It's an old Bible."

Alice looked a bit disappointed. "I don't think they sell well. I mean old Bibles. Maybe they do. I could check. We could sell it in the store, if you wanted. Or display it. Wouldn't that be a nifty conversation piece?"

Leslie hardly heard anything Alice had said. There was something about this book, something about the ribbon, something about how it felt in her hands. It wasn't just a Bible. She was sure of that—even before she undid the green ribbon, tied tightly around the book, in both directions, like a present, but not a present.

This was well used. This was someone's Bible.

She stared at the thick book.

At the back, between the back cover and the last page, there was a thicket of loose pages, just a bit larger than the pages of the Bible, as if someone had stored them in there for safe keeping. The edges of those loose pages were worn, torn in a few spots. Leslie could see that even before she opened the book.

She untied the ribbon and carefully pulled it off as a puff of dust was released into the air, and held it in her left hand. She opened the Bible to the first page, and next to the inside of the front cover she found an old photographic image, the paper a buttery color, the ink a sepia tone. It was the portrait of a man and a woman, dressed as bride and groom.

Leslie gingerly turned one more page.

At the top, in ornate, gilded letters, with scrolls and filigrees spreading out like unchecked ivy in a garden was written:

Dedication.

Underneath that were the words:

Presented to _____ on the occasion of _____:

In black ink filling in the lines that had faded to umber, were the handwritten words, in a most precise writing style: *Presented to Amelia Grace Westland Middelstadt, on the occasion of our Wedding. 10 June, 1886.*

Leslie looked at the words again. She couldn't believe what she was seeing.

She reached out and touched her fingertip to the name, as if trying to feel the vibrations made when it was first transcribed. She traced her finger down the page to the date.

Alice and Jack looked at her, watched her move her hand, as if in slow motion.

"What is it?" Alice asked, "What? Is it a famous person? I can't see."

Leslie shook her head no. "No. No one famous. It's just—"

"Just what?" Alice asked. "What?"

Leslie touched the name again. "This was my great-great-great grandmother's Bible. Amelia Grace Westland. Her married name was Middelstadt. It belonged to her."

Alice and Jack both were astonished—not to Leslie's level perhaps, but very surprised and incredulous.

"That's why I bought this building," Leslie murmured. "That's why I was drawn to it. It had to be. It was because of this Bible."

———◦◦◦———

Leslie took the old Bible upstairs, to her kitchen table, to be with the precious pages by herself. Leslie was not one to believe in apparitions, or in being guided or led by spirits, but this was one situation where she had to wonder.

This is why I am here. This is why I own this building. Gramma Mellie wanted me to have this.

She looked again at the dedication page. She wondered if Amelia's husband had written these words, or if he had paid someone to draft the letters with a calligrapher's flourish. From what Amelia had written in her own hand, she assumed the latter.

She looked again at the photographic portrait, presumably of her great-great-great grandparents on their wedding day. Amelia was twenty-three when she had married. She was beautiful and serene in her white dress and veil. Her husband, Samuel, looked back at Leslie in his morning coat, a kind smile touching his lips. A Bible—especially a fine copy like this one with leather binding and gilded pages—would have been a substantial purchase. A man would not buy an expensive Bible like this for his wife on a whim or if money was tight and resources limited.

She turned to the back page of the Bible.

She had been right. There was a small thicket of hand-written pages, pages torn out of some other book and placed in this Bible for some reason—to safeguard? To hide? To be kept from other's eyes?

Leslie removed the stack of pages. It didn't appear that they were in order, for the rough edges of the torn side didn't line up. They must have been, at one time, rearranged, shuffled.

Yet the handwriting was so familiar. It was Amelia's hand, Leslie could be sure of that. The penmanship matched the pages in the diary on Leslie's nightstand that she had read so many times.

She looked up at the clock. School would soon be out. She didn't want to rush this experience. She wanted to take her time, to savor what she had found, and not consume it like some fast-food meal.

She tapped the diary pages back in order, slipped them back in the Bible, and placed the treasured book on top of the refrigerator—not sure why, exactly, except that space was empty and might be the last place a Bible thief would investigate.

She grabbed her coat, her keys, her cell phone, just in case, and headed for Ava's school.

"I know it hasn't been that long, Leslie," Mike said as the two of them watched Ava and Trevor race around the playground, their breath coming out in little vapor clouds. "I know you said a year. I know all that."

Leslie knew what Mike was going to ask. He had hinted at it during every conversation they had had since their initial discussion. Normally, in the past, before everything that had happened to Leslie had happened, she might have found Mike's sort of persistence annoying, or upsetting, or an adequate reason to say "no." But now that Leslie was older, and less secure—financially and in other ways—than she had ever been in her life, she didn't find Mike's dogged pursuit aggravating or annoying in the least. In fact, it was flattering, even a bit endearing.

Not every woman is so desired, or so wanted.

"My father always said that if you know that you want something, then you should go after it. Simple as that, he said," Mike explained, blowing on his hands in the chilly prewinter air. He hadn't worn gloves, which, for Mike, was an unusual occurrence.

He noticed her looking. "I can't find them. I had them yesterday. You saw me with them when we talked after school. But now they have vanished. I looked everywhere."

Leslie knew what the next line was, and she smiled to herself when he delivered it, without any hint of self-consciousness.

"I guess I really need a woman to help me keep track of things."

She noted that he didn't say that he needed a woman to keep track of things—but that he needed her help to help *him* become more responsible. She wondered if that was a very deliberate choice of words, or only accidental.

Looking at Mike's hopeful expression, much like a puppy's expression as it looks at a not-yet-opened box of Milk-Bones, Leslie figured that Mike was just being Mike.

And would being with Mike be so bad?

He had a lovely home, a nice son, and a good job, as an operations manager at Herr-Voss, a firm that made coil-processing equipment. Leslie had no real idea of what that was, or what they produced, but Mike said he enjoyed the work. "It's like a big puzzle sometimes," he had said. "The people are nice. I really like working with them. And it's got a great pension plan. You can never be too prepared for the future." That was more than a lot of people could say, Leslie thought.

Leslie and Mike had gone out together several more times, for dinner and a movie, had gone for ice cream and coffee with Ava and Trevor in tow on a couple of occasions, and Mike had stopped by, without Trevor, at Leslie's apartment often. Leslie would have admitted the arrangement looked a lot like two people who were dating.

Mike was not aggressive in the "intimacy department," as he once called it. "I can take my time. Don't get me wrong—I like it and all that—but I know that waiting is the proper thing to do. That's what my church, and the Bible, teaches, and I can go along with that."

Even as he said that, even as he stated that he respected waiting, Leslie imagined that if she had been more willing, so would Mike.

Kisses were shared, hugging happened often. Mike was patient and kind, and Leslie allowed herself to feel closer to him, especially in regards to the future "intimacy department." If she waited for sparks and fireworks, she wondered, would she be waiting forever?

Now, this afternoon, he brought the subject up once again—the subject of him and her and her eventual decision. But this time it was a bit more direct than in the past, a bit more forward.

"So … I know you're waiting. I know that. But do you think you can give me a hint? Do you feel any different now than before?"

Leslie reached out with her gloved hand and placed it on his forearm. He looked at her hand and then back to her face, as if this might be some sort of new sign, a signal he was trying his best to interpret.

"Mike, I want to tell you. I want to give you an answer. But the truth of the matter is that I can't. I'm just not ready. I think I'm closer—a lot closer than I was before."

Mike patted her hand. "That's okay. You take your time. I keep asking … well … because I want to be with you and I keep hoping your answer will be yes. We should be together. That's the way I feel."

"I know, Mike. I know that. A little more time. That's all."

He placed his hand over hers, and squeezed a little. "I'll keep asking, you know that. I want to be with you."

They untangled their hands.

"I know, Mike. I know you do."

And she waited and looked at him, carefully, wondering if waiting for, and wanting, a spark—or even a small fireworks display—was just out of the question.

Amelia Westland Middelstadt
Butler, Pennsylvania
Thanksgiving Day 1891

As I pause this day to recount my blessings, I look back on my life and see the hand of God. It has not, of course, been, as I would have imagined as a young precocious farm girl of thirteen in Glade Mills when I commenced recording my thoughts in this dear book. There have been dark days when, despite the great material provision God has wrought, despair threatened to cloud my heart. Nor have I always been as thankful as I should that it has all come about in the way that it has. But God has demonstrated His great faithfulness despite my selfish ways and has lifted me up when my soul was most downcast. I am most undeserving of His grace and mercy.

He has blessed me with a kind and generous husband, of even temperament and upstanding character. I confess, with deep sadness, that I have not always been liberal in my expressions of affection toward him. But his patience knows no bounds, and for that I am grateful.

God has twice blessed me with children—first, my two darling stepdaughters, and then, my precious daughter Ellen, some three years ago, and then my delightful son Seth, whose first year of life we celebrated just one month previous, both strong and healthy and remarkable indeed. After my first travail, it was thought by the doctor that it would never again be possible; however, God in His mercy has looked upon me with favor and has seen fit to grant me a son. How unexpected and wonderful! My lying in with Seth was not as difficult as such I experienced with Ellen. Though Samuel had not voiced his feelings, it was most apparent to me that he was desirous of a male child to carry on the Middelstadt name. He takes much joy in Seth and Ellen both, and I fear they are in danger of becoming exceedingly spoiled, for he is most indulgent of them, as he is with the older girls, who take great pleasure in their stepsiblings as well. Catherine is now with child. It brings me great joy to think of the two of us as mothers together, and our children, should God will, as close as cousins.

It is of the LORD's mercies that we are not consumed,
because his compassions fail not. They are new every morning:
great is thy faithfulness. The LORD is my portion, saith my soul;
therefore I will hope in him. The LORD is good unto them
that wait for him, to the soul that seeketh him.
—LAMENTATIONS 3:22–25

CHAPTER TWENTY-SEVEN

"Has he called you?" Pastor Blake asked. "Your ex-husband, I mean."

At first, when she first began meeting with Pastor Blake, Leslie had asked for counseling sessions twice a week. Then, as she felt better, the sessions were reduced to once a week. For the last month, they had met only twice.

"No. And I am surprised. In the past, if somebody threatened him, that made him all the more angry and dead-set. And if he had an attorney, or wanted to pursue some legal action, an attorney would have notified me right away, right?"

Pastor Blake shrugged. "I have no experience in this, Leslie. But I would guess that they would have—if only to intimidate their opponent."

He reached over and drew the office window closed. There was a hint of snow in the air.

"And how are you feeling, Leslie? Any recent episodes?"

She shook her head no.

"I think I'm more nervous than I should be. I still get distracted over little things sometimes, but … no more panic. Maybe God fixed me."

Pastor Blake smiled. He had previously acknowledged that God can do anything, can heal any illness, can provide any need.

"The bottom line, Leslie, is that He wants us to come to Him. But sometimes He doesn't take us *from* the fire. He walks with us *through* the fire."

He had told Leslie that along with having faith, God expects us to fully participate in seeking out the healing that we desire. We have to want it, a solution, and we should take advantage of the help that others offer.

"And sometimes, Leslie, the healing that God provides comes through sessions like this, and prayer, which makes a change in your mind and heart possible. It's a bit of all of that."

To Leslie, it felt as if they had discussed the panic attack situation to death, or nearly to death—the why, the how, methods of prevention, tips to deal with them, all the practical approaches to the problem. And now, while the sessions may be less needed at the emotional/prevention level, Leslie knew she needed a friend she could trust and confide in, who believed in her and could help her in her growing relationship with God. Pastor Blake was that friend.

He had all but acknowledged the shift a few weeks ago.

"You don't need this anymore," he had said. "But if our meetings help you, and I can advise and guide you, then that's okay. Sort of like disciple making. Jesus wants us to do that. And I'm happy to be here for you."

"Thanks."

"So … how are things with Mike? Are you coming closer to a decision?"

Leslie knew he would ask. And she had not figured out a good answer.

"I don't think so. I keep waiting for a sign. Something that will make it easy for me to decide. And so far, no signs. No skywriting. No wet sheepskins."

"Have patience. You may not see a sign, but you'll know when you know."

Even the pastor laughed at his nearly clichéd response.

———

Leslie hurried down the stairs. Ava was having a sleepover with the Stickles, who were the most perfect de facto grandparents Ava—and Leslie—could have hoped for. The Stickles had two children of their own, fine children now living in California. They both made the return pilgrimage to Butler on an infrequent basis.

Ava was their perfect grandchild. She loved to color with them, and make cookies, and laugh hysterically at Mr. Stickle's incredibly corny jokes, and watch the hours of home movies that Mr. Stickle had taken with an old Kodak 8mm camera. His son had them all transferred to videotape several years earlier. Ava loved those videos—as if Daniel and Henry were the brothers she never had, enjoying their birthday parties and Little League games as if they had happened just last year.

So tonight Leslie had a rare evening to herself. She had no plans other than having no plans.

As she walked past the windows of Alice and Frank's, she noticed someone moving around inside. It was not late, but she didn't expect to see anyone there. The grand opening was planned for the following Saturday. Media would be there. Cameron and her crew would be there—on Friday, actually, to shoot the interiors before the crowds came. Alice expected an overflow crowd.

The figure inside stepped into a pool of light.

It was Jack, holding a drill in his hand, wearing his tool belt low on his hips, a denim shirt, unbuttoned, with a tight white T-shirt underneath, highlighting his muscular build. His hair, a little longer than when they first met, was tousled just a bit, almost like it was planned.

Leslie wasn't surprised at the way her pulse quickened when she looked at him. She didn't have any real reason to talk with Jack—not specifically. But she found herself tapping on the door, lightly, as if saying that she didn't want to raise a fuss.

Jack spun about, saw her, waved, and hurried to the door. "Just doing some last-minute picture hanging," he explained as he locked the door behind her. "Alice had a list six pages long, and most of it had to do with matching her grand-opening wardrobe to the store colors. There were, like, a half dozen items for me to do on my punch list. And one was to finish hanging the pictures."

Leslie felt tongue-tied and only smiled in reply.

"Maybe you could help. I never know if pictures are at the right height. Alice said 'lower rather than higher.' There are—" he looked over at the stack of vintage posters, from very large to medium-sized, leaning against the eggplant-colored wall—"four … no five more to go. Give me a hand?"

She agreed and grabbed the top picture—an Italian travel poster. A sticky note was fastened to the glass.

Far wall from the street … the moss green wall—centered.

"I guess that means this one," Leslie said, pointing.

"Is that moss green? Or is it leaf green or mint green or tea green?"

"No," Leslie said, almost certain, "this is moss green."

The exact same color as Gramma Mellie's diary. Amazing.

She held the picture up, at eye level, no higher. "Do you have a tape measure? We need to find the middle of the space—at this height."

He ran his tape along the wall, Leslie made a bridge with her body, and he squiggled beneath her, their bodies close. She could have simply taken the picture off the wall.

Maybe Freud would say that I meant to do it this way.

Jack marked the center of the wall with a piece of chalk ("It comes off better than pencil," he had said) and drilled a small hole, tapped in an anchorman, added a screw, and then gestured for the picture. He placed the picture's wire on the screw.

Leslie stepped back.

"Level?" he asked.

"Up on your right—just a little. Perfect."

The two of them made short work of the last few colorful posters and a beveled mirror with a thick frame that remained. When they were done, Jack slipped the drill into the holster on his belt, unbuckled it, and set it carefully on the floor.

"I guess that's it, then," he said.

She looked around at the totally renewed space, nodding in agreement. "Everything looks so wonderful. That mirror is beautiful and really adds sparkle to the entry area."

"Alice has an eye for design," Jack answered.

He brushed the back of his jeans with his hands and sat on the sleek cream suede sofa against the interior wall, the sofa that was flanked by two expansive dark wood bookcases, filled "with all my most favorite books," Alice had declared. "They're all for sale, of course, but they are my favorites." The sofa was in the comfortable shadows of the store. Two chrome pharmacy lamps were fastened to the wall on either side of the sofa, neither of them turned on.

Jack took a deep breath.

Leslie took a seat on the sofa—not exactly at the other end, more like on the middle of the cushion next to the cushion that Jack was sitting on. It was a two-cushion sofa, not a love seat, but a full-length sofa, with only two long seat cushions. She could have sat closer; she could have sat farther away.

"This is such a perfect space," she said. "At least the interior is. It's both restful and energetic at the same time."

"I agree. And what they have for sale makes me want to buy—and I'm not much of a shopper," Jack said.

"The feather boas?"

"No," Jack answered with a smile. "Actually, though, I am going to buy one of those cool robots over there. Reminds me of a toy I had when I was small."

"Maybe that's why I like everything here. It's all familiar and comforting. That must be Alice's gift—being able to make those kind of connections."

Leslie turned to face Jack more directly. "Are you all finished? Is everything ready for the grand opening?"

"I think so."

Leslie found that she couldn't keep her eyes off his face. "Are you okay, Jack? Are things okay with you?"

This time, it was obvious that he wanted the question—that he wanted to tell someone that he was better. Not cured—he would never be cured. He would only be better. He would only be well, one day at a time.

"Yeah. I am. Things are going well." He looked at his hands. "I mean, I'm still alone here, and I'm not flush with jobs or money, and it can still be a struggle at times, but I'm doing okay. Comparatively, I'm doing better than okay."

He didn't look at her. "And you? I heard about your ex and all that. Small town."

"No, that's okay. I expected you to hear about that. And that might not be a problem anymore. He hasn't done anything. With the money from selling that safe, if he does go to court, I have the resources to handle that."

"That's good, Leslie. You and Ava … you should always stay together. She is such a great kid."

"She is. Thanks."

Jack looked up at her. There was expectancy on his face, she thought.

"Jack, I wanted to say that I understand. I mean, I've had struggles of my own. Different than yours, but something I've had to work through. All the anxiety over what I've had to go through with Randy … it's had me in its grip. There have been times I've panicked and could barely function. That's why I've been seeing Pastor Blake. He's helped me. A lot. Helped me find my way to peace. Pointed me toward God."

She paused, and when she spoke again, her words were gentler, more tender. "I want that for you, too, Jack."

She stopped speaking and looked at Jack closely, trying to see if he was surprised, shocked, put off by her words.

None of those reactions registered on Jack's face. He just looked back at Leslie with a softness in his eyes that she hadn't seen before.

She didn't move … didn't take her eyes from him. Their eyes stayed on each other for a very long moment, looking deep, looking beyond the words.

If they had been asked, neither of them would be certain whose hand moved first, but their hands did move, and they sought each other out. She could feel how hard and rough his hand was, how strong it was, how firm and enveloping.

He hesitated just a moment, then leaned toward her and embraced her—not so tenderly this time, but with more of a passion, with more yearning, more fiercely. She wrapped her arms around him and pulled him close, feeling the angles and muscles of his shoulders and back and chest.

They did not kiss, though Leslie had hoped they might. He just held her. And she held him, feeling the warmth of another man, another man's tenderness, another man's passion.

They stayed that way for a long time.

Perhaps he let go first. Perhaps it was Leslie.

They came apart, and, holding hands, continued to look at each other—a look of confusion, just a little, but more of acknowledgment and communion, trust and relief.

Jack was the first to speak. "Thank you, Leslie ... for caring, for believing in me. Thanks a lot."

She squeezed his hand. "Jack ..."

She wanted to tell him how very much she cared for him, that she loved being with him, that she felt so ... right, being in his arms.

But instead she simply brought her small hand up to his cheek. She felt the gentle stubble of his whiskers. She saw his eyes grow even more tender. She leaned to him and kissed him, soft like a butterfly, on his lips, just for a single moment, then leaned back, stood up, and walked away, out to the front door, and down the sidewalk to her front door, knowing that his eyes were on her the entire time.

Amelia Westland Middelstadt
Butler, Pennsylvania
January 1, 1895

On this first day of the New Year, I scribe here a prayer that has been most precious to me all my days.

A PARAPHRASE OF THE LORD'S PRAYER
BY REV. H. HASTINGS WELD

Father in Heaven! Oppressed with sacred awe,
We bow before Thee; yet since Thy dear Son
Thus bide us pray, through Him we humbly draw,
In trusting love, before a Father's Throne:
As seraphs honor Thee with tongues of flame,
Awakened be our tongues to hallow Thy great Name.
And as in Heaven, rejoicing in Thy Will,
Myriads of angels on Thy Glory wait,
Thy great behests obedient to fulfill,
So upon earth be known Thy royal state—
Thy Kingdom come, until of men there be,
From least to greatest, none save those who worship
Thee!
Thy Will be done! When, stricken to the dust,
Affliction's cup we pray may pass us by,
Still let us wait in never-failing trust,
Sure that Thou hearest when we meekly cry—
In patience our appointed courses run,
Always content that Thy Almighty Will be done.
Break to us each this day our daily bread,
Nor let earth's fading good alone be given;
Feed us upon Thy Words in Christ our Head,
To find Thy Peace—the Living Bread from Heaven

Since in Thy Mercy only we can live,
Forgive us, Lord, our debts—oh, teach us to forgive!
Shield us, O Lord, from dark temptation's power.
And guide our footsteps, lest they, erring, stray;
Deliver us in the dark and evil hour,
And turn our night, O Father, into day.
Shelter us, in Thine All-protecting Arms,
From specious sin's attacks—from pleasure's gilded
harms.
Thine is the Kingdom, Father, Thine the Love;
Redeemer, Son, the Grace, the Power are Thine;
Thy Glory, Holy Spirit, from above,
Descending, binds a Fellowship Divine.
Creator, Saviour, Sanctifier, deign,
Three persons, and one God, in all our hearts to reign.

CHAPTER TWENTY-EIGHT

THE SUN WAS SHINING, AND despite the chilly day, a crowd gathered outside the Midlands Building. The "Official Grand Opening" of Alice and Frank's would start at 9:00 a.m., and by 8:15, fifty people milled about on the sidewalk outside the storefront. Some of them were drawn to the novelty of it all, and some were drawn to the cameras from *Three Rivers Restorations*, along with most of their crew who were on hand to film the festivities for the wrap-up on the show documenting the storefront's renewal.

Alice was flitting about the place, adjusting this, and turning that. She flew through the kitchen, checking on the chefs. Trays of French baked goods were awaiting customers. Five trained coffee baristas were waiting behind the new granite and dark wood counter, cappuccino and espresso makers ready, cups stacked tall, all in readiness for the first coffee drinkers to charge their position. A fire blazed in the fireplace, giving the space an inviting warmth. Frank, as usual dressed to the nines and working on his third double espresso of the day, remained impassive. This sort of event brought out the peaceful and implacable Frank, the rock to Alice's butterfly.

The Ferrari-style case was filled with an overflow of European delicacies, mostly French and Italian, along with puffy bagels and enormous cupcakes decorated with edible violet petals, and an array of sandwiches—small-but-tasty sandwiches—filling up the rest. Alice planned on adding an actual lunch and dinner menu with a few specials, but for the grand opening, and until all the systems were running smoothly, just brunch items would be offered.

Cameron was there and had been in town since Friday night, when she and Alice and Frank and Jack had filmed all the final questions and responses concerning the building's renewal. Jack was now practiced in speaking—not to the camera but to the interviewer just off camera, unless instructed to look straight into the lens by the director. Jack never really understood why, but he followed directions as told.

The director seemed pleased with the show. Cameron seemed very excited with the story—but her joy might have been caused by baby Riley Margaret Willis, a sturdy Irish name for a sturdy Irish baby girl, who had arrived some three weeks ago and was now bellowing hungrily for her breakfast. Cameron happily obliged. She sat on the back sofa, a bit away from Alice's hustle and bustle, and tended to her child.

Jack came by, looking most dapper in a starched white dress shirt—no tie, of course—with a snazzy sport coat and dressy jeans and shoes. He was the perfect embodiment of the rugged, yet sophisticated and caring, contractor. He sat on the sofa with Cameron, trying not to stare or be intrusive. Cameron smiled at him, her and the baby well covered by a hand-knitted Irish blanket.

"You look really nice, Jack. It's not often we get to see you all dressed up."

He might have blushed a little.

"And I can't say I have ever seen you … with a baby, Cameron," he replied.

She adjusted the infant under the blanket. "The place is absolutely fabulous, Jack. Judging on what happened after Ethan finished the Carter Mansion, you will be swamped with work. He still gets referrals from that job at least once a week."

"Maybe so," Jack replied. "It would be nice to stay busy."

"Oh, you will, Jack. You'll be hiring a crew before long."

The baby made cooing noises, and Jack smiled.

"Have you talked to Ethan?" Cameron asked.

"Ethan? He's here? I didn't see him. I thought your director brought you down."

"He did," Cameron replied. "But Ethan said he wasn't busy this morning, so he thought he would drive down and drive us home. I haven't driven since the baby came. I don't think I want to yet."

Cameron shifted the baby, then pointed to the window. "There he is. The one with the sixty-four-ounce cup of coffee. And a doughnut! Tell him no more doughnuts. Tell him the doughnut police are after him."

Jack agreed and hurried outside.

"Good job, Jack," Ethan said, then stuffed the doughnut into his mouth and offered him his hand.

"Thanks," Jack answered, giving Ethan's hand a firm shake. "I wanted to tell you thanks too, Ethan. I learned a lot working with you."

Ethan finished off the doughnut in two bites. He gestured with his head toward the store. "Did she tell you to yell at me about the doughnut?"

Jack nodded.

"Well, you can tell her you did. With the new baby, she tells me I have to stay in shape, keep healthy. She's right, but what harm does a doughnut do now and then?"

The crowd, now extended almost to where the two men stood, was getting noisy.

"Let's walk around the block. The crowd is bugging me," Ethan said. "Remember, I'm from a small town and just not used to the big city craziness like you folks are."

The two of them walked west, up one block, and headed to the nearby Ritts Park. They walked in silence, as men often did, building a relationship shoulder-to-shoulder, rather than face-to-face.

They came to a hillock that looked down on the creek, hidden by the foliage of oak trees in the summer, now more visible with the leaves gone.

"Ethan, besides what I learned from you on the job ... I wanted to thank you for being a role model for me as well."

Ethan didn't turn to him. He simply remained silent, and let Jack talk.

"You knew I had problems ... with alcohol ... and you still hired me. No lectures. No making me feel guilty. You lived your life in front of me. I saw what happened after you met Cameron. I saw the change in you."

Jack kicked at a rock with his toe. "I've been fighting with God all along. I blamed him for what happened to my family. I blamed him for making me weak. I blamed him for ... everything."

He looked up into the sky. "But that stuff was all my fault. It was just me trying to run things. I was a jerk. I was in bondage to myself. That fight I was having with God—well, now it's over. I finally figured out that it was easier to lay down my guns than to fight a losing battle. I've stopped drinking—this time forever. I have things I want to live for. I want to stay free. I want my life to mean something. Life can be good again."

He waited. "You know what I mean?"

Ethan did not jump at a reply. In time, he simply said, "I do, Jack. I really do. Completely. Hope renewed is a miraculous thing. I'm really happy for you. I know you can do it—only with God's help, of course."

And he put his arm around Jack's shoulder, just for a moment, then slapped him on the back, as men do. "We better head back. If Cameron doesn't see me every ten minutes, she panics. I guess a baby can do that to a woman."

"I guess they can," Jack replied. "I guess they can."

The grand opening of Alice and Frank's remained in high gear. The first fifty people in line had been replaced by a hundred more, and the storefront stayed crowded with happy, smiling people for the entire morning. Alice, exuberant in her smashing, color-coordinated outfit, zigged and zagged through the crowd, greeting and hugging and making sure the lattes were just perfect and that people were being well fed and finding the necessary treasures she had gathered for the store.

Leslie did not understand the retail business, but she assumed that the size of the crowds and the hustle and bustle of the first day was a good sign.

She watched Jack, so very handsome—no, closer to irresistible, she thought—in his sport coat and well-fitting jeans, talking to the reporter from the *Butler Eagle*, and then the radio announcer from WBUT.

Afterward, she walked over to him. They exchanged a few words, then she grabbed his hand and squeezed, wishing him good luck, and he leaned into her, and whispered back, "Thanks for all you've done for me.

And thanks for the other night. I didn't know how much I missed connecting with someone so special." For a moment, with him so close, it felt to Leslie like they were the only two people in the place, and she wished they could stay that way forever.

Later that morning, because Leslie did not draw strength from crowds, she slipped away and went back to her apartment. Ava had gone to Trevor's house. Mike had been one of the crowd of early arrivers, with Trevor along for his hot chocolate, which he loved, and chocolate cupcake. Mike had gathered up both his son and Ava and offered to take them home until five that evening.

"Keep them out of your hair," he'd said to Leslie. "I'm sure you have lots to do."

She didn't, but appreciated his kindness.

She'd had enough lattes to keep her engines running for several days. She poured a large glass of ice water. She sat at the kitchen table with Amelia's Bible again. With lingering disbelief, she ran her hand over the cover and then opened it.

There were twelve more pages of her great-great-great grandmother's diary tucked away in the Bible. Most had dates. A few did not. She had read one page per day since the Bible had been discovered, rationing out the aged sheets, like gourmet chocolates, too dense and rich to eat more than one at a sitting, too precious to consume in great gulps. Instead Leslie took each single page, read it over and over, seeing a clearer picture into the past, a more complete picture of who Amelia Grace Westland was and who she became. Once married, the entries in the diary had become less frequent, as if the duties of being a wife had become all-consuming.

And now Leslie held in her hands the last four pages, the last entries of Amelia's diary that had spanned nearly four decades.

Amelia Westland Middelstadt
Butler, Pennsylvania
September 30, 1895

I suspect the risk that someone unintended read these words is still great, but I find great comfort in scribing them to give record of my life's journey, sort out my thoughts, and shed light on my decisions.

We have been wise in our investments, and we now have capital of a considerable amount in our hands. We desire to know how to use it best. Along with our ongoing contributions to the Butler Asylum for Orphans, I am of the mind to give the majority of the sum to the church, but my husband is not of that mind. He states that we should use most of the sum to construct a building in the growing town of Butler, for a purpose, and that building, along with our offspring, would be our legacy of sorts to the future.

I counter that monies given to the church would do the same, only of more eternal significance, but I fear that being a man, with more temporal aspirations, and concerned about what comes later in this life for our children, he is reluctant to donate the entire sum.

I pray that God will direct us.

> *He hath shewed thee, O man, what is good;*
> *and what doth the LORD require of thee, but to do justly,*
> *and to love mercy, and to walk humbly with thy God?*
> —MICAH 6:8

Amelia Westland Middelstadt
Butler, Pennsylvania
June 10, 1897

On this day was held the ribbon-cutting ceremony for the Midlands Building. Samuel designated it so, deriving it from parts of the names Middelstadt and Westland, so as to stand proudly on its corner as a landmark to our heritage. I was astounded at the considerable throng that gathered for the event. The assemblage was regaled with speeches and toasts, after which a substantial repast for the various town burgesses and councilmen and members of the General Assembly of Butler County, who were in attendance, was served at the Willard Hotel. It was a fine affair.

It was announced that a managerial arrangement has been contracted, whereby Samuel shall set up a Mr. and Mrs. Finch in a pharmacy and variety store, a most welcome addition to Butler, which shall occupy the first-floor space of our building. The Finches' living quarters shall be above the store on the second floor. The Finches are the most delightful of folks, and they have made great plans for their establishment to be the finest to thus far grace the town. Andrew Finch has great skill as a pharmacist. I am drawn to Cecilia Finch's energetic and artistic nature. She has set about procuring an abundant array of dry goods—embroidered silks, fine woolens, laces, and calicos—to be sold in the variety store. This has, of course, caused quite a stir among the ladies of Butler. It will no longer be necessary to journey to Pittsburgh to purchase textiles and many other items of fashion that Mrs. Finch will offer for sale, such as can be seen in Godey's Ladies Book.

And in that day shall ye say, Praise the LORD,
call upon his name, declare his doings among the people,
make mention that his name is exalted. Sing unto the LORD;
for he hath done excellent things: this is known in all the earth.
—ISAIAH 12:4–5

Amelia Westland Middelstadt
Butler, Pennsylvania
October 12, 1903

Today I don my dress of black crape, the mark of my bereavement. Samuel has breathed his last, leaving me a widow in my forty-first year. It is the common lot of men, the just and the unjust alike. Yet even though expected after his long illness, it is not without much pain and sorrow—for the children especially. The servants, too, are all in mourning, for Samuel was a gentle and generous master of this house. All is in readiness for services this day, to be held at our new Second Presbyterian Church. It is fitting, says Reverend Ekstrom, that Samuel's funeral be the first, since he had been so liberal in his contributions to the building and his bequeathment of a large sum to the church. Henry has been most helpful in seeing to all necessary arrangements, and Catherine is my ever-present comfort.

Dear Samuel was good and wise to leave his affairs in order, and shall be greatly missed. I am left, with the help of God, to carry on as best as I am able. I scribe here the Scripture most beloved by Samuel, which is his character portrayed:

> *Be kindly affectioned one to another with brotherly love; in honour preferring one another; Not slothful in business; fervent in spirit; serving the Lord; Rejoicing in hope; patient in tribulation; continuing instant in prayer; Distributing to the necessity of saints; given to hospitality. Bless them which persecute you: bless, and curse not. Rejoice with them that do rejoice, and weep with them that weep. Be of the same mind one toward another. Mind not high things, but condescend to men of low estate. Be not wise in your own conceits. Recompense to no man evil for evil. Provide things honest in the sight of all men. If it be possible, as much as lieth in you, live peaceably with all men.*

> *Dearly beloved, avenge not yourselves, but rather give place unto wrath: for it is written, Vengeance is mine; I will repay, saith the Lord. Therefore if thine enemy hunger, feed him; if he thirst, give him drink: for in so doing thou shalt heap coals of fire on his head. Be not overcome of evil, but overcome evil with good.*
> —ROMANS 12:10–21

Amelia Westland Middelstadt
Butler, Pennsylvania
November 17, 1912

I am close to death. I have asked my faithful Catherine to procure this book from the place where it was secreted, and once more she has proved herself my steadfast friend—though she need not, after all these years of devoted companionship.

I am not long for this world—it is certain. The young doctor is kind, but he has no miracle, no skill, no magic nor vial, that can prevent the eventual death that will befall us all.

I wish now that I had written every day in this, my diary, but when I was younger, I felt the days too filled with such urgencies upon my hours. Now, as I struggle to read, there are so many gaps, so many things unsaid in my feeble words and writings. For all intents and appearances, one could say of my life that, in the end, it has been full and good. And yet ...

I wonder ... if so many years ago ... I made the most fitting choice. I wonder now, perhaps every day, in my isolation and feebleness, whatever became of my dear, dear, Julian Beck. I now confess that, unbidden, my thoughts would go to him so very often—sometimes most distressingly during my most intimate moments with Samuel. But there was no remedy for it. I have come to realize that he had irrevocably claimed in large part my heart, and there was no unclaiming once staked, even from my first glimpses of him while just a very young girl, alone and most susceptible to a virile man of his considerable charms. How utterly smitten was I! How great was his fervor for life, how ardent his love of God, how strong the call of the wider world on his soul.

He made his discreet departure from Butler shortly after Samuel and I were wed. It must have been exceedingly hurtful to him, but I had no opportunity to discuss my decision. To my great regret, I was young and perhaps foolish, or not foolish enough, confused by my trepidations, the instabilities of my youth.

But I ... I loved him, and I see now, after many years distilled by deep longing, of remembering all that he had been to me, and is still, I should have listened to my heart. I should have insisted that we marry and that we, as husband and wife, set off to do God's work.

Would he have complied with such a demand? I will never know, for I made no attempt to find out.

I did not, and therein lies the difference: security, stability, and safety over uncertainties and passion and adventure.

I ask whoever reads these pages to first: follow God, and then to follow their heart, their truest and deepest heart, for not doing so will lead to a life of quiet regrets.

"We take no note of time, but by its loss."

I pray that God may receive me into His Kingdom, despite my human frailties.

But I have trusted in thy mercy; my heart shall rejoice in thy salvation.
I will sing unto the LORD, because he hath dealt bountifully with me.
—PSALM 13:5–6

The LORD knoweth the days of the upright:
and their inheritance shall be for ever.
—PSALM 37:18

TERRI KRAUS

Leslie sat, in disbelief, in utter astonishment, her finger tracing the sentences, stopping at words, reading lines twice, and then once again.

Follow God. Follow your heart.

Leslie had hoped for signs, never expecting to receive them. She had listened for portents, never expecting to hear them. She had asked God for a light upon her path, revealing His will, never really expecting to blink in the brilliance of an answer.

Is this the answer I've wanted? Is this the question I have been asking?

She sat, in silence, for a long time that afternoon, almost forgetting that Ava was to be picked up at five.

At 4:55, she finally noticed the clock, grabbed her coat and keys, and flew down the stairs.

CHAPTER TWENTY-NINE

THE GRAND OPENING OF ALICE and Frank's had been a great success. Alice declared it a triumph beyond her wildest expectations. More than one thousand people passed through the doors that Saturday. All of them, she stated, loved everything about the place.

"They will be back," she predicted. "All of them."

Now the sky was dark, the storefront empty of people and closed for the night. Both Alice and Frank said planning on an early closing was the only sane thing they had done in weeks. They planned, in the future, to be open Sundays, but not until all the systems proved themselves reliable and they both had built up their endurance.

———⋈———

"Can I get a cupcake?" Ava asked. "The ones with the flowers you can eat on top? Mrs. Alice said I could have every cupcake that they didn't sell today. Can we go and look? You have the key, don't you, Mommy?"

Leslie did indeed have the key, to both the front door and the rear entrance. And she was too filled with emotion to argue the point.

"Sure, honey, we can go look. But we'll use the back entrance, okay? And turn on only a few lights, so we don't cause any fuss."

Ava jumped up and ran to the back door of the apartment and bounced down the steps. Leslie followed and unlocked the store's back door. Ava hurried in to the Ferrari-like display case.

"There's still four left, Mommy. I can have all of them, right? Mrs. Alice said so."

"We'll take them all. You can have one tonight. We'll save the rest until tomorrow. Okay?"

Ava was disappointed, a little, but happy for her small victory.

"Can I have some milk?" she asked, sitting at one of the small tables near the kitchen.

Leslie did not want to take any milk from the restaurant.

"I'll go upstairs and get a glass for you. Are you okay down here by yourself?"

Ava looked at her mother with that look that said, "Of course I am. I'm in kindergarten, remember?"

Leslie hurried back upstairs, found a glass, spilled the milk, poured another, and spilled some of that.

That's what I get for being in a hurry, she said to herself as she mopped up the third little puddle. She hated spilled milk because it immediately got invisible and sticky.

As she made her way carefully down the steps, she heard voices. A bit alarmed, she wanted to run downstairs but didn't want to spill more milk. And hopefully it was Frank or Alice, she thought, returning for some forgotten item.

No ... that's Jack's voice.

She stopped in the doorway for a moment, listening, unseen.

"I came back for my drill. Didn't want it to be sold by accident. Where's your mom? Or did you come here all by yourself?"

Ava giggled. "No. You're being silly. My mom is upstairs getting me a glass of milk."

"Milk and Mrs. Alice's cupcakes. That must taste great," Jack said.

"It does," Ava replied, with great enthusiasm. "And you can eat the flowers. Do you eat cupcakes, Mr. Kenyon?"

Jack pulled a chair up next to Ava. "Not so much anymore."

"Why?"

Jack hesitated. "Well ... I had a little girl. She loved cupcakes too. But she's gone now."

Leslie could see the back of Ava's head as she turned to Jack.

"Like to Wisconsin?"

"No," Jack answered, then added, "she's in heaven."

Leslie's hand went to her throat. She had no idea. She knew he had a past ...

"What happened?" Ava asked.

"She died in a car crash ... with her mom."

This had been the first time Jack had ever told any of this story out loud to anyone. Leslie listened, wanting to weep, her heart breaking for him, for his long silence, for his heavy burden.

"That is very sad, Mr. Kenyon."

"It was, Ava. It was very sad."

"Did you get hurt?"

"A little. But I was hurt mostly where you can't see the hurt. Inside."

Like a small sage, Ava nodded. "Are you better now?"

"I'm trying, Ava. I'm trying very hard to be better. It's hard, though, sometimes."

Ava finished her cupcake. "Can I have another one, Mr. Kenyon?"

"Sure. I guess."

She carefully unwrapped the fluted paper, then took a small bite, leaving a bit of chocolate frosting above her lip. "I think my mom really likes you, Mr. Kenyon. Maybe you should get better for her. I think she needs somebody."

If Jack had been surprised, he didn't show it, or at least not that Leslie could see from the shadows.

"But what about Mr. Reidmiller. Doesn't your mom like him?"

Ava shrugged, her shoulders almost touching her ears.

"But don't you like Trevor? If Mr. Reidmiller was here, Trevor could be your brother."

"Eeewww," was Ava's loud and emphatic response. "I don't want him as a brother. I like him as a friend, but he's weird sometimes."

Ava ate while Jack sat almost motionless. "So ... are you going to ask my mom out on a date or something? Like for ice cream? I love ice cream."

Jack only waited a second to answer. "Maybe I will, Ava, maybe I will."

———⬦———

Leslie all but kicked the back door, making her entrance unmistakable to both her daughter and Mr. Kenyon.

Jack stood up.

"I came back for my drill," he said, holding the tool in the air like a captured animal.

Leslie's eyes found his, for a long moment, full of knowing, full with meaning.

Then Jack spoke softly. "How are you tonight?"

"I'm good, Jack."

"The grand opening went very well."

"It did. Everyone was asking about who did the work here."

"Not everyone," Jack said.

"Well, maybe not everyone. But a lot of them did. I talked to at least a dozen people myself. And your stack of business cards was all taken. You'll be busy now."

"I think I will be," he said, agreeing with her assessment. "But not that busy. I mean … not too busy to call you. Maybe take you and Ava for ice cream. If that's okay with you, that is."

Leslie smiled. "That sounds really good to me."

Jack appeared as relieved and as happy as a man might be. "No more locked doors, Leslie. No more secrets."

"No more," Leslie agreed.

Their eyes locked again until Ava said, "Can I have another cupcake?"

EPILOGUE

IN THE COMPLETELY RENEWED APARTMENT over Alice and Frank's place, Jack reached into the freezer and extracted a half gallon of vanilla ice cream—the good kind, from Cunningham's. He took out three bowls and began scooping out generous amounts of smooth creaminess into each bowl.

"Do we have any chocolate sauce, Ms. Assistant Museum Curator?" he asked.

Leslie came up behind him, wrapped her arms tight around him, and hugged him with a loving ferocity. "Don't we always have chocolate sauce?"

She turned him around in her arms and kissed him. He let the scoop fall back into the opened carton of ice cream as his embrace and kiss met hers.

From the living room came Ava's voice. "Eeewwww."

And everyone in that apartment knew Ava didn't mean it—not at all. Not even a little.

After a long, tender minute passed, Jack called out, "Who wants to go for a motorcycle ride?"

POSTSCRIPT

EARL PASSED AWAY SIX MONTHS after first being admitted to the hospital. He came home after a three-week stay, and that is where he died. Jack was at his side. Even though Leslie never considered herself a computer whiz, using her new laptop, she located Earl's son, who was living in California. She took it upon herself to call Earl Jr., and three weeks before his father passed away, they connected via a telephone call. His mother, Earl's ex-wife, had been dead for more than a decade. Both men were cordial, but cautious. Earl Sr. apologized for what he had done and what he had not done in his son's life. His son did not grant him forgiveness but acknowledged what his father had said and thanked him. So Earl passed away in peace, having done his best to atone for his past mistakes.

Mike took Leslie's decision hard. He spent a lot of Saturday mornings drowning his sorrows at the Krispy Kreme doughnut store in Cranberry, fifteen miles north of Butler, alone, so no one could observe his unhappiness, leaving Trevor with his Aunt Denise. It was there, in Cranberry, that he met Susan Mallen, a divorced mother of six-year-old twin girls. Between chocolate-frosted doughnuts—the ones with the crème filling and not the custard—Mike talked and Susan laughed and they began dating. They are now engaged and planning a small wedding, with just family in attendance, in the spring.

No further legal action for custody of Ava was taken by Randy Ruskin.

He and his new wife, Lisa, relocated to Florida. Ava sees them a few times a year.

The money from the sale of the antique safe was used to begin a college fund for Ava.

Alice and Frank's Take Two became an instant success. It became even more popular when outdoor seating was added, with cozy bistro tables and wicker chairs lining the wide sidewalk—just like a café found in Europe, making it the first restaurant in Butler to offer seasonal eating outside.

Leslie has done well in her job as assistant curator at the museum and occasionally walks to the elementary school to have lunch with Ava. Jack sometimes takes a break from his latest renovation projects, including a historic house he'd bought on Taylor, just a block from the Maridon Museum, and joins them. The three of them enjoy their Sunday morning walks through the renewing downtown to Grace @ Calvary Church.

The diary of Amelia Grace Westland Middelstadt still has its home on Leslie's nightstand, along with Amelia's Bible. She continues to find great inspiration from her great-great-great grandmother's writing.

The highest pleasure of the human race is for God to reveal Himself to us.
This is more pleasurable and intoxicating, wondrous,
and terrifying than any other thing in the universe.
We were made to experience His depths, to search the vast ocean of His Deity,
to mine the treasures that creation longs to look into.

—ALLEN HOOD

ABOUT THE AUTHOR

 After eleven coauthored books with husband, Jim, Terri Kraus has added her award-winning interior designer's eye to her world of fiction. She comes to the Project Restoration series naturally, having survived the remodel, renovation, and restoration of three separate personal residences, along with those of her clients. She makes her home in Wheaton, Illinois, with her husband; son, Elliot; miniature schnauzer, Rufus; and Siberian cat, Petey.

Visit Terri Kraus at her Web site: www.terrikraus.com.

Other Books by Jim and Terri Kraus

MACKENZIE STREET SERIES
The Unfolding
The Choosing
Scattered Stones

THE CIRCLE OF DESTINY SERIES
The Price
The Treasure
The Promise
The Quest

TREASURES OF THE CARIBBEAN SERIES
Pirates of the Heart
Passages of Gold
Journey to the Crimson Sea

PROJECT RESTORATION SERIES
The Renovation

His Father Saw Him Coming

The Micah Judgment

The Silence

... a little more ...

When a delightful concert comes to an end,

the orchestra might offer an encore.

When a fine meal comes to an end,

it's always nice to savor a bit of dessert.

When a great story comes to an end,

we think you may want to linger.

And so, we offer ...

AfterWords—just a little something more after you

have finished a David C. Cook novel.

We invite you to stay awhile in the story.

Thanks for reading!

Turn the page for ...

- **A Note from the Author**
- **Discussion Questions**

A Note from the Author

Writing a novel set in the world of the restoration of old buildings has always been a dream of mine. The idea of renovation is in my family's blood. I'm an interior design professional. My brothers are rehabbers. My husband, Jim, and I have survived the renovation of three houses.

I know the upheaval well, the despair of having no control, the agonizing over style decisions, the budget constraints, the disagreements between contractor and owner, and the emotional roller coaster of unexpected problems and unanticipated gifts along the way. Together my clients and I have accepted big disappointments, celebrated tiny successes, and experienced the inexpressible elation at seeing what was once in ruins—old, broken, useless—become, with all its quirks, a beautiful, completely renewed, and usable place for people to share life again. Looking back on all those projects, I can echo the sentiment in the opening line of Dickens' *A Tale of Two Cities*: "It was the best of times, it was the worst of times."

Many of you are probably, like me, HGTV fans who watch the many shows about fixing up old houses. You find yourself glued to the glimpses of contractors and owners engaged in the process. You live vicariously through the rehabbing, renovating, and restoring.

I can relate. I've always been captivated by old buildings. Poring over books about art, architectural styles, and decoration from all over the world has always been one of my favorite pastimes. As I've traveled internationally and visited many of the places I've studied independently and in the course of my education in design, I've become even more passionate about restoration. (I'm the woman you might see sitting on a bench along the wall of the Sistine Chapel, silently weeping as I take in Michelangelo's magnificent masterpiece in the simplicity of that sacred space.) I can talk forever about the importance of preserving buildings that are testaments to the creative impulse, the hours of painstaking effort, the motivation and dedication of artists, designers, craftsmen, and artisans from previous eras. All were, no doubt, imperfect people—but people used as instruments in God's hands to create perfectly rendered works of art that endure and can stir our hearts so many, many years later.

For me, there's something quite magical about walking into an old place, with all its history, where so much life has been lived, where so many events and significant moments have taken place—the happy ones, the sad ones, and all the everyday moments and hours in between. Imagining who might have inhabited a house, how the family came together, the love they shared, their conversations, the tears and laughter, is irresistible to me. I find inspiration as I imagine how they celebrated and grieved, how they overcame adversity, how they survived tragedy, then moved on to enjoy life within the old walls once again.

One of the joys of my life was visiting the little northern Italian village, nestled among olive groves high up in the Apennine Mountains, where my maternal grandparents were born, grew up, and married before emigrating to America in 1920. A short lane connects their two families' farmhouses. In between them stands a small, now empty house of ancient, mellowed stone where my grandparents lived as newlyweds. How full my heart felt as I walked over that threshold! I pictured them as a young couple in the first blush of matrimony, with all their hopes and dreams ... before their brave journey (separately) across a wide ocean to a strange land where all was unknown. Within those aged walls, did they speak of their fears as they prepared to leave their homeland, certain they'd never see their parents and siblings again? What kind of courage did that require? What words did they use to comfort and reassure one another? I wondered. I could see, in my mind's eye, my grandmother stirring a pot of pasta as my grandfather stoked the fire. I could even hear the crackling of the firewood, smell the slight wood smoke....

A few artifacts remained of their time there, and I was delighted to be able to take them back to America with me. Now I treasure and display them in my own home because they connect me with that place and time and remind me of my rich heritage—all stemming from that small structure, still standing, solidly built so long ago.

I love the metaphor of restoration, which is why I came up with the idea for the Project Restoration series—stories that would follow both the physical restoration of a building and emotional/spiritual restoration of a character. Perhaps in the Project Restoration series, you'll find a character who mirrors your own life and points you toward the kind of restoration you long for.

After all, God is in the business of restoring lives—reclaiming, repairing, renewing what was broken, and bringing beauty from ashes. I know, because I've seen it firsthand. For many years, I've worked in women's ministries. I've seen many women—as well as the men and children they love—deal with scars from their past that shape their todays and tomorrows. They all long for restoration—to live hopefully, joyfully, and productively once again—but that also requires forgiveness. Forgiveness of others (whether they deserve it or not) and, perhaps most importantly, forgiveness of oneself in order to be healthy and available to God. Clinging to past hurts or "unfairness," hostility, anger, grudges, resentment, bitterness, or allowing abuse to alter your self-worth renders your life virtually useless. Unforgiveness shapes your perception of yourself, your outlook on life, the kind of relationships you have, and keeps you in "stuck" mode. It leaves you without hope, in a dark, emotionally paralyzing, spiritually debilitating, physically draining state and causes so much unnecessary pain ... even addiction.

Yet God Himself stands and waits, extending the gift of restoration. The light of His love shines on all those dark places deep within us, exposing what needs His healing touch, renewing hope, providing freedom from bondage. This is the type of restoration I've become passionate about too. For when our souls are gloriously freed through God's renovation, we become whole, useful, and able to extend the forgiveness we have experienced to others. Our hope is renewed. Then individuals, families, churches, and entire communities can be transformed!

What event in your past do you need to let go of? It is my hope and prayer that you, too, will experience the renewal that awaits you through saying yes to God's invitation of heart restoration ... and the life-transforming joy that will follow.

Discussion Questions

1. What hints do you see, early in the book, that Leslie is struggling with anxiety? When do you first understand, from her behavior, that her anxiety manifests itself in panic attacks?

2. From her diary entries, when do you first see that Amelia Westland, Leslie's great-great-great-grandmother, struggled with anxiety attacks as well? Have you, or has anyone you know, ever struggled with anxiety or panic attacks? If so, tell the story.

3. When do you know that Jack has an addiction? In what way(s) does he set himself up for failure in staying sober? Do you or someone you love struggle with an alcohol or other drug addiction? If so, how has this influenced your life and your actions?

4. Put yourself in Leslie's shoes. Did you think, initially, that her relationship with Mike held great promise for the future? Did your feelings change later in the book? If so, when—and why?

5. What were your feelings about the initial attractions between Leslie and Jack? Were you concerned? Supportive? Did those feelings change as the story developed? If so, when—and why?

6. How did Amelia's relationship with Julian and Amelia's relationship with Samuel parallel the relationships between Leslie and Jack? Between Leslie and Mike? What kind of life would you be tempted to choose, based on your personality? Why?

7. What was it about Amelia's diary that was so intriguing to Leslie? Why do you think she was so attached to it?

8. Trace the development of Leslie's spiritual journey. What situations, people, and events in the story were instrumental in pointing her toward God?

9. Trace the development of Jack's increasing awareness of God in his life. What situations, people, and events were catalysts in his spiritual journey?

10. How did you feel about the counsel and advice that Pastor Blake gave to Leslie? Was it sound? Why or why not? Who has acted as your counselor or mentor? In what ways did that help you—or not help you?

11. Leslie comes to the realization that no one in her life had ever really believed in her. When Pastor Blake tells her that he believes in her, what happens in Leslie's heart? How does this influence her recovery? How can encouragement make a difference in someone's life? When has someone encouraged you, and made a difference? When have you played the encourager and seen the impact?

12. Jack finally comes to understand that he is in bondage to himself. How does that help in his recovery? How does bondage to self relate to addiction?

13. Describe your reaction to the scene when Jack revisits the grave site of his wife and daughter with the bottle of liquor. Did you think he would keep his vow? Why or why not? Is there a "place" you need to revisit to end the grip of a past event on your present and your future?

14. What did you think of Randy Ruskin? Do you know someone like him? How do you respond to that person?

15. What did you think of Alice and Frank Adams and their venture? Have you ever "risked" to do something unusual in an unusual place? What happened as a result? In what ways did you surprise yourself and others—for the good?

16. What parts did Ava, Mrs. Stickle, and Mrs. DiGiulio play in Leslie's spiritual growth?

17. What role did Ethan Willis, Jack's former boss, play in Jack's recovery? What kind of influence did Earl, the bartender, have on Jack? Why?

18. What did you think was in the locked storage room of the Midlands Building? Were you disappointed? Why or why not?

19. Were you surprised by the outcome of Amelia's story and her words in the last journal entry? What lessons could be learned from her life? Which lesson touches your life the most—and why?

20. What was your reaction to Leslie's choice between Mike and Jack in the end? Did you surprise yourself? If so, in what ways? Do you think it's always best to follow your heart? Would you have followed Amelia's advice to do so, or would you have taken a safer route? Explain.

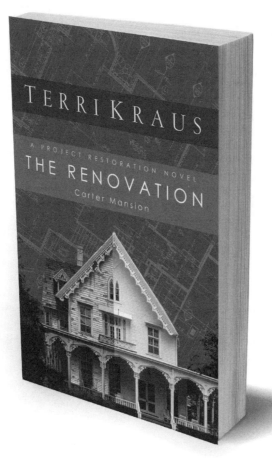

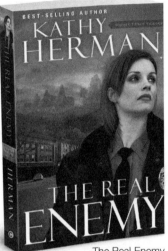

Gloucester County
Library System